... that it has received throughout the Spanish-speaking world . . . Señor Gallegos has caught the spirit of the *llanos.* He knows the people of the great silent plain, their primitive fears, their superstitions. For him the plain itself is a living creature; the people but puppets under its control." —G. M. KEEFFE, *New York Herald Tribune*

"It is an exciting heroic tale of the life of the Venezuelan plainsmen, masters and peóns, ranchers and cowboys and horse thieves . . ." —C. A. PEARCE, *New Republic*

"The characters and circumstances go to make up a plot as delicate and credible and psychologically convincing as it is absorbing. . . . If Señor Gallegos is one-half as good a President as he is a novelist, Venezuela is a lucky land."
—F. T. MARSH, *New York Times*

"A rattling good yarn, and Señor Gallegos (admirably translated by Robert Malloy) obviously knows every detail of what he is writing about." —BONAMY DOBREE, *Spectator*

"A drama thrust at us with admirable creative power, *Doña Barbara* is one of those books the readers never forget."
—JORGE AMADO

"Gallegos's most outstanding work and one of Spanish America's best regionalist novels . . . *Doña Barbara* is a work of social, cultural, and aesthetic import. . . . Not only did it fill a cultural vacuum, but Doña Barbara also made a clear optimistic prediction about the great future of a new Venezuela, which would be ushered in by the triumph of the forces of progress over the prevailing lawlessness and primitivism."
—CLAUDETTE ROSEGREEN-WILLIAMS, *Symposium*

"A story of the Venezuelan plains, with a fiercely dominant woman, a female embodiment of *caciquismo,* its dynamic center, *Doña Barbara* is a portrayal of the *llanero's* turbulent existence. While much of its interest derives from the violence of plot and actors, much also is due to the author's skill in recreating the atmosphere of the wild and lonely Venezuelan plains. Through a narrative echo the tales, legends, and improvised songs of the plainsmen; and along with these, birds call and beasts cry. Gallegos makes such detail a vivid, integral part of his novel." —MUNA LEE, *The Americas*

"*Doña Barbara* gives us the first great Latin American novel and one of the most typically novelistic literary works written in Spanish." —RICARDO BAEZA

"The emotional excellence and the powerful description make the novel a prose epic." —*Boston Transcript*

"*Doña Barbara* . . . marks the peak of the regionalist novel in Spanish America. . . . *Doña Barbara* . . . is the paradigmatic novel of a quest for the 'cultural essence' of some given area of Spanish America (and, by extension, perhaps of Spanish America itself). . . . The struggle between Barbara and Santos provides the dramatic interest of the novel, while the latter's efforts to overcome the attraction of macho self-assertion . . . deepens the symbolism of his character."
—VERITY SMITH, *The Encyclopedia of Latin American Literature*

"A superb example of the well-made novel."
—DONALD SHAW, *Hispanic Review*

DOÑA BARBARA

BY

Rómulo Gallegos

Translated by

Robert Malloy

WITH A NEW FOREWORD
BY LARRY MCMURTRY

The University of Chicago Press ∗ *Chicago & London*

RÓMULO GALLEGOS (1884–1969) was the first democratically elected president of Venezuela, whose works have been translated into many languages. After publishing *Doña Barbara* in 1929, he left Venezuela for Spain, but returned in 1936 to hold a variety of political offices. He was again forced out by the 1948 Venezuelan coup d'état, returned in 1958, and was elected senator for life. His honors include the National Literature Prize and a nomination for the Nobel Prize for Literature; his many published works include three acclaimed novels: *Doña Barbara* (1929), *Cantaclaro* (1934), and *Canaima* (1935).

The University of Chicago Press, Chicago 60637

Originally published in Spanish in 1929 by Editorial Araluce, Barcelona

University of Chicago Press edition 2012
Printed in the United States of America

21 20 19 18 17 16 15 14 13 12   1 2 3 4 5

ISBN-13: 978-0-226-27920-6 (paper)
ISBN-10: 0-226-27920-0 (paper)

Library of Congress Cataloging-in-Publication Data

Gallegos, Rómulo, 1884–1969.
[Doña Barbara. English]
Doña Barbara / by Rómulo Gallegos ; translated by Robert Malloy.
p. cm.
ISBN-13: 978-0-226-27920-6 (paperback : alkaline paper)
ISBN-10: 0-226-27920-0 (paperback : alkaline paper) 1. Matriarchy—Venezuela—Fiction. 2. Landowners—Venezuela—Fiction. 3. Upper class families—Venezuela—Fiction. 4. Families—Venezuela—Fiction. 5. Women—Psychology—Fiction. 6. Farmers—Venezuela—Fiction. 7. Mothers and daughters—Fiction. 8. Venezuela—Social conditions—Fiction. I. Malloy, Robert. II. Title.
PQ8549.G24D613 2012
863'.62—dc23

2011029353

♾ This paper meets the requirements of ANSI/NISO Z39.48-1992 (Permanence of Paper).

CONTENTS

FOREWORD

Rómulo Gallegos was a Venezuelan jack-of-all-trades: educator, journalist, diplomat, politician—he was the first democratically elected president of Venezuela—and novelist. *Doña Barbara,* his masterpiece, was written from exile and published in 1929. It was Englished in 1931, was republished in the 1940s, and then vanished, except in Venezuela, where it was recently the basis for a popular soap opera.

When I was asked to do this foreword I had never heard of Gallegos, though I run a bookshop containing 250,000 books. The novel, which richly deserves republication, is both very late Gothic and very early Magical Realism. Within a few pages we are introduced to the Turk, the Toad, and the Evil Eyed, the last a creepy master of aphrodisiacs, in which Doña Barbara frequently indulges in order to fuel a vast spring of couplings with gross and unsavory men. As for the Turk, he is "a leprous and sadistic Syrian, who has become wealthy through exploitation of balata (rubber)." The Turk keeps a harem of young Indian girls, whom he buys. He would have liked to buy Barbara when she was but a beautiful Barbarita, but was foiled.

The book is in its way a paean to the Venezuelan *llano,* or plain. I am a son of the *Llano Estacado* myself, but Gallegos's plain is nothing like mine. In one of his rivers, for example, is a giant one-eyed alligator; this beast is said to be centuries old and can eat horses, bulls, or anything that wanders near. And, if one escapes this monster, there is the Great Bog, a bottomless swamp that swallows up any creature that attempts it.

Unlike the austere plain I grew up on, Gallegos's *llano* is steamy, tumescent, lust driven. Doña Barbara may have been a kind of anticipation of Eva Perón. She owns a great ranch, the Altamira, but must struggle constantly to keep it. She is, in her way, a tragic heroine, seeking to attract a decent lover, while giving herself day and night to very coarse lovers indeed.

She is, however, very vividly drawn, a Bovary of the *llano.*

In the prose one will now and then hear Conradian echoes, and certainly there are echoes of Gallegos in García Márquez, Vargas Llosa, and Fuentes.

Let us hope this attractive reprint will bring Rómulo Gallegos the readers he deserves.

Larry McMurtry

PART I

I

WHO IS WITH US?

A LARGE dugout was making its way up the Arauca, keeping close to the right side of the gorge.

Two boatmen propelled it by means of a slow, painful, and slavish manœuvre. Bronzed body bathed in sweat, apparently insensible to the torrid sun though but meagrely covered by dirty trousers tucked up above the knee, each in turn plunged a long pole into the muddy bed of the stream; then, with the upper end pressed against his powerful chest, set the craft in motion by tramping from bow to stern with heavy, measured stride and back bent from the strain. And while one struggled aft, panting, the other would return to the bow, renewing the desultory talk which lightened the bitter toil, or singing, between mighty indrawings of breath, some significant ballad of the boatman's life—the laborious poling of league upon league upstream, or the cautious gliding among overhanging boughs during the descent.

The *patrón,* a guide of long experience in the streams

and channels of the plain of the Apure, sat in the stern, the bar of the tiller in his right hand, and kept a sharp watch for the currents which form among the tangles of waterlogged limbs and tree-trunks strewed on the river-bed, and for the eddies which would indicate the presence of an alligator lurking in ambush.

There were two passengers. Under the awning sat a young man whose strong, though not athletic, stature and decided expressive features gave him an air of almost aristocratic hauteur. His bearing and attire were those of the city dweller who is careful of his appearance. As though indicating a conflict of emotions concerning his affairs, the quiet pride of his expression would change for moments to a look of enthusiasm, and his eyes would light up joyously as he gazed at the surrounding country; but this would be followed by a frown and a dejected contraction of the corners of his mouth.

His fellow-passenger was one of those men of disturbing aspect and Asiatic cast of feature who make one think of the possibility of a strain of Tartar blood mysteriously introduced into South America at some unknown time. They belong to an inferior race, cruel, gloomy, and entirely unlike the inhabitants of the Plain. This man was stretched out beyond the awning, with his poncho beneath him, pretending to be asleep — a feint which did not influence either the *patrón* or the boatmen, who did not lose sight of him for an instant.

A blinding sun, the sun of the Plains at midday, flung

its glare over the yellow waters of the Arauca and the trees along its banks. Through the open spaces occasionally breaking the almost continual density of the growths along the riverside could be seen, on the right, the basin of the Apure, a succession of small grassy plains enclosed by chaparral and palm trees, while on the left was the immense basin of the Arauca — its sides, vast green prairies stretching as far as the eye could reach, dotted at wide intervals by the blackness of wandering herds. In the deep silence the tread of the boatmen on the deck of the boat resounded monotonously, monotonously to the point of exasperation. Now and then the *patrón* would put a conch-horn to his lips, drawing from it a hoarse, groaning note which lost itself in the depths of the surrounding silence and was succeeded by the disagreeable chatter of the chenchena-fowls and the hurried plunges of the alligators dozing on the sunny deserted sand-banks — the fearful lords of the wide, silent, lonely stream.

The oppressive heat of midday increased in intensity. The sloughy smell of the tepid water broken by the boat became irritating. The boatmen had ceased to sing. The spirits of those on board were weighed down by the crushing atmosphere of the desert.

"We're coming to the Big Tree," remarked the *patrón* at last, turning to the passenger under the awning and pointing out a giant tree. "You can eat your lunch comfortably and have a good siesta there."

The disturbing passenger opened his slanting eyes a little and murmured:

"It's not far to the Bramador Pass, and there's a fine place there for a siesta."

"The *señor* gives orders here," the *patrón* said sharply, alluding to the passenger under the awning, "and he's not interested in the resting place at the Bramador Pass."

The man looked at him craftily and answered, in a voice as smooth and sticky as the quagmires of the Plain:

"All right, then, I didn't say anything, *patrón*."

Santos Luzardo turned his head suddenly. All at once, although hitherto oblivious of the man's presence, he had recognized that peculiar voice.

He had first heard it when crossing the gallery of an inn at San Fernando. Some cowboys had been talking about their work, and one of them broke off what he was saying and exclaimed,

"That's the man!"

The second time he had heard that voice was in a roadside lodging-house. The suffocating heat of the night had forced him to go out into the patio. In one of the galleries there were two men swinging in hammocks, and one of them had ended the story he was telling with these words:

"What I did was shove the dagger at him. He managed the rest himself. Went on pushing as if he liked the cool feeling of the steel."

Luzardo had heard the voice again, the night before. Just as he came to the inn at the place where he intended to cross the Arauca, his horse had a sunstroke, and he found that he would have to spend the night there and continue his trip on a river boat which at that season shipped hides for San Fernando. He had arranged for departure the following day. Just as he was falling asleep, he heard someone say:

"You go on ahead, partner. I'm going to see if there's room for me on the boat."

The three scenes flashed clearly and exactly across his memory, and Santos Luzardo drew this conclusion, which was to be responsible for a change in the purpose for which he had come to the country of the Arauca:

"This fellow has been following me all the way from San Fernando. That business of the fever was just a blind. I wonder why that didn't occur to me this morning?"

As it happened, the man had appeared that morning at dawn, just as the boat was about to leave. He was shivering, wrapped up in his poncho, and had asked the *patrón:*

"Will you take me along a little ways? I've got to get to the Bramador Pass and I can't sit on a horse with this fever. I'll pay well, you know."

"I'm sorry, my friend," answered the *patrón,* after a keen glance at the stranger. The *patrón* was, like all *llanero,* or Plainsmen, a bit suspicious. "I can't give you a lift, because the *señor* has hired the boat, and he wants to go alone."

But Luzardo, without any question, and without noticing the significant wink of the riverman, had allowed the man to come aboard.

Now he watched him out of the corner of his eye, and asked himself:

"I wonder what this fellow is about? He's already had plenty of chances to knife me, if that's what he was sent for. I'll bet he's one of the El Miedo outfit. I'll find out, pretty soon."

And putting his sudden thought into words, he asked the *patrón,* raising his voice:

"Tell me, *patrón:* Do you know this Doña Barbara of whom there are so many tales told in the Apure country?"

The boatmen glanced at each other, and the master, after a moment's pause, answered with the phrase used by the Plainsman confronted with an indiscreet question:

"I'll tell you, young man: I come from a place a long way from here."

Luzardo smiled knowingly; but he was determined to carry out his idea of sounding the disquieting stranger, and so added, without taking his eyes off the latter:

"They say she's a desperate woman, and leader of a troop of bandits she orders to assassinate anyone who shows any signs of opposing her."

A sudden movement of the *patrón's* steering hand made the boat swerve roughly, and one of the boatmen, pointing to what looked like a mass of tree trunks washed up on the right bank, exclaimed, turning to Luzardo:

"Look! You wanted to shoot alligators. See how they're piled up on the sand there!"

Luzardo smiled again, with the same knowing expression on his face; and standing up, brought the stock of his rifle to his shoulder. But the shot missed its mark, and the huge reptiles slid hurriedly into the water, churning it until it boiled.

When he saw the beasts plunge unharmed into the water, the stranger muttered, "Fine beasts, but they got away alive."

But only the *patrón* could hear him, and he looked the man over from head to foot as though he wanted to drag the dark meaning of his remark out of his body. The stranger pretended to be unaware of this attention, and when he had gotten to his feet and had stretched himself, slowly and freely, he said:

"Good. Here we are at the Big Tree, and my fever's all sweated out. Too bad it's gone."

Now Luzardo was the one who remained silent—a sombre silence—and in the meantime the boat had come to a stop at the place selected by the *patrón* for their midday rest. All got out. The boatmen drove a stake into the sand and moored the craft to it. The stranger went into the thicket, and Luzardo, seeing him go away, asked the *patrón:*

"Do you know that man?"

"Know him? Well, not exactly, because it's the first time I've come across him; but I think he's the one people around here call the Wizard."

One of the boatmen intervened:

"And you're not making a mistake, chief. That's the man."

"And this Wizard, what sort of person is he?" Luzardo asked.

"Think the worst things you can about a person, and put a little more with that, and don't be afraid that you're going too far," replied the riverman. "He's not from these parts. A *guate,* as we say here. A footpad from San Camilo, and he came down here some years ago, from ranch to ranch, all through the Arauca basin, until he got to Doña Barbara's place, where he works now. You know the saying: 'God makes them and the Devil brings them together.' They call him the Wizard because he is so good at catching wild horses. They say besides that he knows prayers that never fail to cure worms in horses and cattle. But if you ask me, his real business is something else. I mean what you spoke of before—Really, you nearly made me upset the boat!—That is, he's Doña Barbara's chief cut-throat."

"Then I wasn't mistaken."

"Where you were mistaken was in giving him a place on the boat. And let me give you a bit of advice, since you're a young man and a stranger here: Don't travel with anybody you don't know as well as the palm of your own hand. And since I've made free to give one bit of advice, I'm going to give you another, because I like you. Be very careful of Doña Barbara. You're going to Altamira, and that is, so to speak, her back gate. I can tell you now that I *do* know her. She's a woman who has pocketed heaps of men, and she never misses when she begins sweet-talking. She gives a man a love potion and ties him to her apron-strings, and then does what she likes with him, because she knows witchcraft. And if it's a case of an enemy, she don't shed tears at sending somebody who's daring enough to put him out of the way. And that's what she keeps the Wizard for. I don't know what you're looking for around here, but let me tell you again: Be careful. That woman's got a cemetery of her own."

Santos Luzardo remained wrapped in thought, and the *patrón,* fearing that he had said more than he had been asked to, added reassuringly:

"But I'll tell you the other side, too. All this is what people say, but you don't need to put much faith in it, because the Plainsmen are a born race of liars, I'm sorry to say, and even when they are telling the truth they exaggerate it so much that it might as well be a lie. Besides, there's nothing to worry about for the time being.

We've four men and a rifle, and The Little Old Father is with us."

While they were talking on the beach, the Wizard, hidden behind a hummock, was listening to the conversation· as he ate, with the slowness characteristic of his movements, the lunch he had in his knapsack. Meanwhile the boatmen had spread Luzardo's blanket under the tree, placing upon it the bag in which he carried his provisions. Then they fetched their own food from the boat, and the *patrón* joined them. During the time they spent eating their frugal lunch in the shade of a tree, the leader told Santos some of the incidents of his life on the streams and channels of the Plains. At last, wearied by the heat, he lapsed into silence, and all was still save for the gentle lapping of the waves against the sides of the boat.

Worn out with their toil, the boatmen flung themselves on their backs and soon began to snore. Luzardo leaned against the trunk of the tree and, crushed by the loneliness of the wild surroundings, he let sleep overcome him.

When he awoke, the watchful *patrón* said to him:

"You've had a good siesta."

And in truth, the afternoon was nearly at an end, and the breath of a fresh breeze was moving over the Arauca. Hundreds of black points bristled on the wide surface — the snouts of alligators breathing just flush with the level of the stream, motionless, lulled by the warm caress of the muddy waters. Then, in the middle of the river, slowly arose the head of an immense alligator. He came entirely to the surface, lazily blinking his scaly eyelids.

Santos Luzardo grabbed the rifle and stood up, eager to make up for his earlier failure. But the *patrón* intervened:

"Don't shoot him."

"Why, *patrón?*"

"Because—Because another of them might pay us off if you hit him, or even if you miss him. That's the One-Eyed Alligator of the Bramador Pass, and bullets don't go into him."

And as Santos seemed determined, he repeated:

"Don't shoot, my boy. Listen to me."

As he said this, his gaze turned, with a swift expression of warning, towards something which seemed to be on the other side of the tree. Santos turned and discovered the Wizard, leaning against the trunk and apparently asleep. He left the rifle where he had got it, went around the tree, and stopping short in front of the man, demanded, without paying any attention to the feigned slumber:

"So you like to hear what other people are saying, eh?"

The man opened his eyes, slowly, as the alligator had done, and replied with perfect calm:

"I like to be quiet when I'm thinking."

"What do you think about when you're pretending to be asleep?"

The man bore the gaze of his interlocutor without flinching, and said:

"The *señor* is right. The land is wide, and there's room for all of us without bothering each other. Excuse me for coming to rest against this tree. *Sabe?*"

And he went farther off to lie down, flat on his back with his hands under his neck.

The little scene had been watched expectantly by the *patrón* and the boatmen, who had, upon hearing voices, awakened with the rapidity characteristic of men whose lives are spent among dangers and who pass immediately from heavy sleep to watchfulness. The *patrón* murmured:

"Hoho! The tenderfoot isn't afraid of the Terror of the Savannah?"

Luzardo suggested at that moment:

"Whenever you're ready, *patrón,* we can go on. We've had our bit of rest."

"Right away, then," replied the *patrón;* and addressing the Wizard in a tone of authority:

"Get up, my friend! We're going."

"Thank you, *señor,*" the man answered, without budging. "Very much obliged to you for wanting to take me all the way, but I can go on from here by shanks' mare. I'm not very far from home. I won't ask how much I owe you, because I know that people of your class aren't used to making dead beats pay you for favours. But, at your service! My name is Melquíades Gamarra, your servant, and I wish you a good voyage indeed, *señor*."

Santos was already going towards the boat, when the *patrón,* after exchanging a few words in a low voice with the boatmen, stopped him, determined to anticipate any emergency:

"Just a minute. I won't let this man travel behind us in this jungle. Either he goes ahead or we take him in the boat."

The Wizard, whose ears were of the keenest, heard what was said.

"Don't be afraid, *patrón*. I'm going ahead of you. And thank you for the good character you've given me."

And saying this, he stood up, gathered up his poncho, slung the knapsack over his shoulder, all with entire calm, and set off along the open plain which stretched out, a little way from the forest, along the bank.

The others got into the boat. The boatmen untied the rope, and after pushing the craft into deep water, leaped on board and seized their poles, while the *patrón,* already at the tiller, asked Luzardo out of a clear sky:

"Are you a good shot? Excuse my curiosity."

"It looks as though I'm a very poor one, *patrón*. So bad that you didn't want me to try again. No doubt, I've had better luck at other times."

"Evidently!" exclaimed the riverman. "You're not

a bad shot. I knew that, from the way you took aim. And yet the bullet was about six yards away from the alligators."

"The hare gets away from the best hunter, you know."

"Yes. But in your case there was something else. You didn't hit, good shot as you are, because there was somebody near you who didn't want you to hit those alligators. And if I'd let you shoot the next time, you'd have missed again."

"The Wizard, you mean? *Patrón,* do you believe that man possesses supernatural powers?"

"You're a young man and you haven't seen anything yet. Witchcraft does exist. If I was to tell you a tale I've heard about that man — and I will tell it, because you ought to know what to expect."

He spat out his wad of tobacco and was on the point of beginning the story when one of the boatmen interrupted him:

"We're going alone, *patrón!"*

"That's so, boys. This is the work of that damned Wizard, too. Let's go back again."

"What's happened?" asked Luzardo.

"We've left our Little Old Father on land."

The boat returned to the point of departure. The *patrón* headed her out once more, while he asked in a loud voice:

"Who is with us?"

"God!" answered the boatmen.

"And the Virgin!" added the *patrón;* and turning to Luzardo: "That was the Little Old Father we'd left on shore. When you go out on these streams, and leave shore, you've got to leave with God. There are many dangers to be avoided, and if the Little Old Father isn't in the boat, no riverman feels safe. The alligators are watching for you without making a ripple, and the electric eel and the ray are waiting, and the school of caribs is there, and the buzzards overhead ready to strip your bones before you can say Father, Son and Holy Ghost."

Wide plains! Wild vastness! Illimitable deserted prairies—deep, silent, solitary streams! How useless is a cry for help when the tail of the alligator lashes against the boat, how useless in these lonely spots!

Santos Luzardo already knew why the rivermen wanted the "Little Father" with them; but now he could also apply the wish to himself, for he had begun the voyage with one plan, and now he was embracing another totally different from the first.

II

THE DESCENDANT OF THE CUNAVICHERO

IN THE wildest and most deserted part of the Arauca basin was situated the ranch of Altamira, originally some two hundred leagues of fertile savannahs giving pasture to the immense herds which grazed in its fastnesses and containing one of the finest flocks of wild herons in the country.

It had been established years and years before by Don Evaristo Luzardo, one of those nomad cattle-men who used to — and still do — scour with their herds the vast prairies of the Cunaviche basin, passing from this to the basin of the Arauca, which was less remote from the centers of population. His descendants, real Plainsmen of " bare feet and side buttons " who never went beyond the boundaries of the ranch, improved and extended the property until they had converted it into one of the most important in the country; but when the family became rich and numerous, some of its members turned towards the cities, while the others remained under the palm-thatched roof of the ranch-house; the peaceful patriarchal life of the earlier Luzardos was succeeded by separation, and this brought the discord which was to give them tragic fame.

The last owner of the original Altamira was Don José de los Santos, who, in order to save the property from the ruin of wholesale division, bought the interest of his fellow-owners, an undertaking which cost him a long lifetime of toil and privation; but, upon his death, his children José and Panchita — the latter married to Sebastian Barquero — chose to divide, and the old establishment was succeeded by two, one the property of José, keeping its original name, the other taking the name of La Barquereña after its owner's surname.

Beginning at that time, because of an ambiguous phrase in the will which described the boundary line as "the palm grove of La Chusmita," discord arose between the brothers-in-law, for each declared that the phrase should be interpreted, to *his* advantage; and thus they commenced one of those endless litigations which make the fortunes of several generations of lawyers. It would have ended by ruining them, had not the same intransigeance which was making them waste a fortune over an unproductive bit of land also made them determine, when a settlement was proposed, to have "all or nothing." And since both could not have all, they agreed that both should have nothing, and engaged to build a fence around the grove, which thus became enclosed and no part of either property.

But the matter did not end there. In the centre of the grove was the bed of a channel which had dried up. In the winter this became a quagmire, a mudhole which was death to any man or beast attempting to cross it, and one day, when he spied in it a drowned steer belonging to the Barquero herd, José Luzardo protested to Sebastian Barquero, declaring that this was a violation of the neutral ground. The dispute became heated; Barquero swung his whip at the face of his brother-in-law, and the latter, whipping out his revolver, toppled Barquero from his horse with a bullet through his head. Then the reprisals commenced, and with the partisans killing each other off, the population, composed as it was of practically nothing but the various branches of the two families, was in the end nearly wiped out. And the seed of tragedy was born again in the breast of every single one.

When war broke out between Spain and the United States, José Luzardo, "true to his race," as he phrased it, sympathized with the mother country, while his eldest son Felix, a symbol of the new times, took the part of the "Yankees." The Caracas newspapers came to the ranch, about once a month, and with the very first items of news, read by the son, for Don José was rapidly losing his sight, they became engaged in a fierce dispute which led to these bitter words from the old man:

"Anybody'd have to be mighty stupid to believe that those Chicago sausage-packers can beat us," to which

Felix, livid and stammering with rage, replied, facing him defiantly:

"Maybe the Spaniards will win, but I won't stand for your insulting me for nothing."

Don José looked at him from head to foot, with an expression of scorn, and burst into a loud laugh. The son ended by losing his head, and drew his revolver from its holster; whereupon the father cut his guffaw short, and without any change of voice or position, but with a proud expression, said slowly:

"Shoot! But don't miss me, or I'll nail you to that wall with my lance-head."

This happened in the ranch-house, shortly after supper, when the family was gathered around the lamp. Doña Asunción hastened to interpose, and Santos, who was about fourteen years old at that time, was stupefied with horror.

Whether overcome by the terrible calm of his father, or certain that the latter would carry out his threat if he shot and missed, or repenting of his violence—at any rate, Felix replaced the revolver in his holster and left the room. Shortly afterward, he saddled his horse, determined to leave his father's house, and it was in vain that Doña Asunción pleaded and wept. Meanwhile, as though nothing had happened, Don José had put on his glasses and read stoically the news items ending with the disaster at Cavite. But Felix was not content with leaving his home. He made common cause with the Barqueros against his own family in that war to the death, whose most pitiless advocate was his aunt Panchita, and which was winked at by the authorities, for it was the day of the caciques, and the Luzardos and Barqueros shared the lordship of the Arauca.

Nearly all the men of both families had fallen in personal encounters, when one night, when he knew there was to be a cockfight in the village and that his father would be there, Felix also went, under the joint influence of alcohol and his cousin Lorenzo Barquero, and burst in, shouting:

"Here's a Porto Rican bantam. Not even a Yankee, but I want to see if there's any Spanish *cripple* to match him! I'll put him in with his spurs clipped to fight to the finish."

The unequal struggle had already ended with the victory of the "Yankees," and Felix had of course said that to provoke his father. Don José wanted to use a whip in correction of this insolence, but Felix flew to arms. So did the father, who returned home shortly afterward, dejected, grim, and suddenly grown old, to deliver this news to his wife:

"I've just killed Felix. They're bringing him in."

Going to the room where the first scene of the tragedy had occurred, he shut himself up in it, gave strict orders that he was not to be disturbed, removed the lance-head from his belt, and buried it in the wall where he had threatened to nail his son with it, that night of the tragic newspaper reading. For it was there, where he had threatened to kill his son, that he wished to have the murderous steel before his eyes until they should be closed for ever, as a sign of expiation.

Shut up in that room, without so much as bread and water, without moving, almost without blinking his eyes; with the light from a single shutter, and eyes which would soon learn to do without light in the darkness, with his whole will bent on a horrible expiation for his deed—there he waited day after day for the death to which he had condemned himself, and there death found him, sitting up rigid in his chair, his gaze fixed on the blade stuck in the wall.

When the authorities came to perform the farce usual in such cases, there was no further need of punishment. Indeed, it was with difficulty that they managed to close his eyes.

Within a few days, Doña Asunción left the Plain for ever, moving to Caracas with Santos, the sole survivor of the hecatomb. She wanted to preserve him by educating him in another environment, hundreds of leagues away from that tragic scene.

The first years in the city were so much lost time for the boy. The sudden transplantation from the midst of the Plain, rude, yet full of intense, character-forming emotional life, to the smooth, lulling atmosphere of the city, existence between four walls in the society of a mother broken by terror, produced a peculiar slumber of his faculties. He had been a boy of spirit, keenly intelligent, full of high courage; the pride of his father, who enjoyed watching him break a wild horse or retrieve himself with dexterity and assurance from amidst the constantly recurring dangers of the cattleman's life; a worthy representative of the fearless race that had furnished more than one epic with its centaur and the Plain with many a lord. His mother, with another concept of life, had placed so many hopes in him when she heard him express ideas revealing a subtle and reflective mind; he now became dull and procrastinating, and changed into a misanthrope.

"I don't know you any more when I see you, son. You're like a captive broncho," said his mother, a Plainswoman still in spite of everything.

"He's growing," her friends observed. "That's how boys are at his age."

"It's the ruin caused by the havoc we've seen," declared Doña Asunción.

It was due to both, but the transplantation was to blame too—the longing for an endless horizon before one's eyes and the hot wind of the open country in one's face, the memory of ballads sung as one rides ahead of the herds, a nostalgia for the wild isolation of the broad, silent land. Santos was like a tuft of grass from the Plains forced to languish in a flowerpot. Sometimes Doña Asunción found him in the yard, daydreaming, lying flat on his back in a clump of neglected mignonette. He was "bushed," as the Plainsman says of the bull seeking refuge in the thicket, and lying there for days upon days without food or drink, roaring with helpless rage at the mutilation which has deprived him of his spirit and his leadership of the herd.

But in the end, the city conquered the exiled soul of Santos Luzardo. Coming to himself after the sorceress nostalgia had lost her power, he realized that he was in his nineteenth year and not much richer in knowledge than he had been when he first came from the Arauca. He resolved to make up for the time he had lost, and plunged eagerly into his studies.

Despite the reasons she had for loathing Altamira, Doña Asunción had not been willing to sell the ranch. Her soul was the robust, unchangeable soul of the Plainsman, for whom there is nothing like his native soil, and although she had no thought of returning to the Arauca country, neither had she considered breaking the bond which joined her to it, especially as the ranch, managed by a loyal and honest overseer, brought her an excellent income.

"Let Santos sell it when I die," she used to say. But when she was dying, she said to him:

"Don't sell Altamira as long as you can avoid it."

And Santos kept it, out of respect for his mother's last wish, and because the income made it easy for him to cover the expenses of his temperate existence. Otherwise, he would have had no struggle in parting with the land. His native soil had no attraction for him, neither Altamira nor all the rest of it, since in losing his feeling that he was a part of that territory, he had lost all feeling for his fatherland. Urban life and intellectual habits had barred from his spirit all urge toward the free and savage life of the ranch. At the same time, however, they had produced an aspiration which that city itself could not permanently satisfy. Caracas, with all its excellencies, was far from being that ideal city, intricate and perfect as a mind, in which all movement becomes converted into ideas, and every reaction bears the seal of conscious efficiency. And as this ideal seemed to be realized only in the aged civilization of Europe, he embraced the plan of permanently expatriating himself as soon as he had completed his studies at the university.

As a means to this end, he counted upon the income from Altamira, or, if that were sold, upon the earnings of the money invested in city real estate, since his profession as lawyer would afford him but little hope abroad. But meanwhile Altamira was no longer in the hands of the upright overseer of his mother's day, and while Santos was content with a grudging glance at the statements, always so clear on paper, which the managers presented, the latter were making ducks and drakes of the hacienda. Besides, they allowed the cattle thieves to sack it and permitted the neighbours to brand as their own the very calves clinging to the udders of the Luzardo cows.

Then began the legal struggles with the notorious Doña Barbara, into whose hands were passing leagues and leagues of the savannahs of Altamira as the result of arbitrary boundaries fixed by the Tribunal.

His studies finished, Santos went to San Fernando to see if he could find evidence to make it still possible to institute action for restoration. But there, after a minute analysis of the judgments in Doña Barbara's favour, if he proved to himself that everything — bribes, violence, and justice — had been astonishingly easy for the boss woman of the Arauca, he also discovered that whatever designs on his property had succeeded had done so because his right to Altamira suffered from the weaknesses common to the acquisitions of all squatters, and his ancestor, Don Evaristo of the Cunaviche, had been hardly more than that.

So he decided to sell the ranch. But as no one wanted to make himself Doña Barbara's neighbour, and moreover, the revolutions had impoverished the Plain, he spent considerable time trying to find a purchaser. At last one appeared, but he declared:

"We can't close the deal here, Doctor. You'll have to see, with your own eyes, what Altamira is like. It's pretty well run down. A few soapbark trees are all that's left of the savannahs. The cattle are all thin. If you wish to, go there and wait for me. I'm going to Caracas now, to sell a herd, but I'll be at Altamira within a month, and we can talk about the property then."

"I'll wait for you there," said Santos, and the next day he left for Altamira.

On the journey, before the spectacle of the deserted Plains, he thought of doing many things: settling on the ranch to struggle against the enemy; defending his own property and his neighbours,' outraged by the chiefs of the country, of whom Doña Barbara was but one of many; struggling against nature herself, against the unhealthful conditions which were wiping out the race of Plainsmen, against the alternate floods and droughts which fought over the land all during the year, against the desert which shut off the Plain from civilization.

These, however, were not yet plans, but thoughts, the soliloquies of a man reasoning; and an optimistic mood would be succeeded immediately by pessimism.

"To carry all this out," thought Santos," needs something more than the will to do it. What good will it do to put an end to the authority of Doña Barbara? It will just reappear under another name. The really necessary thing is to change the circumstances that lead to these evils, to populate the country. But before you populate, you must have sanitation, and before you have sanitation, you have to populate. It's a vicious circle."

But a single incident, his meeting with the Wizard and the words of the riverman warning him against crossing the path of the dread Doña Barbara, had roused his impulse to struggle. It was the same aggressiveness which had ruined the Luzardos; but here it was subordinated to an ideal. To struggle against Doña Barbara, symbol of the times, was not only to free Altamira, but to destroy the forces which were holding back the Plain. And he decided to throw himself into the task, with the impulsiveness of the Cunavicheros, men of a vigorous race, and also with the ideals of a civilized man, in which they had been lacking.

III

THE OGRESS

FROM beyond the Cunaviche, from beyond the Cinaruco, beyond the Meta — from beyond everything, said the plainsmen of the Arauca, for whom, undoubtedly, *everything* is " right there, behind that thicket." Thence came the dread *guaricha.* Fruit of the sowings of white adventurers in the dark passion of the Indian, her origin was lost in the dramatic mystery of the virgin forest.

In the deeps of her hazy recollections, in the first glimmerings of her memory, she saw herself on a pirogue which plied through the great waters of the Orinoco forest. There were six men on board, and she called the captain " daddy." All of them, except old Eustaquio, the pilot, made the same brutal gestures toward her — cuffs, and kisses tasting of rum and chimó.

Going between Bolivar City and Río Negro, the boat carries on piracy under patent of legitimate enterprise. It set out laden with barrels of rum and boxes of trinkets, cloth, and spoiled food, and returned bursting with tonka beans and balatá. They exchanged the former for the latter at some settlements, and were content merely to cheat the Indians from whom they secured their rich cargo; but in other places the crew landed with nothing but their rifles slung over their shoulders, and plunged into the woods. At these times, when they returned to the pirogue, the fragrant tonka beans or black balatá came aboard dyed in blood.

One afternoon, as they were leaving Bolivar City, up came a hungry-looking ragged young man, whom Barbarita had seen several times along the wharf gazing at her with bulging eyes as she, as cook of the pirogue, was preparing dinner for the pirates. He said simply that his name was Hasdrubal, and made a proposition to the captain:

"I've got to go to Manaos and I haven't the money to pay my way. If you'll be good enough to take me to Río Negro, I'll be willing to work my passage. I can be useful at anything from cook to purser."

He was ingratiating and insidious, with the winning grace of the intelligent vagabond, and making a good impression upon the captain, was engaged as cook, so that Barbarita might have a little rest. The captain was beginning to indulge her, for the mestiza was fifteen and very pretty.

Some days passed. When they were resting, or at night, when they were seated around the fire on the beach where they camped, Hasdrubal would enliven the meal with entertaining stories of his vagabond existence. Barbara nearly split her sides laughing; but if he interrupted his story to dwell on her strong, fresh laughter, she would stop suddenly and lower her eyes in maidenly embarrassment. And one day she murmured in his ear:

"Don't look at me that way, because Daddy is getting suspicious."

It was a fact that the captain was repenting his having taken the strange young man on board, for his services were going to cost dearly, especially those of teaching Barbarita to read and write, which had not been required. These lessons, on which Hasdrubal laid great stress, and her writing, with his hand guiding hers, were drawing the two together a bit too much.

One evening, after the lessons, Hasdrubal began to tell her the sad part of his history: The tyranny of his stepfather which had driven him away from home, his unfortunate adventures, wanderings without direction, hunger and need. Then came the hard work in the Yuruari mines and the struggle with death on a wretched cot in the hospital. Finally, he spoke of his plans. He was going to Manaos to make his fortune, for he was tired of wandering, and was going to give it up and devote himself to work.

He started to say something more, but stopped short and sat watching the river glide silently before them through the impressive landscape.

She understood that she did not occupy in the young man's plans the important place she had imagined, and her lovely eyes filled with tears. The pair remained thus for a long while. She would never forget that afternoon. Far off, in the profound silence, could be heard the hoarse roar of the Atures rapids. Suddenly Hasdrubal looked her straight in the eyes and asked:

"Do you know what the captain intends to do with you?"

Oppressed by the sudden force of a horrible intuition, she exclaimed:

"Daddy!"

"He doesn't deserve having you call him that. He intends to sell you to the Turk."

This was what they called a leprous and sadistic Syrian, who had become wealthy through exploitation of balatá. He lived in the heart of the Orinoco fastnesses, apart from men on account of the wasting disease, but surrounded by a harem of Indian girls of marriageable age whom he had seized or bought from their fathers, not only to sate his lust, but also to avenge the hatred of an incurable towards every healthy being by giving them the disease.

Hasdrubal had learned, from conversations among the crew which he had overheard, that this rubber-trading Moloch had, on their previous trip, offered twenty ounces of gold for Barbarita, and that if the business was not settled then and there, it was simply because the captain wanted a better price for her; and this would not be difficult for him to get, because in a few months the girl had become an alluring woman.

She had not been entirely unaware that this was the fate in store for her; but until then, the horror surrounding it had not succeeded in producing more than a certain feeling, half pleasure and half fear, which arose from the lascivious glances of the men with whom she shared the intimacy of the pirogue.

But when she became enamored of Hasdrubal she had resurrected her buried soul, and the words she had just heard strangled her with horror.

"Save me! take me with you!" she was about to say to him, when she saw the captain coming. He was carrying a rifle, and he said to Hasdrubal:

"Well, young man, you've talked enough. Now let's have you do something more profitable. The Toad is going to look for a bit of tonka beans they ought to be keeping for us here, and you're going with him." And then, giving him the rifle: "This is to defend yourself with, if the Indians attack you."

Hasdrubal thought a moment. Could the captain have heard what he had just said to the girl? What about this commission? . . . At any rate, he had to face the music.

As he rose, Barbarita tried to stop him with a pleading glance, but he winked swiftly at her, and getting up with his decision made, he left the camp, following The

Toad. This man was the mate, and the captain's right hand when there was dirty work to be done. Hasdrubal knew that; but he knew that he would be irretrievably lost from that moment if he showed fear or unwillingness to obey the command. At least, he had a rifle and would be pitted against only one man, while here were five against him. Barbarita's glances followed him, and for some time her eyes remained fixed on the gap in the bank through which he had disappeared.

While this had been going on, the crew had exchanged significant glances; and when the captain, a few minutes later, ordered them to beat about up the beach, under pretext of a possible attack by the Indians — he had already given such an order to old Eustaquio — they understood that he wanted to get them away from the camp so that he might be alone with the girl, and answered, after a brief session of muttering:

"Leave that for later on, Captain. We're tired now."

This was the mutiny which had been brewing for some time on account of the girl's disturbing beauty. The captain, not daring to make the attempt to crush it, for he knew that the three men were in complete accord and ready for anything, postponed the punishment until the return of The Toad, of whose blind adherence he was certain.

Suddenly the song of the screech-owl reached their ears, a knell to strike icy fear to the traveller's heart in the desolate silence of the savage twilight.

"Tu-hoo! tu-hoo!"

Was it an evil omen or Hasdrubal's death cry? was it an illusion caused by the snapping of overstrained nerves, or the mysteriously relayed prolongation of a mortal blow in another body, the slitting of Hasdrubal's throat by The Toad? Barbarita could remember only that overcome by a sudden rush of feeling, she had fallen face downward to the ground with a cry that rent her throat.

The rest happened seemingly without her having realized it: The death of the captain and of The Toad, who had returned alone, and her rape at the hands of Hasdrubal's avengers.

When old Eustaquio, hearing her shriek, came running to her aid, wholly spent with his exertion, the others had had their fill, and one remarked:

"Now we can sell her to the Turk, and the twenty ounces he offered will be enough."

The night is red with the gleam of fires, and wild cries ring out. They are hunting the heron. The natives light heaps of straw around the inaccessible bogs, and their cries raise the frightened birds. The wings show red in the fiery glare enclosed by the pitchy darkness. The hunters cease their shouting, the fire is put out, and the bewildered birds drop helpless within easy reach.

In Barbarita's life, Hasdrubal's affection was a brief flight, scarcely more than a flutter, in the gleam of the first pure affection she had ever experienced, a gleam forever extinguished by the violence of the hunters of pleasure.

She was rescued from them that night by Eustaquio, the old Baniba Indian who piloted the pirogue simply to be near this daughter of the woman of his tribe who, dying of the captain's cruelty, had begged him never to abandon the girl. But neither the quiet life of the settlement to which they fled, nor the peaceful sense of fatality roused now and then in her Indian soul by the doleful sound of the native flute, had succeeded in lulling her bitter torments. A hard, ceaseless frown creased her forehead, and a hateful gleam lighted her eyes. Her heart had room for nothing except bitterness, and nothing pleased her so much as the sight of the male caught in destructive toils: In the bane of Camajay-Minare, the sinister deity of the Orinoco, in the hellish power of the glances of the Evil-Eyed, in the terrible effects of the herbs and roots used by the Indian women in preparing the aphrodisiacs which inflame the passions and destroy the will of men struggling against their caresses. These things attracted Barbarita to such an extent that she lived only to gain the secret knowledge necessary for bewitching men. And the entire troop of enchanters who watched over the savage life of the Indian initiated her into their shadowy lore. The Evil-Eyed, who claimed to produce the most strange and terrible diseases by a mere malign glance at the victim, the Breathers, who claimed to cure the diseases by the power of their miracle-working breath on the injured part, the Prayers, who possessed abracadabras against every ill, which were sufficient if murmured in the direction of the sufferer, however distant — all revealed their secrets to her and it was not long before the half-breed girl was entirely possessed by the grossest and most extravagant superstitions.

At the same time, her beauty was troubling the peace of the settlement. The youths coveted her, the women kept a jealous watch over her, and the prudent elders were forced to advise Eustaquio:

"Take the *guaricha* away. Go away from here with her."

And once more she led a wandering life on the wide waters, on a dugout with two Indian boatmen.

The waters of the Orinoco are yellow, those of the Guainía are black. The waters meet in the heart of the wilderness, but run on for a long distance without mingling, each retaining its own hue. Just so, it was some years before the mestiza's hot sensuality combined with her bitter loathing for men.

The first victim of this hideous mixture of passions was Lorenzo Barquero. He was the youngest son of Don Sebastian, and had been educated in Caracas. His studies were nearly completed, the future was bright with the love of a beautiful and cultured girl and the prospect of a profession in which his talent would not fail to triumph. At this time, when the trouble between the Luzardos and Barqueros broke out in the Plain, a strange moral retrogression began to appear in him. Seized with a sudden access of misanthropy, he abandoned the university and the pleasures of life in the capital for a nearby ranch, where he passed days on end lying in a hammock, silent and gloomy, like a steer shut up in his stall, until he at last definitely renounced all that could make life agreeable in Caracas — his fiancée, his studies, the brilliant society — and set off for the Plain to be swept into the whirling drama in progress there.

There he met Barbarita, one afternoon when Eustaquio's boat, ascending the Arauca with a cargo of provisions for the Barquereña ranch, stopped at the Bramador Pass, where Lorenzo was directing the examination of a herd.

"When I saw you the first time you reminded me of Hasdrubal," she told him, after she had narrated the tragic tale. "One day you will be the captain, and another day The Toad."

He replied, with the vanity of possession:

"Yes — every one of those men you hate. But when I play their parts, I make you love them, one by one, in spite of yourself."

"But I'll ruin them all, in you," she shrieked.

This savage passion, which actually lent a touch of

originality to the adventure, ended in the total perversion of Lorenzo's already unstable spirit.

Not even motherhood could quench the ogress' hatred. On the contrary, it deepened that hatred. A child in her womb was to her another victory for the male, a new injury undergone. And under the influence of this feeling she conceived and bore a girl child, who was perforce suckled at another breast, for her mother would not so much as look at her.

Nor did Lorenzo, a mere prey to the insatiable woman, pay the child any attention. Victim of the aphrodisiacs she mixed in his food and drink, it was not long before the stalwart youth of the man apparently destined for a brilliant career became no more than the life of an organism subject to the lowest vices, with a broken will and a degenerate spirit well on the way to bestiality. And while the increasing torpor of his faculties, manifested in days of unbroken stupor, was hurrying him to the hideous misery of vital exhaustion from the poisonous potions, greed despoiled him of his patrimony.

The suggestion was made to Doña Barbara by a certain Colonel Apolinar who had come to the vicinity in search of lands he wished to buy with the proceeds of graft gathered during his term in the Civil Court of a village in the region. An expert in all sorts of pettifogging, when he became aware of Lorenzo's moral ruin, and realized that this woman should be an easy conquest, he rapidly formed his plans, and when he commenced his courtship, spoke these words between compliments:

"There's a sure, simple way for you to get control of La Barquereña. Without marrying Don Lorenzo, since you say you couldn't bear being called any man's wife. A dummy bill of sale. It all depends on his signing the deed, but that won't be hard for you. If you like, I'll draw it up so there won't be any chance of complications with the family."

The idea found a warm reception.

"All right. Draw up the deed. I'll get it signed."

It was done without any resistance on Lorenzo's part. But when it came to registering the deed, Barbara discovered a clause by which she acknowledged receiving the stipulated price from Apolinar, and surrendered the property as security.

Apolinar explained:

"It was necessary to insert the clause as a blind for Don Lorenzo's family, because if they discover that the sale is a dummy, they can demand annulment on grounds of illegality. So that there won't be any doubt, I'll pay you the money before a notary. But don't worry about it. Just a little game between us. Then you give me back the money and I give you the counter-deed nullifying the clause."

And he showed her a secret document whose invalidity was his own affair.

It was too late to back out, and besides, she had made

her own plans for getting hold of the money Apolinar wished to change into land. So, returning the counter-deed, she replied:

"Very well. Just as you like, Apolinar."

Apolinar understood that she was also surrendering to his advances, and felt quite pleased with himself. First the woman who had signified her capitulation by addressing him familiarly, then the property, and then his money intact.

Some days later Doña Barbara informed Lorenzo:

"I've made up my mind to have the Colonel in your place. So you're in the way here."

Lorenzo thought of a very poor reply:

"I'm ready to marry you."

She answered with a coarse guffaw, and the wretched man was obliged to flee with his daughter, for good and all, to a hut in the palm grove, which was not his own either because of that agreement between his mother and his uncle José Luzardo.

Not so much as the name La Barquereña remained, Barbara changing it to El Miedo (Fear) the name of a strip of savannah where the ranch-houses stood, at the starting point of the famous wasteland.

Her greed loosed, she determined to own the entire basin of the Arauca, and aided by the advice of the experienced Apolinar, began to sue all her neighbours, winning through the corruption of the judges whatever she could not gain from justice. When the novelty of the new lover began to wear off, and all his money had been used in improving the property, she recovered her proud independence by causing, in some mysterious way, the disappearance of the man who prided himself on calling her his own.

Altamira, neglected by its owner and in the hands of easily corrupted overseers, was the chosen prey of Doña Barbara's acquisitive ambition. Lawsuits brought her league after league, and between one thing and another the boundary of El Miedo crept farther into Altamira by means of a simple change of boundary posts — this helped by the deliberate ambiguity and lack of precision the well-bribed judges wrote into their verdicts, and by the collusion of the Luzardo overseers who winked at it and let it pass.

Santos Luzardo was accustomed to change overseers upon report of each of these robberies, and thus Altamira, going from hand to hand, fell in the grasp of a certain Balbino Paiba, a former horse-dealer who had had the opportunity of buying some animals from the owner of El Miedo and the audacity to flatter her at the very moment of her needing a henchman at Altamira without having anyone suspect collusion.

She had just won another case against Santos Luzardo by cajoling his lawyer, who was susceptible in addition to being unscrupulous. The fifteen leagues of savannah belonging to Altamira went to increase the spread of El Miedo, but she was not content with this, and persuaded the lawyer to recommend Balbino Paiba for the then vacant stewardship. From then on, they worked busily, and any unbranded cattle or stray calves entering Altamira during rodeos, or stampeded, were burned with the El Miedo mark, and the uncertain boundary line went cutting deeper and deeper into Altamira. And while the adjacent properties were becoming hers by these methods and the neighbouring ranch was swelling her herds, all the money which fell into her hands disappeared from circulation. People spoke of numerous earthenware jars full of twenty-dollar gold pieces, her favourite coins, and said that she did not count money, but measured it. Perhaps there was a good deal of the legendary in the talk about her fortune; however, there was no doubt that she was very rich and extremely stingy.

As for the tales of her powers as a sorceress, neither was all here the mere fancy of the Plainsman. She really believed herself endowed with supernatural powers, and often spoke of a "Partner," who had saved her life one night by blowing out the lamp to wake her just as a peon paid to assassinate her was entering her room, and who had appeared since then to counsel her in difficult situations or to acquaint her with such distant or future happenings as might interest her. She said that he was the Nazarene of Achaguas himself, but she called him simply and naturally "my Partner"—and from this arose the legend of her compact with the devil.

Whether God or tutelary demon, it was all the same to her, for religion and witchcraft, incantations and prayers were in her mind all changed and confounded into a single mass of superstition; so that scapulars and the amulets of Indian medicine men hung on her breast in perfect harmony, and the mantel of the room where the " Partner " appeared was occupied by holy pictures, crosses of blessed palm, alligators' teeth, flints, *curvinata* stones, and fetiches from the native settlements, all sharing the same votive lamp.

In the matter of love, the ogress was no longer the wild mixture of lust and hatred. Her appetites were strangled by her greed, and the last fibres of femininity in her being were atrophied by the habits of the virago — she personally directed the labour of the peons, tossed the lasso, and could bring down a bull out in the open as well as her most skillful cowboy. She was never without her lance-head dagger and her revolver, nor did she carry them in her belt as a mere threat. If reasons of pure expediency — such as the need of a docile henchman, or in the case of Balbino Paiba, of a personal representative in the enemy camp — moved her to be generous with her caresses, she was so more as a man who takes than as a woman who gives. A deep disdain for men had replaced her implacable hatred of them.

In spite of this sort of life and the fact that she was over forty, she was still an alluring woman, and if she was entirely lacking in womanly delicacy, the imposing appearance of this Amazon put, in exchange, the stamp of originality on her beauty: there was something about her at once wild, beautiful, and terrible.

Such was the notorious Doña Barbara: a compound of lust, superstition, greed, and cruelty, with a pathetic little remnant in her bitter heart of something pure and sad—the memory of Hasdrubal, and the frustrated love which could have made her a good woman. But even this took on the characteristics of a barbarous cult demanding human sacrifice. The memory of Hasdrubal always came to her when she encountered a man who was a worthy prey.

IV

A THOUSAND DIFFERENT PATHS

THE Algarrobo Pass was the entrance to the Altamira ranch. It was marked out by two sloping clearings in the banks of the Arauca, which were high and steep at that point.

Hearing the horn which announced the boat's arrival, several girls hurried to look over the bank and three boys and a couple of men came down to the beach.

Santos recognized one of these, a good-looking Araucan with a round face and olive skin, as Antonio Sandoval, Antoñito the calf-tender in Santos's earlier days on the ranch, and his comrade in searches for wild honey and birds' nests.

Antonio removed his hat respectfully in greeting, but when Santos embraced him, as he had done upon his departure thirteen years before, the peon, deeply touched, murmured:

"Santos!"

"Your face hasn't changed, Antonio," said Luzardo,

putting both hands on the man's shoulders. The latter replied, this time with a more respectful address:

"But you have. So much so that if I hadn't known you were coming on the boat I wouldn't have recognized you."

"So I haven't surprised you, eh? How did you know I was coming?"

"It seems the peon who was with the Wizard brought the news to El Miedo."

"Oh! Yes, there were two of them, and one must have come last night."

"The messenger, Juan Primito, told me," said Antonio. "That's a booby at El Miedo, a regular telegraph for every bit of news he finds out. You can be sure I've spent the whole day worrying because the Wizard insisted on coming in the boat with you. That's what I was talking about with my partner when we heard the horn."

He was referring to his companion, whom he immediately introduced.

"Carmelito Lopez—a man you can trust with your eyes shut. He's new, but a *Luzardero* to the bone, for all that."

"Servant," replied the man, laconically, and without more than touching the brim of his hat. He was a man of angular features, with eyebrows that joined, by no means prepossessing at first sight; one of those men who are always hiding inside themselves, in the Plainsman's phrase, above all in the presence of strangers.

Despite this, and because of Antonio's recommendation, Lopez made a good impression on Luzardo, but the latter saw immediately that this had not been mutual.

Actually, Carmelito was one of the three or four peons at the ranch on whose loyalty Santos would be able to depend in the struggle he intended to undertake with his enemies. He had come to Altamira a short time before, and if he stayed in spite of the fact that he was *persona non grata* with the overseer, Paiba, it was to please Antonio, who, carrying the traditional loyalty of the Sandovals to an extreme, not only bore with the treacherous overseer but even managed to keep the few remaining honest peons in the hope of Santos's some day making up his mind to take charge of the ranch. Like Antonio, Carmelito had been happy over the prospect of the owner's arrival; it meant that Balbino Paiba would be dismissed at once and obliged to acknowledge his thefts, that Doña Barbara's abuses would cease, and that everything would be put in order.

But Carmelito's idea of manhood excluded everything he had noticed about Santos Luzardo as soon as he stepped out of the boat: the aristocratic bearing, which Carmelito considered insolent; the smoothness of his face and the delicacy of his skin, already burned by the exposure of a few days' travelling; the absence of a mustache, a characteristic of males; the pleasant manner, which he considered affectation. Then there was the unused riding habit—the tight-fitting coat, the breeches baggy in the seat and tight at the knees, the leggings in place of chaps, and a necktie! which was a fine rag for this lonely country, where covering is plenty and everything else superfluous.

"Hm!" he muttered between his teeth. "And so this is the man we expected so much from?"

At that moment Antonio's father, an old man with a face full of wrinkles and a head of jet black hair, came limping down the ramp to the beach, wreathed in smiles.

"Old Melesio!" exclaimed Santos, going to meet him. "And not a grey hair yet!"

"Indians don't paint them, Santos my boy," answered the old man, and then, after some moments of noiseless laughter, scarcely more indeed than a grin which showed his toothless gums and the mouth full of tobacco juice: "So my boy Santos hasn't forgotten me! You'll let me call you that, because I always have, you know, and we old dogs find it hard to learn new tricks."

"Whatever you like, Melesio."

"But always with respect, eh, my boy? Come rest in my house, poor as it is, before you go to yours."

The weather-beaten palisades of the corrals for the herds received at that point stretched out on the right of the sloping path. On the left were the typical Plainsman's lodgings: two houses of adobe and palm, the dwellings of Melesio's family, and between these a low shed with a thick thatched roof beneath which stood a large table encircled by benches. There was, a little farther off, another log cabin, longer and higher than the first, with untrimmed corner posts over whose short projecting branches were slung the bridles of three horses, and still another cabin apart from the houses, with newly stripped and stinking skins of deer and *carpinchos* hanging from the palm-wood beams.

Beyond this a clump of trees reared their heads: small pines, tan-barks, and the lofty carobs, the *algarrobos* which gave the Pass its name. The rest was a naked plain, the enormous grazing lands; and in the distance, above its circular horizon, floated in mirage a vast fringe of foliage, the *mata* — native forest — isolated in the midst of the savannah.

" Altamira! " Santos exclaimed. " Think of the years since I have seen it! "

The girls who had been looking over the river bank when the boat arrived came out of the house.

" My granddaughters," said Melesio. " Fly-aways, *cimarronas* as we say. All afternoon they haven't done anything but look down the river, and now that you've come they go and hide."

" Your daughters, Antonio? " Santos asked.

" No, *señor*. I'm still single, thank God."

" My other sons' children," Melesio explained. " The dead ones', God rest their souls."

They had gone into the shade of the open cabin. The ground had been carefully swept, and the benches arranged as neatly as they would have been for a dance.

An armchair, the pièce de resistance of the Plainsman, had been brought as a place of honour for the guest.

"Come out here, girls," called Melesio. "Don't be so countryfied. Come say 'How do you do' to the master."

The granddaughters, hiding behind the door, yet anxious to be presented, concealed their shyness by giggling and elbowing each other.

"You first."

"*Guá!* why not you?"

Finally they appeared, all in a row, as though on a narrow path, and greeted Luzardo, each with the same phrase as the other, pronounced in an identical sing-song, offering reluctant hands.

"How are you?" "How are you?" "How are you?"

"This is Gervasia, Manuelito's girl. This is Francisca, Andres Ramon's. Genoveva, Altagracia . . . the Sandoval heifers, they call them. The only boys are those three lumps that took your things from the boat. That's the fortune my sons left me. Eleven hungry mouths to feed."

The embarrassment of the introduction over, the girls sat on the benches in the order of their arrival, uncertain what to do with their hands or where to look. The eldest, Genoveva, was not more than seventeen. Some were quite pretty, with dark skins and rosy cheeks and black eyes. All were strong and healthy-looking.

"A fine family, Melesio," said Santos. "Strong and well. I can see there's no malaria here."

The old man shifted his wad from one cheek to the other and replied:

"I'll tell you, my boy. It's true that it's healthier here than in those other places you've passed through, but we've got our troubles with malaria too. I had eleven sons and seven grew up. Now only Antonio is left. And lots of people could say the same thing I do. What happens is that some of us are too strong for the fever. With God's help, all of us here, I hope. But the malaria has its way with the others."

He spat the juice of his tobacco, and, returning to the metaphorical speech of the man bred among cattle, added, with the Venezuelan's typical cheerful resignation:

"I wonder that the two of us are left. The worms took the whole herd, cows and calves alike."

And he laughed again, silently. Santos, taking his cue from the old man, chatted and joked with the girls a bit. They were both pleased and frightened; the old man looked on, his face contorted with noiseless mirth, and Antonio fixed his loyal gaze on the master.

Then one of the girls brought the cup of coffee which is the Plainsman's inevitable offering to his guest.

"You'll drink it from your father's cup, peace to him," said Melesio. "It's never been used since — then. To think I didn't die without seeing my boy Santos!"

Santos thanked him.

"No, no thanks, my boy. I was born a *Luzardero* and

I'll die one. You know what they say about the Sandovals, that they've all got the Altamira brand on their backsides."

"You've stuck to us, that's the truth."

"And knock wood, so these boys listening to you will go the same way. Yes, *señor*. We stick and we've always stuck, and we talk when we're asked and keep quiet when we're not asked, and do our duty. There's no two ways about it. The Sandovals with the Luzardos, as long as they don't kick us out."

"All right, Father," Antonio interrupted. "Nobody's asking us about that now."

Santos understood what Melesio had been getting at with that phrase "keep quiet when we're not asked." He was anticipating the reproaches Santos might direct at them for not keeping him informed of the swindling of the administrators, and inferred the resentment of people who, in spite of their proven and traditional loyalty, found themselves under adventurers like this Paiba, whom Luzardo did not know even by sight.

"I understand," he said. "I admit that I'm the one really to blame, because you were here, and I couldn't have found anyone better to turn my affairs over to. But the truth is, that I didn't bother and didn't want to bother with Altamira."

"Of course, your studies didn't leave you any time," said Antonio.

"Nor my own indifference to the place."

"That was bad, Santos," Melesio observed.

"And I know," Luzardo continued, "what a hard time you've had at Altamira."

"Keeping the herd quiet, as the saying is," declared Antonio.

The old man emphasized this with the typical native metaphors:

"And the stampedes have been no joke. There's Antonio, first of all. He's had to knuckle down, specially to that Don Balbino, and even pretend to be against you to keep his place."

"And with all that, he was ready yesterday to fire me."

"And now it will be your turn. It's good for him that he hasn't come to meet me, and I hope he'll clear out before I get at him. Because, after all, what kind of account can he present but the same kind his predecessors gave? And what can I accuse him of, when I'm the one really to blame for his thieving?"

When he heard this, Carmelito, who was tightening the cinches of the horses tied to the cabin posts, muttered:

"What did I tell you? Here's the man already hoping he won't have trouble with the overseer. The rule never fails: Don't expect anything from a tenderfoot. The one they're going to get rid of is me, this very night, because I'm going at sun-up."

Possibly Antonio, despite his profession of affectionate loyalty to Santos, had similar thoughts when he saw his master ready to leave the overseer in untroubled enjoyment of his stolen gains; but he frowned and maintained an obstinate silence.

Santos went on enjoying, sip by sip, the fragrant, deep-brown coffee, the Plainsman's great predilection; and at the same time he enjoyed a forgotten emotion.

The lovely approach of night over the silent immensity of the prairie; the pleasant, dark, fresh shelter of the rustic roof over his head; the timid girls, who had waited for him all afternoon, dressed in their best frocks with flowers of the savannah twined in their hair as though for a feast; the old man's delight at seeing that "his boy Santos" had not forgotten him, and the fine discretion, the resentful loyalty of Antonio: all these things told him that not everything was evil and unfriendly in the Plain, that unredeemed land in which an upright race loves, endures and hopes. With this emotion reconciling him to his home, he left Melesio's house, just as the sun was setting, to cross the well-known prairie, which was, after all, but a single land with a thousand different paths.

V

THE LANCE-HEAD IN THE WALL

BESIDE the path of the horsemen, a trail worn by the hoofs of cattle, the owls and cowbirds rose in noiseless flight, still dazed by the light of day, and the bitterns sleeping in the open prairie emitted their harsh cry of warning as the cavalcade went by.

Flocks of deer fled on all sides until they were lost to sight. Far away against the reflection of the gorgeous, warm-hued twilight, was the silhouette of a horseman driving a herd. Here and there a solitary steer stood proudly and menacingly, or a shy one bolted with tail in air as he saw the horseman. Others, tamed, jogged along their trail towards the point of the horizon where arose the white smoke of dry dung-heaps which it was customary to burn near the ranch-houses at nightfall, so that the scattered herd would seek shelter in the corrals. In the distance, a scrimmage of wild horses raised a cloud of dust. A flock of herons sailed southward, one after the other, in quiet, harmonious flight.

Nevertheless, the vast frame of the prairie enclosed a

picture of desolation. Santos Luzardo had already been told that nothing was left in Altamira besides a few soapbark trees, and in truth the herds moving over the savannah numbered scarcely more than a hundred, horses and cattle together, where once, up to the time of José Luzardo, there had been myriad studs and herds.

"This is done for," Santos exclaimed. "Why did I come, if there's nothing left to save?"

"Just consider," said Antonio. "There's Doña Barbara on one side, and a procession of overseers, each one a bigger thief than the one before, on the other side, playing their game with our herd. And as if that wasn't enough, there's the Cunaviche rustlers flooding Altamira whenever they feel like it. What with the revolutionists there and the Government Commission there, coming for horses — and here's where they take them from, because Doña Barbara shies them into Altamira to keep them from taking hers."

"And there I was in Caracas, without a worry," said Santos, "in all this disaster."

"But there's a something left yet, Doctor. Wild steers, and thank God for that, because if they weren't wild, you wouldn't have them either. It's a lucky thing that the herd has been growing ever since the dairy was given up. That's from 1890 on. The straying usually means ruin, I know, but it's been a godsend here, because since they put up such a good fight, the overseers in league with the neighbours have been satisfied to steal the tame heads. One of these nights I'm going to rob that mint thicket at Mata Luzardera just to give you an idea of how much money there is left for you to save. But if you'd put off coming a few days longer, you wouldn't have found even that, because Don Balbino was ready to start a stampede so he could divide the strays with Doña Barbara. She's not fooling with him for nothing."

"What! So Paiba is Doña Barbara's new lover?"

"You didn't know that, Doctor? *Caramba!* that's why he's here! At least, Doña Barbara herself says that she got Balbino his place at Altamira."

This explained to Santos that his lawyer had betrayed him, by recommending Paiba, after he had deliberately lost the case confided to his care.

A faint smile, perceptible only to the sharp-eyed Antonio, crossed Carmelito's face, and Antonio began to regret having revealed Luzardo's uncomfortable situation. But he discovered in the master's fierce bearing the evidence of that virility which Carmelito clearly did not believe in, and which he too had doubted a moment before.

"We've got a man," he said to himself, pleased at the discovery. "The Luzardo blood is alive yet."

The faithful peon maintained a respectful silence. Carmelito remained wholly mute, and for a long time nothing could be heard but the ring of the horse's hoofs. Then, from afar, where the black silhouette of the horseman following the herd stood out against the gleam of twilight, a song, one of long cadences, floated through the vast silence. The peaceful emotion aroused by his presence in his native soil recovered possession of Santos. His frown vanishing, his gaze wandered over the broad plain, and the names of places he recognized in the distance rose to his lips:

"Mata Oscura . . . Uveral . . . Corozalito . . . the palm grove of La Chusmita."

It was the work of the merest instant: as he pronounced the name of the baleful spot, the cause of the discord which had wiped out his family, he felt suddenly welling from the depths a flood of grim emotions, darkening his newly recovered peace of spirit. Was it the hatred of a Luzardo for the Barqueros, from which he had thought himself exempt? As he was asking himself this question, so revealing to his alert consciousness, he heard Antonio, loyal even to the hatred of what the Sandovals called by antonomasia "the family," murmuring:

"The unlucky grove. . . . Yes, *señor*. The man who set a son against his father is suffering there in this life for his crime."

He meant Lorenzo Barquero, and the hatred quivering in his voice seemed like his very own. Santos, on the contrary, was glad to find, after a moment, that only a compassionate interest led him to ask:

"Is poor Lorenzo still alive?"

"If you call just having a breath left, living. They call him 'the spectre of La Barquereña' around here. He's just the wreck of a man. They say Doña Barbara made him like that, but as far as I'm concerned, it's the punishment of God, because that man began to dry up alive the very minute Don José — stuck that in the wall."

Although Santos did not understand the full significance of Antonio's last sentence, the thought of having his father's name drawn into the affair was distasteful to him, and he changed the subject with a question about the herds grazing nearby.

The sun had set at last; but the long twilight of the Plains still hung over the scene, a girdle of dark clouds cut by the sharp circular horizon of the savannah, while in the east, beyond an invisible stretch of silent land, the full moon was rising. The spectral radiance, silvering the prairie, became brighter and brighter, floated like a veil in the depths of the distance; and it was night when the riders arrived at the *hato*. This was a group of cabins surrounding a large house of adobe and tiles, with sagging walls, a crumbling roof, tin-sheathed over the encircling porches, a palisade in front for protection against the cattle, and a few trees behind, in what was called the patio — not very high trees, for the Plainsman will not permit them near his dwelling, for fear of lightning. At the back of the house were the kitchen and several store-rooms for the cassavas, kidney beans, and lima beans grown for home consumption; to the right, the harness-cabin and the houses for the hands, and between them the smoke-house, where salted meat dried in the open sunshine and nourished innumerable flies. On the left were the granaries, where the corn was kept, and the calabash tree and the leafy merecure in the poultry yard, the rope-cutters, sheepcotes, and stables, and lastly, the pig-sty. Such was the Altamira ranch-house, just as Don Evaristo had built it generations before, save for the tiles and tin roofing of the residence, these being improvements introduced by Santos' father. It was a primitive establishment, the centre of a primitive industry, sheltering a semi-barbarous life in the heart of the desert.

The only people to be seen were two women looking out of the kitchen door to see what the master looked like, and three peons, who hurried out to meet him.

Antonio introduced them according to their names, occupations, and condition. Thus he presented a yellow-faced man with a moustache composed of three or four straight hairs:

"Venancio, the cattle-breaker. Son of Ño Venancio, the dairyman. You remember Ño Venancio?"

"How could I help it?" answered Santos. "Our people from time immemorial."

"Then I don't need to tell you anything," said the cattle-breaker; but Santos noticed the same expression of misgiving he had seen on Carmelito's face.

"The driver, María Nieves," Antonio continued, introducing the next man, a short, heavy blond. "A fine Plainsman, except for his woman's name. You'll find out all about him. I'm only telling you the good things."

As for the third man, a thin, ungainly, pleasant-looking half-breed, Antonio did not have the chance to present him.

" By your leave, Doctor, I'll introduce myself. I don't want my partner to give me a bad name, and I can see that coming in his eyes. Juan Palacios is my name, but they call me *Pajarote,* The Big Bird, and you can call me that too. I haven't been here from time immemorial, as you just said, but you can count on me, because I'm open and above-board."

And he stuck out his hand. Santos took it; he liked the peon's rude frankness. Exchanging a few words with his men, he went into the house, and Antonio asked a question which would have been imprudent in the master's presence:

" Why is it so quiet here? Where are the others? "

" They've gone," replied Venancio. " You'd no more started for the Pass than they saddled up and rode off to El Miedo."

" And Don Balbino? Wasn't he here? "

" No. This was his plan, you know. I suspected a long time ago that he was drawing the boys away."

" It's no great loss. They were all a set of crooked loafing cat's-paws," said Antonio, after a moment's thought.

Meanwhile, physically wearied by the hardships of his long journey but excited by the emotions he had that day experienced, Luzardo lay in the hammock hung for his use in one of the rooms and analysed his feelings.

They ran in two contrary currents of reflection and impulse, determination and hesitation. There was on one hand, as the result of his emotions upon seeing the Plain once more, the desire to devote himself to a patriotic duty, the struggle against evil both in man and nature, and the search for effective remedies. It was, up to a certain point, an unselfish desire, for the thing least important to him was recovering his wealth by salvaging the ranch.

But in the determination to do this, Santos felt that there was a great deal of the intellectual man's rationalization of the impulse to escape when the path of least resistance — in this case, the half-savage country, " man's country " as his father had used to say — appeared. Furthermore, the riverman's warning of the dangers in store for anyone daring to oppose Doña Barbara had been sufficient to shake his decision to sell Altamira. Finally, that very discovery of this path of least resistance, and that sudden access of the old family hatred when he saw the palm grove; were not these a warning against himself? The Plainsman's life, the irresistible attraction of the land's lordly barbarity, the exaggerated belief that manhood was produced by the simple act of riding over the immense prairie, would be ruinous to the work of his best years, given to crushing the savage tendencies of the man-at-arms latent in him.

The sensible thing, then, was to carry out his first

plan and sell the ranch. Besides, this was in agreement with his real plan of life. That feeling which had come upon him in the boat had been but a temporary exaltation. Was he prepared for the task he would set himself? Did he actually know anything about a ranch, how to manage it, or how to correct the deficiencies of an industry which had preserved its primitive character for generation after generation? The broad aspects of his tremendous task of civilizing it could not escape him, but could he master the details? If his intelligence were removed for a moment from the ideal realms through which it had roamed heretofore, would it yield any practical results when faced with real and minute emergencies, such as those of managing such a property would assuredly be? Hadn't he already shown his impotence in his stupid method of dealing with Altamira up to then?

Here was the weakness of his otherwise well-tempered character. Luzardo was unaware of his real latent strength; he was afraid; he exaggerated the need of vigilance.

The appearance of Antonio, announcing that supper was ready, put an end to his deliberations.

"I'm not hungry," he answered.

"Being tired takes away the appetite," Antonio observed. "You'll have to put up with sleeping in this room just as it is, for to-night, because we only had time to sweep it. To-morrow we'll whitewash the walls and clean up a bit more. Unless you intend to have the whole house overhauled, and it really isn't fit to live in the way it is."

"We'll leave it just so for the present. I may sell the ranch. Don Encarnación Matute is coming here in a month's time. I proposed selling Altamira to him, and if he makes a good offer, I'll close the deal immediately."

"Ah! How is it that you're thinking of getting rid of Altamira?"

"I think it's the best I can do."

Antonio was thoughtful for a moment, then he said:

"If you've made up your mind, you'll do it, of course." And handing over a bunch of keys:

"Here are the keys. This rusty one is the key of the living-room. It may not work, because the room was never opened again. Everything is there just as your father left it, God rest his soul."

"Just as your father left it. . . . From the very minute your father stuck that in the wall. . . ."

The rapid association of Antonio's two phrases came at a crucial moment of Luzardo's life. He got out of the hammock, took the candle, and said to the peon:

"Open the living-room."

Antonio obeyed, and after a short struggle with the rusty lock opened the door which had been closed for thirteen years.

A rush of stale, foul air drove Santos back. Something

black and loathsome — a bat coming out of the darkness — fluttered against the candle and extinguished it. He lighted it again and entered the room, followed by Antonio.

Everything was actually just as Don José had left it. There was the rocking chair in which he died, and the lance head plunged into the wall.

Without a word, Santos, deeply moved and aware that he was doing something far-reaching, went up to the wall, and with a movement as vigorous as that his father must have used to plunge it in, he drew out the fatal lance head. The rust on the blade was like blood. He flung the weapon away, saying to Antonio:

" You see what I've done with that? You do the same thing with those feelings I heard you express a while ago. It isn't your hate, after all. One Luzardo imposed it upon you as a duty, but another frees you of such a monstrous obligation, this very moment. That feud has already done enough damage in this country."

As Antonio, impressed, was withdrawing in silence, he added:

" Get things ready so we can begin to repair the house to-morrow. I'm not going to sell Altamira."

He went back to the hammock and lay down, calm and full of confidence in himself. And, without, the sounds of the prairie lulled him to sleep as they had in his childhood: The strumming of guitars in the peons' houses, the braying of donkeys seeking the warmth of the dung-heap smoke, the croaking of frogs in nearby ponds, the persistent concert of the crickets scattered over the savannah, and that mighty silence of the Plain asleep in the moonlight, a stillness more audible than any sound. . . .

VI

THE MEMORY OF HASDRUBAL

THE same night, at El Miedo.

The Wizard came out of the darkness. Informed that Doña Barbara had just sat down to supper, he nevertheless went into the house, as he had money to give her and news to tell her, and was anxious too to lie down and rest. He did not care to wait until she had finished eating, and entered, with his poncho still slung over his arm.

As he went in, he repented of his haste. Doña Barbara was having supper with Balbino Paiba, whom he did not like. He attempted to retreat, but Doña Barbara said at that moment:

" Come in, Melquíades."

" I'll come back later. Go on eating and don't disturb yourself."

Balbino, wiping the grease of the stew from his heavy moustache with the back of his hand, added languidly:

" Come in, Melquíades. Don't be afraid. There are no dogs here."

The Wizard flung a hostile glance at him and replied cuttingly:

" Are you sure about that, Don Balbino? "

But Balbino did not understand this sort of remark, and Melquíades continued, addressing Doña Barbara:

" I came to tell you that the cattle got to San Fernando all right, and to give you your money."

He laid the poncho on a chair, pulled the wallet fastened to his belt around in front of him, and took out a number of gold pieces which he proceeded to place in a stack on the table, saying:

" Count it and see if it's all there."

Balbino looked at the coins out of the corner of his eye, and said, alluding to Doña Barbara's habit of burying all the gold which came into her hands:

" Twenties! My eyes have seen them! " and went on chewing the chunk of meat which filled his mouth, but without once removing his gaze from the money.

Doña Barbara frowned sharply, her eyebrows meeting and parting with the rapidity of a sparrow's fluttering wings. She was no more accustomed to brook jests from her lover in the presence of others, than she was to allow endearments or anything which might place her in a position of inferiority. It was not in the spirit of dissimulation that she took this course, for in this as in everything else she was entirely unconventional, but because of her natural feeling towards the man.

Balbino Paiba was not unaware of this; but as he was

dull-witted and a braggart, he never lost an opportunity of showing that he held absolute control over her, although every one of his boasts had failed. The jest he had just allowed himself was one of those which Doña Barbara could least bear, and he swiftly got what was coming to him.

" It must be all there," she said, looking at the money without troubling to count it. " You never make a mistake, Melquíades. *You* haven't that bad habit."

Balbino stroked his moustache, a trick he performed mechanically whenever he was displeased. She had never shown him a single mark of confidence; on the contrary, she always counted the money he paid her with the utmost care, and if any happened to be missing, which was frequently the case, she stood and looked at him without a word, until he pretended to become suddenly aware of his carelessness and made up the amount with what he had left in his purse. Moreover, it was evident that the remark about *that bad habit* referred to him. In spite of the splendid service he had rendered her in his position as overseer of Altamira, he had not yet succeeded in gaining her confidence. As for his position as lover, he could not even count on her precarious caprice. He was a hired employee, and paid by Luzardo for his stewardship at Altamira.

" Good, Melquíades," Doña Barbara continued. " What more have you got to tell me? Why did you send the peon ahead? "

"Didn't he tell you?" Melquíades inquired, anxious to avoid explaining in the presence of Balbino, before whom he was always extremely reticent.

"Yes. He told me a bit, but I want you to give me the details."

She pronounced these words, like her earlier ones, without looking at his face, intent on her plate. Melquíades reciprocated by speaking without looking at her either. Both, being sorcerers, had learned from the Evil-Eyed Indian spellbinders never to look each other in the face.

"Well, I heard them say in San Fernando that Dr. Santos Luzardo had come to bring counter suits against you for all you won from him. I was curious to know the man and at last I got him pointed out to me. Then I lost sight of him until yesterday afternoon, when I was saddling my horse so as to leave at night and get here at sun up. Then I heard a traveller come in and say that his horse was sunstruck, and then arrange for the boat that was taking on a cargo of hides there for Algarrobo Pass. That's my man, I said to myself, and I unsaddled the horse and took my poncho and smuggled myself into the cabin where he was getting supper so that I could hear what he said."

"And you heard plenty, I don't doubt. I can imagine."

"Well, yes, but nothing to get up a sweat about, as they say. But while I was listening to the Doctor, and it's a pleasure to listen to him, because he's a sweet talker,

I thought to myself: This is a man who loves to hear himself talk and won't be able to keep quiet long. It's just a matter of patience and keeping your ears open. So last night I said to the peon: Take my horse and go on ahead, I'm going to see if there's room for me in the boat."

And he told her what he had heard during the siesta, describing Santos Luzardo as a reckless and dangerous man.

Doña Barbara's henchman was one of those elusive and dissimulating human beings who always feel the need of saying the opposite of what they think. His smooth manners, quiet way of speaking, and habit of showing great admiration for the manhood of others concealed a cold and calculating wickedness beyond the limits of atrocity.

" Don't humble yourself so," said Don Balbino, hearing Melquíades exalt the excellencies of the owner of Altamira. " We know you're not the man to feel small beside a tenderfoot."

" All right, Don Balbino, but see here: It's not that I'm humbling myself, see? It's because the man is a big fellow and he stands on tiptoe besides."

" Well, if that's so, we'll bring him down to size tomorrow so we can polish him off," said Paiba, who, quite the opposite of Melquíades, was not disposed to concede any point to the enemy.

The Wizard smiled, and said sententiously:

"Remember, Don Balbino, that it's better to reap than to sow."

"Don't you worry, Melquíades. I'll be able tomorrow to reap what I sowed today."

He meant by this the plan he had laid for intimidating Luzardo: to lure the peons away, absent himself from Altamira that night, go there next morning, and then, upon the first pretext that offered, provoke a dispute with the first peon he came across and dismiss him without any attention to the presence of Luzardo. Since he was never satisfied unless he could divulge the idea he had in his head, and moreover felt it necessary to show Melquíades that he was going to stand up to Luzardo, he did not stop at this vague allusion to his scheme, and taking the bit in his teeth, began to explain it:

"Early to-morrow Dr. Luzardo is going to find out what sort of man his overseer Balbino Paiba is." But he interrupted himself to watch what Doña Barbara was doing meanwhile.

She had just poured herself a glass of water and was putting it to her lips, when, with a gesture of astonishment, she jerked her head back and continued to stare fixedly at the vessel, holding it at eye-level. Her expression changed immediately from one of surprise to one of startled amazement.

"What's up?" Balbino inquired.

"Nothing. It's only Dr. Luzardo allowing himself to be seen," she replied, continuing to stare in the glass.

Balbino started. Melquíades approached the table, and leaning on his right elbow bent over to look in the bewitched tumbler for himself. Doña Barbara continued in a rapt tone:

"A very pleasant looking blond. What a complexion! Anybody can see that he isn't used to the sun of the plains. He's good-looking, too!"

The Wizard moved away from the table, saying to himself:

"Dog don't eat dog. Balbino can believe you. But the peon told you all that."

It was one of Doña Barbara's many tricks for furthering her prestige as a witch and heightening the fear it inspired in others. Balbino suspected something of this; but the business had evidently impressed him.

"Father, Son and Holy Ghost!" he muttered between his teeth, immediately adding: "If she really saw it."

Doña Barbara had put the glass back on the table untouched; she was struck by a sudden recollection which made her face cloud over: She was on a pirogue. . . . Far off, in the profound silence, could be heard the hoarse roar of the Atures rapids. . . . Suddenly the note of the screech owl. . . .

Several moments passed.

"Aren't you going to finish eating?" Balbino demanded. The question remained unanswered.

"If you haven't any more orders for me —" said Melquíades after a brief silence; and taking his poncho, he stopped another moment to add:

"Well then, I'm going, by your leave. Good-night."

Balbino went on eating alone. Then he pushed back his plate, brusquely, wiped his moustache, and left the table.

The lamp began to flicker, and finally went out. Doña Barbara remained seated at the table, and her thoughts, bitter and gloomy, were fixed on that hideous moment of the past.

Far off in the profound silence could be heard the hoarse roar of the Atures rapids. . . . Suddenly the note of the screech owl. . . .

VII

THE TAWNY BULL

A NIGHT of full moon is favourable to tales of apparitions. The cattlemen, in their cabins, or seated in the doorways of the corrals, always find at least one of their group to tell of the terrors he has experienced.

The illusive clarity of the moon, altering every perspective, peoples the prairie with hobgoblins. These are the nights when little things seen from afar become vast, when distances are incalculable and shapes fantastically distorted; nights of white shadows at the foot of trees, and mysterious horsemen abroad, stark and still in the glades of the savannah, whisked away if any stop to regard them; nights of travelling with a chill no coat may prevent and a Magnificat on one's lips, as Pajarote said.

In Altamira, it was always Pajarote who told the most blood-curdling tales. The wandering life of the rancher, and a vivid imagination, afforded him the material for a thousand stories, each more strange than the last.

"Dead men? I know hair and hide of everyone that

appears from the Uribante to the Orinoco and from the Apure to the Meta," he would say. " And as for the other terrors, they've given me every fright they know."

The souls in torment, who must gather up their sins where they were committed; The Weeping Woman, genius of the river banks, channels and ponds, whose lament may be heard miles away; the choruses of spirits, praying with a loud hum in the stillness of the solitary thickets or in the clearings, and The Lonely Soul, who whistles at the passerby to make him say an Our Father, because he is the neediest soul in Purgatory—Pajarote knew all these, and had seen the Vampire, a lovely woman in mourning, scourge of the concupiscent night-wanderer, who comes upon him, saying " Follow me! " and suddenly turning shows him her hideous phosphorescent teeth, and the black swine she leads as Mandinga, and reveals all her other forms.

It is therefore not surprising that on that very night, he suddenly put down his guitar and announced that he had seen the Familiar of Altamira.

According to an ancient superstition, of unknown origin but common in the Plain, whenever a ranch was established a live animal was buried beneath the posts of the first corral to be built, so that his spirit, imprisoned in the earth of the property, might watch over this and its owners. Thence came the title " Familiar," and the fact that his apparition was considered an omen of future success. The animal entombed at Altamira was a tawny bull, which Don Evaristo had buried, said the legend, at the gate of the sheepfold. He was also called "Ragged-Hoof" because he was supposed to have had fibrous, spongy hoofs in his old age.

Although Pajarote's visions were not usually taken very seriously, at the same time María Nieves stopped shaking his calabash rattle, and Antonio and Venancio sat up in their hammocks. Only Carmelito seemed indifferent.

Antonio's expression revealed more than mere curiosity. Many years had passed since the Familiar had been seen; the years making up the Luzardos' period of adversity, so that of all those present on the ranch only Antonio's father remembered having heard, in his childhood, of the Familiar's frequent apparition to Don José de Los Santos, the last of the Luzardos to enjoy prosperity. If Pajarote had not lied, the vision promised the return of good times with the arrival of Santos.

"Out with the yarn, Pajarote, so we can see if we can believe you. How did the thing happen?"

"At sunset, when I was rounding up the yearlings. I thought I saw a yellow bull in a mirage of water, pawing the ground. That was at the mouth of La Carama. The dust he was raising was like gold and it couldn't have been anything but 'Ragged-Hoof' because when I yelled at him he disappeared just as if the ground had swallowed him up."

Venancio and María Nieves exchanged glances with

which each tried to estimate the credulity of the other, but Antonio was thoughtful. And when the other two had expended considerable effort without shaking Pajarote's insistence that the bull he had seen was the Familiar, Antonio, thinking that the story of the apparition would be a good means of spreading confidence in Santos, especially among such as Carmelito, who had become indispensable since the disloyal peons had left, said to Nieves:

"So you don't think Pajarote is telling the truth?"

"Well, I'll tell you. It don't surprise me, because I thought I saw the bull too, some days ago. But not in a mirage of water, or pawing the ground, the way the old folks say he always appeared, and like my partner here saw him — he always sees more than anybody else."

He added the last as a fling at Pajarote, and paused to note the effect of his words. But Pajarote did not change countenance in the least.

"Come on, partner, let's have a show down," he said to Nieves. "Tell us how *you* saw the Familiar. Nobody will be satisfied now not to have seen it, because the world is like a ranch, and first comes the guide and then the followers."

"Guide or follower, I saw him standing on a dune." And he looked straight at Pajarote, to make him understand what he pretended not to:

"That's the way I told you about it. You put in the dust and the mirage to bluff me out, but I'm calling your hand. It was a giant bull, tawny-coloured and well set up. He was sniffing in this direction a long time, and then he turned towards El Miedo and let out a roar that you could have heard from there. Then he disappeared, as if the ground had swallowed him up."

Pajarote grinned. He had made up the entire story on the basis of what María Nieves had told him, simply because he wanted to stimulate his companions to confidence in the arrival, with the master, of better times. For Luzardo had made a good impression on him, perhaps just because he had so evidently made the opposite impression on the others.

"It's not far from the sand bank to the place where I saw him. There's nothing unusual about him appearing one time on the sand dune and another time in a mirage of water. That's his hangout around there."

"Why didn't you say anything about it, María Nieves?" asked Antonio, interested.

"Because that wasn't the way the Familiar appears here, and I thought it was just some yellow bull or other."

"But that business of sniffing towards Altamira and then roaring in the direction of El Miedo must have struck you, knowing how things are—" Antonio insisted.

"Don't think I didn't have any notion, but—"

Pajarote interrupted him.

"But there are some people that grow old between thinking and doing."

Nieves and Pajarote, sworn friends to the death, could never exchange two words without getting into a contest of sarcastic and incredulous gibes, to the delight of all present. Venancio had begun to egg them on, as was customary, but that night Antonio was interested in keeping them on the track, and he continued:

"How long ago did this happen, María?"

"How long ago—? Well, I'll tell you. . . . It was last Monday."

"Look at that!" Antonio exclaimed. "That was the very day the master arrived at San Fernando."

"There you are, then!" added Pajarote, and Venancio, leaping out of his hammock, said:

"Now I'm going to tell my story."

"You see what I told you? Everybody's seen the thing, now."

"It isn't just now with me. I've been saying for a long time that strange things were happening here."

"That's so," said Nieves.

"Tell us, then. What did you see?"

"To tell the truth, I didn't see anything. But I had a sort of hunch. There was the thing we all saw the time of the last branding."

"You mean the herd taking fright?"

"Yes. It didn't look natural to any of us. All those steers milling and crying and trying to shove each other aside, all night. Nobody can get it out of my head that there was something there trying to turn them. And besides, I heard their hoofs and saw the grass trampled down without anything to be seen going over it. And wasn't it queer that we couldn't round up that prairieful of animals? Why, you could see that the prairie was black with them, and when you rode up they scattered like the seeds of a gourd."

"It's the truth," Nieves agreed. "There wasn't anything but soapbark trees left."

But Pajarote was eager to have it all to himself, and raising his gruff voice still higher, in the manner of the cattleman used to making himself heard at a distance, he took up the theme.

"You remember, Carmelito, the morning we started out with some of the men from El Miedo after the herd of strays that turned up at La Culata? It was impossible to rope a single stray, and we were all good hands at it, too. The best noose slipped off, and the best horses twisted up the lassos like God playing tricks on the devil. Old Don Torres, the best rope in the Arauca, was with us, and when we divided up, he got a bull, a tawny-coloured one, if you don't believe me. The old man chased him up between the sides of the hills, and had the rope around him when that bull stopped dead and stood there looking at him. And listen to this, Antonio. You know what a wrangler Don Torres is, and not afraid to take chances with the strays in El Caribe, and they're the wildest in the Apure. Well, that morning he turned as white as a sheet, and you know how dark he is. He didn't even try to pull back the rope, and he called his crowd together right there. I heard him say: 'I was so anxious to rope him that I didn't notice that he was the Familiar of Altamira. As long as I live, I'll never toss another rope in this place.' "

Carmelito remained wrapped in silence, and Antonio asked, to draw him out:

"What about that, Carmelito? Is Pajarote telling the truth?"

But Carmelito merely replied evasively:

"I was 'way off, see? tending to something else."

"Still buried in himself," muttered Antonio.

"God strike me dead to keep me from telling another lie, if it isn't the truth," said Pajarote. "You don't need to believe about 'Ragged-Hoof,' if you don't want to; but my partner María saw it too, and everybody knows *he* never tells a lie. Now this business of the Familiar appearing again means that that witch is losing her spell, and it's our turn. So put up your money, Carmelito, if you want a chance at the pot."

Carmelito shifted his position in the hammock and replied shortly:

"How long are you people going to keep up this nonsense about Doña Barbara's spells? The real truth is that she's got hair on her chest, that woman, and you've got to have it if you want to be respected in this country."

"You're right about that, Carmelito," said Pajarote, "but listen to me — the ones that show it aren't the only ones with hair on their chests, because lots of people would rather hide it, and that's what shirts are for. Now, nobody can deny that Doña Barbara knows witchcraft, and if you don't believe it, listen to what I'm going to tell you, exactly as I heard it."

He spat through his teeth and continued:

"It was about a week ago, early in the morning, and some of the El Miedos were getting ready for a rodeo at Corozal, and that's the best picking in the whole prairie, you know that. Well, Doña Barbara looked out of the window, still in her nightgown, and told them: 'Don't waste your time, because you won't catch a single calf today.' But the peons went anyway, because they were all ready. And it turned out just as she said it would. They didn't get a single yearling. There wasn't even a steer grazing there, and it's the best grass on the ranch."

He paused briefly. "But that's nothing," he went on. "Here comes the big show. A couple of days after that, before the roosters had crowed even, she woke the peons up and told them: 'Saddle up quick and go right away. There's a pack of strays at Lagartijera. Seventy-five of them, and easy game.' And that's how it was. Now, Carmelito, tell me this: How could the woman count those strays in Lagartijera, from her house, two leagues away?"

Carmelito did not deign to reply, and María Nieves intervened to save his friend from embarrassment.

"What's the use of denying that this woman learned

witchcraft from the Indians? I know of a case where a woman she knew told her to watch out for her lover, because he was robbing her, and all she said was: 'Nobody, he or anybody else, can take a single steer away from here unless I let him. He can take all the cattle he wants to lead away, but none will go past the boundary of the ranch. They'll stampede and come back to pasture, because I've got some one helping me.'"

"I should say she has! The Mandinga, that's what. She calls him the 'Partner.' What else are those talks for, that she carries on with him in that room where she won't let anybody go?" said Venancio. The talk about Doña Barbara's sorcery would have gone on endlessly had not Pajarote changed the subject by saying:

"But that's all going to end now. The tawny bull roaring like María Nieves heard him means that the jig is up. Already, we've gained a lot in having Don Balbino's business finished, the thief! as soon as the Doctor came. Oh, what a slick crook that is! He's even robbed the Holy Soul of Ajirelito, and that's everything in a word."

"Not about that, partner," declared María Nieves in his bantering tone. "I know somebody else that's had his fingers in the Holy Soul's box."

The Holy Soul of Ajirelito—one of the many to be found in the Plain—was the favourite patron of the settlers in the Arauca basin. They never set out without commending themselves to his aid, nor came near the thicket of Ajirelito without going there to burn a candle or drop a coin. For this purpose there was a shelter beneath one of the trees in the clump, under which was a shrine, with votive candles burning and a box where travellers put their alms, collected from time to time by the village priest for the masses said monthly for the Holy Soul. No one watched over the box, and it was said that it was not unusual to see ten- and twenty-dollar gold pieces among the coins, sums vowed by travellers in grave need. As for the legend, there was nothing fantastic about that — a traveller found dead at the foot of the tree, another who thought of saying when he found himself in danger: "Holy Soul of Ajirelito, deliver me!" Delivered unscathed from the danger, he alighted from his horse when he came to Ajirelito, built the little shrine, and burned the first candle. Time had done the rest.

When he heard María Nieves' pointed allusion, Pajarote replied:

"Don't shoot me in the dark, partner. The man that put his fingers in the Soul's box was me. But since you don't know that story, I'm going to tell it myself so you won't believe all you hear from the wagging tongues around here. I was broke and wanted some money, two things that always go together, and when I passed Ajirelito I thought of a way of getting the coin I needed. Well, I went up to the tree, got off my horse, made the sign of the cross, and said to the Spirit: 'How's things, partner? How's the old collections?' The Holy Soul didn't answer, but the box said to my eyes, 'Here's four or five silver dollars among the pennies.' Then I scratched my head, because an idea was coming to me, and I said, 'Listen, partner. Let's try a throw or two with the dollars. I've got a hunch that we'll break the bank in the first town I come to. We'll go halves on it. You furnish the money and I furnish the hunch.' And the Holy Soul answered me, you know how — you can't hear it — 'Why not, Pajarote? Take all you want. How long are you going to stand there thinking about it? If we lose the money, it was going to be lost anyway, when the priest got this hands on it.' So I took the money and went to the gambling house in Achaguas, and played it dollar by dollar."

"And did you break the bank?" Antonio asked.

"No more than you did. They stripped me clean, one by one, because those demons in gambling houses don't even respect the Holy Souls. But I whistled it down and went to bed, and the next time I was at Ajirelito I said to the Holy Soul: 'Of course you know we didn't win, partner. Another time. Here's a little something for you.' And I lit a candle for him, a twopenny one, which was all the light he'd ever have got from those four dollars if the priest had got hold of them."

Pajarote's tale was greeted with roars of laughter. Then all began to discuss the Holy Soul's recent miracles, and ended by getting back into their hammocks.

Silence reigned in the cabin. The night was well on its way, and the moonlight deepened the shadowy perspectives of the savannah. The rooster there in the calabash tree dreamed of hawks, and his frightened crowing alarmed his mates in the chicken-yard. The dogs, sleeping stretched out in the patio, raised their heads and pricked up their ears, but hearing nothing but the fluttering of bats and owls around the trees, put their muzzles back on their forepaws. From the distance came the terrified roar of a bull, perhaps scenting a tiger.

Pajarote, who was nearly asleep, exclaimed:

"Old bull! I need a rope and a horse, and I'm the man for him!"

One of the men laughed, and another inquired:

"'Ragged-Hoof' maybe?"

"Just what we need," said Antonio.

They said no more after that.

VIII

THE HORSE-BREAKING

THE Plain is at once lovely and fearful. It holds, side by side, beautiful life and hideous death. The latter lurks everywhere, but no one fears it. The Plain frightens, but the fear which the Plain inspires is not the terror which chills the heart; it is hot, like the wind sweeping over the immeasurable solitude, like the fever lying in the marshes.

The Plain crazes; and the madness of the man living in the wide lawless land leads him to remain a Plainsman forever. In the Revolution, The Good War, this madness appeared in the irresistible charge through the flaming brake, and in the heroic deeds of Queseras del Medio. In work, there it is, in wrangling and horse-breaking, which are not tasks, but risks; during the hours of leisure, you will find it in the witty yarns, the sparkling anecdotes, in the sensuous melancholy of the ballads. There is madness in the languid desolation —the vast land with nothing to be called a goal, the unbroken horizon enclosing nothing but emptiness. In friendship, there is the initial distrust and the final absolute frankness; in hatred, the violence of the sudden attack; in love "horse first and woman afterward." The Plain, always the Plain! the sprawling wilderness, land of struggle and peril, with as many horizons as hopes, as many ways as wills.

"Up, me boys! The hares of the dawn are coming!"

It was the voice of Pajarote, who always arose in high spirits. "The hares of the dawn"—the ingenuous metaphor of the cowboy poet—are the little round clouds on the horizon behind the dark fringe of the thicket, golden in the sunrise.

Already an oiled taper hung from the kitchen ceiling between the soot covered walls gave light for the morning service of coffee, and the peons were coming through the doorway, one by one. Casilda, the cook, was serving the fragrant brew, and the men talked between sips of the day's work, all apparently full of expectation except Carmelito, who already had his horse saddled to go away.

Antonio was saying:

"The first thing we've got to do is break in the sorrel colt, because the master needs a good saddle horse, and that broncho is one of the best."

"I should say he is!" agreed Venancio, the horsebreaker. And Pajarote added:

"Don Balbino knows a bit about horses, too, and you

can't take that from him; he's already been making eyes at it."

Carmelito said to himself:

"It's a pity for the horse, he was made to carry a better man." When the peons started for the corral where the colt was, he stopped Antonio and said to him:

"I'm sorry to tell you that I've decided not to stay at Altamira. Don't ask me why."

"I won't ask, because I know what's the matter, Carmelito," Antonio answered. "And I won't ask you not to go, although I counted on you more than anyone else. But I will ask you a favour. Wait a little while, just a couple of days, until I can get used to the idea of losing you."

Carmelito, understanding that Antonio was asking him that with the hope of seeing him change the opinion he had formed of the master, agreed.

"All right. I'll do it for you. Since it's you ask me, I'll stay until you get used to it, as you say. But there's some things you can't get used to in this country."

The swift dawn of the Plain was advancing. The fresh morning breeze came up with its smell of mint and cattle. The hens began to scramble down from the calabash and merecure tree; the insatiable rooster threw over them the golden mantle of his arched wings and made them, one by one, yield to his passion. Partridges piped in the grass. A *paraulata* on the fence of the sheepfold opened his silver throat. Noisy flocks of parrakeets passed overhead, and higher up the wild ducks quacked, and the red herons went by like a long garnet rosary; higher still, the white cranes, serene and silent. And under the wild clamour of the birds dipping their wings in the gold of the soft daybreak the free rude life of the prairie beat out its full, powerful rhythm over the broad land of wandering herds and studs of unbroken horses neighing a clarion call to the day. Luzardo surveyed the scene from one of the galleries, and knew that the feelings in his heart of hearts were in accord with that rugged swing.

Excited voices in the nearby corral interrupted his reflections:

"This colt belongs to Dr. Luzardo, because it was caught in Altamira. Don't come to me with your stuff about it being the foal of a mare from El Miedo. That sort of rustling is all over now on this ranch."

Antonio Sandoval was standing face to face with a large man who had just arrived and was demanding to know why Antonio had given orders for bridling the sorrel colt. Santos realized that the newcomer must be his overseer, Balbino Paiba, and went over to the corral to put an end to the quarrel.

"What's going on?" he inquired. But as neither Antonio, choked with rage, nor the other man, evidently not deigning to explain, replied to his question, he insisted, authoritatively, and coming face to face with the newcomer:

" What's happening? I asked you."

" This fellow has been impertinent to me," replied the big man.

" And who are you? " Santos asked, as though he had no idea who it could be.

" Balbino Paiba, at your service."

" Ah," exclaimed Santos, " so you're the overseer. This is a fine time to come here and pick quarrels instead of coming to me to make your apologies for not being here last night, as it was your duty to be."

This was followed by a twisting of Balbino's mustache, and a response not included in the plan he had made for impressing Luzardo right from the start.

" I didn't know that you were coming last night. I just found out that you were here. I suppose you must be the owner, to speak to me like this."

" You suppose correctly."

But Paiba had now recovered from the momentary confusion produced in him by the unexpected vigour of Luzardo's attitude, and in an attempt to recover lost ground, he said:

" I've already made my apologies. It seems to me that it's your turn. The tone you've used in speaking to me is not the one I'm used to hearing."

Santos replied quietly and with a faintly ironical smile:

" You don't ask very much, do you? "

" We've got a chief! " Pajarote said to himself.

Balbino's desire to bluster had vanished, as well as his hopes of stewardship.

"Does this mean that I'm discharged, and that my connexion with you ends now?"

"Not right yet. You have to give me an account of your administration. But that will come later."

Antonio looked at Carmelito, and Pajarote, turning to Nieves and Venancio, who were in the corral waiting for the climax of the little drama although apparently busy preparing lengths of rope for hobbling the colt, shouted meaningly:

"Come on, cowboys! Haven't you got that broncho hobbled yet? Look how he's shaking with rage. You'd think he was afraid. And he's only seen the hobbles so far. What will he do when we've got him on the ground?"

"We'll see pretty soon."—"Let's see him try to throw off this hobble as he did the others," added the two peons, laughing at the double meaning of their friend's words.

Spirited, beautifully formed, magnificently proportioned, his coat gleaming and his gaze defiant, the untamed animal had burst the bonds placed on him when he was captured, and knowing by instinct that he was the object of these preparations, protected himself by staying in the middle of the stud of unbroken horses there in the corral. Pajarote finally succeeded in getting hold of the trailing rope, and bracing himself with his feet dug into the ground and his weight thrown back, he struggled with the broncho and threw him to the ground.

"Pull his tail between his legs, you!" he shouted to María Nieves. "Don't let him stand up."

But the sorrel immediately got to his feet, quivering with rage. Pajarote let him quiet down and regain confidence before approaching him very gradually with the blinders.

Quivering, his eyes bloodshot with fury, the colt allowed him to come near, but Antonio, divining the animal's intention, shouted:

"Careful! He's going to kick you."

Pajarote slowly advanced his arm, but he did not succeed in getting the blinders on, for the moment he touched the colt's ears the animal charged straight for his face. The cowboy, with an agile leap, managed to get out of reach, roaring:

"You vicious son of a whore!"

This brief respite was sufficient to allow the colt to seek refuge once more in the middle of the stud, his head held high, and his ears pricked up.

"Tie him up," Antonio ordered. "Throw a lasso over him."

The sorrel trussed up in the noose, Nieves and Venancio hastened to hobble him. Fettered and strangled by the noose, the beast sank to earth, cowed and winded. Once they had put the blinders on him they undid the hobbles and allowed him to stand, Venancio immediately throwing over him the light breaking-in saddle. The broncho, struggling to his feet, let fly kicks in all directions, but seeing that it was useless to resist his captors, he stood still, rigid with rage and bathed in sweat, under the torture of the saddle his back had never before felt.

Luzardo had watched all this from the gate of the corral, excited by old memories of his boyhood — riding bareback into the teeth of the wind across the prairie. Just as Venancio was about to fling himself on the colt, Santos heard Antonio say to him:

"Santos, do you remember when you used to break in the horses the old man picked out for you?"

Luzardo needed no explanation of the meaning behind the loyal fellow's question. Horse-breaking! the great test of the cowboy, proof of the courage and skill these men were waiting to attribute to him. He involuntarily glanced at Carmelito, who was sitting on the fence on the other side of the gate, and said, with a swift decision:

"Let him alone, Venancio. I'm going to ride him."

Antonio smiled, pleased at not having been mistaken in his estimate of the master; Venancio and María Nieves looked at each other, surprised and distrustful, and Pajarote said, with his rude honesty:

"That isn't necessary, Doctor. We all know you're a man with nerve. Let Venancio break him."

But Santos did not listen, and flung himself astride

the untamed beast, who bent nearly to the ground as he felt the rider on his back.

Carmelito made an astonished gesture and then remained immovable, staring at every move of the horseman under whose legs, which were resting on the ground, the sorrel, restrained by the blinders and held up by the bridle in the hands of Pajarote and Nieves, was still trembling with fury, his coat dripping sweat and his gaping jaws flecked with foam.

Balbino Paiba, who had hung around in hopes of another chance to "show Luzardo," if the latter addressed him, smiled depreciatingly and said to himself:

"Now this tenderfoot is going to bury his head in his own ground."

Antonio was eagerly giving useless advice, useless, for Santos had naturally not been able to forget the tricks of breaking.

"Let him go all he wants to at first, and then work him around a bit. Don't put the spurs to him unless you have to, and get ready for a bolt, because this sorrel is not one of the curvetting kind, he's a stampeder and the kind that runs as if the devil was after him. Venancio and I will go along with you."

But Luzardo was occupied with his own thoughts, the overmastering impulses that shook his nerves, just as the colt's were shaking him. Leaning over to remove the blinders, he called out:

"Turn him loose!"

"In God's name!" said Antonio.

Pajarote and Nieves released the animal, getting quickly off to one side. The ground shook under the furious prancing, horse and rider like one creature. A cloud of dust arose, and it had not settled before the sorrel colt was far away, drinking in the air of the endless prairie.

Antonio and Venancio rode behind, hunched forward over their mounts but falling farther and farther in the rear.

"I was wrong about the man," muttered Carmelito, emotionally, and Pajarote exclaimed:

"Didn't I tell you the necktie was to hide the hair on his chest, eh? Look at him hold on! If that horse wants to throw him he'll have to turn over on his back first." And then he added, with the open intention of provoking Balbino:

"Some of the *tailors* will find out what kind of pants a man wears now. We're going to see soon if everything that roars is a tiger."

But Balbino pretended not to hear him, for Pajarote, when he started anything, did not stop at words.

"Everything in time," he thought to himself. "The dude has got some nerve, but the colt hasn't come back yet and maybe he never will. The prairie looks very smooth from here, but it's got its ups and downs."

Nevertheless, after a turn around the cabins to meddle with what was no longer his business, he remounted his horse and left Altamira without waiting for anyone to demand an account of his thefts.

Endless land of vigour and daring!

The mirages circling the prairie danced before his eyes in a vertiginous whirl. The wind whistled in his ears, the brakes parted and closed immediately behind him, the rushes tore and cut his flesh, but his body felt no hurt. At times the horses' feet rested on nothing but air, but leaps and obstructions, mortal dangers indeed, were passed flying. The drumbeat of the galloping hoofs filled the prairie. One might ride on for days; there would always be more prairie ahead.

At last the colt's courage began to flag. He had already slackened to an ever-quieter trot. Now he was pacing—snorting, shaking his head, dripping sweat, white with foam, beaten, but still proud. Now he was approaching the ranch houses between the other houses, and he neighed arrogantly, for if he was no longer free, at least he had a man on his back. And Pajarote greeted him with the Plainsman's praise:

"Dead before he'd tire."

IX

THE SPHINX OF THE SAVANNAH

BALBINO PAIBA had left a good thing behind him, and he was losing it just as he was about to get real profit out of it. Until that time Doña Barbara had been the one who really benefited by his administration of Altamira, for while she had taken from there thousands of strays to be burned with the El Miedo mark, he had managed to lay hands for himself on no more than some three hundred horses and cattle, a number insignificant in comparison with his "skill."

He now had left only the prospect of being "overseer" of El Miedo — the title given there to rustlers — since, precarious as was his position of lover, Doña Barbara would nevertheless have to make up to him for his loss of easy pickings at Altamira, for which the efforts he had put forth in her behalf were to blame.

Besides these things, Balbino was meditating on other vexations. His withdrawal was equivalent to recognition of the qualities he had refused to concede to Luzardo the night before, and it might easily occur to Melquíades to receive him with:

"What did I tell you, Don Balbino? It's better to reap than to sow."

He had nearly reached the ranch-house at El Miedo when he was joined by three men going in the same direction.

"What are the Mondragons looking for here?" he inquired.

"*Guá!* Don't you know the latest thing, Don Balbino? The *señora* has ordered us to get out of the house at Macanillal. It seems she don't need us there now."

The Mondragons were three brothers, born on the plains of Barinas, and nicknamed, on account of their ferocity and misdeeds, the Leopard, the Tiger, and the Lion. Fugitives from justice in Barinas, they had come to the Apure country, and after some time spent in marauding and rustling had entered the service of Doña Barbara, whose property was asylum for whatever blackguards strayed into the Arauca basin.

The Macanillal house was situated on the boundary of Altamira established in accord with the last judgment Doña Barbara had won. But the house had changed position as often as the boundary stakes, going farther and farther into Altamira. The Mondragon brothers were there under orders to advance from time to time the boundary line, whose point of reference in the intentionally vague decree of the Tribunal was "the house on stilts" where the three brothers lived, a shack easily taken down and rebuilt in a few hours without leaving any immediately visible traces of its removal, because of the monotony of the immense prairie. By means of this stratagem, Doña Barbara had in six months taken an additional half league or more from Altamira while she was getting another suit started.

The information he had received from the Leopard did not please Balbino. Still more disconcerting was what the Tiger added:

"It wasn't so much that she told us to vacate the house, but this morning Melquíades came there to order us to take it down tonight and put it and the boundary posts back where they were before. As if that was easy, to move a house and a line of stakes in one night. Besides, we never did like to go back after we'd pushed up. So we're going to tell the *señora* that she'd better send somebody else to do this job."

Balbino frowned thoughtfully, and the Lion added:

"I don't understand. Unless the *señora* is afraid of her neighbour."

"Don't take down the house or move the posts," Balbino told him. "And don't have any talk with her, either. Leave that to me." And when they reached the cabins, he said:

"Wait here while I have a talk with her."

The brothers struck up a conversation with the other peons thereabout and Balbino turned his steps towards the house.

His first disagreeable impression was produced by

the change which had come over the woman since the night before. She was not dressed in the simple white frock with high collar and sleeves entirely concealing her arms which was the maximum of femininity she allowed in her attire, but had replaced it with another Balbino had never seen her wear, low necked, sleeveless, and adorned with ribbons and lace. Moreover, she had her hair better arranged, with a certain grace even, which made her handsomer and more youthful looking.

Despite this, the transformation did not please Balbino at all. He frowned, and a grunt of displeasure escaped him.

The second disagreeable impression resulted from her bitingly sarcastic smile as she inquired, alluding to his trumpetings of the preceding night, concerning his plot against Luzardo:

"Did you polish him off?"

Annoyed and disconcerted by this mocking reception, he replied gruffly:

"I've decided to wait for him to call me to account. I hope he does, and we'll see who'll give it."

She kept looking at him without ceasing to smile, and after three or four strokes at his mustache, he added:

"If I was there, it was to please you."

The smile disappeared from her face, but she maintained her disconcerting silence. Balbino's expression now changed to one of discomfiture, and he said to himself:

"I don't like the looks of this a bit."

In fact, the woman's superiority, her domination over others, and the awe she inspired seemed to spring from that very ability to observe and say nothing. It was useless to attempt to wring a secret from her. No one knew a single detail of her plans, nor anything of her attitude towards a person. Her favour gave such a one everything, including the eternal uncertainty of really possessing her, but when the favourite approached her, he never knew what he would find. Whoever loved her, as Lorenzo Barquero had, spent a life of torment.

Balbino was very far from experiencing a passion like Barquero's, but still, Doña Barbara's favours were not to be despised, and besides, they were profitable. The legend of that supernatural power which aided her and rendered it impossible for anyone to steal a horse or steer from her may very well have been an invention of the cunning of overseer-lovers who defrauded her; while she, entirely superstitious as she was, thinking herself really assisted by such powers, relaxed her vigilance and allowed herself to be robbed.

Balbino decided to make use of the Mondragons to draw out this enigmatic woman.

"The Mondragons are here, just come from Macanillal," he announced.

"What did they come for?" she inquired.

"To speak with you, it seems." It appeared best to treat her with deference, now. "Because they're not entirely pleased at the idea of undoing all they've done there."

Doña Barbara turned her head brusquely with an imperious expression:

"Not entirely pleased, eh? And who asked them whether they liked it or not? Call them here."

"I meant to say: Not because they don't want to do what you ordered, but because they're only three men, and can't move the house and the posts all in one night."

"Let them take the men they need, then. But tomorrow morning I want to see that house back where it was before."

"I'll tell them so," answered Balbino, shrugging his shoulders.

"You should have begun with that. You know very well that I won't have my orders discussed."

Balbino went out to the yard, called the Mondragons to one side, and said to them:

"You were wrong. It's not because she's afraid of that man, but because we want him to feel confident. You go back there and do all she told you to, and take the men you need to get that house back where it was, and the posts where the judge ordered them to be, by tomorrow morning."

"That's another tune," said the Leopard. "If that's the case, we'll get right at the moving, posts and all."

He and his brothers returned to Macanillal, taking sufficient men for the rapid execution of the task.

Balbino returned to Doña Barbara, and after he had made several unanswered remarks to her, he determined to clear up his doubts about her feelings toward Santos Luzardo.

"Look at the way Melquíades throws away chances," he said. "After he goes and gets himself on the boat, he can't do anything. With all those fine spots on this side of the plateau for stopping Dr. Luzardo. And a river full of alligators like that, enough to take care of all the dead men you could throw into it. Now the thing is going to be more complicated, because even if it's only a matter of form, the authorities will have to make an investigation."

Without any change of attitude, Doña Barbara replied to the sinister insinuation, in a smooth, measured, sombre tone:

"God help the man that dares to do anything to Santos Luzardo. That man belongs to me."

X

THE SPECTRE OF LA BARQUEREÑA

IT WAS a thicket of mapora palms, high and thin, covering a wide low-lying part of the prairie. Its name was derived from a small blue heron, *chusmita,* which, according to an old legend, used to be there, the sole inhabitant of the spot. The place was under a curse, surrounded by an unforgettable silence; there were numerous palm trees blackened by lightning, and in the centre was a quagmire in which any living thing that tried to cross perished in the quicksand.

The *chusmita* which gave the grove its name, La Chusmita, was, said the legend, the tormented soul of an Indian woman, daughter of the cacique of a settlement of Yaruros living there at the time when Don Evaristo Luzardo led his herds to the Arauca basin. The man of prey despoiled the aboriginal settlers of their just domain, and when they tried to defend it, exterminated them with fire and sword. But the cacique, when he saw his settlement in ruins, laid a curse upon the grove, so that the invader and his descendants, as victims of the lightning, would find there only ruin and calamity. He prophesied, too, that the grove would return to the Yaruros whenever one of them should pick up the talismanic flint from the ground.

The traditional curse had been fulfilled. Not only did every storm never fail to wreak its wrath there in destructive lightnings, at times killing whole herds of the Luzardo cattle, but that spot was the cause of the feud which had wiped out the Luzardo family. As for the prophecy, it was currently said, up to the times of Santos' father, that after every storm an Indian, from whence nobody knew, was to be seen there searching for the magic flint. But years had passed since the Indian had been seen. Perhaps the tradition had vanished from the settlements. No one in Altamira would admit belief in the legend, but all preferred to make a long detour rather than pass the fateful spot.

Santos skirted the bog along a patch of black mud, slippery, but not dangerous, which splashed noisily under the horse's hoofs. The ground bordering the deadly quagmire was covered with soft grass, but notwithstanding the freshness of this pleasant verdure, there was something forbidding about the scene. Instead of the legendary heron a lonely crane standing on a clayey shoal accentuated the note of funereal quiet.

Santos was going along absorbed in the plan which had brought him there, when something moving just within his field of vision made him turn his head. It was a girl, tousled and dressed in filthy rags, carrying a bundle of wood on her head and trying to conceal herself behind a palm.

"Hello!" he called to her, reining in his horse. "Whereabouts is Lorenzo Barquero's house?"

"Don't you know then?" the girl replied, after giving a cry like that of a frightened animal.

"I don't know, that's why I asked you."

"*Guá!* what do you think that roof peeping out there is, eh?"

"You could have said that at first," Santos declared and went on.

A miserable dwelling, half cabin and half hut — the latter aspect deriving from wattled walls without a window and an open doorway, the former from untrimmed posts supporting the end of the blackened and ruined palm thatch roof; within, a wretched hammock slung between two of the posts — such was the house of Lorenzo Barquero, the Spectre of La Barquereña, as he was called in the vicinity.

Having seen him once in childhood, Santos had some vague recollection of his appearance, but had the memory been of the clearest, he would not have recognized the man who sat up in the hammock upon hearing him approach. Extremely thin and wasted, a genuine physical ruin, he had grey hair and every aspect of an old man, though he was barely over forty. His large, skinny hands shook continually, and his dark green eyes held a glint of madness. His head hung down as though under a yoke. His features, like the condition of his body, revealed a fundamental decay of the will; his mouth was deformed by the leer resulting from sodden debauchery. It was with a visible effort that he managed to force out, in a hollow voice, the words:

" Whom have I the pleasure . . . ? "

The visitor had dismounted and after hitching the horse to one of the posts, came forward.

" I am Santos Luzardo," he said. " And I've come to make friends with you."

But the old implacable hate was still burning in the wreck of humanity before him.

" A Luzardo in a Barquero's house! "

Santos saw him stumble and blunder about, in search of a weapon perhaps, but he advanced and held out his hand:

" Let's be sensible, Lorenzo. It would be ridiculous for us to insist on keeping up that miserable feud. For me, because I don't feel that way, and for you — "

" Because I'm not a man any longer? Isn't that what you were going to say? " Lorenzo interrupted with the stammer of a man whose mind is giving way.

" No, I hadn't any such idea," answered Santos, beginning to feel a real pity for the man, though he had gone there with the sole intention of ending the family quarrel. But Lorenzo insisted:

" Yes, yes, that was what you were going to say."

Up to this point he had kept his gruff tone and insolent manner. Suddenly he collapsed again, as though he had used up with that burst of energy the little force left in him, and continued in another voice, spent, painful, and stammering more than before:

"You're right, Luzardo. I'm not a man any more. I'm the ghost of a man that's dead. Do what you like with me."

"I said I'd come to make friends with you, and be ready to do anything I can for you. I've come to take charge of Altamira, and — "

Lorenzo again interrupted, exclaiming, as he laid his skeleton hands on the young man's powerful shoulders:

"You too, Santos Luzardo? You've obeyed the call too? We all have to obey it! "

"I don't understand. What call do you mean? " As Lorenzo did not release him, but kept his delirious gaze fixed on his face, and since it was impossible to bear any longer the reeking alcoholic breath, Santos added:

"But you haven't asked me to sit down yet."

"That's so. Wait. I'll get you a chair."

"I can get it. Don't bother," Santos said, noticing that Lorenzo staggered as he walked.

"No, stay out there. You can't come in here. I don't want you to. This isn't a house, it's a pig-sty."

He went into the house, stooping still more to pass under the low doorway. Before getting the chair he meant to offer his guest, he went to a table at the back of the room, on which stood a carafe with a glass inverted over the neck.

"I beg you not to drink, Lorenzo," Santos intervened, approaching the door.

"Just a swallow, that's all. Let me take a swallow. I need it at these times. I won't offer you any, because it's hogwash. But if you like — "

"Thanks. I'm not in the habit."

"You'll soon get into it." A hideous smile creased the degenerate man's hollow face, and his trembling hands made the glass click against the neck of the carafe.

Santos, seeing the size of the drink Lorenzo was pouring himself, would have interfered, but the air within was so foul that he could not cross the threshold. Besides, Lorenzo had already raised the glass to his lips and was swallowing the liquor in great gulps. Then, with the movements of a baby unable to make proper use of its hands, he wiped his moustache by passing his forearm across it, picked up a stool and a chair with a greasy leather seat, and came out, saying:

"Think of it! A Luzardo in a Barquero's house! and both still alive. The last two left."

"I beg you — "

"No. You've already said so. I know . . . the Luzardo has not come to kill him, and the Barquero offers the best chair he has — this one. Sit down — and he sits on the stool. So."

The stool, a very low one, obliged him to draw up his

knees and place his elbows on them, with the shaky hands hanging down, in a grotesque attitude which made the wretchedness of his physique even more repulsive. His only clothes were ragged trousers of what the Plainsman calls "turkey's claw," open at the sides as far up as the knees, and a scanty striped shirt, with the hair of his chest showing through the holes.

Before this repugnant image of ruin, Santos felt a moment's unavoidable horror. The man before him had been one in whom were centred pride, hope, and love. To do something which would enable him to speak to Lorenzo without looking at him, he took out a cigarette, and said while he was lighting it:

"This is the second time we've seen each other, Lorenzo."

"The second?" replied the derelict in a questioning tone, with an expression betraying painful mental effort. "Do you mean that we've already met?"

"Yes. Some years ago. I must have been about eight then."

"In your house? Then —"

"No," Santos interrupted. "The feud hadn't broken out yet."

"Then my father was still alive?"

"Yes. And at home; everybody praised you and your unusual intelligence. You were the pride of the family."

"My intelligence?" Lorenzo repeated, as though he had been told of something he had never possessed.

" My intelligence! " he repeated, putting his hands to his head in an agonized gesture and directing a pleading look at Santos. " Why have you come here to talk to me about that? "

" Because I've just remembered something," replied Santos, concealing his intention of producing some healthy reaction in the debased spirit. " I was a small boy, but hearing everyone say fine things about you, especially my mother, who was never tired of saying ' Learn from Lorenzo ' whenever she wanted to stimulate me, I had formed the loftiest idea of you an eight-year-old mind could form. I hadn't ever seen you, but I lived with the thought of ' the cousin studying in Caracas,' and I never heard of any word or way or gesture of yours without immediately beginning to copy it. I don't remember feeling all through childhood such a profound excitement as I felt the day my mother said to me, ' Come meet your cousin Lorenzo.' I can still see it. You asked me the three or four questions usually asked children when they are introduced, and when Papa said to you, with a real Plainsman's pride, that I was ' well in the saddle ' you answered with a long discourse that sounded like heavenly music to me, as much because I didn't understand it as because the words, being yours, were naturally eloquence itself for me. One of the phrases did make an impression on me. You said, ' We must kill the centaur inside every one of us Plainsmen.' Now, of course I had no idea what a centaur was, much less any idea of how we Plainsmen had them inside us. But the expression pleased me so much and made such an impression that I must confess my first attempts at oratory — and all Plainsmen, being an emphatic race, are in some way attracted by eloquence — were based on that same 'we must kill the centaur' which I declaimed to myself without understanding one jot of what I was saying, and without being able to stop, either. I don't need to tell you that I had already heard of your fame as an orator."

He paused, apparently to flick the ashes from his cigarette, but actually to allow Lorenzo time to show what effect the words had produced. They had produced some, for he displayed considerable agitation, running his hands through his hair from his forehead to the back of his neck in a troubled gesture. Santos proceeded:

"Years later, in Caracas, I got hold of a printed copy of one of the speeches you made at some patriotic celebration, I don't know which one, and you can imagine my sensations when I came across that same phrase. You remember that speech? The theme was 'That centaur is barbarism, and therefore we must put an end to him.' I learned then that you had stirred up a commotion among the traditionalists with that theory, which pointed out a more useful direction for our national history, and I had the satisfaction of proving that your ideas had marked an epoch in the manner of viewing the history of our independence. I was capable of understanding the thesis at that time, and I agreed with you in thought and feeling too. I ought to have retained a little of it after repeating it so much, don't you think? "

But Lorenzo did nothing but run his trembling hands through his hair, over the head in which the agony of recollection had been released.

His brilliant youth, his future, all promise . . . the hopes placed in him . . . Caracas . . . the University . . . the pleasure, the vanity of success, the admiring friends, a loving woman, everything which could make life agreeable. His studies, about to be completed with the doctor's degree, the aura of sympathy with the well-earned triumph, the pride in possessing a fine intellect — and suddenly, the Call! The fatal reclamation of barbarism in his mother's hand: "Come home. José Luzardo killed your father yesterday. Come and avenge him."

"Now do you understand why I can't consider myself your enemy? " Santos concluded, in an attempt to help the soul struggling in the abyss. "You were the object of my admiration when I was a child, and you helped me after that, indirectly, because lots of things in Caracas were made easier for me, in my studies and social life, by the admiration and friendship you aroused there. . . . And spiritually speaking, I feel I owe you a debt, because in trying to imitate you, I formed my ideals."

The terrific sarcasm lent by circumstances to these well-meaning words ended by exasperating the derelict. He rose brusquely from the stool where he had sat bowed down under the weight of his misery and torment and rushed through the doorway. The clink of the glass against the neck of the carafe held by the trembling hands was immediately audible, and Santos murmured:

" It's no use. There's nothing left for this poor devil but to stupefy himself with liquor."

He was preparing to go when Lorenzo reappeared, with a firmer step and a more intelligent expression, as though galvanized by the shock of alcohol.

" No! No! you can't go away now. You've got to listen to me. You've talked, and now it's my turn. Sit down and hear what I have to say."

" Leave it for another day, Lorenzo. I'll come often to see you."

" No! right now! I beg you to listen to me." And again, violently: " Beg you? No. I command you to listen to me. You came here to aggravate me, and now you've got to listen to me."

" All right, then. I'll please you," Santos agreed, good-naturedly. " I'm sitting down again. Talk about whatever you like."

" Yes, I'll talk. At last, I'll talk. What a great thing, to be able to talk, Luzardo! "

" Don't you have anyone to talk to? Don't you live with your daughter? "

"Don't talk about my daughter. Don't talk. Listen. Listen, that's all. So. Ah! Look at me well, Santos! This ghost of a man that used to be, this human wreck, this carrion talking to you was your ideal. I was what you were talking about just now, and now I'm what you see. Doesn't it frighten you, Luzardo?"

"Frighten? Why?"

"No! I'm not asking you so you'll answer, but so you'll listen to this. That Lorenzo Barquero you spoke of was a lie. The truth is what you're looking at now. This land never relents. You've already heard the call of the ogress, you too, and I'll soon see you fall into her arms. When she opens them, you'll be the wreck of a man. Look at her. Mirages everywhere, one here, one there. The Plain is full of mirages. What fault of mine is it that you've been under the illusion that a Luzardo — a Luzardo, because I am one, though it hurts me to say it — that a Luzardo could be any man's ideal? But we're not alone, Santos. That's our only comfort. I've known many men, and you're one, certainly, who showed great promise at thirty. Double the age — they're done for, ruined. The mirage of the tropics. But let me tell you this: I never made any mistake about myself. I knew that everything others admired in me was a lie. I found that out right after one of the greatest triumphs of my student years, an examination for which I wasn't well prepared. I had to develop a theme I was totally ignorant of, but I began to talk and the words, pure words, did it all. Not only was I well rated, I was all but applauded by the very teachers that were examining me. The scoundrels! From that time on I began to observe that my intelligence, what everybody called my great talent, operated only when I was talking. Whenever I shut up the mirage was destroyed and I understood nothing about anything. I recognized the lies — my intelligence, my sincerity. You understand, realized the falseness of my own sincerity, the worst thing that can happen to a man. I felt the old hidden sore of that hereditary cancer in the bottom of my soul, just as it must feel in the deepest part of an apparently healthy body. I began to loathe the University, and city life, the friends who admired me, my sweetheart, everything that was the cause or effect of that self-deception."

Santos listened with lively interest and a hopeful feeling. The man who could still think and express himself with such clarity was not hopelessly lost.

But this could not last long. It was the lash of alcohol, and the long-habituated organism responded to the stimulation only for brief moments followed by rapid descents into stupefaction. In fact, this brief pause of Lorenzo's was sufficient for the disappearance of the effect.

"Kill the centaur? Ho-ho! Don't be an idiot, Luzardo. Do you think that business about the centaur is mere rhetoric? I assure you that the centaur exists. I've heard him neigh. He's around here, every night. Not only here, but in Caracas, too. And still farther away. No matter where one of us is, he hears the centaur neighing if he's got Luzardo blood in his veins. And you've heard it, too, and that's why you're here. Who said that it was possible to kill the centaur? I? Spit in my face. The centaur is an entelechy. He's been galloping through this land for a century and he will be for centuries more. I thought I was a civilized man, the first civilized man of my family, but it was enough for me to be told 'Come and avenge your father' to make the barbarian inside of me appear. The same thing has happened to you. You heard the call. I'll soon see you falling in her arms and going mad for her caresses. And she'll kick you aside and when you say to her 'I'm ready to marry you' she'll laugh at your misery and — "

He clutched his hair. The fixed idea which had begun to appear in the earlier part of his discourse had finally succeeded in obtaining mastery over him. His hands, with tufts of hair between the fingers, fell to his sides, and lowering his head to his breast, he stood muttering:

"The Ogress."

Luzardo looked on in silence, with a heavy heart, at this dramatic spectacle of human degradation and then asked in an attempt to awaken him:

"And your daughter?"

But Lorenzo, with his gaze fixed on the horizon, went on muttering: "The Plain! The cursed Plain, the Ogress!" And Santos thought: I really believe this poor devil has fallen under the spell of the desert more than the wiles of Doña Barbara.

A sudden gleam of lucidity re-animated the derelict's features. The debauched leer momentarily disappeared.

"Marisela!" he called. "Come here and meet your cousin." But as there was no answer from within, he added: "You couldn't drag her out of there by the hair. She's wilder than a tapir . . . than a tapir."

His head drooped again and slow trickles of saliva began to run out of his drawn lips.

"Well, Lorenzo," said Santos, standing up, "I'll come back, often."

The drunkard got immediately to his feet and stumbled into the hut.

"Leave her alone," said Santos, thinking he had gone in search of his daughter. "I'll meet her some other day," and he began to unhitch his horse. He was about to put his foot in the stirrup when he saw that Lorenzo was raising the carafe of brandy to his lips, pouring the liquor into his mouth, as he could not get the neck into it. He hastened into the house to take it from him. But the drunkard had already taken enough to stun him. He fell into Luzardo's arms and exclaimed, gazing deliriously at him:

"Santos Luzardo, look at me! This land never relents."

XI

THE SLEEPING BEAUTY

On his way back to Altamira, weighed down by the impression of the scene he had just witnessed, Santos again met the girl of whom he had asked the way to the house he was to visit. Only after he had seen the wretchedness reigning in Lorenzo Barquero's house did he suspect that the wild, dishevelled, barefooted girl, barely covered by those tatters she wore, could be his daughter.

She had put down her bundle of wood and was stretched out beside it with her forearms resting in the sand. Her face, propped up on her hands, held a wondering look. Santos stopped to look at her. The curve of her back and the line of her hips and thighs were of a statuesque beauty beneath the scant, dirty rags that clung to her body; but the broad, thick feet, toughened and cracked by going barefoot, broke the spell, and it was on this lamentable ugliness that one's pitying gaze finally rested.

A snort from Luzardo's horse roused her from her

abstraction, and becoming aware of the presence of the man who had stopped a few paces away, she bundled herself into a heap to conceal the nudity of her legs, and after several protesting grunts, burst out laughing as she lay face downward on the sand.

"Are you Marisela?" Santos inquired.

She had him repeat the question, and then answered, with the rudeness of her rustic breeding emphasized by confusion:

"If you know what I'm called, then what do you ask for?"

"I didn't really know. I imagined you were Lorenzo Barquero's daughter by that name, but I wanted to be assured."

Shy as the wild animal to which her father had compared her, she replied, upon hearing that unknown word:

"To be assured? Well, you're off your track. Run along."

"Not so bad if her wildness protects her innocence," thought Santos. He said aloud:

"What did you think 'be assured' meant?"

"Ho! ho! what a question-box you are!" she exclaimed, bursting into another laugh.

"Is this innocence or slyness?" Santos asked himself, realizing that, far from displeasing her, his having stopped to talk was producing quite the opposite effect; and no longer smiling he continued his pitying contemplation of the heap of rags and tatters.

" How long are you going to stay there, eh? " Marisela grumbled. " Why don't you finish talking? "

" What I want to know is, how long are you going to stay there? It's time for you to go home. Aren't you afraid of being alone in this deserted place? "

" *Guá!* and why should I be? Are the wild animals going to eat me, maybe? And what's it to you if I go alone wherever I want to? Are you my daddy, maybe, to come around scolding me? "

" Don't be so rude, child. Haven't you even been taught how to answer people? "

" Well, why don't you teach me? " And once more the prone body shook with mirth.

" I *will* teach you," said Santos, whose pity was beginning to change to liking. " But you've got to pay me in advance for the lessons by showing me that face you're so bent on hiding."

" What a thing to say! " she exclaimed, shrinking herself up more than ever. " You'd better stop talking right away, because the night will come on you."

" I won't move from here until you show me your face. I came just to meet you, because I've heard you were very ugly and I don't want to believe it until I see it with my own eyes. It's hard for me to think that a relative of mine could be ugly. That's right, I didn't tell you we were cousins."

" Get along! " she exclaimed. " I haven't got any relative but my dad, because I can't even say that I know my ma."

The mention of her mother drove away the good spirits Santos had derived from his talk with the girl, and she, fearful of having really displeased him, persisted, after peeping at him from beneath the arm which covered her face:

"Don't you see that you're no relative of mine, as you say? If you were, it wouldn't have been such a secret."

"Yes, I am," he declared. "I'm Santos Luzardo, your father's cousin. Ask him, if you want to be assured of it. And don't put a bad meaning on that word again!"

"All right. If you really are my cousin. . . . But I'm not sure I believe it, see? Ho! ho! and they say women are curious. Take a peep then, and get it over with now," she said, and without waiting for Santos to insist upon it, she raised her head and immediately lowered it, but with her eyes closed and her lips puckered so that she would not laugh, a shy and innocent piece of coquetry.

She must have been about fifteen years old, and although poor food, bad water, neglect, and the wildness of her life had spoiled her youth, under the dirt and tangled hair one could see that her features were perfect. It required no more than an instant for Santos to grasp the fact that she was really beautiful.

"How pretty you are!" he exclaimed, and found himself looking at her with a totally different sort of compassion. The girl, no longer timidly surly, but modestly shy now, as though humanized by the first spark of pleasure in herself which the exclamation had produced, said to him in a soft, pleading tone:

"Now go away."

"Not yet," Santos answered. "You haven't shown me your eyes. Let me see them. Ah! now I understand why you won't open them before me. You're cross-eyed, of course. They must be very ugly."

"Me cross-eyed? Looka-here."

Raising herself up, gayly, she opened her eyes. They were beautiful, the loveliest thing about her. She stared at him, motionless, and he exclaimed again:

"The girl's a treasure!"

"Now go away," Marisela repeated, blushing under the dirt on her face, but without taking her eyes off him.

"Look here. I'm going to give you the first lesson you paid for in advance, right away."

He got down from his horse, went up to the girl, whose eyes revealed a cringing fear, made her get up by seizing her arm, and said to her:

"Come here, little cousin. I'm going to show you what water is for. You're pretty, but you'd be much prettier if you didn't neglect yourself so."

Freed of her instinctive fear by the voice, without a shade of malice, with which this man from a different world addressed her, Marisela allowed herself to be led to a pool of clear water at the side of the marsh, hiding her face under her arm and laughing, half ashamed, half pleased.

Santos made her lean over, and then, scooping the water in the hollows of his hands, began to wash her arms and her face, like an infant's.

"Now take a lesson from this, and learn to appreciate water, because it will make you still prettier," he said to her. "Your father does wrong in not giving you the care you deserve, but it's a sin against the nature that made you so pretty for you to neglect yourself so. You could at least have been clean, since there's no lack of water around here. I'm going to have some decent clothes sent to you in place of those things that don't even cover you, and a comb for you to use on your hair, and some shoes so you won't have to go barefooted. Now, there! How long has it been since you washed your face?"

Marisela abandoned her face to the freshness of the water, her lips shut tight, her eyes closed, and her maiden body tense under the touch of a man's hands. Santos, not having a towel, took his handkerchief to wipe her face, and when he had done that made her raise her head, holding her under the chin. She opened her eyes and looked at him, and they filled with tears.

"Good," said Santos. "Now go home. I'll go with you, because it's not safe for you to be around this place at this time of day."

"No. I'll go by myself," she replied. "You go first."

She was again the girl he had first met. But he had left her two beautiful things: The freshness of water on her cheeks and the emotion roused by words she had never before heard.

For the first time in her life Marisela did not go to sleep the moment she lay on her mat. The dirty, miserable bed of leaves felt strange, as though a new body were lying on it, a body unused to discomfort. She resented the contact of those dirty rags which she did not even take off when she slept, as though she had just put them on. All her senses shrank from the sensations to which they had become accustomed; they had suddenly become intolerable, as to a new-born finer sensibility.

The woman's soul in her had just awakened, complicating her life, hitherto simple as the wind that knows nothing but its own flight over the savannahs. Confused feelings began to stir in her heart, a pleasure full of pain, a hope tense with fears; one time it seemed necessary to beat her head against the wall to banish a thought, and then it would seem necessary to lie motionless so that it might return. There were many other things, too, which she was unable to grasp.

The crane, the harbinger of day, was already singing: "Up, Marisela!" he seemed to say. "There is cool water in the well. The stars passing all through the night over the kerb-stone have chilled it. Some fell in and are still at the bottom. Go draw them up with the bucket and pour them over you. They will leave you pure and shining like themselves."

The sun was rising, the moon setting, the palm grove lay like a sacred wood in the silence of dawn.

The bucket went down and rose out of the well without rest, and the water from deep in the earth where it had never known the light of day ran bewildered over the young naked body.

XII

THE DAY WILL COME

ANTONIO'S surprise was great when, next day, having taken Santos to Macanillal to show him how the boundary of El Miedo was advancing, he discovered that the Mondragons' house had returned to its former site.

"They moved it last night," he exclaimed. "See where the boundary post came from. The hole is still there."

"Good," said Luzardo. "Now it's in its place and we won't have any more trouble on that score, at least for the present. To keep it from being moved overnight after this, we'll put a fence on this side."

But Antonio objected. "Do you mean to say that you're going to accept this boundary? Are you going to be satisfied with the suits Doña Barbara has won from you unfairly?"

"They're completed actions and they have the authority of legal judgment. I could have successfully appealed some, if not all, of these decisions of the tribunal, but I didn't know how to take care of my own interests. Besides, as for land, there's still plenty, in spite of everything. But there are not cattle enough, hardly more than a bit of a herd here and there."

"Cattle aren't lacking either," replied Antonio. "What's happened is that nearly all of them have run away. There are lots of strays in Altamira, as I told you, because we, the only friends you had left here, have encouraged the strays instead of wiping them out. That was the only way to save the herd, to let it run away. What was missing here was an owner and now what we need is hands to work."

"It's true. I can see that Altamira has changed into a perfect desert. Before, there were houses everywhere."

"Don Balbino dispossessed the few settlers that were left when he took charge, so that when there were no *Luzarderos* near the boundary to watch them, the neighbours could come in just when they pleased and lead out all the cattle they came across."

"So that Doña Barbara was not the only enemy?"

"She has done whatever she was tempted to do with your property, but the others have handled it any way they pleased, too. For example, they've done away with the water holes in Altamira and put them where they thought best, so that the herd from here would walk right into their hands. At every water hole over there you'll find four or five men from the ranch it belongs to catching the Luzardo herd with lassos. Do you see that bunch of steers? All those animals are going to the

Bramador Pass water holes in lands that used to belong to us and belong to El Miedo now, and any unbranded steer that puts his foot in the water is as good as lost. Doña Barbara's men themselves have driven the herd in that direction until the beasts have got used to it, and we couldn't stop them. As for the gentleman over by the La Barquereña salt lick, it's impossible to say. That's the Señor Danger I told you about this morning. That man has learned every trick a slick cattleman knows and any animal that passes through the Gap of Corozalito never comes back here. I think the first thing we ought to do is dig the waterholes again and make the herd get used to giving up the neighbours', and then throw up the barricade that closed up the Gap right up to your father's time to keep the herd from going to gather around the La Barquereña Licks. If you like, we can begin this very day to dig the holes for the posts."

"There's no need to hurry. Before that I have to study the deeds to determine the boundary lines, and consult the Law of the Plain."

"The Law of the Plain?" Antonio replied insinuatingly. "Do you know what it's called around here? 'Doña Barbara's Law.' Because they say that she paid to have it made to measure."

"There wouldn't be anything strange in that, the way things go around here," said Santos. "But as long as it's a law, it's got to be obeyed. Some day we'll be able to get it rewritten."

That evening, after a study of the titles of Altamira and the Law of the Plain, Santos sent a written notice to Doña Barbara and to Señor Danger, informing them of his intention of fencing off the property so that they might proceed legally to take out their respective herds grazing on lands belonging to Altamira. At the same time he asked their permission to remove his own cattle from El Miedo and from The Licks.

Antonio himself delivered the letters and entertained these reflections on his way:

"This is just like taking money from Doña Barbara. This business about the fence that's in the law I don't like much, but she'll like it even less. There had to be someone to come some day and put her in her place."

At nightfall the following day Santos went off in the direction of Mata Luzardera accompanied by Antonio. After they had ridden for two hours over bare savannah they came to a strip of land overgrown with dry mint and broom where there were no cattle trails to be seen.

The moon was rising behind the dark clump of foliage, suffusing the wide bristling tract in a melancholy glow. Antonio slowed his horse down to a walk, and after he had advised Luzardo to be cautious and quiet they rode to the top of a dune.

"Watch now," Antonio said to him. "Now you're going to hear something you never even dreamed of," and making a trumpet of his hands he sent from the top of the hill a piercing call to shatter the silence of the night.

Immediately a vast, steadily increasing roar arose, and all the face of the prairie commanded by the dune swayed and trembled under the trampling of a multitude of wild cattle.

"Listen!" exclaimed the peon. "There are thousands and thousands of unmarked steers that have never seen a man. It's over seven years since there was a horse in this strip of the prairie, and what you are hearing now is nothing compared to other flocks of strays farther on, towards the Cunaviche. Altamira is prospering in spite of everything. The stray flocks have been a godsend, but it's time to put an end to them. I'd like to try a few stampedes on this bunch, if you think we might. Right now we need special ropers, because everyone can't manage stray herds, but I know where to find some and I can get them. Besides, it seems to me that it would be a good idea to start operating the dairies again. When we had them before we had good results. The dairying is good, not only because it brings in more money, but it helps too in taming the herd, and these cattle around here are the wildest of the wild. There's many a horse killed in rounding them up."

These practical reasons would have been sufficient for commencing the re-establishment of the dairies, but Luzardo saw something else besides, a reason of a different order and just as interesting to him as the economic one.

Anything making for the suppression of ferocity had great importance in his eyes.

Finally, another idea came to him as the result of a conversation with Antonio the next day, an idea even more closely in accord with his plans for reclaiming and civilizing the Plain.

"Today we'll smuggle about fifty strays in a single lassoing," Sandoval had said.

Smuggling, that is to say, lassoing unbranded cattle found within the boundaries of the ranch, is the favourite sport of the Apure Plainsman. Since the lands in these limitless prairies are not enclosed, the herds are free to wander, and ownership of the cattle is acquired by every ranch owner either in the round-ups undertaken in concert with the neighbours, and in which each gathers and brands whatever stray yearlings or unmarked steers from the group he collects; or outside of these round-ups, at any moment, by natural right of the noose. This primitive form of acquiring property, the only one which can prevail under the circumstances was sanctioned by the law itself with the one limitation of the extent of land and number of cattle which must be possessed as a qualification for pursuing it. It had, beyond doubt, some tinge of the old-time rustling, and that is why it was not so much work as it was the preferred diversion of the men dwelling in the open Plain, where might is always right.

Reflecting on this, Santos concluded:

"All this hinders the development of breeding because it kills the incentive. But it would all disappear with the obligation to fence the ranches that the Law of the Plain would impose on the owners."

"Maybe you are right," Antonio said," but to do that you'll have to change the Plainsman first. The Plainsman won't have fences. He likes to have his land open the way God gave it to him, and he likes it that way just because he likes smuggling whatever animals he can lasso. If you took that pleasure away from him he'd die of grief. A Plainsman is only satisfied when he can say: Today I smuggled so many head, and it's nothing to him if his neighbour is saying the same thing, because the Plainsman always thinks his own herd is safe, and that the cattle his neighbour took belonged to somebody else."

Luzardo nevertheless kept thinking of the necessity of implanting the custom of fencing. Through that the civilizing of the Plain would begin. The fence would be a bulwark against the omnipotence of force, the necessary limitation of man prior to his undertakings.

Meanwhile, he had other ideas which made him feel as though he were riding a wild horse in the dizzy career of his breaking, sending the mirages spinning on the horizon. The fence-wire, the straight line of man before the curving line of nature, would represent one sole unswerving road towards the future in this land of untold paths where wandering hopes had been lost since time immemorial.

He made all these plans, talking aloud to himself in his enthusiasm. It was really beautiful, that vision of the Plain of the future, civilized, prosperous, as it welled up in his imagination.

The afternoon was sunny, with a high wind. The pastures undulated within the shimmering rings of the mirages, and across the distant dunes on the horizon ran funnel shaped clouds of sand, whirled up by the wind, like plumes of smoke.

Suddenly the dreamer, as though actually tricked by the illusion, or else deliberately indulging his fancy, exclaimed:

"The train! there goes the train!"

Then he smiled sadly, as one smiles at the deception when he has ceased to fondle hopes perhaps impossible of fulfilment. But after gazing for a while at the joyful sport of the wind over the dunes he murmured confidently:

"The day will come. Progress will come to the Plain and barbarism will be conquered and retreat. Perhaps we shall not see it, but our blood will sing with the emotion of the ones who do."

XIII

SEÑOR DANGER

HE WAS a great mass of muscles under a reddish skin, with a pair of very blue eyes and hair the colour of flax.

He had come to the Arauca some years before with a rifle slung over his shoulder as a hunter of tigers and alligators. The country pleased him because it was as savage as his own soul, a good land to conquer, inhabited by people he considered inferior because they did not have light hair and blue eyes. Notwithstanding the rifle, it was generally believed that he had come to establish a ranch and bring in new ideas, so many hopes were placed in him and he was cordially received. But he had contented himself with placing four corner-posts in land belonging to somebody else, without asking permission to do so, and throwing over them a palm-thatch roof; and once this cabin was built, he hung up his hammock and rifle, lay down, lighted his pipe, stretched his arms, swelling the powerful muscles, and exclaimed:

"All right! Now I'm at home."

He said his name was William Danger and that he was an American, a native of Alaska, son of a Danish woman and an Irish prospector; but that this was his real name was doubted, for he always added immediately: "Señor *Peligro*"—and as he was a humourist in his own particular fashion, that of a naïve child, it was suspected that he called himself Danger merely to be able to add the disconcerting translation.

For the rest there was a certain mystery about him. It was said that in the first period of his settling in the country he had several times displayed clippings from New York newspapers, always headed "The Man Without a Country" and containing protests against some injustice done to a citizen who was unnamed, himself, according to Señor Danger's version. And although he had never satisfactorily or clearly explained what the injustice had been or why his name was concealed in such a description, all doors had opened to him in expectation of the flood of money about to over-run the Plain.

In the meantime, Señor Danger displayed industry only in the shooting of alligators, whose hides he exported every year in large quantities, and, for sport's sake, of tigers, lions or whatever wild animals came within range of his rifle. One day, after he had killed a female jaguar which had recently borne cubs, he took the little ones and succeeded in rearing and taming one of them. He played and frolicked with this one, exercising the humour of the great brutal boy that he was. The cub had given him many a scratch already, but he enjoyed showing the scars, and these added to his prestige as much as the clippings.

Within a short space of time the hunter's cabin changed into a house sufficiently furnished for comfort and surrounded by extensive corrals. The history of this transformation, which seemed to indicate that "The Man Without a Country" had found one, touches at certain points upon Doña Barbara's story.

It was in the time of Colonel Apolinar, when they were founding the recently baptized El Miedo. Señor Danger, having learned about the legend of the Familiar, wished to witness the barbarous rite which the superstitious Amazon could not forbear, and with this object he went to pay a visit, owing to her anyway, since the bit of land on which he had built his cabin was her property.

To see the stranger, hear him express his desire, fall in love with him, and form her plans was all the work of an instant for Doña Barbara. She had Apolinar ask him to dinner, took upon herself the service of the drinks they both liked so well, and as the native was a weakling and senselessly drunk, he took no notice of the glances with which his wife and the guest, during the meal, concerted their plan for his betrayal.

The peons had meanwhile rapidly dug the trench

where they were going to bury an old lame horse, the only thing at hand to serve as Familiar.

"We'll bury him at midnight, which is the right time," said Doña Barbara. "And just us three, because the peons ought not to see the business. That's the way it ought to be according to the legend."

"Fine!" the foreigner exclaimed. "The stars overhead and we beneath them throwing earth over a live horse. How pretty! How picturesque!"

As for Apolinar, he was neither familiar with the custom nor in any state to make an objection, and it was necessary for Danger to pick him up and set him on his horse when it came time to go to the new foundations, some distance from the present ranch-houses.

The trench was all ready, and the lame old horse, victim of the barbarous sacrifice, was tied to one of the posts of the corral in process of construction. Three spades for the buryers lay beside the trench. The starry night enveloped the lonely scene in a thick darkness.

Señor Danger untied the old horse and led him to the side of the pit, speaking compassionate words to him between noisy guffaws which roused Apolinar to idiotic hilarity; then, with a fearful push, he flung the beast into the pit.

"Now pray to your devilish friends, Doña Barbara, not to let the horse's spirit escape, and you shake yourself, Colonel. We're buryers now and the thing must be done right."

Apolinar had seized one of the spades and was struggling with the laws of gravity in his attempt to lean over and fill it with the earth heaped beside the trench, meanwhile muttering obscenities which seemed to give him huge delight, for he nearly split himself laughing over every atrocious remark he brought forth. At last he succeeded in filling the spade and swung it stupidly, stumbling after it with each sway.

"What a load you've got on, Colonel!" Señor Danger had just said. He was absorbed in his rôle of buryer and was throwing in spadeful after spadeful with remarkable dexterity when he saw Apolinar, staggering, his face hideously distorted, clap his hands to his sides, and giving a mortal cry, pitch into the trench with his own lance-head in his back.

"Oh!" the American exclaimed, interrupting his task. "This wasn't on the program. Poor old Colonel!"

"Don't waste any pity on him, Don Guillermo. He had me marked out for death, too. What I've done was to get there first," said Doña Barbara, and she added, taking the spade which had fallen from the Colonel's hands: "Help me with this! You're certainly not the man to shed tears over such things. You must have done worse in your own country."

"*Caramba!* How you talk! Señor Danger doesn't shed any tears, but Señor Danger doesn't do anything that isn't on the program. I came here to bury the Familiar, and nothing else."

And with these words, he flung down the spade, mounted his horse, and returned to his cabin to frolic with the jaguar.

But he kept the secret, first to keep from being involved in any difficulties which might be complicated by his own mystery and secondly, because for him, the scornful American, there was little difference between Apolinar and the horse buried beside him. He allowed the rumour to prevail that Colonel Apolinar had been drowned in Bramador Channel trying to swim across it, the only proof of this story being the discovery, in the stomach of an alligator he had killed in the same channel, of a ring Doña Barbara identified as the Colonel's.

As his reward for secrecy he converted the cabin into a house and built corrals on land belonging to La Barquereña, changing himself from alligator-hunter into cattleman, or more properly speaking, cattle-hunter, for those he branded as his own were either from Altamira or El Miedo. Some time passed thus without his being molested by Doña Barbara or bothering himself with her, until one day he presented himself at El Miedo with this declaration:

" I have learned that you are thinking of taking from Lorenzo Barquero the bit of land next to the palm grove, which you have allowed him to keep, and I've come to tell you that you can't commit this injustice, because I'm protecting his rights. I'm going to take charge of that strip of land for him, the only land he owns, and you can't send your people in there to take out cattle, either."

But Lorenzo Barquero's rights did no more than pass from the hands of one usurper to those of another. The only earnings he saw from his land were the bottles of whisky Señor Danger sent him upon his return from San Fernando or Caracas, with a good supply of his chosen beverage, or the flagons of the latter Señor Danger had sent from the El Miedo Commissary, and that without paying a cent to Doña Barbara for them.

In return for this the foreigner enriched himself by smuggling cattle at pleasure. The remains of the old La Barquereña were scarcely more than a plot of savannah crossed by a creek, dry in winter, called The Lick, whose salty banks attracted the cattle belonging to neighbouring reaches. Numerous herds were always to be seen there licking the creek bed, and thanks to this it was very easy to capture unbranded heads within the limits of the piece of land, which did not attain to the size required by law for the common right to unmarked herds wandering over the prairie. Señor Danger, however, found it easy to vault over legal obstacles and seize his neighbours' cattle, for the Luzardo overseers were always corruptible and the owner of El Miedo did not dare to protest.

When he had reaped his little harvest in this manner he departed to sell it as soon as winter came; and since the creek was full during the rainy season and the cattle ceased to come to it, he stayed in San Fernando or Caracas until the water ran out again, spending his money on extravagant sprees, for he was not very much attached to it, and his hands were never quite equal to squandering all of it.

He had made up his mind to treat himself to this yearly pleasure when he received Luzardo's note declaring his intention of rebuilding the old barricade at Corozalito where the Altamira herds passed through the Gap and were lost in The Licks.

"Oh! *Caramba!*" he exclaimed after he had read Luzardo's letter. "What does the man want? You tell Dr. Luzardo, Antonio, that Señor Danger read his letter and says this—listen carefully—that Señor Danger must have the Gap of Corozalito open, and has the right to keep him from putting up any barricade."

Santos Luzardo did not think so, and went next day to clear up the matter.

The barking of the dogs brought the Yankee's imposing bulk to the door with great show of friendliness.

"Come in, Doctor. Come in. I knew you'd come here. I'm very much upset about having to tell you that you couldn't close up the Gap. Do me the favour of coming in."

He ushered Luzardo into a room whose four walls

were covered with trophies of his hunting: heads of deer, tiger, puma and bear skins, and the hide of a gigantic alligator.

"Sit down, Doctor. Don't be afraid, the jaguar is in his cage."

And going up to the table where stood a bottle of whisky:

"Let's have a 'good-morning,' Doctor."

"Thanks," replied Santos, rebuffing the offer.

"Oh, don't say no! I'm very glad to have you call, and I want you to have a shot with me, as you say."

Annoyed by this insistence, Santos nevertheless accepted, and then getting immediately to business, said:

"I think you've made a mistake, Señor Danger, concerning the limits of La Barquereña."

"Oh, no, Doctor," replied the foreigner. "I never make a mistake when I say anything. I've got my map and I can show you. Wait a minute."

He went into the adjoining room and came out immediately with several papers in his trousers' pocket, spreading out another which he held rolled up.

"Here you are, Doctor. Corozalito and Alcornocal de Abajo are within my property and you can see with your own eyes."

It was a map drawn by himself, on which the places referred to were shown as belonging to La Barquereña.

Luzardo, out of courtesy, took it in his hands, but he replied:

"Allow me to call your attention to the fact that this diagram is not authentic proof. It will have to be compared with the titles of La Barquereña and Altamira, which I'm sorry I didn't bring with me."

Without ceasing to smile, the Yankee protested:

"Oh! that's bad! Does the Doctor think I draw things that are only in my head? I don't say anything I'm not entirely sure of."

"You shouldn't take my words to mean that. I merely said that it wasn't a proof. I don't doubt you may have others which are, and since you're willing to show me them, I beg you to do so." And since the attitude of the American, intent on the smoke from his pipe, was frankly insolent, he added in a more decided tone: "I'd like you to know that before taking this step I've gone into the matter thoroughly with my deeds before me, and I want to call your attention to the fact that I'm perfectly sure of what I say when I declare that Corozalito and Alcornocal de Abajo belong to Altamira, and that consequently I have an undeniable right to put the barricade at the Gap. Besides that, there was one up to my father's time, not so very long ago. Some of its posts are still standing."

"In your father's time?" exclaimed Señor Danger. "You're so sure you still have those rights. I shouldn't like to tell you that you don't know what you're talking about."

"Do you think they've been written off?" Santos inquired, without giving any notice to the tone in which Danger had spoken.

"Oh, I don't want to go on talking in the air," said Danger, and taking out the papers he had in his pocket, he added: "Here it is in writing. You can see for yourself that you can't put up the barricade."

He placed in Luzardo's hands a document signed by Lorenzo Barquero and one of the administrators in charge of Altamira after the death of José Luzardo, according to which the owner of La Barquereña had acquired by purchase the hills of Corozalito and Alcornocal de Abajo, and the owner of Altamira engaged neither to construct fences nor to obstruct with any other kind of construction the free passage of herds over the boundary.

The object of such an agreement was precisely to obviate the interference of the barricade referred to by Luzardo, which, closing up the Gap, would prevent the Altamira herd from gathering at the salt licks on the neighbouring property; but Santos had had no news of such a sale or consequent engagement, just as he was doubtless ignorant of many other encumbrances and impairments of his property by means of which his agents had made themselves rich, documents not duplicated in the legacy in his possession.

The deed Danger showed him was duly authenticated and registered, and Santos was mortified at having taken this false step and having to confess now that he did not know the actual status of Altamira. Another document accompanied this one, from which he learned of Lorenzo Barquero's sale of The Lick to the American, and when he saw the signature of the vendor, written in unintelligible, irregular, twisted letters, giving the impression that they had been traced by some illiterate guided by another hand, it seemed certain to him that he had before his eyes material proof of coercion exercised by the American over Lorenzo's broken will. For he could be certain, without any risk of libel, that this sale had been nothing but a piece of plundering carried out in the manner of the other dummy sales Doña Barbara had forced Lorenzo to sign.

"I'm forgetting my plans," he thought, contemplating the illegible signature. "I told myself I was going to set up as a defender of injured rights, and here it never even occurred to me to find out if this poor fellow's are defensible. There wouldn't be anything strange about it if these sales were subject to defects permitting one to bring action for restoration."

Meanwhile Danger had gone to the table and poured out two glasses of whisky to celebrate his triumph over the neighbour who had come to demand lost rights. An insolent self-satisfaction impelled him to insult this man of the inferior race who had dared to challenge his claims.

"Another swig, Doctor?"

Santos leapt up and gave him a look of offended dignity, but the American did not attach any importance to his gesture and went on quietly filling the glass.

Luzardo returned the deeds to him and said:

"I didn't know of this sale of Corozalito and Alcornocal de Abajo. Otherwise I shouldn't have come to claim what I had no right to. Please excuse me."

"Oh, don't worry about it, Dr. Luzardo. I knew you were talking without knowing the case. But let's take another bit of whisky to make peace, because I want to be your friend and whisky is good for that."

Recovering his self-command, Luzardo replied:

"Pardon me if I don't accept."

Señor Danger understood that he did not accept the offer of friendship either, and when Luzardo withdrew he said as he looked at the retreating figure:

"Oh, these little men. They never know what they're talking about."

On his way to Altamira, as he passed near Lorenzo Barquero's house, Santos decided to take the opportunity of asking an exact explanation of the loss of La Barquereña.

Slumped down in the dirty hammock, Barquero was still sleeping off the previous night's drunkenness, alone in the house. Stertorous snores issued from his throat, a viscous spittle was running out of his half-opened mouth, and his face, in the deep sleep of intoxication, bore a deathlike expression. Alarmed by this appearance, Santos went up and felt the pulse of the arm dangling out of the hammock. He could feel under his fingers the characteristic hammering of arterial tension. He stood a moment looking compassionately at the man.

"There's very little life left in this poor devil, but something has to be done for him."

Beneath the hammock was a pail and at the bottom of it a pitcher, a glass, and a rustic dipper of calabash bark. By merely stretching out his arm, and with the aid of the dipper, Lorenzo had consumed all the liquor in the vessel, pouring it into his mouth sip by sip — "soaking," to use the popular word for this brutal method of getting drunk.

Luzardo, on tiptoe, took the glass away, and then seizing the carafe from the table, which contained a good quantity of brandy, he flung it out of the house. This done, and in view of the uselessness of attempting to waken Lorenzo, he prepared to leave, when the pink and smiling bulk of the American appeared.

He pretended to be surprised at finding Luzardo there, but as the latter saw very clearly that he had been followed, and made a movement by no means friendly, Danger inquired, nodding in the direction of Lorenzo:

"Drunk, eh? If he hasn't drunk all the brandy I sent him yesterday!"

"You're doing a great wrong, giving this man liquor," replied Santos.

"There's no help for him, Doctor. Let him finish

killing himself. He doesn't want to live. He's still in love with the fair Barbarita. Terribly in love, and he drinks and drinks to forget her. I've said to him many a time: 'Don Lorenzo, you're killing yourself.' But he won't pay any attention to me and he never takes the bottle from his lips."

He went up to the hammock, and shaking it by the ropes said:

"Hey! Don Lorenzo! You've got a visitor, old boy. How long are you going to lie snoring in that hammock? Here's Dr. Luzardo come to see you."

Lorenzo half opened his eyes and muttered something unintelligible. The Yankee gave him a brutal slap with the back of his hand and guffawed.

"What a bun you've got, old fellow!"

As he turned around he stood for an instant looking in the direction of the palm grove, and then he shrank, curved his fingers as though he were about to scratch, showed his teeth, and let out a growl, as he did in imitation of the jaguar when they were frolicking.

"What's the matter with the man?" Santos was asking himself in astonishment at these antics, when the American guffawed and explained:

"It's the girl, by God."

It was Marisela, coming with a bundle of firewood, as she had been on the evening of the meeting in the grove; but she was a different person from that dirty, unkempt girl. She was wearing one of the dresses made by Melesio Sandoval's grandaughters which Santos had sent to her, and everything about her was neat and clean, in spite of the menial work she had been doing.

Santos was pleased by this change in her, the work of a few words of his, and he was more so when he realized that the house was no longer the same dirty, filthy, ill-smelling stall. The floor had been swept clean, and if poverty still reigned, neglect had disappeared.

Meanwhile Señor Danger continued:

"Now she's Señorita Marisela, but still wild as a jaguar." He shook an admonishing forefinger at her. "You drew blood yesterday with your nails."

"*Guá!* What did you touch me for, then!" Marisela retorted.

"She gets savage with me because I tell her: 'I've bought you from your father, and when he dies I'm going to take you with me, because I've got a male jaguar and I want a female too so I can have little jaguars.'"

While Señor Danger showed his appreciation of this brutality with a stentorian laugh and Marisela whined in annoyance, Santos thought of the danger the girl was exposed to under the patronage of such a man, and felt once more the profound aversion he inspired.

"This has gone too far!" he exclaimed, unable to contain himself. "You make a drunkard of her father, take her inheritance away from her, and then you haven't even the decency to treat her well."

The man's laughter ceased, his blue eyes darkened,

and the blood left his face. Nevertheless, his voice was unchanged as he replied:

"That's bad! that's bad! You want to show yourself as my enemy and I can keep you from putting your feet on the very ground where you're standing. I've got the right to keep you off it."

"And I know all about your rights," Santos replied with decided emphasis.

The Yankee was thoughtful for a moment. Then, pretending not to understand, he took out his pipe, filled it, and replied, while he was drawing at it, with the match cupped in his great hairy hands:

"You don't know anything, man. You don't even know your rights." And he started off, the hard dry ground shaking under the huge feet of this conqueror of badly defended lands.

Santos felt his indignation changing into mortification, but he reacted immediately.

"You'll soon have proof that I do know them, and know how to defend them."

He decided to take Lorenzo and Marisela into his house to free them from this humiliating and dangerous patronage.

PART TWO

I

AN UNUSUAL EVENT

WHEN Doña Barbara received the letter from Luzardo announcing his decision to enclose Altamira, the tactics she employed were cunning indeed. Nothing could have pleased her less than this news of a boundary; she usually answered mockingly, when her ambition for territory was mentioned:

"But I'm not so grasping as I'm painted. I'm satisfied with only a bit of land, enough so that I can be in the middle of my property, no matter where it may be."

Nevertheless, when she had finished reading the letter, she replied, in a tone indicating that she was a good-natured, simple-hearted woman:

"Good, then! At last these suits about that blessed Altamira boundary will be done away with, since Dr. Luzardo's going to fence his land, and from now on there won't be any more mistakes. That's the best thing, a fence. Yes, then everybody will know how far his property extends, and we can be as says the proverb:

'Everyone in his own house and God in everybody's.' I've been thinking about a fence for some time, but I haven't been able to give myself the pleasure because it costs a great deal of money. The Doctor can afford that pleasure because he's wealthy."

Balbino Paiba, who at mention of a letter from Luzardo had come up to see if it referred to him, stood looking fixedly at her without in the least understanding that what she said was directed at Antonio Sandoval, who was waiting for the reply, to make him return to Altamira with a tale about the good humor Doña Barbara had shown at receiving the news.

But as Antonio knew that she used that tone only when she was hatching some clever plan, he reflected:

"*Now,* this woman is dangerous."

"Tell Dr. Luzardo, then," she concluded, "that I agree to his proposal, but that respecting the partition fence, I'm not in a position to spend the money for it. If he wants to and is in a hurry—and I see that the Doctor is one of those people that come knocking down and gelding, as the vulgar saying is—let him go ahead and put up the posts right away, and we'll have an understanding later. He can tell me what he spent and we won't fight about that."

"And *respecting* the round-up the Doctor asks you for," Antonio inquired, with special emphasis on the word she had used, "What is your answer?"

"Ah! I'd forgotten that he spoke of that too. Tell him

that my land is not in condition to permit round-ups, but that I'll advise him as soon as we can have them. From now until the time we put up the wire there's enough time for him to collect his herds from here and for me to recover mine from there. Tell him that, and give him my best regards."

Scarcely had Antonio left when Balbino Paiba expressed the sinister idea he could not help attributing to Doña Barbara:

"I suppose Dr. Luzardo won't ever have the time to put up that fence."

"Why not?" she replied, folding the letter to replace it in the envelope. "It's just a question of a few weeks, that's all. That is, if he doesn't make a mistake and put it up on this side of the line."

Returning to her natural tone, without insinuations, which had no further object, she said:

"Call the Mondragons."

The next morning found the boundary posts and the Macanillal house moved, not into Altamira as before, but in the opposite direction, giving ground, and to a site whose landmarks could not correspond to those of the boundary last in force.

The object of this stratagem was naturally to make Luzardo go out of his territory in putting up the fence, which he would certainly do, with only the posts and the house as landmarks, the most tangible point of reference in the vague terms of the decision. Then it would be easy to show that the change had been his doing, and that he had taken advantage of the fact that no one was there to stop him, it being three days since the Mondragons, the only inhabitants of the desert at Macanillal, had left the " house on stilts." It was not for nothing that she had so disposed matters.

Even Balbino Paiba, who was not accustomed to grant anything to anybody, had to admit:

" There's no question about it, that woman sees the worms before anybody else can see the steer. I don't know if it's the 'Partner's' advice, but what I do know is that it's a well-laid plan."

The truth was that the order for vacating the house at Macanillal, together with the one providing for replacement of the boundary posts where the last decision had placed them, had not been directed towards this last stratagem, for the possibility of Luzardo's putting up a fence had not even crossed Doña Barbara's mind. But as the two former ideas had turned out useful for the last bit of cunning, she deceived herself into considering them as preliminary steps of her plan, as though that had been traced out complete from the beginning in anticipation of the enemy's undertaking—a miracle due to gift of divining future events which she was convinced she possessed, thanks to the "Partner." She had always proceeded in this way, by isolated sudden impulses which later and lucky circumstances joined together, and as fortune was always with her, looking at the thing from outside, which was her own way of regarding it, the whole always appeared to be an effective and extraordinary piece of foresight. Actually, Doña Barbara was incapable of conceiving a real plan. Her skill lay solely in the ability to derive the best immediate profit from the chance results of her impulses.

But this time circumstances did not come to her aid. Warned by Antonio's misgivings over the woman's false attitude of conciliation, and taught by his recent experience with Señor Danger, Santos studied the matter carefully before proceeding to drive in the fence posts, and when she saw that he had put them just where they belonged, without falling into the trap, her intuition told her that something new to her was beginning at that moment.

Nevertheless, her pride roused by the embarrassing situation in which she had been left, she decided upon hostility, and when Luzardo, several days later, repeated his request for permission to take his cattle from El Miedo, she roundly refused.

"And now, Doctor," Antonio insinuated, "I suppose you're going to pay her in her own coin by putting up the fence without allowing her to take her cattle out of here. Isn't that so?"

"No. I'm going right to the nearest authority and force her to comply with the law. At the same time I'll have Señor Danger summoned before the Civil Magistrate, and the two difficulties will both be overcome at the same time."

"And do you think Ño Pernalete will pay any attention to you?" Antonio persisted, referring to the Civil Magistrate under whose jurisdiction Altamira and El Miedo were situated. "Ño Pernalete and Doña Barbara are hand in glove with each other."

"We'll soon see if he refuses to do me justice," Santos declared with finality, and the next day he set off for the chief village of the District.

It was a heap of ruins in the midst of a thicket, the remains of a once prosperous village: old houses of adobe and palm thatch scattered over the prairie, others farther off, lined up along the sides of streets with no sidewalks and full of deep ruts; a plaza, now a field of creeping weeds in the shadow of century-old scabby trees. At one end of it was an unfinished structure—looking more like a ruin—a church, which would have been too large for the actual population; at the other end were several old houses, solidly built, mostly uninhabited, some of them without even a known owner. Over one, with crumbling roof and sagging walls, lay the huge trunk of a tree blown over by a hurricane many years before. It was a village whose chief families had disappeared or emigrated entire, a place without commerce or any sign of activity—one of those numerous Venezuelan villages which war, malaria, ankylostomiasis, and other calamities have left changed to heaps of ruins along the roads. This was the chief village of the District, theatre of the deadly contest between the Luzardos and Barqueros.

Santos had gone through nearly all of it without encountering a single person when he at last saw a group of men on the porch of an inn, silent, idle, but all looking as though they expected something to happen at any moment: a group of pot-bellied, sunken-cheeked men with thin moustaches and dull, languid eyes.

"Can you tell me where the Civil Magistrate's office is?" Santos asked them.

The men looked at one another as if annoyed at being forced to speak, and one of them was finally beginning in a plaintive tone to give the desired information, when someone else ran out of the inn exclaiming:

"Luzardo! Santos Luzardo! You here, old boy?"

But as Santos did not respond to his demonstrations of cordiality, the man came towards him with open arms and asked:

"Don't you know me?"

"Well, honestly—"

"Think, old fellow. Try to remember. . . . Mujiquita! Don't you remember Mujiquita? We were students together at the University, in the first year of Law School."

Santos did not recall him, but as it would have been too cruel to disappoint him, he said:

"How could I forget? Mujiquita, of course."

Like the men on the porch, Mujiquita seemed to belong to a race different from that peopling the prairie, generally composed of vigorous, light-hearted men. The men in the villages of the Plain were, on the contrary, sad, pathetic, wasted by swamp fever, Mujiquita especially was a pitiful sight: his moustache, hair, eyes, skin, everything about him seemed to be powdered with that yellow dust which lay in the village streets, and gave the same impression as one of those pitiful wayside trees of indeterminate colour. It was not really neglect of his person, it was a patina, the swamp sickness and alcohol.

Nothing but a series of muttered exclamations escaped from him:

"Right, man! Your fellow-student. What times those were, eh Santos? Ortolan, Dr. Urbaneja! . . . Mujiquita, old chap! That's what you called me and my friends still call me that. You were the best student in the class. Don't try to deny it! I haven't forgotten you. You remember how you helped me with my lessons on Roman Law? while we were walking through the halls of the University? *Pater est quem nuptiae demonstrant.* How some things do stick in your mind! I couldn't get Roman Law into my head, and you used to get into a fever with me because I couldn't understand it! Ah, Santos Luzardo! What times those were! I seem to hear those perorations of yours that left us with our mouths open. Who would have said that I'd ever see you again? You've graduated, I suppose? . . . No? You were the best in the class. And what are you looking for here?"

"The Civil Magistrate's office."

"You've left it just behind you. You didn't notice because it was closed. The General isn't in town today, he's gone out to one of his ranches, so I didn't open it. You must know that you're talking to the Secretary."

"Oh, yes? Well, I'm glad I did meet you—" said Santos, and he explained the reason for his visit.

Mujiquita remained thoughtful for a moment, and then said:

"You've had good luck, old boy, in not meeting the Colonel, because you'd have wasted your time with him. He's a great friend of Doña Barbara's, and as for Señor Danger, you know that that gentleman has pull in this country. But I'm going to fix the thing up for you. Why not, Santos? We're not friends for nothing. I'm going to summon Doña Barbara and Señor Danger in the name of the Civil Magistrate, as if I didn't know what's going on, so that when they come to the office there won't be any way out of it and you can make your complaint."

"So that if I hadn't met you . . ."

"You'd have had rough going. Ah, Santos! you've just come out of the University, and you think it's as easy to get your rights as it seems in books. . . . But don't be worried, the principal thing is already accomplished—having Doña Barbara and Señor Danger made to appear before the magistrate. I'm going to send a messenger with the summonses, taking advantage of the Colonel's not being here. At the exact time specified, I'll say. So that day after tomorrow at this time they should be here. In the meantime you stay here, without letting anyone see you. Then the Colonel won't find out what you've come for and I won't have to explain ahead of time."

"I'll have to shut myself up in the inn. If there is any in the village."

"I can't recommend it very highly, but . . . If it weren't for the fact that the General mustn't find out that we're good friends, I'd have you stay at my house."

"Thanks, Mujica."

"Mujiquita, old boy! Call me as you used to. Now and forever the same to you, you know. You can't imagine the pleasure you've given me. Those days at the University! And old Lira? Still alive? and Modesto, always growling? What a good chap that Modesto was! Isn't that so?"

"Very good. But listen, Mujiquita; I'm grateful to you for your goodwill and wish to help me, but since what I'm claiming is perfectly legal, I haven't any reason for using all these dodges. The Civil Magistrate, I don't know yet whether he's General or Colonel, since you call him both in turn—he'll have to take care of my demand—"

But Mujiquita did not let him finish.

"Look, Santos, you follow my lead. You've got the

theory, but I've got the experience. Do as I advise. Go to the inn, make out that you're sick, and don't go out in the street until I tell you to."

He was like nearly all of his peers in office, as nearly like them as one bull to another of the same colour, for he possessed neither more nor less than the necessary qualifications for Civil Magistrate of such a village—absolute ignorance, a despotic temperament, and a military rank. The rank he had gained in youth was that of Colonel, but although his friends and subordinates were wont to give him at times the title of General, the rest of the population preferred to call him *Ño* Pernalete, á corruption of *Señor* Pernalete.

He was attending to correspondence in company with Mujiquita, under the aegis of a sabre hanging on the wall, sheathed, but with the nickled handle showing signs of use, when they heard horses in the street.

Suddenly turning pale, although he had everything in readiness for that very moment, Mujiquita exclaimed:

" Ah, *Caramba!* I forgot to tell you, General." And he told the story of what he had done, giving as justification of his haste in summoning Santos's neighbours the fear that Luzardo would take justice into his own hands if he did not find the authorities ready to give it to him.

" Since you'd gone off to Las Maporas without telling me how long you would be there," he concluded, " I thought it was best to take immediate steps."

Ño Pernalete looked him over from head to foot.

"I knew you were up to belling some cat or other, Mujiquita. Since yesterday you've been like a dog with the worms, and as for today, if you haven't looked out of that door a hundred times you haven't done it once. So it was best to take immediate steps, eh? Look here, Mujiquita: Do you think I don't know that the Doctor fellow at the inn is a friend of yours?"

But Doña Barbara and Señor Danger had already stopped before the door of the office, and Ño Pernalete kept what he was going to say to the Secretary for later. He did not want the subpoenaed pair to know that anything could be done there without his consent, and went out to greet them, accepting the rôle Mujiquita was forcing him to play, but determined to make him pay dearly for it.

"Come in, *mi señora. Caramba!* We never see you here unless it's at a time like this. Sit down, Doña Barbara. You'll find this more comfortable . . . Mujiquita! Take your hat off that chair so Señor Danger can sit down. I've told you time and again not to put your hat on the chairs!"

Mujiquita obeyed with alacrity. That was the price, the inevitable taunts he had to suffer at the hands of Ño Pernalete every time he dared to move his hand to help some justice-seeker; it was his crown of martyrdom, made up of insulting reprimands delivered in public, bellowed, for the better stripping of his dignity as a man.

His ears were already hardened to them, but the people in that village never considered how much they were in debt to Mujiquita. " How long are you going to keep on playing the saviour? " his wife would ask when she saw him come into the house after one of those scoldings, cast down, with tears in his eyes. But he always answered: " But, my dear girl, if I don't, who'll watch the Colonel? "

So, distressed by his mortification, he was a long time finding a place to put his hat.

" Well. Here we are, at your disposition," said Danger.

Doña Barbara, without attempting to hide her annoyance at the whole business, added:

" We just missed getting our horses sunstruck, to be here at the time you ordered."

Ño Pernalete directed a furious look at Mujiquita and said to him:

" Go and find Dr. Luzardo. Tell him not to make us wait long, because the lady and gentleman are already here."

And Mujiquita left the office, saying to himself, under the weight of a gloomy presentiment:

" What a fool I am! I'll lose my place for this. My wife is right. Who told me to play saviour? "

A few moments later, when he returned with Luzardo, Doña Barbara's attitude had undergone a transformation. She had recovered her usual impassible expression, and only a very keen eye could have found on her face any index of her understanding with Ño Pernalete.

Nevertheless, she had a moment of uneasiness when she saw Luzardo, a flash of intuition telling her that the final drama of her life was about to be played.

"Good," said Ño Pernalete, without returning Luzardo's greeting. "Here are the lady and gentleman who have come to hear the complaint you are going to make against them."

"Splendid," said Luzardo, taking a chair when none was offered, for Ño Pernalete was not courteous, nor was Mujiquita anxious to make any demonstrations of friendship which would end by compromising him more. "First of all, and I hope the *señora* will pardon the delay of her case, we'll have Señor Danger's." And seeing the rapid glances the latter exchanged with the magistrate, he understood that they had come to an agreement between them, and paused to allow them to enjoy their roguery.

"The matter is, that Señor Danger has in his corrals—and I can easily prove it—cattle, marked with his brand, which nevertheless can be identified as belonging to Altamira."

"And what does that mean?" the American demanded, surprised by this attack, which he had not expected.

"That they don't belong to you. That's simple."

"Oh! *Caramba!* Everybody knows that you're pretty

green in these matters. Don't you know that the marks of identification have no importance whatever, and that the only witness to the ownership of a beast is the brand, provided it's rightfully taken possession of? "

" So that you can take unbranded cattle with marks of identification showing that they belong to someone else? "

" And why not? I've been so long at it that I'm tired of it, and so would you be if you'd paid any attention to your ranch. Isn't that so, Colonel? "

But before the latter had time to confirm Señor Danger's affirmation, Luzardo said:

" That's enough. I was interested in getting you to admit that you round up unbranded cattle in La Barquereña."

" Well, doesn't La Barquereña belong to me? I've got my deeds right here in my breast pocket. Do you imagine that you can keep me from doing in my ranch what you can do in yours? "

" I actually do propose to do something like that. Colonel, be good enough to require Señor Danger to show those deeds."

" But, then," replied Ño Pernalete, " what is it that you propose to do, Dr. Luzardo? "

" I propose to point out that Señor Danger is outside the law, because he doesn't possess the amount of land fixed by the Law of the Plain as the minimum qualification for the right to round up unbranded cattle."

"Oh!" ejaculated Señor Danger, turning white with rage, but unable to make any denial, for what Luzardo said was true.

The latter, without giving him time to recover from his surprise, continued:

"Do you see whether I know my rights or not, and whether or not I know how to take care of them? Did you think I came here to talk about the barricade at Corozalito? Now you'll be the one who *has* to put it up, because since you haven't got the right to take cattle, your property must be enclosed."

"Well, well!" exclaimed Ño Pernalete, banging his fist on the writing table before which he was seated. "And what part do I play here, Dr. Luzardo? To judge from your tone, anyone would think you were the magistrate."

"Absolutely not, Colonel. I speak in the voice of a man demanding that the Authorities insist upon fulfilment of the law. And now that I've made out my case against this man, we'll turn to the *señora*.

Meanwhile, Doña Barbara, without taking sides in the quarrel, had shown an increasing interest as Santos talked. Greatly impressed, and that much against her will, from the moment he appeared at the door of the office, she ended by enjoying the skill with which he had drawn the admission he wanted from the American. This was partly because of the keenness he displayed, the one thing Doña Barbara most admired in anyone;

partly because Danger was the object of it, and nothing could be more pleasing to her than the downfall of the one man who could boast of having spurned her, the only man who had until that time forced her to do his will, because of the secret he possessed; and finally, because he was a foreigner, and Doña Barbara hated foreigners with all her heart.

But the next words Santos spoke removed the complacent expression from her face, and made him her sworn enemy.

" The matter is," Santos continued, " that the *señora* refuses to allow me to have a round-up on her land. A round-up which I need urgently, and which the Law of the Plain obliges her to allow me."

" What the Doctor says is perfectly true," declared Doña Barbara. " I have refused once and I refuse again."

" That's as clear as cockcrow! " exclaimed the magistrate.

" But the law is clear too, and final," replied Luzardo. " And I ask the *señora* to abide by it."

" I'll abide by it; certainly! "

Smiling at thought of the design they had formed, Ño Pernalete turned to the Secretary, who had all the while maintained the appearance of attending only to what he was writing in one of the two books lying on the table.

" Let's see, Mujiquita. Bring me here the Law of the Plain in force now."

He seized the pamphlet from Mujiquita, almost tearing it out of his hands, wet his finger and turned several pages, exclaiming:

" Aha! Here it is. Let's see what the majesty of the law has to say. Yes, *señora.* The Doctor is right: the law is final. Listen to what it says here: ' Every owner of a ranch or such establishment, must — ' "

" Yes," Doña Barbara interrupted. " I know that article by heart."

" Therefore," Ño Pernalete commenced, keeping up the farce.

" What, therefore? "

" You must abide by the law."

" I will abide by it, I've already said so. I refuse to allow the Doctor the round-up he asks for. Now impose the penalty the law provides."

" The penalty? Let's see what the majesty of the law says."

But Luzardo interrupted him, saying, as he stood up:

" Don't bother, Colonel. You won't find it. The law does not provide fines or arrest or any punishment, which are the only things the civil authority you represent can provide."

" And then? Now I ask you: what do you want me to do if the law doesn't give me any authority? "

" I don't want you to do anything, except this: make the *señora* understand that, although the law does not provide for fines or penalties or arrests, it is binding *per se.* It obliges everyone to fulfil it, purely and simply.

And if the *señora* interprets it differently and does not accord with my demand, at the end of eight days I shall hail her before the Tribunal, and Señor Danger too. And that's enough of explanation."

Having said this, he left the office. There was a moment of silence, while Mujiquita said to himself:

"Ah, Santos Luzardo! Always the same."

Suddenly the Civil Magistrate burst out:

"This won't be the end! Somebody's going to pay for that Doctor's insolence. Coming to talk to *me* about the law!"

He could not forgive Luzardo for having talked to him in that manner, especially concerning laws which were imperative in themselves, without need of *manu militari,* which was his recourse when the law was in question. However, in addition to this jealousy of his authority, as the savage understands it, or more exactly, because of that jealousy, Ño Pernalete had something of a grudge against Doña Barbara because of the as-one-power-to-another attitude he was forced to take with her, and he immediately turned against her. As soon as he was convinced that Mujiquita, for whom his remarks had been intended, had turned as crimson as was humanly possible, he added, in a different tone:

"Now. I'll tell you one thing, Doña Barbara. And the same to you, Señor Danger. What the Doctor says is absolutely true: the laws must be fulfilled because they are laws, that is, orders from the Government to do this or that. And since it appears that this Doctor knows where the shoe pinches, I advise both of you to settle with him. So, put up your fence, *señor,* because you're really outside the law. Even if it's only for the sake of the formula. After that, if a post falls today and another tomorrow, and the herd only needs a little opening to pass through, who's going to pay any attention to that? Put the posts up again, if your neighbour demands it, and they'll fall again, because that land of yours isn't very firm, you know. Eh? "

" Oh! Soft ground, Colonel. Just as you've said."

And clapping a hand on the Magistrate's shoulders he added:

" This Colonel of ours has more twists than a riddle. I'm keeping two milch cows over there for him, good ones, too. One of these days I'm going to send them to him."

" I'll be very glad to receive them, Señor Danger."

" Aha, the efficient Colonel! Would you like to come and have a little drink with me? "

" In a little while. I'll look for you later at the inn. I suppose you won't go right away."

" All right. I'll wait for you there. And you, Mujiquita, will you go with me? "

" No, thanks, Señor Danger."

" Well! Here's something unusual. Mujiquita doesn't want to drink today! Well then, see you later. Until then, Doña Barbara." He laughed. " Doña Barbara seems to be very thoughtful."

Frowning and thoughtful, indeed. With her hand resting on the Law of the Plain which Ño Pernalete had just consulted during the farce they had planned—" Doña Barbara's Law " as it was called because she had paid to have it made to suit her—the Amazon had sat nursing the rancour Luzardo's words had aroused.

It was the first time in her life she had heard a threat of that sort; and what increased her fury was that this very law, her very own law, paid for with her money, was obliging her to give in when she had planned to refuse. She tore up the pamphlet in a rage, muttering:

" To think that this paper that I can crumble and tear into bits can make me do anything against my will! "

But these angry words expressed something besides rancour: an unusual event, a feeling of respect she had never felt before.

II

THE TRAINERS

FOR several days Carmelito had been keeping close watch over La Catira, one of Black Mane's stud. In all Altamira there was no more lusty stallion than the fierce bay, who could not see a mare in another stud without trying to snatch her away from it, and it was by no means easy for the others to prevent him, for the stallions could not resist the furious attack of his kicks and bites. For the rest, no man had yet found a way of capturing him. They had chased him many a time, but no matter how well the disguised corral was hidden in the gullies, he always discovered it and escaped.

La Catira, white and slender as a crane, was the handsomest filly in his stud. But the time came when, forbidden to the savage stallion as his daughter, she had to be expelled from the group. Black Mane laid back his ears, showed his teeth at her, giving her to understand that they could not stay together, and she stood still in the middle of the prairie, watching the disappearance of the family she no longer belonged to—

her slender legs planted close, her pink jaw quivering, her clear eyes sad.

She wandered around alone, listlessly, slowly, through the familiar paths, and Carmelito, on his way back to the ranch-house, saw her far away gazing at the golden dust raised on the horizon by the joyous gamboling of her lost companions.

Next day he lay in wait at the water hole, hidden among the branches of a lofty terebinth with his lasso in readiness; but the filly was as wily as her father, and it was necessary to keep watch over her for a full week.

At last she fell into the trap. While he was hobbling her, Carmelito consoled her by saying:

"You won't mind, Catira. Stay still, now."

When she saw the splendid animal the peon was leading in, Marisela exclaimed:

"What a pretty horse! Who ever had one like that?"

"I'll buy her from you, Carmelito," Santos proposed. But the peon replied shortly:

"She's not for sale, Doctor."

In the Plain—where, as the proverb says, moving property is nobody's property—whoever catches a wild horse is the owner of it, and it is customary for the master, if he wants the beast for himself, to purchase it for a sum which is actually no more than the proper pay for capturing and training it. But the capturer has entire right to refuse to sell it, provided the animal is for his own use.

The breaking-in and training was laborious, because La Catira had a bad trick or two, the *corcoveo jacheado,* and only a master horseman could have stayed on her. But a horse broken in by Carmelito became finally as steady as a chair and as gentle as a lamb, no matter how tricky it had been.

" How's Catira coming along, Carmelito? " Luzardo would ask him.

" Ah, Doctor. She's learning her gaits little by little. And how's your little job going? "

He referred to the task of educating Marisela which Santos had undertaken.

Marisela had a few capers of her own, too. It was not because learning was difficult for her, but she sulked every now and then.

" Let me go back to my woods again."

" All right, go. But I'll come after you with: 'Don't say " seen " but " saw " or " met "; don't say " looka " but " look " or " see." ' "

" It slips out without my noticing it. See what I found, then, snooping . . . searching around here. Doesn't it look pretty on the table with flowers in it? "

" Well, the vase is really not very pretty."

" I knew beforehand you'd find some fault in it."

" Look here, infant. You didn't let me finish. It's not your fault that the vase isn't handsome. I'm very much pleased that you thought of putting flowers on the table."

"Then you see I'm not so stupid after all. You didn't teach me to do that."

"I never did think you were stupid. Quite the contrary. I've always told you that you were a smart girl."

"Yes. You've said that enough, already."

"It seems that you don't like it. What else would you like me to say?"

"*Guá!* What should I want? Am I asking for anything else?"

"There goes that '*guá!*' again!"

"Oop! . . ."

"Don't lose patience," he told her. "I'm keeping count of those '*guá's*' and the number is getting smaller every day. Only one has got out the whole day."

He corrected her diction constantly. The real lessons were given at night. Reading and writing were coming back to her, out of the long years of disuse, quite well. These were the only things her father had taught her, and that when she was a very small girl. Everything else was new and interesting and she learned with extraordinary ease. Her models in manners and habits were young ladies from Caracas, always cultured and dainty, friends of Santos', whom he remembered at opportune moments during the after-dinner talk. Marisela always smiled at mention of them, for it did not escape her quick perceptions that these lengthy dissertations on the ladies in Caracas were intended to give her something to imitate. Nevertheless, she would sulk at times if Santos seemed to take too much pleasure in depicting the models, for it generally happened that he began for instruction's sake and ended up with nostalgia for city life; but it was then Marisela learned the most, for if the teacher became distracted, her instinct was awakened.

Neat, even vain, she was still a rustic, but rustic like the *paraguatán* flower which sweetens the air of the thicket and perfumes the wild honey; and nothing remained in Marisela's appearance to recall the girl who carried bundles of wood on her frowzy head.

Santos bought from the Turk, who came every year at that season to the ranches in the Arauca basin, the best things in his pack, so that Marisela might be well shod and well dressed. Melesio Sandoval's granddaughters had helped him out of his difficulties when she first came, but later on Santos played the part of modiste, sketching designs for her dresses, and this led to merry scenes, for if the sketches were not very bad, the patterns were always inimitable and sometimes in deplorable taste.

"Hm! I'm not going to wear that fright," she would protest.

"You're right," he admitted. "It's come out a little overladen. It's got a bit of everything on it, tucks, flounces, and what not. We'll take this off."

"And this too. I certainly won't wear that business on the neck."

"We'll agree about that, but say 'collar.' Take it off. Your instinct is sure in these things, as in a lot of others," Santos concluded, pleased at the happy results of her alternately rude and docile naturalness, and seeing Marisela as a personification of the soul of the Plainsman, open as the prairie and improved by every experience.

As compensation for the rough work of the ranch, he derived spiritual occupation from the task of regenerating Lorenzo Barquero. By gradually reducing his allowance of liquor and providing him with physical and mental work, he had succeeded in bringing Lorenzo to the point of determining to rid himself of his vice. Santos took him out during the day, and during their after-dinner talks made persistent efforts to interest him in subjects which would spur his lethargic intelligence, for years helpless save under alcoholic stimulation.

But in addition to giving him the incomparable satisfaction of successful accomplishment, Marisela made the house a happy place for him and brought in the necessity of personal orderliness. When she arrived at Altamira, it was no longer the dirty bat-roost Santos had settled in a few days before, for he had seen to the whitewashing of the walls, spattered with the filth of the loathsome creatures, and the scrubbing of the floors, covered with a hard coating of clay brought in on the peons' feet for unknown years; but it was still a house without a woman. As to material things, there was no one to stitch and mend; his meals were served by a peon.

Spiritually, and most important for Luzardo, there was the lack of any control, the liberty to go around any way he pleased, the fact that it did not matter if the peons' obscene speeches disturbed the silence, or if he neglected his appearance or forgot his little refinements.

Now, on the contrary, it was necessary to return from the rough toil of pursuing and herding cattle with a bunch of flowers for the young lady of the house, to change his clothing, get rid of the rank odour of horses and cattle clinging to his skin, and sit down to table to give an example of good manners and maintain an agreeable, carefully regulated conversation.

Thus, while Santos was polishing away her rusticity, Marisela served him as a defense against the adaptation of the roughness of his environment, the irresistible force with which the wild, simple life of the desert puts its seal on anyone who abandons himself to it. Sometimes the discipline irked her, she got her blood up, to use her own phrase, and refused to take a lesson or responded to his admonitions with a curt "Let me go back to my woods, then."

But these were merely passing attacks, signs of character proceeding from the very feelings he was trying to rouse in her. She would come immediately around to what she had rejected:

"Well, shan't I have any lesson tonight?"

She was very like La Catira, who after a few leaps struck the proper gait of her own accord. But Carmelito completed his task first. He presented himself before Santos one afternoon, leading the filly by the bridle, and said:

"I'm going to take a liberty, Doctor. As there isn't any fine horse here for Señorita Marisela, I've broken Catira in for her. Here she is, if you want to try her yourself first. I haven't got her bridled for that, but I've got the English saddle and harness out there, complete."

For a moment Santos saw no more in this than an indication of the character of Carmelito, who had given him that curt answer when he offered to buy the filly, instead of responding that he wouldn't sell her because he intended to make Marisela a present of her. But he thought afterwards that Carmelito's having chosen to give him a demonstration of friendship through Marisela to atone for the cool reception he had been accorded might also signify that the peons thought him in love with his cousin; and as this had no part in the purely disinterested feelings she inspired in him, Santos was not pleased at having his attitude interpreted in this way.

He called Marisela so that she herself might be the one to acknowledge the gift.

"How lovely!" she exclaimed, clapping her hands with delight. "So she's for me? And why didn't you tell me before, Carmelito? Here you've had me envying you the beast all these days. Saddle her for me so I can take a ride." And then: "The trouble is that Papa's in one of his touch-me-not humours today and won't want to go with me."

"That's all right," said Santos. "I can go with you."

"Let me go too, Doctor," Carmelito requested. "I want to see how Catira turns out with the *señorita* riding. Because horses when you ride them and horses with women up are two different things."

This reason was acceptable, but it was not the real one. Along the way, talking with him, Santos determined to bring him to some degree of frankness—Antonio Sandoval never tired of commending Carmelito, and Santos had confidence in him—but for a long time he succeeded in bringing forth only short, dry responses. Finally, upon a question from Santos, he decided upon the confidence he had wanted to give for days.

"I was not born a peon, Dr. Luzardo. My family was one of the best in Achaguas and San Fernando, and even in Caracas, I have lots of relatives you perhaps know." He cited several, people of good position. "My father, while he wasn't rich, had a good bit of property. The Ave Maria ranch was his. One day, when I was about fifteen or a little more, a gang of rustlers attacked the house. They were all over the Plain during the rainy season, plundering. They had come for horses, but the old man saw them in time and said to me: 'Carmelito, we've got to get those forty bronchos in the corral out of there quick and hide them in the woods. Take the peons that are here and don't come back until I tell you to.' Well, we got the horses out, and tied branches to their tails, so they would rub out their own tracks, and we shut ourselves up in the woods, three peons and I. We stayed there more than a week, hungry, taking the horses where they could graze in the daytime and keeping watch at night, with the water up to the saddle girths most of the time, because that was a fierce winter and nearly all the woods were under water. The fever got us and the mosquitoes bit us until we didn't know one another, our faces were that swollen, and the horses were skinny and covered with sores, because the ticks ate them and they had worms. Then, when I saw that the Old Man hadn't told us to come back yet, I made up my mind to go back, by myself, to see what was going on. I say going on? It had happened days before. A buzzard came flying out of the house when I stepped into the hall. Skeletons were all that was left of my father and mother, and there in a corner was Rafaelito. That's the brother I told you I'd sent for to work for you, the other day. He was just crawling then, only a few months old. I picked him up from the floor dying of hunger."

He continued, after a brief pause:

"The man they call Ño Pernalete was one of those murderers. He's still alive because although he was with the others, he was the only one who didn't put his hands on my father and mother, as I found out later. The others have all paid for it, one by one. I know that revenge is not a good thing, but it's all we have here to wipe out blood. I won't bother to tell you how it is I came to be a peon, though I like working for you."

He returned to his habitual silence; Luzardo spoke to him about this terrible story with the warmth characteristic of him when he discussed anything relating to the ruling violence of the Plain.

Marisela had been listening all the while, but as the theme in which Santos became engrossed was rather uninteresting to her, and she couldn't forgive him for having talked a whole hour without giving her a word, she put spurs to Catira, forcing her to a livelier trot, and burst out singing one of the ballads the Plainsman has ready for every shade of feeling.

The words could not be heard, but the agreeable voice carried the melody gracefully. Santos stopped talking to listen, and Carmelito, the bitterness of his recollections vanished, was likewise delighted with the well-sung ballad, and when Marisela came to the end, he said:

"Ah, Doctor! I guess we're not such bad trainers. Look at the way Catira's pacing."

III

THE FURIES

FOR stabbing, Melquíades; for general knavery, Balbino; for messages, Juan Primito. Only some of the messages Juan Primito delivered were just like stabs.

Unkempt, louse-eaten, with a bristling beard nothing could bring him to trim, Doña Barbara's messenger was a simpleton with a tendency to fits of madness, although these were not without some method. His most singular manias consisted in refusing to drink water in the houses at El Miedo, although this made it necessary for him to travel miles for it, and in placing upon the roofs of the cabins pans full of the oddest liquids, to be drunk by certain grotesque birds he called "furies."

From what could be gathered from his nonsensical prattle, the furies were a sort of materialization of Doña Barbara's evil inspirations, and there was a certain relation between the particular kind of perverse activity she was contemplating and the liquids he placed on the roofs to slake the birds' thirst: Blood, if she were scheming to assassinate someone; oil and vinegar, if she were preparing a suit; and a mixture of wild honey and the bile of cattle if her enchantments were being directed towards a future victim.

"Drink, birdies!" Juan Primito would growl when he set the pans of the roofs. "Fill up so you can leave the Christian in peace."

And as the birds were always at least a trifle thirsty, Juan Primito would not drink water at El Miedo, because he didn't wish to change his luck, and he assured everyone that wherever those devilish birds put their beaks the water changed into the liquid they wanted, and any Christian — that is to say, human — who drank it, received the injury destined to someone else.

"Now the furies will be loose again," the simple fellow had said to himself when he heard of the arrival of the owner of Altamira, and from that day on he was often seen gazing up at the sky in expectation of the diabolical flock, his pans already filled with the requisite liquid.

"What's happened, Juan Primito?" Doña Barbara's peons would ask the poor fellow, with whom they amused themselves. "Don't you see them yet?"

"That seems to be one coming," he would reply, pointing with his hand at eye level, as though there really were something in that part of the brilliant heavens he was indicating.

Nevertheless, Juan Primito was considered more sly than foolish by the peons at El Miedo. Only Doña Barbara, who alone was not in the secret, considered him an utter idiot.

Finally, one afternoon, Juan Primito exclaimed:

"Here are the furies! *Ave Maria Purísima!* Look, lads, at the way that flock is turning the sky black!"

But those who were in the secret understood that it was not at the sky they were to look, but at Doña Barbara, who was returning from the village with the deep vertical crease of a fierce scowl on her forehead.

From that moment, for several days, Juan Primito spent his time—either through madness or slyness, although he himself could not have said where his madness ended and his slyness began—watching the flight of the grotesque, sinister birds in order to find out what kind of thirst they had. His idiotic contemplation of the sky was interspersed with occasional knowing looks at Doña Barbara's face.

"Will it be oil and vinegar they want to drink this time? I can't seem to tell. Because when there's a suit in hand there's a clerk of records up there too. Everybody knows that flutter. . . . Honey and bile? But if that was the case they'd be flying around flapping, and now those furies up there are very quiet. . . . Hm! How can it be that it's blood they're looking for?"

Several days passed in this fashion, without respite for the propitiatory offerings, or for the pool of blood left by the steers killed for use on the ranch, or the oil and vinegar from the commissary, or for the hives of wild bees; and as the days went on without the disappearance of that mighty frown from Doña Barbara's brow, Juan Primito's silly mania was changing into frenzied madness.

The same sort of frenzy was taking possession of Doña Barbara, a furious spite at her failure to silence forever the lips which had spoken the first threat she had ever listened to: "And if the *señora* interprets it differently and does not accede to my demand, at the end of eight days I shall hail her before the Tribunal."

During the day she gave herself up to a feverish activity, astride a horse, a repellent Amazon with her man's trousers, down to her ankles, under the skirt thrown over the saddle-bow, lasso in hand behind the Altamira herds grazing within her lands — insulting the peons for the least slip, and cutting up the horse's flanks with her spurs. At night, she shut herself up in the room where she conferred with the "Partner" and remained awake there until the roosters crew.

"We'll see if he dares," she would say, over and over to herself in a long soliloquy, walking from one end of the room to the other. Juan Primito was always listening outside the door, and he declared that he had several times heard the words with which the "Partner" responded, saying:

"He will dare!"

It was her intimate conviction, cherished in spite of herself and formulated aloud in a voice hoarse with useless rage, that Luzardo would be as good as his word.

The last day of the term he had set was almost over when she called her messenger.

"Your orders, *señora,*" said Juan Primito, standing before her with the smile produced on his idiot's features by superstitious fear and unconditional submission, while he jerked at his dirty beard with his clawlike black nails.

"You are going to Altamira right now. Ask for Dr. Luzardo and tell him for me that he may go ahead whenever he wishes with the round-up he requested, and ask him to advise me of the exact time to send my men."

Juan Primito saw her black eyes gleam with a sinister intention, and before he set out he hurriedly filled all his pans from the pool of blood in the *abattoir* and put them up on the cabin roofs, muttering:

"It was blood they wanted! Drink, birdies! Fill up and leave the Christian in peace."

No one could cover ground as Juan Primito did, with his rapid long strides, turning his head every moment and muttering:

"These hellish women!"

But he did not refer especially to Doña Barbara nor to the task she had just given him, but to women in general, the theme of a strange paranoia which attacked him whenever he was going through the deserted prairie.

That afternoon the desire to see Marisela was another

spur to him. The only love of his simple soul, Marisela, with her conversation, gave him a pleasure never exceeded by any other. It was only to her that he showed the small reasonable part of his being: the bitterness of the man within the simpleton. He had been with her at birth, the name they gave her had been his whim. Repudiated by her mother and abhorred by her father, she had been cradled in his arms. Some tender contradiction in his idiot soul had made him a devoted nurse, and if Marisela heard any kind words they were the things he called her: "My heart's darling," coming forth from his gaping jaws, out of the dirty beard, like honey from the black hives of the wild bees. Whatever money came into Juan Primito's possession went to delight the darling of his heart, with whatever pretty trinket the passing peddlers had in their bags, and later, when Lorenzo Barquero, thrown out of his own house, sought refuge in the hut within the palm grove and abandoned himself to drunkenness, the only reason why Marisela did not suffer from hunger the greater part of the time was that he brought daily the food left over in the peons' houses at El Miedo.

"Here are your leavings, my heart's darling," he would say to her, showing her his knapsack full, and who knows what bitterness was hidden in his foolish laugh. And then the many foolish things he scattered over his heedless chatter, and the laughs with which she showed her enjoyment of them, and his delight in hearing her laugh, and her pleasure in being told that! And deep within, reciprocal affection, the light of the poor fellow's life.

Santos Luzardo had deprived him of this pleasure by taking Marisela to Altamira. Until that time he had gone daily to see her, for distance was no matter to him; but after that the peons had said to him, between gross jests:

"They've taken your sweetheart away, Juan Primito."

This, maddening him, was like the stirring up of a stagnant pool. Animal jealousy and hideous thoughts, the miry dregs of his simple soul, clouded his pure affection for Marisela and changed her suddenly into one of the women of his paranoia who ran naked behind him in the deserted prairie.

Tormented by this hallucination, he had a fit of madness, and Doña Barbara was very nearly obliged to have him put in a strait-jacket. When the fit had passed, he ceased to speak Marisela's name, and if anyone asked about her he replied:

"*Guá!* Don't you know she's dead? The girl at Altamira is another person."

Nevertheless, his fleet legs could not go fast enough for him, that afternoon he was going to see her.

The Marisela who came out to meet him really did seem like another person.

"My heart's darling!" he exclaimed, stopping, out of breath. "Is it you?'"

" Who should I be, Juan Primito? " she replied, laughing from embarrassment and pleasure.

" But how you've changed, girl! You've even got fatter! Anyone can see that you're getting enough to eat, now. And that pretty gown, who bought that for you? And those shoes? You with shoes on, darling! "

Marisela blushed with shame at the words. " Don't tease me, Juan."

" It's just because I'm glad to see you like this. You're prettier than a marigold. What a few rags can do! "

" Well, if you know that, then change the ones you're wearing, because they're disgusting.'"

" Dress myself in new clothes? That's all right for you, you've got someone to show off to. Is he very fond of you? Tell me the truth."

" Don't be an idiot, Juan," she replied, blushing again. But this was a different kind of blush which reddened her cheeks and made her eyes like black velvet.

" Hm! " the simpleton grunted, with a suspicious inflection. " Don't deny it to me, I know all about it."

Marisela smiled and was about to protest, but he added:

" A little bird over there told me."

" One of your furies? " she replied with a sudden inspiration. The word, carelessly pronounced, seemed to disturb her happiness. She became immediately serious, and inquired:

" Is there trouble over there? '"

She was really speaking of her mother whom she never mentioned by name.

" Don't ask me, little girl! " answered Juan Primito. " There's no living in El Miedo. The fuss those birds make flying all the blessed day over the cabins! *Ave Maria Purísima!* I'm disgusted with bothering with the devilish things. I'd come here, willingly to be with you, my girl, but I can't. I've got to be there, sticking to those birds, so I can give them their drinks at the right time. . . . Because if I don't . . . Ah, *caramba!* You don't know what those furies are. They're very bad, those birds, very wicked, heart's darling."

" And what have you been giving them to drink these days? " Marisela asked gravely.

" Blood, my child," he answered, smiling broadly. " Those birds are up to something this time. If they want to drink blood, it must be something pretty bad, eh? I filled their pans just now, before I came here. They must be satisfied now." He added immediately: " Before I forget it, where's Dr. Luzardo? I've got a message for him from the *señora.*"

This, added to his earlier words, was Juan Primito's way of warning any one to whom he delivered a message of his suspicion of Doña Barbara's designs. It made Marisela tense with apprehension.

" How long are you going to serve her, booby? " she

inquired angrily. "You're going to send your soul to the devil with all this bringing and carrying. Get away from here, and right away!"

But at this point Luzardo, who had been near by for some time listening to Juan's conversation with the girl, intervened.

"Let him alone, Marisela. Tell me, Juan Primito, what message have you brought me?"

Juan turned around with feigned surprise. He had already begun to suspect that the man who had been looking at them from the doorway was Luzardo. While he twisted his fingers in his tangled beard, he delivered his message in Doña Barbara's exact words.

"Tell her that I'll be at Mata Oscura with my men, at daybreak," Luzardo replied, and went immediately into the house.

Marisela waited until he was out of hearing to say what she had to tell Juan Primito, and the latter, noting her state of consternation, spoke first, soothingly.

"Don't be afraid, little girl. Those furies won't do anything now. They must be full of blood by this time."

But she replied, seizing him by the arms and shaking him angrily:

"Listen to what I'm saying: If you come here again with messages from there, I'm going to turn the dogs on you."

"On *me,* my heart's darling?" he exclaimed, divided between resentment and fear.

"Yes, on you. And now get out of my sight. Go away from here, right away!"

Juan Primito returned to El Miedo, sad because his heart's darling had given him such a farewell, when he had been so happy merely because he was going to see her. Besides, hadn't he done a good deed, saying that about the blood so that Luzardo would know what to look out for?—But when he arrived at El Miedo his resentment had vanished, and after he had repeated Santos' reply to Doña Barbara, he burst out talking about Marisela.

"If you could see her, *señora.* You wouldn't know her. Ah, that girl has changed into a fine woman. Such beautiful eyes! Prettier than yours, *señora.* And so neat it's a pleasure to look at her. The Doctor certainly keeps her well dressed, from the shoes up. It ought to be nice for a man—eh, *señora?*—to have a girl as pretty as that one at his side!"

Nothing referring to Marisela had ever interested Doña Barbara, for she had never felt toward the girl even the instinctive love of an animal for her suckling young; but where maternal feeling did not exist, Juan Primito's words brought out a sudden impetuous womanly jealousy.

"Good. That doesn't interest me," she told the messenger. "You may go."

But if Juan Primito had paid any attention, he would have discovered immediately how thirsty the furies were then.

IV

THE RODEO

THAT night there was much discussion among the Altamira peons. It was the first time they had ever heard of Doña Barbara letting anyone lead her by the nose, and next morning, when they were saddling the horses, Antonio suggested:

" It wouldn't be a bad thing for those that have revolvers to bring them along; cattle aren't the only thing we'll have to contend with today," to which Pajarote replied:

" I won't carry a gun, because mine's in hock, but I'm putting this little lance head of mine under the saddle in case I need it. It's not very long, only about nine inches of steel, but an arm's length makes it long enough."

In this mood they departed for Mata Oscura before it was light, with Santos Luzardo at their head.

There were only the five loyal peons Luzardo had found upon his arrival and three other cowboys, secured by Antonio after a great deal of insistence, for Doña

Barbara had engaged all the hands in the vicinity to keep them from swelling the ranks at Altamira. But these three were real Plainsmen, good riders, and ready to outdo themselves for the sake of the man who had come to stand up to the *cacica* of the Arauca.

The prairie was still asleep, black and silent beneath the twinkling heavens, and as the horses left the ranch farther and farther behind, their hoof beats were echoed in the distance by the trampling of studs of wild horses and stray cattle fleeing to their hiding-places as they scented the men. They were scarcely visible masses, blacker than the night itself, moving among the brakes, and no more than a faint rustling came from the thickets parted by their flight; but the Plainsmen's keen senses needed no further indications:

"That's the herd from the muddy ground at Uverito. More than a hundred running away."

"There goes Black Mane's stud, towards Corozalito."

They reached the appointed meeting-place at dawn. The El Miedo men were already there, captained by Doña Barbara, and told how to stampede the herd Luzardo collected, since there were among the Altamira cattle which had taken shelter there a great many cows whose calves, still suckling, had already been burned with the El Miedo brand. This was Doña Barbara's favourite method of stealing her neighbours' cattle, with the aid of overseers of ranches neglected by their owners.

But Antonio's alertness was a step ahead of Doña Barbara's plans. Noting the large number of cowboys she had with her, he said to Santos:

" She's brought such a crowd to make you confident, so that you'll begin the drive on a large scale, and then they'll stampede the herd and drive it away, just as they've done at other times."

Antonio's suggestion led Santos to go hurriedly over his plan a second time. He greeted his neighbour by lifting his hat, without going up to her. She came forward to give him her hand, with a treacherous smile. He started at seeing her, for she was almost another person, entirely different from the disagreeably mannish woman he had first seen several days before at the Civil Magistrate's office.

Her eyes were brilliant with that disturbing light of a sensual woman's, her full lips were gathered as though for a kiss, with an enigmatic twist at the corners. He noticed that her complexion was warm and rich, and that her hair was coal black, abundant, and straight. She wore a blue silk bandana, knotted around her neck, with the points lying between the collar of her blouse, and a rather severely tailored skirt; but she wore all, even the wide velvety sombrero, the only masculine detail of her costume, with a certain feminine grace. Lastly, she rode side-saddle, a thing she did not usually do at a rodeo, and all this made one forget the notorious woman she had become.

It could not escape Santos that her show of femininity

had the sole object of making an agreeable impression on him, but prepared as he was, he could not help admiring her.

For her part, when she looked in his eyes, the treacherous smile vanished from her face, and she felt once more, but this time with all the force of that peculiar intuition of the fatalist, that her life was from that moment taking an unforeseen direction. She forgot her studied attitude of flattery — the aims inspired by the fundamental passion of her being, hatred of men, put it to flight within the dark confines of her spirit — but she noticed that her habitual emotions were suddenly leaving her. What would replace them? It was a question she could not answer for the moment.

They exchanged a few words. Santos Luzardo seemed to be doing his best to be courteous, as though he were addressing a lady of quality in some drawing-room. She, hearing his words, so correctly, yet so drily pronounced, was scarcely conscious of her replies. She was overcome by this unaccustomed sort of masculinity, a mixture of dignity and refinement she had never encountered in the men she dealt with, and by the impression of strength and self-control she received from the quiet fire of his gaze, his precise manners, his carefully pronounced words, and although he said to her only the indispensable things referring to the work in hand, it seemed to her that she enjoyed talking to him only for the pleasure of hearing his voice.

Balbino Paiba had not taken his eyes off them all this time, and he disguised his displeasure by making obscene jokes about Luzardo to the delight of the El Miedo peons, while, a little distance off, the Altamira men exchanged their impressions of this encounter.

Then Santos began to give orders about the work; but Balbino Paiba, in whose head no perverse idea could remain quiet, hastened to interrupt:

" There are thirty-three of us, and we can make a good round-up by starting the herds in the open."

Satisfied with his own perspicacity, Antonio exchanged looks with Santos, who replied:

" That won't be necessary. Besides, we're going to work in groups, in a fair proportion — one of my men for three of yours, since you're three to our one."

" What for? " Balbino objected. " We always round-up separately here, every ranch after its own brand."

" Yes. But today we're going to work another way."

" Do you think he doesn't trust us? " Paiba insisted, protesting against this proceeding which would frustrate Doña Barbara's plans, since the El Miedo men, controlled by the cowboys from Altamira, would be unable to carry out the instructions they had received.

But before Luzardo could answer, Doña Barbara intervened:

" It will be done as you like, Doctor. And if you think I have too many men, I can send them back immediately."

"It isn't necessary, *señora,*" Santos replied dryly.

Surprised by her unheard-of compliance, the El Miedo peons looked at one another, some with visible disgust and others with an expression of malice, depending upon their degree of loyalty to Doña Barbara, while Balbino Paiba gave his moustaches the customary stroking and Pajarote, with apparent unconsciousness, hummed between his teeth the first two lines of a significant ballad —

Oh, the old bull goes at the cow
And the young bull runs away —

With it he expressed the thought occurring to everyone: "The woman has fallen in love with the Doctor. Balbino might just as well say good-bye to his seat at her table."

Meanwhile, Luzardo had said:

"Antonio, you take charge of the affair," and Antonio, as field captain, began to give his orders.

"You on the black and white, with five men and Carmelito and Pajarote, go and beat about that clump. All the herd that spends the night around here runs up there, and they've got to be started. I mean you, friend."

He was speaking to the Leopard. He left the man at liberty to have his brothers with him, but made it necessary for them, in that case, to join Carmelito and Pajarote, who were just as tough.

"You know my name," the Leopard grumbled, without stirring to execute the order, and it was the turn of the Altamira men to exchange glances as if to say: "Now things are going to come to a head." But Doña Barbara interfered.

"Do what you're told or get out."

The man obeyed, not without continuing to grumble, and after he had chosen his two brothers as companions, he said:

"There's room for two more who want to come with us."

Carmelito and Pajarote exchanged swift glances, and the latter muttered between his teeth:

"Now we'll see if they wear pants or corsets."

Antonio went on dividing the cowboys into groups which went in different directions, and then said to Balbino:

"If you wish to come with me . . ."

He said this out of respect for the other's position as leader of the El Miedo group; but, at the same time, he sought an opportunity such as he had given Carmelito and Pajarote, for Balbino's insolent words on the morning of the horse-breaking were still unaccounted for. But Balbino refused the invitation, saying slyly:

"Thank you, Don Antonio. I'll stay here with the *blancaje*."

By this he meant the gathering of the owners of ranches taking part in the rodeo, without sharing the work, merely staying to keep an eye on their own interests when the time came for dividing the cattle rounded up. In José Luzardo's time, during the general rodeos the *blancaje* had been composed of more than twenty ranchers dwelling in that part of the Arauca, of whose properties, now swallowed up in Doña Barbara's huge territory, only the names remained to designate thickets and savannahs in El Miedo.

Reflecting on this, Santos remained a long while inattentive to the remarks with which his neighbour was trying to carry on a friendly conversation, apparently directing them at Balbino, but choosing subjects such as would oblige Luzardo to intervene out of politeness.

Finally she decided to speak openly to him.

"Haven't you ever seen a rodeo, Dr. Luzardo?"

"When I was a boy," he replied, without turning to look at her. "This is practically new to me now."

"Really? So you've forgotten the ways of the Plain?"

"Why not! So many years away, you know."

She looked at him steadily for some time, a caressing light in her eyes, and then said:

"Nevertheless, I've heard about your exploit with the sorrel colt, just after you arrived. So I think you can't be quite as forgetful as you pretend to be."

Doña Barbara's voice, the instrument of the half-masculine demon within her, was now like a slow rustling of the forest, now like the harsh lament of the wind-swept plain, and had a peculiar timbre which was the enchantment of every man who heard her; but Luzardo had not stayed there to delight himself with it. It was true that, for a moment, he had been curious in a purely intellectual way to see into the depths of her soul, to solve the riddle of that mixture of the pleasing and repulsive, interesting, beyond doubt, as are all monstrosities; but a sudden feeling of aversion for the woman immediately overcame him, not because she was his enemy, but because of something much more intimate and profound which he could not distinguish at the moment. This led him to cut short the absurd prattle, which he did brusquely, and to go away towards the spot where some of the Altamira hands were guarding the young calves, nucleus of the rodeo.

Balbino Paiba smiled and pulled at his moustache, but although he kept looking at her out of the corner of his eyes for some time, he did not see the appearance of that fluttering motion of her eyebrows joining and separating, a sign of her fits of temper. He saw instead an expression he did not recognize, an air of far-away thoughts.

Now, driven by the cowboys the herd commenced to fill and animate the prairie, until then apparently deserted. Numerous groups of cattle surged out of the thickets and distant sand dunes; groups composed of steers used to being herded were in moving bands, with the leaders at the head. Then there were the suckling calves frisking about their mothers; others, more shy, a few at a time, roaring with fright. The cries of the horsemen rang out. Old steers kept running about on all sides, trying to break through the ring formed by the horses, and here and there wild bulls gathered, eager to attack;

but the stampedes became irresistible at times, bringing troops of tame cattle from the distant part of the plain, and these, forming in front of the wild beasts who were trying to stampede, converted their rage into fear.

Some small troops were already beginning to run together where the calves were herded; others resisted, and the cowboys, in a ring around the animals, had to strain their utmost to drive them from the more distant points, whirling their mounts around, bringing them to their haunches with rude jerks of the bridle which stopped them in full career.

The round-up grew from moment to moment, becoming more and more riotous as the streams of wild cattle poured in from all parts towards the centre. Clouds of dust arose, the yells of the cowboys became louder:

"Halloo! Halloo! — Hold on there! — Close in! Close in!"

Luzardo watched the thrilling spectacle, his thoughts fired by the recollection of his boyhood, when, beside his father, he had shared with the peons the dangers of the round-up. His nerves, which had forgotten this wild emotion, tensed once more with it, vibrating in accord with the trembling fury of horsemen and beasts shaking the plain. And the prairie seemed to him wider, more impressive, more beautiful than ever.

The round-up had come to a stand. There were hundreds of cattle gathered together. The work had been hard, the horses were panting, bathed in sweat, white with foam; their flanks were bloody, and many had been badly gored by the bulls. But the rodeo was not over. There were many wild steers, and they were fidgety, running around the ends of the herded groups or making their way through them with furious charges, smelling the air of the open prairie, eager to run away, to give their conquerors no rest. A deafening clamour filled the plain — the mooing of cows calling their lost calves, and the pitiful squeals of the calves, seeking their mothers in the turmoil; the roars of the leaders who had lost the government of their herds, and the frightened cries of the latter; the noise of horns locking, the thumping of powerful ribs in the crush, the yells of hoarse cowboys.

Now it seemed as if the herd would surrender. The leaders began to recognize their groups, and as they gathered around their followers, the restless animals became quieter, the crying of the others diminished, and the reassuring chant of the riders could be heard. The men had taken their places, forming a wide circle around the cattle, while those whose horses had been hurt went to a nearby thicket to change them for remounts. Antonio was about to give the order to take out the leaders and proceed with the division of the stock when suddenly, the carelessness of a cowboy, who had dismounted to tighten the cinch of his saddle at the same moment that a bull had made his way through the centre of the herd in a furious charge, started an avalanche of stampeding beasts.

There were sudden cries from the horsemen, and a number of riders rushed in a body to check the imminent scattering of the herd.

But it was already too late. With a terrific concerted shove, the herd flung itself through the breach made by the bull, and scattered in small units over the plain.

"The damned witch!" exclaimed the Altamira peons, attributing the event to the evil powers of Doña Barbara. But it did not escape Antonio that the apparent carelessness of the cowboy — the Leopard — had been deliberate. Since the Leopard had noticed the presence of a large number of Altamira cows whose suckling calves already bore the fraudulent El Miedo brand, he made use of the pretext of tying the cinch just as the bull, breaking through the cattle around him, was threatening to lead them with him. His loyalty to Doña Barbara cost him dear. The rushing horde bowled him over, horse and all, and when the cloud of dust raised by the trampling hoofs had cleared away, those who had hastened to the spot where he fell found no more than a shapeless inert mass covered with blood and dirt.

Luzardo, with the Plainsman's instinct, had given free rein to his horse and had joined the group of cowboys. Someone shouted at him:

"The herd is going to break up at that clump there, and there's a wild bull in the lead."

It was Pajarote, galloping to join him. Antonio and Carmelito and two men from El Miedo were likewise coming up, all with their lassos in hand, ready to rope the bull which had caused the outbreak. Santos realized that he had forgotten to take this precaution, and he quickly untied the loops holding his rope to the saddlebow and spread the noose, going towards the clearing in the midst of the clump pointed out by Pajarote.

The herd immediately commenced to pour forth from the place. The cries of the horsemen drove them back and they sought a ford in a nearby channel crossing the prairie; but a huge, long-horned bull separated from the moiling beasts, and offered battle.

"That's the white-faced fellow that's been giving us trouble for two years," said Pajarote. "But he won't get away this time."

The animal stopped an instant, and then rushed about, here and there, his head down, his gaze going from one to another of the men worrying him; then he shot out in the direction of the edge of the thicket Luzardo was skirting.

"Quick with that rope, he's right on top of you," Pajarote shouted, while Carmelito and Antonio, seeing Santos in danger between the thicket and the bull, called to him while rushing to his aid:

"Come away from that side of the clump where the bull is driving you."

"Get the horse clear."

Luzardo did not hear this advice, but he did not need it; he had not forgotten his boyhood experience and skill.

With the rapid movement of the experienced horseman, he rushed forward, cutting off the charging bull, and flung his lasso over the rump of the horse. The rope fell over the bull's horns, and Pajarote cried enthusiastically:

"Right in the head, if anybody wants to know!"

Santos immediately pulled his horse up short, to tighten the rope, but this was a bull of terrific strength, and more than one rope was needed to bring him down. As it tightened, vibrating with the powerful tug of the beast, the horse, cruelly dragged backward, sat down on his haunches with a strangled shriek, and the bull turned and was rushing at him when Antonio, Carmelito, and Pajarote flung their lassos at the same time, with a triple yell as they caught around the horns:

"We dressed him that time!"

The horses stopped short, the ropes tensed, and the bull rolled over in a whirl of dust. He had no sooner fallen than the cowboys were on top of him.

"You put his tail through his legs, Pajarote," Antonio ordered, "and I'll take him by the horns while Carmelito ties him up."

And Luzardo, remembering:

"Put the rope through his nose and castrate him right here."

Pajarote caught hold of the bull's tail, passed it through his hind legs, and pulling with all his might, rolled the animal over on one side, while Antonio pinned him to the ground by the horns. When he had been rendered helpless in this manner, Carmelito, before the beast could recover from his stunning fall, made the holes in his nostrils, strung the nose rope through them, castrated him with a swift, sure stroke, and notched his ears with the Altamira mark.

"This fellow won't give us any more trouble," he said, as he concluded the operation. "Now let's tie him to the foot of a tree."

"I guess this big devil must be a loyal *Luzardero,"* said Pajarote, "and didn't want any other brand on him but the one his mother had. He was just waiting for the owner to come to fall into his hands. That's why we couldn't rope him last time."

"Well, he was roped this time," said Carmelito. "If this is the way beginners pull them down, what'll be left for us?"

"A Plainsman is a Plainsman for five generations," said Antonio, delighted with his master's prowess.

At this moment Doña Barbara came up, smiling.

"What a cattleman you are! And you'd forgotten the ways of your country, had you?"

She no longer remembered the rebuff she had suffered a short while before, nor recollected that she also could, and better than Luzardo, throw a bull and castrate him right out in the open. She was now merely a woman who had seen an interesting man perform a difficult feat.

"I didn't do it by myself, and there's no great credit in it," replied Santos. "On the other hand, from what

I've heard, you can bring down a bull as well as the best of your cowboys."

It was a brutal answer. Nevertheless, Doña Barbara took it with a smile.

"So I see you've heard them talk about me. How many things have they told you? I could tell you more than they have, and interesting things, too. But there'll be time for that, won't there?"

"Time won't be lacking, certainly," answered Luzardo, whose voice expressed his small pleasure in talking to her. Doña Barbara, however, did not so interpret his words, and said so herself:

"Here's something else fallen in the round-up."

But Luzardo, spurring his horse to catch up with his peons, who had gone after tying the bull to one of the trees in the thicket, once more left her in the middle of the prairie. She remained there a time, watching Santos ride away, smiling with her illusion of triumph, and saying:

"Let him go. He's already dragging the rope."

In the other direction, the mutilated bull, his head bowed to the ground at the foot of the tree, stood in silent woe.

Doña Barbara's smile changed.

V

MUTATIONS

THE singular transformation which showed itself in Doña Barbara from that day brought sly comments from the peons at El Miedo.

"Aha, partner! What's come over the *señora.* She doesn't come around here as she used to when her blood was up, ruffled and noisy as a chenchena hen! She doesn't even come to play the guitar and wrangle with us when she is in a good humour. Now she spends her time shut up with her business, and playing the lady, even with Don Balbino. 'I don't remember having met you,' you know."

"Ah, *caramba,* partner! Don't you know that it's 'like fish, like line'? This fish is not the kind that swims into shallow water and falls in the net no matter how you cast it. She's got to play him with the line to make him take the hook."

But days passed and Luzardo did not come.

"Aha, partner. This fish isn't swallowing the hook? You can't even see a ripple anywhere."

"He must be a man who won't get drunk and can't be doped," the other answered, referring to the potion Doña Barbara used to weaken the will of her lovers.

They did not fail to allude to the mysterious watches she held in the conjuring-room.

"And there's that about the 'Partner' not having any rest all these nights. He's being kept away from Hell until late. Every night the roosters crow just when he's going."

"Do you think they've got the spell-breaker over there?"

"Either that, or the spells are wearing out from being used too much."

"Hm! Don't you believe it," replied Juan Primito. "The *señora* left her eyes over there that morning when they had the rodeo at Mata Oscura, and no matter how he struggles against it, he'll have to bring them back to her."

This was the peons' explanation of the change in Doña Barbara, though it did not lessen their respect for her or the loyalty with which they served her.

Neither could she herself explain these changes, for all this was the work of feelings, new in her life, over which she had no power. For the first time, she had felt, in the presence of a man, that she was a woman. She had gone to Mata Oscura with the intention of involving Santos Luzardo in the fatal web of her seductions, so that he might repeat the history of Lorenzo

Barquero; but, although she felt that only greed and her implacable hatred of men were the forces that moved her, there was also, in the vehemence of the soul tormented by these feelings and in the appetites of her nature—a nature made for love—an unsatisfied longing for a genuine passion. Up to then, all her lovers, victims of her greed or instruments of her cruelty, had been hers as the steers marked with her brand were hers. Now, when she saw herself repeatedly rebuffed by this man who neither feared nor desired her, she felt that she wanted to belong to him, although it had to be as one of his cattle, with the Altamira sign burned on their sides; and she felt this with the same overmastering force which had driven her to ruining the men she loathed.

At first there came a violent need of activity, not that which, in its gloomy fury, had heretofore led to the exercise of her rapacity, but an ardent longing to enjoy for its own sake this unknown part of her soul which had unexpectedly shown itself to her. She spent whole days riding about the prairie, without object and without direction, merely for the sake of spending the excess of energy her sensuality had developed, fired with the desire of real passion coming to her in the critical forties. She rode drunk with sunlight, sweeping wind, and the open plain.

At the same time, her gaiety moved her to acts of generosity. Once she divided among her peons whole fistfuls of money for them to spend on amusement. They looked and looked at their handfuls of coins, tried them with their teeth, made them clink against stone, and still could not believe that they were genuine. Avaricious as Doña Barbara was known to be, how could anyone trust her largess?

She prepared to have a real feast for the reception of Luzardo when he came for the reciprocal rodeo at El Miedo. She wanted to overcome him with hospitality, turn the house inside out, so that he and his men might go away pleased, and the enmity separating owners and peons of the two ranches might come to an end. The idea of being loved by this man furnished her powerful excitement. He had nothing in common with the men she had known, neither the repugnant sensuality she had seen from the first in Lorenzo Barquero's glances, nor the brutal masculinity of the others; and as she made this comparison she was ashamed of having brutalized herself in the embraces of lascivious and gross lovers, when there were other men in the world like this one who could not be caught with the first smile directed at them.

She thought for a moment of making use of her "powers" as a sorceress, of conjuring up the baleful spirits obeying the will of the Evil-Eyed, asking the "Partner" to lead her to the elusive man, but she immediately rejected the idea with an inexplicable repugnance. The woman who had appeared in her that morning at Mata Oscura wanted to win him with a woman's arts.

And when Santos Luzardo did not put in his appearance there, she went around in bad humour, yet always well-dressed and composed, walking through the halls of the house, her gaze fixed on the floor and her arms crossed. Or she spent hours out by the palisade of the corrals, watching the horizon in the direction of Altamira, or went out to wander over the savannahs. The horse did not return as before, covered with foam and with bleeding flanks. The ride was always one of quiet pensive wandering.

At times she neither saw the horizon with her eyes, nor Altamira in her imagination, but that river and the pirogue where Hasdrubal's words had made her feel the first quivers of this finer desire which was now trying to master her heart, long sated with violence.

Finally, one morning, she saw Santos Luzardo coming.

"It had to happen," she said to herself.

As she formed this sentence saturated with the superstition of a woman who believed herself assisted by supernatural powers, the intimate and profound truth of her being overcame the nascent desire of renewal.

Santos tied his horse to the cassia tree growing before the house and came into the hall, hat in hand.

One look should have been enough to convince Doña Barbara that not much was to be hoped for from that visit, for Luzardo's bearing revealed only self-control; but she was conscious of nothing but her own emotions, and received him cordially.

"Good things are always to be wished for. What a pleasure to see you, Dr. Luzardo! Come in. Please be seated. At last you are giving me the pleasure of seeing you in my house."

"Thank you, *señora*. You are very kind," Santos replied, and added immediately, without giving her time for more flattery: "I have come to make a demand and a plea. The first, respecting that fence I wrote you about."

"Are you still thinking about that, Doctor? I thought you had been convinced that it was neither possible nor convenient here."

"As far as the possibility goes, that depends on the resources of the people concerned. Mine are very limited at present, and I shall be obliged to wait some time before I put the fence around Altamira. As for the convenience, each person has his own basis for judging that. But, for the moment, I'm interested in knowing if you are willing to share the construction of the dividing fence, as it is only right that you should. I wanted to discuss this matter before taking any other steps—"

"Don't say any more, man," she interrupted with a smile. "That's in all friendliness, you know."

Santos, with a gesture expressing injured dignity, replied:

"With a little money, which you don't lack—"

"The money that must be spent is the least part of it, Dr. Luzardo. People must have already told you that I am immensely rich. They must have spoken to you of my stinginess too, isn't that so? But if one listens to gossip—"

"*Señora,*" Santos replied quickly, "I beg you to stick to the subject I have proposed. I am not at all interested in knowing whether you are rich or not, or in finding out whether you have the faults attributed to you, or lack them. I came to ask you a question and I am waiting for a reply."

"Goodness, Doctor! what a dictatorial man you are!" exclaimed Doña Barbara, recovering her smiling expression, not for the purpose of flattering him, but because she found a real pleasure in finding this man so authoritative. "You don't let a person beg the question for an instant."

Santos realized that she was mistress of the situation, that he had lost his control over it, and that whether it was cynicism or something else that was responsible for this change of position, it was at any rate an evidence of well-balanced character on her part. He reproached himself for his excess of severity and replied, smiling:

"Nothing like that, *señora.* But, I beg you, let us get back to our subject."

"Very well. The idea of the fence seems an excellent one to me. With that up, we'd solve this disagreeable question of our boundaries, which has always been so much in the dark."

She accented the last words in a manner that would again test the self-control of her interlocutor.

"Exactly," he replied. "We should establish a situation of deed, if not of right."

"You ought to know more about that than I do, since you're a lawyer."

"But not very fond of lawsuits, as you must already understand."

"Yes, I see that you are an unusual man. I confess that I have never come across anyone more interesting. No. Don't be impatient. I'm not going to get away from the subject again. God deliver me from that! — But before I can answer I have to ask a question. Where shall we put up this fence? At the Macanillal house?"

"Why do you ask that question? Don't you know where I have set the posts? Unless you mean to say that the boundary isn't in its proper place."

"It isn't, Doctor." She kept looking fixedly in his eyes.

"You mean that you don't want to meet on friendly ground, as you said just now?"

But she answered, giving a caressing inflection to her words:

"Why do you add, As I said? Why don't you say it yourself?"

"Señora," Luzardo protested, "you know very well that we cannot be friends. I can compromise to the

point of coming here to deal with you, but don't think I am so likely to forget."

The quiet energy with which he pronounced these words overcame Doña Barbara. The insinuating smile, half-cynical and half-lascivious, vanished from her face, and she looked fixedly at the man bold enough to address her in such a way, her glance respectful and at the same time impassioned.

"If I told you, Dr. Luzardo, that the fence would have to be put up very much farther this side of Macanillal? Where the Altamira boundary used to be, before those lawsuits which keep you from considering me as a friend?"

Santos frowned, but once more managed to keep his temper.

"Either you are making fun of me, or I am dreaming," he said, slowly, but without asperity. "As I understand it, you are promising restitution, but I do not see how you can make it without injuring my feelings."

"I'm not making fun of you, and you're not dreaming. You don't know me well, Dr. Luzardo. You know what it amounts to, and what it means to you: that I have taken that land we spoke of away from you, unjustly. But listen to this one thing I have to say, Dr. Luzardo. The person to blame is yourself."

"We agree about that. But it already has the authority of legal judgment, and the best thing is to say nothing about it."

"I haven't yet said all I have to say. Do me the favour

of listening to this. If I had, during my life, met men like you, my story would have been a different one."

Luzardo felt again that impulse of intellectual curiosity which had been on the point of moving him to look into the abyss of that soul, wild and uncouth as the Plain where it lived its agitated life, but possessing nevertheless like the Plain its cool shady retreats and placid pools. There was some hidden, uncontaminated place in that soul, whence those words had come—words at once confession and protest.

In all truth, what they had expressed was sincerity and the obstinacy of a strong spirit facing its destiny; for Doña Barbara, in pronouncing them, had no intention to deceive and no sentimental softness in her heart. In that moment, the enamoured woman, in need of caresses, had disappeared; she was sufficient unto herself, and proudly facing the inner truth. Luzardo felt that he had heard a soul turned into words.

But she immediately recovered and said:

"I'll return these lands to you, through a dummy sale. Tell me you will accept, and we'll draw up the document instantly. That is, you will draw it up. I have official paper and seals. We'll have it certified and registered whenever you like. Shall I get the paper?"

Meanwhile, Luzardo had concluded that this was the auspicious moment for proposing the second object of his visit. He replied:

"Wait a moment. I am grateful to you for the good will you've shown me. But I've already told you that I had two objects in coming to your house. Instead of giving me back these lands, which I consider restored, morally speaking, do another thing which would please me more. Give La Barquereña back to your daughter."

But this, in its profound and intimate truthfulness, shattered the desire for reform. Doña Barbara sat back in the rocker she was about to rise from, and said in a disagreeable tone, looking at her nails:

"Look here, man. Now that you speak of her. I have been told that Marisela is very pretty. That she is another person since she has been living with you."

The slanderous significance hidden under the double meaning of the word "living," pronounced as it was with a malignant accent, brought Santos to his feet with an involuntary movement.

"She lives in my house, under my protection, which is another thing from what you have just seen fit to say," he corrected her, his voice trembling with indignation. "And she lives under my protection because she hasn't a crumb of her own, while you are immensely wealthy, as you told me a moment ago. But I have made a mistake in coming to ask you for what you cannot give: maternal feeling. We'll let things be just as if we hadn't spoken a word about this or anything else."

And he strode out without taking his leave.

Doña Barbara rushed to the desk, where she kept her revolver when she was not carrying it. But something held her hand and said to her:

"You won't kill him. You're not the same any more."

VI

THE TERROR OF THE BRAMADOR

HOLY Thursday. Day of abstinence from the flesh of all animals that live on the earth, for the earth is the Body of the Lord who is suffering on the Cross, and whoever eats of the flesh nourished upon it profanes and martyrizes with his teeth the Body of God Himself. Day when none must work, neither on the savannahs, nor in the corral, for this would bring ruin for the whole of life. The day when the dairies must be emptied, for milk churned on holy days does not turn to butter, but is changed into blood. A day only for tortoise-fishing, alligator-hunting, and the removing of honey from the hives.

The first has for its object the securing of the Plainsman's favourite food for Holy Thursday and Good Friday, and the second follows the traditional custom of using two days' leisure in forming parties to beat up the creeks where alligators live, both to rid the waters of the beasts and because the musk and teeth of the alligator caught on holy days have greater healing powers and are more valuable as amulets.

The palisade, concealed by branches of trees, was already stretched from one side of the creek to the other, with an open space or " door " left in the middle, and the gate-keepers were in place, up to their waists in the water. Upstream, the whippers, armed with long poles and shouting at the top of their lungs, churned up the surface of the creek to drive down whatever living thing the muddy water was harbouring.

Hidden behind the branches, with their hands under water, one over the other, ready to be joined instantly when they sensed the coveted prey between them, the " gate-keepers " waited in silence, and an occasional sudden contraction of their facial muscles, or an instant pallor, was the only sign that an alligator had passed between their hands.

Santos stopped to watch this rash sport, and within a few minutes saw a pool, dug for the purpose on the bank, fill with tortoises. Then he went over to join the rest of the peons who had gathered to watch the alligator hunting.

Like all the streams running through the Plain, this creek was a breeding place for alligators, whose teeth had lately been the death of several head of cattle, and for this reason Antonio had chosen it for the traditional Holy Thursday hunt. It was customary to hunt the beasts with rifles, or to harpoon them from a place on the shore, but when Luzardo came up the shots had long ceased to ring out, and a large number of the terrible inhabitants of the stream lay belly upward littering the beach.

"Is the hunt over?" Antonio inquired. "The Doctor was anxious to take a shot or two."

The hunters, all silent and at a distance from the water's edge, but intent on something which was going on in the creek, signalled him to be quiet, and Antonio, after a glance in the direction indicated by their expectant attitude, said to Luzardo:

"Do you see those two gourds floating in the middle of the creek? There are two men underneath them waiting for an alligator to come to the surface so they can spear his tail under water. This is the most difficult kind of alligator hunting, and it must be Pajarote and María Nieves hiding under there."

"That's right," said Carmelito. "And waiting for the One-Eyed, too. He's let himself wander as far as this."

This was the alligator Luzardo had meant to shoot during the siesta under the Big Tree, the day of his arrival. He was the terror of the Arauca fords, and the number of his victims, both horses and cattle, had gone beyond reckoning. He was supposed to be centuries old, and as he always escaped unharmed from the bullets which bounced off his thick dorsal scales, legend declared that he was invulnerable because he was under a spell. His usual location was at the mouth of the Bramador Creek, now part of El Miedo, but from there he ruled the Arauca and its tributaries, making long journeys through them and returning with gorged stomach for the placid digestion of his prey, basking on the sunny banks of his home. Here he was safe, for Doña Barbara, believing in the protection attributed to him, forbade anyone to attack him, especially as his chosen victims were the Altamira cattle going upstream.

"You shouldn't have let Pajarote and María Nieves risk their lives this way, Carmelito," said Santos. "Motion them to come out of there."

"It's useless to do that now," Antonio intervened. "Because the holes in the gourds, where they look out, are on the other side. Besides, it's already too late. Neither one of them can even make a movement now. The alligator is coming to the top, right near them. Look at that ripple."

A few yards from the gourds, the smooth surface of the creek had begun to crinkle faintly.

"Sh!" came from all the spectators as they crouched to make themselves imperceptible, and the anguished anxiety of that silent minute made it seem like an eternity. With the majesty of his age and ferocity, the alligator slowly brought up his hideous head and immense back studded with a crest of thick scales. The gourds, as though a gentle current were moving them, glided slowly over to the other side of the creek, and the spectators breathed, while Antonio murmured softly:

"They've got on his blind side."

The gourds continued to slide over toward the alligator, and although he could not see the men, since he was completely above water and his good eye was toward the beach, the danger was not past. They were within reach of his jaws, and the slightest carelessness might cost their lives.

The reptile turned his head and looked at the things floating on the water. Three rifles were pointed at him from the shore, putting the lives of the two men near him at the mercy of a poor aim; and he was about to go under again when the sudden drifting of the gourds indicated that Pajarote and María Nieves had abandoned them, risking everything for the attack, now their only salvation.

The muddy waters boiled, an enormous mass thrashed convulsively around, the fearful tail rose again and again in the air, with a terrific splash each time it struck the water — and finally the alligator turned over and was still, the gigantic white belly floating upward, the mutilated tail bloody. Pajarote and María Nieves came up, exclaimed:

"God Almighty!" and a roar of applause came from those on shore.

"That's the end of the 'Terror of the Bramador'!"

"And there'll be an end of spells from El Miedo, because we've got the spell-breaker here."

VII

WILD HONEY

THE carob tree at the Pass was vibrating like a harp with the buzzing of wild bees.

Melesio's grandsons, having climbed up to the branches where the bees had built their hives, were driving them out with the fumes of an oiled taper, and the brown honeycombs passed from the boys' hands to the hands of their sisters who were gathered at the foot of the tree. The girls ran away, with shrill shrieks, if an angry bee chanced to light on any one of their heads, but they returned, choked with laughter, to quarrel over the sweet, piquant morsels.

"You already had yours. It's my turn now."

"No, mine! mine!"

There were seven of them quarreling over the honeycombs, for Genoveva, the eldest, had stayed in the little open cabin where the chairs and table stood, to have a talk with Marisela. It would be more exact to say that she was listening to Marisela, with her elbows resting on the table and her chin propped up on her hands.

"I get up very early and have a bath," Marisela was saying. "How nice that cold water is! And if you could only hear the fuss, because I sing while the water is running over me, and the hens and roosters cackle, and the ducks quack, and the *chacalacas* in the rain tree. Then I go into the kitchen to see if the coffee's made, and when Santos comes out of his room, I give him a cup of the strongest there is, black, because that's the way he likes it. Then I tidy up the house. My hands are blistered from so much sweeping. If there's any mending to be done, I do it, and then I start to study my lessons. And when it's time for him to come back from the prairie, I go into the kitchen again to fix his dinner, because he hates the cook and won't eat anything but what I fix. He's crazy on the subject of cleanliness. I have to be chasing flies all day, and shooing the hens out of the house. I've already taught them to lay in their nests. He always brings flowers in with him, and I've already got the vases full with the ones I picked near the house. At first I wanted to have flowers everywhere but on the roof. The house was a perfect beehive! You should have heard him laugh when he saw it! I was furious, but I saw afterwards that he was right. Ah! What am I talking about, my dear? You didn't know that the Indians came in the house? I was feeling a little timid at the time, because he had gone with Papa and the peons, and I was alone in the house. The women had gone to wash the clothes in the brook. All of a sudden I heard somebody say, 'Call your dogs, lady.' And I looked around, and there were about twenty Yaruros that had come in the hall, just as if they owned the house."

"And weren't you afraid?"

"Afraid! I went out to meet them and yelled at them: 'Get out of here! of all the cheek! How do you dare to come in without asking? I'm going to loose the dogs on you —!' The poor things! They were just some civilized Indians that had been picking changuango and had come to the house to ask for salt and sugar. You know there's nothing they like as well as a piece of sugar. But look out if you give one more than the other! You've got to divide it up evenly. But I was wild, and shouting 'You cheeky pigs! Look how you've got my floor tracked up with your dirty feet! I wish those Cuibas around here would come!' That was just like saying 'I wish the devil would come!' They opened their eyes very wide and asked me, 'You've seen Cuibas, lady?' But . . . Why am I telling you this? Oh yes. I know now. You should have seen how worried Santos looked when he found out that the Indians had found me alone in the house. Even that night, when he was teaching me my lessons, he was still thoughtful."

Genoveva sat looking at her in silence. Marisela fidgeted and smiled.

"No. It isn't what you think. It isn't anything like that. *Jesús!* why are you looking at me like that?"

"Because you're very pretty. Although that won't be a surprise to you, because you must have heard enough of that already."

"Well, let me tell you — you needn't worry about that."

"I don't believe it. Even today, I'll bet you've had a compliment."

"The ones you paid me. What he tells me is that I'm very intelligent. He's already made me tired of hearing that. Sometimes I feel I won't study my lessons, to see if he'll say something different. But why do you keep looking at me that way?"

"Because that dress looks so nice on you."

"Thank you. But don't think I don't know what you're thinking."

Marisela went on to tell about Santos' designs, and they laughed a long time over the ruff on the collar of the pattern he had drawn. Then Genoveva lowered her gaze, and drummed with her fingers on the table, saying after a little:

"How lucky you are, in spite of everything."

"Hm!" Marisela grunted. "Careful, now."

"Careful about what?"

"You know what I mean."

"I? what should I know?"

"Don't be a hypocrite. Confess. You're in love with him, too."

"A ragamuffin like me in love with the Doctor?" Genoveva exclaimed. "Are you crazy, woman? He's a very nice fellow, but honey isn't made for donkeys, you know."

Marisela asked what she had already been told, for the pleasure of also saying it herself.

"Is he really very nice?"

Her words, however, had the intonation used in speaking of the completely impossible. It was involuntary; and as she heard her own voice, she realized that she too had been having her illusions, for Santos' attitude towards her revealed everything but love: the severity of a father or teacher when he gave advice or criticism, the camaraderie of an older brother when he was in a playful humour; and if, at times when she sat and looked at him in silence, he too became silent and gazed into her eyes, the smile on his face had such an air of superiority that her anxiety changed to shame. Besides, especially during the last few days, Santos spoke at table of nothing but the ladies he knew in Caracas, not to bring them forward as examples, but for the purpose of enjoying his memories. And there was, above all, Luisana Luján, whose name he never spoke without becoming thoughtful.

"I say just what you do, Genoveva. Honey was not made for donkeys."

Now both of them drummed on the table with their fingers, and the wild bees swarming about there took possession of the honeycombs, whose sharp sweetness was no longer being touched by greedy hands.

Marisela cleared her throat, to conceal the lump that had formed there, and Genoveva asked her:

"What's the matter?"

"My throat's burning from eating so much honey."

"That's the trouble with wild honey," Genoveva concluded. "It's very sweet, but it burns like fire."

VIII

THE PHOENIX

THE thunder heralding the rainy season had been heard rumbling far off in the lonely silence, and scuds of cloud were passing on their way to their watery descent over the hills, where the rains begin before coming down to the Plain. The crackle of jagged lightning on the horizon began in the first hours of night. Summer was saying farewell in the chirping language of the cicadas hidden in the dry chaparral, the pasture lands were yellow as far as the eye could reach, and the beds of creeks and pools were cracked and gaping like thirsty throats in the burning sun. The air, laden with the smoke of the fires spreading over the prairie, hung in a suffocating calm for days on end, and only at intervals did brief hot gusts spring up like the gasps of a man with fever.

The languor of the dog-days had reached its height that afternoon. The flashing sunlight was filling the Plain with mirages, and nothing moved in the crushing silence of the desert beyond the shimmer of the rarefied air. Suddenly, as the grass began to sway and yield to the rush of a storm wind, a strange thing happened. Flocks of marsh birds were seen in flight to leeward, uttering panicky cries, studs of horses, single steers, small herds, all fled in the same direction, the cattle to the shelter of the corrals, the horses in wild career towards the open.

Luzardo, about to fall asleep—he was having his siesta in the shade of the front porch—asked aloud, as he heard this unheard-of movement of the animals:

"Why has the herd come to the corrals at this time of day?"

Carmelito, who had come twice to that part of the house, to gaze out over the prairie as though he were expecting something from there, replied:

"They've smelled the fire. Look over there. The fire is breaking out behind that clump. You can see the smoke back of here, too. It's all burning, the whole way from Macanillal here."

Certain primitive ideas deeply rooted in the Venezuelan Plainsman's mind, and the helplessness of the meagre population before the immensity of the land demanding all their efforts, make it seem advisable to set these fires, when the first heavy rains of the year are approaching, as the sole effective method of bringing about a flourishing rebirth of pastures parched by the drought, and of exterminating the ticks and worms so fatal to the herds. It is customary, even obligatory, for every ranch owner to set fire to the dry brakes he meets with, even though they belong to other properties. But Santos had not permitted the setting of such fires in Altamira, as he considered the primitive practice a harmful one, and he insisted, against Antonio Sandoval's advice, on making the experiment of depending upon rotation of grazing to get rid of the ticks, and waiting for the pastures to grow again of themselves when the rains commenced, so that he might compare the results, while he was making a study of the way to introduce a rational system for the cultivation of the prairies.

Therefore, since all Altamira was dry, the fire could spread with violence, and thus, no sooner had the reddish ring of flame appeared on the horizon than it spread in a few moments over the entire huge bosom of the savannah. The thickets of evergreens here and there offered a desperate resistance, but the tongues of fire swept over them, swirling and roaring with fury, becoming fiercer with the struggle, plumed with black smoke; then the crackling of the skirmish with the creeping vegetation, and when that nucleus of the defense had disappeared, the victorious blaze, with serried ranks, resumed its swift advance, threatening to surround the houses.

The latter were not in danger, thanks to the natural protection of the sand banks and enclosures that encircled them; but the heated air passing over them became stifling at moments.

"It looks as if this had been done on purpose," Santos remarked.

"Yes sir," muttered Carmelito. "These fires don't come here on their own account."

He was the only peon there. The others, including Antonio, had gone after lunch to resume the hunt for alligators in the creeks, and Carmelito had remained, wandering about the house as though on guard, because a tobacco planter whom he had met the night before had told him that, while he was in the El Miedo commissary, he had heard the Mondragon brothers talking about something being planned against Altamira for the following day. He kept the news to himself, because he wanted to give it to Santos, he alone, as an unequivocal proof of his loyalty, though without making any show of that.

"No matter how many of them come from there," he had said to himself, "between the Doctor and me, he with his rifle and I with my carbine, we won't let them get near."

But now he had just now realized that the fires were what had been coming from El Miedo, and he reflected:

"That's not so bad, because the bare spots on the prairie will stop them."

They did stop the fire; but when the blaze, broken up by the dunes into random bonfires, and abandoned by the wind as the evening calm came on, finally died out, the wide surface of the charred prairie stretching out to the horizon under a dark sky was like some vast funereal spectacle lighted by a long row of smouldering torches at Macanillal, where the posts for the fence had been set. It was the rebellion of the Plain, the work of the indomitable breath of the limitless land against civilizing changes. Now it had finally destroyed them and was resting like a contented giant, breathing in great gusts and raising whirlwinds of ashes.

But next day, and for several days after that, the fire reappeared at different points. The stray cattle, dislodged from their retreats, scattered to all sides, increasing the peril of the ranchers in their hurried attempt to drive the herds to pastures inaccessible to the flames. It came to pass that entire herds of wild steers were sunstruck as a result of their ceaseless flight, and whatever tame cattle did not yield to the contagion of panic and run away, returned in the evening famished and exhausted. Only a few strips of savannah, protected by the creeks running through the property, had been saved from the fire, and it cost labor untold to make what cattle were not scattered about the neighbouring ranches, take refuge in them.

"This is Doña Barbara's work," declared the peons at Altamira. "Fires like this have never been seen around here."

And Pajarote suggested:

"Give us permission, Dr. Luzardo, and a couple of boxes of matches, and that's all my partner María Nieves and I will need to set fire to El Miedo from all four corners."

But the enemy of reprisals replied:

"No, Pajarote. We'll try to catch the culprits, if there are any, and turn them over to the authorities."

Even Lorenzo Barquero, coming out of his usual self-absorption, counselled reprisal:

"If they are any, do you say? Do you still doubt that this is your enemy's doing? Doesn't the fire come from the El Miedo side?"

"Yes. But if I'm going to accuse somebody of responsibility for a natural event, I've got to be certain, and so far I have only simple suspicions."

"Accuse? And who said it was necessary to go to the authorities? Aren't you a Luzardo? Do what the Luzardos always did: kill your enemy. Armed force is the law of this land. Use that to make yourself respected. Kill the woman who's declared war on you! What are you waiting for?"

It was the brusque rebellion of the man within him, the rancour buried for long years in his degraded soul, masculine, brutal, but for all that less ignoble, less abject than the surrender of his self-respect that had made him give himself up to alcohol to forget his wretchedness. This healthy reaction had begun with the first days of his residence at Altamira, but until now he had not ventured to make the faintest allusion to Doña Barbara. His conversation turned entirely upon his memories of student life, and the exactness he gave to these evocations, citing names and describing the peculiarities of feature of his former friends, and furnishing the most minute details of things and events he mentioned, showed a certain painful determination. Sometimes his ideas would take a sudden turn towards the unmentionable subject; but at these moments he would interrupt himself, and to make sure that Santos would not become aware of the drift of his thought, would lose himself in disconcerting digressions and contradictory circumlocutions, giving, in this way, the impression that his thoughts were rushing around in the ruins of his intellect like mad shadows, seeking and avoiding one another at the same time. Now, for the first time, he referred to the woman who had caused his downfall, and Santos saw a feverish ferocity shining in his eyes.

"It hasn't come to that, Lorenzo," Santos told him, and added, to divert him from the painful subject:

"It's certain that the fires have been coming from El Miedo, but it's also true that I am in some way to blame, because if I hadn't opposed the customary burning in sections, all the savannahs wouldn't have caught at once. That experiment of rotating the grazing was an innovation that cost me dear. The prairie fought for the old ways."

But Lorenzo now had a passion whose burning intensity made up for the lack of alcoholic stimulation, and it was useless for Santos to attempt to dissuade him from his homicidal idea.

"No. Never mind words. There are only two possible

alternatives here, kill or be killed. You're strong and vigorous and can make yourself feared. Kill her and make yourself cacique of the Arauca. The Luzardos never were anything else but caciques, and you can't be anything else, no matter how much you want to. Nobody is respected in this country unless he's killed someone. Don't be afraid of the red glory of murder."

Meanwhile, in El Miedo, too, old roots were putting forth shoots. After the shattering of her intention to reconstruct her life, the afternoon of her conversation with Luzardo, Doña Barbara had passed days and days in a sinister mood, abandoning herself to the machination of terrible revenge, and to whole nights in the room where she held her conferences with the "Partner"; but as the latter did not hasten to her when she conjured him, her temper was such that no one dared to approach her.

Interpreting this as a sign of definite declaration of war on Santos Luzardo, Balbino Paiba had planned the Altamira fires in the hope of recovering his mistress' lost favours, executing in advance the designs he attributed to her, and gave the carrying out of the plan to the surviving Mondragon brothers, who were again lodged in the house at Macanillal and were the only people in El Miedo who obeyed his orders. But as he kept his responsibility a secret, on account of that "God help the man who dares to touch Santos Luzardo" Doña Barbara, in her turn, interpreted the conflagration which had razed Altamira as the work of the "powers" assisting her, especially as the destruction of the fence Luzardo expected to put an end to her outrages had been no more than the realization of her own desire. And thus she became calm, perfectly confident that all the other barriers separating her from the man she wanted would fall at the proper time, and that when she wished him to, he would come to give himself up with alacrity.

It really seemed as though some malign influence were reigning in Altamira. After the painful day's toil, driving the thirsty herds to accustom them to the water-holes which had not dried up, and risking their lives among the scattered strays, the men had to be on the watch at night against attacks from the ravenous foxes that scoured the plain in packs and invaded the houses, and against the snakes fleeing the fire and likewise laying siege to the ranch. And if this was not enough, Santos, whenever he entered the house, had to bear the disagreeable spectacle of Lorenzo Barquero, his voice now trembling with his helpless rage, insisting that Luzardo should hurl himself into reprisals against Doña Barbara, so that he, Lorenzo, might put his arm at the service of the vengeful passion boiling within his breast.

And finally, to cap the climax, there was Marisela. The despair following upon her romantic disillusion was changing her into a most disagreeable person. All the vulgar expressions and incorrectly pronounced words he had rooted out of her with so much trouble reappeared in her speech whenever she opened her mouth to respond to any question of his — a premeditated plan to do everything which might make her disagreeable to him; a constant ill-humor reigned over her, and whenever he made some tactful correction, he received the provoking response:

"Why don't you let me go back to my woods, then?"

The scudding clouds passed overhead, thicker and thicker, the rattling of the thunder on the horizon at night became more frequent, and every morning brought the cackling of the cranes, heralds of the rainy season.

Observing the weather indications, Antonio finally said:

"It's already raining in the hills. The lightning will change around before very long and then we'll have the Barinas wind."

The very next day, after a period of suffocating calm, the disagreeable wind began to blow down from the high Barinas plain, a certain warning of the rain's coming. The lightning changed, the rumble of thunder was heard over towards the low Apure country, and long plumes of rain cloud commenced to speed over the prairie, toward the Cunaviche, where they condensed into violent showers accompanied by furious tempests. Lead-coloured cloud banks filled the sky from one moment to another, a hurricane flung them down to the prairie, the jagged tree-shaped lightning ripped off its branches between them with a continuous deafening clamour, and within a few minutes the entire savannah was filled with pools.

And some days later, the morning found it covered with green.

"It's an ill wind that blows nobody good," said Antonio. "Those fires have made Altamira brand new. The pastures will grow out strong now, for there's nothing like fire. And when we begin the general herding, the whole property will be covered with steers, because they'll come back to their own pastures, and the cattle that belong to other people will come to pay for those the fire killed."

The strays returned to their old haunts, the tame herds to their quiet wandering, the studs of horses to their playful battles. The guitar returned to the hands of the peons in the nights as they sat in their cabins, and Marisela returned to her good manners and her lessons under the lamp in the living-room. And everything happened like the growth of the grass after the fires.

IX

THE DANCE

IT WAS now time for the general herding, undertaken during the rainy season. The rules of this annual round-up, brought about by the lack of boundary fences and sanctioned by law, provide for the common working of the herds by neighbouring ranches, once or twice a year. The work consists in a search of the entire region for the cattle scattered through it, so that the ranchers may proceed with the branding of steers marked but not yet burned with the brand of the ranch. It is done within the boundaries of the neighbouring ranches, each in turn, under the direction of a herding leader previously elected in an assembly of the different groups of cowboys. The work lasts several days, and constitutes a genuine contest of wrangling skill, for each ranch takes pains to send its most cunning cowboys to the one where the herding is held. They take their best horses, display their best equipment, and make every effort to shine in all the departments of the *centaur's* trade.

The roosters were just beginning to crow when the tumult of preparation commenced at Altamira. The ranch now had over thirty peons, and there were, in addition to these, several more cowboys from the Jobero Pando and El Ave Maria establishments.

They saddled in haste, shouting and arguing with each other over their equipment, for it was necessary to fall upon the herd in its shelter before it began to wander.

"My knife! Where is it, I can't find it! Whoever's got it had better give it up, because everybody knows it. It's got a notch at the point, and I'll know it by the cut it makes."

"What's happened to the coffee?" Pajarote roared. "Here the day is already coming on and we're still milling around here."

"Hurry, boys," Antonio called. "And those of you with bobtail horses had better plait them now; we're going to start the drive immediately."

Those who had already saddled up, burst into the kitchen. "Here with the coffee! Señora Casilda."

A hearty fire of pine logs was crackling on the hearth, under the black tripod holding the kettle. The aromatic brew was hissing in this, and Casilda's hands gave no rest to the pot she was using to transfer the coffee to the flannel filter which hung from a hook in the ceiling, while the other women busied themselves with rinsing and filling the cups and giving them to the impatient peons. For a while there was heard in the kitchen a lively exchange of witty talk, the crude and biting jokes of the men and the laughs and answers of the women.

When the coffee had been drunk — and nothing else would enter the men's stomachs until the afternoon meal when they returned to the ranch, except muddy water and the bitter saliva resulting from tobacco-chewing — the party of cowboys left, with Luzardo at their head, happy, excited by the prospects of a thrilling day, cursing, joking with each other, remembering perils undergone at previous herdings when they risked their necks between the horns of a bull or were almost disemboweled by the hoofs of their horses, and spurring each other on with dangerous challenges.

" We'll see who's going to take me on," said Pajarote. " I've bet that I'll bring down twenty, and my knife will show the proof."

It was a hard struggle and it lasted until midday. The ropes never rested in the cowboys' hands, many horses were killed, and those that were not could scarcely stand on their aching legs; but the round-up itself was quiet enough, for the cattle were exhausted from so much running. Only the men were still lively, sitting upright on their panting horses, insensible to hunger and thirst, hoarse with yelling, but neverthless gaily chanting the tunes they used to keep the herd quiet.

It was mid-afternoon when Antonio gave orders to proceed to the division. María Nieves went among the herd shouting at the calves, and the latter, who already knew the herdsman's voice and were accustomed to the process, left the round-up to stand in the place where the small herd for his ranch, the first lot to be separated, was forming.

And, as though the arduous struggle of driving the herd in had been a mere nothing, separating the cattle still gave the men a chance for the display of their skill in catching and throwing the bulls in the different groups.

Then they proceeded to the taking out of the El Miedo cattle, and those belonging to the Jobero Pando ranch, forming the herds by means of the shouts of the cowboys. Finally, when some calves and their mothers appeared, marked with the La Amareña brand—this ranch, situated a long way from Altamira, had not taken part in the herding—Balbino Paiba began to take them out, as if they belonged to him.

Luzardo watched the operation, without saying a word; but each time a steer from La Amareña passed, he looked at its brand and then at the one borne by Paiba's horse. Paiba at last became impatient, and asked him:

"Why do you look at my horse's flank every time a steer goes by, Doctor?"

"Because the horse came here to work for his own brand."

As he said this, Santos's own words sounded to him like those of another. Antonio or any other genuine Plainsman would have expressed himself in this way.

Balbino was forced to give an explanation:

"I am authorized to take the La Amareña cattle with me."

"Show me the authorization," Santos answered. "Until you prove that you're doing what you have a right to do, you can't take anybody else's cattle from here."

"Do you expect to keep them yourself, then?"

"I don't have to give any explanations to you," answered Santos. "However, I will. These animals were driven here when they were wandering free over the prairie, and they'll go back to La Amareña the same way unless they're sent for."

"Caramba!" Paiba exclaimed. "So you're thinking of changing the customs of the Plain?"

"Exactly. That's what I intend to do. To put an end to some of them."

Santos had already put an end to Balbino's dealings with the Altamira cattle. Now, Balbino had to give up the La Amareña steers. There were not many of them, it was true, but they would have brought him something, once the brand was burned over in the way he knew.

Now the herd was entering the enclosure. This was the most exciting moment of the day. The wild animals crowded between the palisades, which formed a sort of funnel with the narrow end leading into the corrals, urged on by the horses who seemed to share the riders' enthusiasm for mastery of the cattle, and through the dust clouds raised by the hoofs, and above the noise of horns rattling against horns, the cries of the yearlings, the roars of the bulls, the pawing and violent shoving of the horses, rose the deafening cries of the cowboys:

"This way! Hold on! Hold on!"

They formed a trampling fence, pricking the cattle who resisted the drive into the corral, shoving them with the horses' flanks, without giving them room for a charge, checking their turns, yelling in the frenzy of the drive.

The drive was finished, the corral gates swung to. The guards stayed behind, humming their tunes, and the others went to the ranch-houses, to unsaddle and groom their horses.

"You did fine," said Pajarote to his mount, a chestnut with a white mark on his head, rubbing the animal's neck. "Not a single beast got by you without getting what was coming to him. Think of those jealous fellows at El Miedo calling you an old plug this morning. I'm sorry I didn't find out who it was so I could pay him back for you."

The return from work brought the clearing in front of the cabins to life. As evening came on, the cowboys came back in noisy groups, began to talk, and ended by singing their thoughts in ballad form, for if there is anything which must be said, the Plainsman always has a ballad which says it and says it better than speech. Life in the Plain is simple and devoid of novelty, and the spirit of the people lends itself to the use of picturesque, imaginative forms.

After the men had groomed their horses and tethered them where there was good forage, they returned to the clearing between the cabins, where the fire was lighted, with the veal on the spits exhaling its appetizing odour. They provided themselves with a bit of *aji de leche* sauce, a few bananas and stewed yuccas, and with this and the roast veal, stood or squatted around the fire and satisfied their temperate appetites, after going all day with no more food than the early morning cup of coffee. And between one mouthful and another they talked of the events of the day's work, exchanged jibes, boasted, and their speech bubbled with the friendly joke and the swift sharp retort, the epigram springing from the picturesque life of the cowboy and guide, the man of hard toil and patient tramping with the lines of a ballad always on the tip of his tongue.

And then, while the watchers by the corrals took their turns going the rounds, singing and whistling continually, for the herd was still restless as it smelled the open air of the prairie and a sudden stampede might have demolished the palisade, the others were finding boisterous amusement in the cabins, with the music of the guitar and the calabash rattle, the *corrido,* which is the popular romance, and the dizaine—poetry coming to birth.

It was usually Pajarote and María Nieves, the latter with the guitar, the former with the rattle, who improvised alternately.

When Christ came into the world
It was on a sorrel jade,
And he went and spoiled his life
Just to catch a calf that strayed.

When Christ came into the world
It was on an August morn;
How glad Christ would be to get at
Custard apples and stewed corn!

And thus, each starting from the other's verse, and with every quatrain the breath of the Plain, springing from the ingenuous and sparkling muse of the man in contact with nature—each leapt in his agile answering lines from the tender to the picaresque, from the amusing to the tragic, without pause or hesitation as long as there were strings on the guitar and seeds in the rattle. For if one's inspiration runs dry, or the right idea does not come quickly, he gets out of the difficulty by borrowing from Florentino, Florentino the Araucan, the great singer of the Plain who expressed everything in verse, and whom even the Devil himself could not vanquish in the contest to see which could improvise the most, one night when he came disguised as a Christian: Florentino's voice was giving out, but his well of inspiration was still running over, and when it was almost time for the cocks to crow, mentioning the Holy Trinity in a stanza, he drove his opponent back into Hell, head over heels with his rattle and everything.

And there were Pajarote's stories.

"That was an ugly light I saw one night when I was on the Meta. We saw lights all of a sudden on the bank, and thinking that they came from houses, we steered close to the land to see if we could find something to eat, because our provisions had run out and we were half dead with hunger. The bank there was a dune, and what do you think the lights were? *Ave Maria Purísima.* Just a thousand snakes rolled into one, wriggling against each other in the sand. It was like when you rub a match on your hand."

"Don't make it too thick, partner," said María Nieves.

"Ah, *caramba!* You've never seen anything, Indian! Go out on those rivers if you want to see strange things. It's just like that story I told you before, of when I was working on the Orinoco, fishing for turtles."

"What was that?" asked one of the new peons.

"*Guá!* Well, a certain day of the year, I don't remember which, an old man went by just at midnight in a long canoe, all by himself and unarmed, and without anybody ever being able to find out who he was or where he came from. Some said it was Our Lord Jesus Christ himself. What I do know is that he stopped on a part of the beach and let out a yell that every turtle in the Orinoco heard, right up to the source 'way beyond the Roraima. That's the signal the turtles wait for, to come out and lay their eggs in the sand. Right there we began to hear the thunder of those millions of shells bumping against each other. And that's the signal you wait for to know when to go out and catch them tame."

And before the listeners laughed, he added, during the short period of credulity:

"And that El Dorado the Spaniards saw? I've seen it too. That brightness you can see from here some nights, over toward the Meta."

"Those are prairie fires, Pajarote."

"No sir, partner Antonio. I tell you positively that's El Dorado that the books you read to us once spoke about. You can see it big and bright over the Meta, like a city of gold."

"This Pajarote has seen everything," said someone, and the others burst out laughing.

"How was it that you saved yourself from being shot, partner?" asked María Nieves.

"That's a good one!" exclaimed those who knew the story. "Tell it, Pajarote, because there are a good many here who've never heard it."

"Well, we'd fallen into the hands of the Government forces, and since we'd given them plenty to do wherever we came across them—and Pajarote got the credit—they put the blame for everybody's doings on me, and made up their minds to shoot me. That happened near the mouth of the Apure; the river is wide there. The men who were watching me went down to the shore, to water the horses. We were all covered with mud up to the nose, and the captain of the company took a notion to bathe, but to stay near the bank, because he wasn't fond of water. My idea came to me, and I said, so he would hear it: 'Ah, Captain, what a man of nerve you are! If I was in your skin I wouldn't be bathing there so quietly, with all the alligators there are in this river.' The man heard me, and just as God is there whenever a man is trying to get out of a scrape, the Captain had an idea too, and not a blessed one, and he asked me: 'You're not a Plainsman, then?' 'Yes, *señor mi Capitán,'* I answered, very tame. 'I'm a Plainsman, but only on horseback, and water's a different thing. Look for me on land, you won't find me in the water, not even on the beach.' He believed me, because God was taking care that it would turn out that way, and to have a good time with me and not have the unpleasant job of shooting me, he ordered them to undo the rope they had me tied with and throw me into the river, and he said to me: 'Come here, friend, so you can wash your feet and not go around dirtying Heaven tomorrow when Saint Peter tells you to come in.' The soldiers started to laugh, and I said to myself: 'You've saved yourself, Pajarote.' And then I went on, playing my part: 'No, *mi Capitán!* Not on your life! I'd rather be shot, if that's what I'm in for, than die eaten by an alligator.' But he yelled at the soldiers: 'Throw this coward in the water!' And they threw me in the river to drown. That was on the other side of the Apure. I did as I'd planned. . . ."

Pajarote left the story hanging, and one of the audience demanded:

"Well, what happened, partner? Is the story going to break off without any end?"

"I swam under water and then stuck my head out on the other side and yelled at them: 'Give me another scare like this, one of these days.' They took I don't know how many shots at me, but who ever catches Pajarote when it's time to say: 'Feet, do your stuff?'"

"And why did you join the rebels?" asked Carmelito.

"Because I was tired of battling with stray cattle, and everybody's strong box was full after all the peace we'd had, and it was time to divide up the coppers."

Pajarote had the Plainsman's individual ideas on the subject of war and the distribution of wealth.

Saturday night. A watch with dancing until daybreak.

The harness-cabin had been emptied, the floor had been swept and sprinkled, and a lantern hung from every notch in the posts. The cracklings were frying, and Casilda had the corn liquor and plum pudding ready. There was, besides, a cask of brandy. Ramón Nolasco, of Las Piñas, the best harpist in the Arauca basin, had already arrived, bringing as singer and rattle-player One-

Eyed Ambrosio, who was, after Florentino, the best improvisor known in the region. The merry cavalcades of girls from Algarrobo Pass and the El Ave Maria and Jobero Pando ranches had come. The benches, placed along the walls of the big cabin, were not sufficient for the number of women.

Marisela did the honours of the house. She came and went here and there, and all had something to say to her, and all said it in a whisper. She laughed and replied:

"But where did you get that idea?"

And so she went from group to group.

"Really and truly?" Genoveva insisted. "Nothing's happened?"

"Nothing. And now less than nothing. He's become very mean these days."

"I can't believe you. As pretty as you are."

"I'll tell you about it."

Now the harpist was tuning up, and Ambrosio had given two or three shakes with his rattle.

"Listen to that, partner!" exclaimed Pajarote. "That man is something else with the seeds."

"And what about the harp? Listen to those treble strings!"

Ramón Nolasco made a sign to the rattle-player. The latter coughed to clear his lungs, spat through his teeth, and announced:

"Here goes 'Chipola.'"

And he burst into song, while the men rushed to the benches to find partners.

Chipolita, put my head
On your breast and let me pet you.
I must do my petting first
Before some other fellow's met you.

and the *joropo* began, with a lively step which made the women's skirts whirl about. Marisela alone remained seated. Santos, the only one who could have chosen her as partner, since the peons would not presume to, had not even come near her. He danced with others, nevertheless.

The treble notes sang over the hoarse booming of the bass, and the swarthy hands of the harpist, as they swept over the strings, were like two black spiders pursuing each other over a web. Little by little, the rhythm quieted down to a sensuous strain, of melancholy cadences. The dancers did not stir from where they stood, marking the beat with swaying bodies. The swishing of the wonderful rattle was followed by breathless pauses, and the singer repeated again and again:

If the Holy Father knew
Of Chipola's flying-skirted
Turns, he'd take his cassock off,
And the Church would be deserted.

the announcement of the "turn" to which the harpist was leading. At the end, the skilful fingers leapt from the treble to the bass, and then back, the dancers gave a cry of satisfaction, and the *joropo* returned to the original measure. The ground shook under the frenzied stamping of the dancers, and the partners, separated in the figure, pursued each other in the confusion, embraced again, and the skirts whirled once more in the final swing of the music.

The women sought the benches, the men the keg of brandy. The drink increased their animation, and Pajarote demanded:

"'The Vulture,' Ramón Nolasco. Now you'll see something good, Doctor. Señora Casilda! Where's Señora Casilda? Come here. You play the dead steer so the folks can see how this buzzard eats his carcass."

"The Vulture," one of the many tunes bearing the name of an animal or bird, is a dance with a pantomime added whenever there is a clown willing to play the fool. The pantomime consists of an imitation, in time with the music, of the grotesque movements of the vulture before he darts upon the feast furnished by the steer lying dead on the prairie. Pajarote was known to be the best dancer of "The Vulture" in the region, and he was greatly aided by his thinness and awkwardness. As for Casilda, who played the part of the carcass, she was the only partner available for the rôle. She was always ready to encourage Pajarote's nonsense, and the two were never at a dance but this music was played for them.

The floor was cleared for them, and the harpist struck up the tune:

Vultures on the marshy ground
By the cork trees of Abajo
Come and see old Nick, *señores*
Starting on a day's *trabajo*.*

Vultures on the marshy ground
By the cork tree of Frío
Pay me for the news, *señores*
Florentino now is *mío*.

This was the ballad of the legendary contest between the Devil and the famous singer of the Arauca.

Standing in the middle of the cabin floor, her body rigid and her eyes closed, Casilda beat time with movements of her shoulders, while Pajarote danced around her with grotesque movements of his arms and leaping steps in imitation of the beating wings and suspicious hopping of the loathsome bird around the carrion.

The spectators laughed to split their sides, but Santos did not enjoy the dance, and said after a while:

"That will do, Pajarote. You've already made us laugh enough."

The harpist changed the tune and the dance went on, Marisela again remaining seated. Santos was listening to Antonio's story of a certain well-known escapade of Pajarote's, and the latter had come up to them, when Marisela suddenly interrupted, asking him:

* Work.

" Will you dance with me, Pajarote? "

" Will a dead man like a Mass? " exclaimed the peon in answer to the question; but catching Antonio's eye, he immediately added:

" That's too much of an honour for me, Marisela, my child."

" Dance," said Santos. " Dance with her."

Marisela bit her lips, and Pajarote swung her in his arms, shouting to the harpist as he passed:

" Take notice of this, Ramón Nolasco, and you shake up those seeds, Ambrosio, and they ought to be gold ones. Here comes Pajarote with the flower of Altamira, though he don't deserve it. Make way, boys, make way! "

X

A PASSION WITHOUT A NAME

"GENOVEVA, if you knew what's happened to me!"

"What, woman of God?"

"Come and hear. There, by the corral fence, where nobody will hear us. Feel my hands. Listen to my heart beating!"

"Ah, I know. He's told you, at last."

"No. Not a word. I swear! It was I told him."

"Woman! the deer running after the dogs?"

"I did it without thinking. Listen. I was very angry with him because he didn't dance with me."

"And you asked Pajarote, to make him jealous. Yes. We all saw it. And afterwards the Doctor took you from Pajarote and danced with you."

"But let me tell it. I was very angry, so angry that there were tears in my eyes. All of a sudden he began to stare at me, and to hide my feelings, so that he wouldn't think I was hurt, I smiled. But not as I wanted to smile. You understand?"

"Yes. I can imagine how you smiled."

"Well then. You know the idea I had then to make things up? To make them worse than ever. I stared at him and said:

"Disagreeable!"

She blushed and added:

"What do you think, girl? Did you ever see anyone so outspoken?"

The exclamation was ingenuous, but another idea had come into Genoveva's mind:

"Well, he is your property, now. Just as grandfather says, 'Inheriting is no stealing.'"

"What's the matter, Genoveva? Do you think I've done wrong?"

"No, dear. I was waiting for you to go on with the story."

"What is left? Do you think it was so little? Wouldn't that one word tell him everything?"

"And will he understand it that way?"

"Well, let me tell you, he got out of step dancing, with all his fine sense of time! He didn't answer a word, he didn't look me in the eye again. . . . That is, I don't know if he looked at me again, because after that I didn't dare to raise my own eyes any more."

Genoveva became pensive again. Marisela was silent too, while her gaze sank into the clear distances of the savannah sleeping in the radiance of the moon. Suddenly she clapped her hands together and exclaimed:

" It told him! It told him everything! "

" And now, Marisela? " Genoveva asked.

" What, now? " Marisela responded, as though she had not understood, and then immediately: " But, my dear! What could I do? Put yourself in my place. All day I've been dreaming about this dance, thinking: 'He'll speak today.' Besides, I tell you, it came out without my wanting it. You yourself are to blame, because every time we've met you've asked me: 'Hasn't he told you yet?' And last of all, you're jealous of me, aren't you? "

" No, Marisela. I'm thinking of you."

Pajarote, who came in search of Genoveva, for they were beginning the dance he was to have with her, interrupted these confidences. Marisela remained in her place, waiting for someone to come and ask her to dance too, but as no one came, she stood thinking of Genoveva's words and of her situation.

" And now, Marisela? " she thought, " do you think everything can go on as it was, after what's happened? Do you think you've cleared up the situation by telling him that he was disagreeable? Don't you see that, on the contrary, you've made it more complicated than ever? How will you appear to Santos tomorrow, if he doesn't come to you this very night to tell you that he loves you?

" He isn't coming. He won't come all night. And all for not knowing how to hide what you feel. Just imagine what he'll have thought of you. He's so . . . disagreeable! "

She imagined a long conversation with Santos in which he reproached her for dancing with Pajarote.

"They say that moonlight on the Plain upsets the brain," he seemed to say.

"There you are. Mine is perfectly all right," she replied.

"Nevertheless, this business of falling in love with Pajarote, just like that, without reflecting, is nothing but madness. Pajarote is all very well in his place, but as a sweetheart for you . . ."

"*Guá!* And why not, then? Wasn't I just an animal from the woods when you picked me up? 'Whoever your father is, your mother is good enough for him.'"

"I knew this would be a night for '*Guás!*' and vulgar sayings, but anyone can see a mile away that you're saying them on purpose. So if you want to fool me, think up something more clever."

"And why didn't you think up something more clever, too, instead of that about my being in love with Pajarote? Now it's my turn to laugh."

He stood looking at her. Then he asked:

"Have you finished laughing?"

"For the moment, yes. Say something else, one of those clever things that come into your head, and see if I want to again. Say, for instance, that you came to stand here, by the palisade, to think about one of the *friends* you left in Caracas, who wasn't a friend at all really, but your sweetheart."

"Well, if you're going to laugh at me . . ."

"Even though you don't say anything. I'm laughing again now. Don't you hear me?"

"Go ahead, go ahead. I like your laugh."

"Then I'll be serious again. I'm not anybody's monkey."

"I'm coming up closer to you, and I'm going to ask you: Do you love me, Marisela?"

"I adore you, Disagreeable!"

But this took place only in Marisela's imagination. Perhaps it would really have happened, had Santos come out to the palisade, but he didn't come anywhere near there.

"But who said it was necessary for him to declare himself to me? Can't I go on loving him on my own account? And why must the affection I feel for him be called love? Affection? . . . No, Marisela. The whole world can feel affection, and for many people at one time. Adoration? . . . But what reason is there why everything must have a name?"

And the difficulty was thus cleared up in the complex simplicity of her spirit. As far as that went, Marisela's love might well be something equally removed from the simple and material side of desire, as from the simple and spiritual side of worship. Life, bending it from one side to the other, would determine its future form; but at that point of balance between reality and dreams, it was still a passion without a name.

XI

IMAGINARY SOLUTIONS

THE strange thing was, that imaginary solutions occurred to Santos Luzardo, too.

With the cold impartiality he assumed in analysing his feelings and the difficult situations depending on them, he stated the problem, seating himself at his desk, clearing it of the turmoil of papers and books, putting them in order one above the other, or separating them, as though it were a matter of analysing law books and the accounts of the ranch and determining their status. Fingering first this one and then that one, as if he found it necessary to objectify and convert into concrete things the feelings he needed to reflect upon, he said, looking at the paper he held in his left hand:

" That Marisela has fallen in love with me is evident, and I hope my vanity will be forgiven. It was logical that it should happen. 'The age, the opportunity . . .' She is pretty, a perfect type of creole beauty, pleasant, spiritually interesting, a pleasant companion, and no doubt a useful one for a man who has to live indefinitely this life of solitude and struggle among peons and cattle. She is industrious, courageous when it comes to facing difficult situations. . . . But this cannot be! "

He moved his hand over the paper before him as if to erase what was written on it. Then, settling his right hand a bit more on the books:

" There is nothing here but a friendly feeling, a very natural one, and the disinterested wish to save a poor girl condemned to a sad fate. Perhaps, at most, I feel the purely spiritual necessity of a woman's companionship. But if this is going to give rise later to sentimental complications, the prudent thing is to find a remedy immediately."

He withdrew his hands from the books and papers, and leaning back in his chair, with his head thrown back, he continued his soliloquy:

" Marisela ought not to stay here in my house any longer. It's clear that she can't go back to the house in the palm grove, even for a moment. That would be turning her over to Señor Danger. I wonder if those two old aunts of mine in San Fernando would consent to take her in? Marisela would be very useful to them, and they would do her a great favour in turn. They would finish her education, complete the work I have begun, with those touches only a woman's hand can give to a woman's soul — that gentleness she lacks, that depth of soul I have never been able to reach. As for Lorenzo, it's evident that I'm not going to ask my aunts to take him in too.

He'll stay here, with me. Now that I've brought him up to where he is, I'll have to take charge of him until the end. And that's not very far distant. That's another reason for finding a solution to the problem of Marisela. As long as Lorenzo is alive, even if he's shut up in that room he never wants to leave now, not even to sit down to meals, Marisela's residence with me is justifiable, but with her father dead, the aspect of things will change. Besides, Marisela will be an impediment which won't allow me to dispose freely of my life. If I should make up my mind, for instance, as I have before and may again at times, to return to Caracas or go to Europe, what shall I do with Marisela? To leave her uncared-for would be inhuman. To a certain degree, I have assumed a moral duty in undertaking her education; I've changed the destiny of a soul. She was the prey Danger had already picked out for himself, and she was on the way to follow in her mother's footsteps. Shall I say to her now, 'Turn around, go on the way you were going'?"

He lighted a cigarette. It was pleasant to think while he was watching the smoke vanish into air, especially since his thoughts were vanishing as soon as they were formulated.

"No. The only solution is having my aunts agree to take Marisela. But first of all I'll have to prepare the ground, in person, because to write them would be time lost. I can imagine how they would exclaim when they finished reading the letter: 'A daughter of The Evil-Eyed Woman in this house!' I'll have to explain the situation to them and persuade them that they can take her in without scruples of conscience or fear of witchcraft."

He threw away the cigarette whose smoke had suddenly become bitter, and began in an absent-minded way to arrange the papers so that none would project unevenly from the others, while he said aloud:

"But I must wait until the herding is finished to go to San Fernando. Now I can't move from here. Meanwhile, if they can repair the cottage at El Bruscal, Lorenzo and his daughter could live there."

He called:

"Antonio!"

"Antonio is not here," responded Marisela from near by. And, strangely, the problem suddenly disappeared, or at least the pressing need of solving it immediately. Perhaps, after what he had discovered the night before, when he asked Marisela to dance with him, things had really changed? Did not the very ingenuousness of that silent confession of love she had made give her love a special character, a certain transparency of childish sentiment, before which his scruples looked out of all proportion?

Perhaps, too, the clear voice that had answered him from in there made him think, involuntarily, of days to come when the house would be lonely and silent. Whatever it was, one or the other, or both at once, it was certain that Santos concluded his reflections with these thoughts:

"Come, old fellow! It's all right to busy yourself with finding a solution of the problem, but not in such a hurry. A little more and I'll be as proper as my aunts. What disadvantage is there in having Marisela live under the same roof with me, near or distant, as she's been doing? It adds a certain charm to life — an affection demanding no more than the mutual consciousness of its existence, without changing things or being changed by them either. Something sufficient unto itself, that doesn't need to be converted into words or actions. Something like the gold coins of a miser, who is perhaps the most idealistic of all men. A wealth that is all a dream, the certainty that disillusion will never be bought with it."

But in reality, when one hasn't a simple soul, like Marisela's, or a too complicated one, which Luzardo's was not, solutions always have to be positive ones. If they are not, it happens as it happened to him — he lost control of his emotions, and became the plaything of contradictory impulses.

Marisela, near or far? always nearer, to such a degree that there was no way of being in the house without being conscious of her presence. Was she in the kitchen, preparing his meals as he liked them? Her voice could be heard from there, or her laugh, or the song she was singing. Was the house quiet? Wherever he looked, he was almost certain to see a flower, placed there by her. If he went to sit down, he had to remove the book or work she had left on the chair. Let him look for something, he would find it right there, because everything was in its place and within arm's reach. Let him come in, and he could count on meeting her in the doorway, for she would be going out at that moment. If he were on his way out, he would have to move to one side or step back to permit her to pass. Did he want to take his siesta? Not even the swarming of the flies would bother him, for Marisela had declared such a war upon them that they did not dare to enter the house, and while he was sleeping, she would be going around, on tiptoe, and biting her tongue to keep from singing. But when he no longer wanted silence, she would burst out singing, like the prairie larks with their silver throats, or she would talk aloud to herself of what she was doing, and he would not have to see her to know what she was about.

"Now I'll get to my mending. Now I'll sweep the hall. Now I'll water the plants. Now I'll study my lessons."

But for this very reason, it was to his advantage to put distance between them, and forgetting his project of taking Marisela to his aunts' house, Santos began the following conversation one day when they were at table:

"Well, Lorenzo. Marisela has already acquired the necessary foundation for an education, and I think it would be best to send her to an academy. There are good schools for young ladies in Caracas, and I think we ought to send her to one without delay."

"What shall I pay her board and tuition with?" Lorenzo inquired.

"I'll take care of that. What I want is your permission to go ahead."

"Do whatever you think best."

Meanwhile, Marisela was biting her lips and was about to get up from the table in annoyance when "her idea" came to her. She went on eating quietly, and Santos thought that she too consented to his plan.

But when he returned to the house that same afternoon, he found over the door a piece of paper on which Marisela had written:

SCHOOL FOR YOUNG LADIES. THE BEST IN THE REPUBLIC.

He laughed heartily at the incident, took down the piece of paper, and never spoke of that subject again.

They were alone at table. Certainly it was much pleasanter thus, without the repugnant presence of old Lorenzo. She was serving him, and stimulating his appetite by saying to him:

"This is very good; you'll like it."

She poured his glass of water without giving him time to do it for himself, and meanwhile she prattled,

prattled without any respite. Her voice was agreeable, her laugh delicious, her conversation picturesque, her movements and manners graceful; and there was such animation and sparkle in her eyes!

"Child, you've got me bound hand and foot."

"But you may talk too, man of God."

"At the same time as you? Really, I'll have to resign myself to doing that."

"Exaggerator! This morning, at breakfast, it was you who talked all by yourself."

"But that's not the same thing, because you were thinking of something else. I could catch you in a trap if I asked you what I said to you."

"How nice of you! So you can't repeat what I have said, either?"

"That's true. Not because I haven't paid attention to you, but because it's impossible to follow you. You simply leap from one subject to another."

"Then everything a person says must be a discourse?"

"That would be boring. As I was this morning."

"I didn't mean that; everyone has his own way of thinking, and he speaks as he thinks. You can talk for two hours straight and run on like a drizzle."

"Thanks for the comparison. You didn't say I was boring."

"It isn't that, *señor*. I meant that you change the subject without knowing that you're doing it. My way is different."

"Yes. Your conversation could be compared to a series of heavy showers, one after the other. But showers with sunshine in between."

"The Devil fighting with his wife? But we don't fight." She blushed and burst into a laugh. "What have I said?"

Santos smiled as he looked at her. "I'm not the Devil —"

But she did not let him finish.

"*Sabe?*"

"What?"

"I've already forgotten what I was going to tell you."

And as Santos continued to look at her, she exclaimed:

"Oh, yes!" but immediately she pretended to forget again, a pure piece of fiction.

Santos mimicked her:

"Ah, no!"

How pretty she was becoming! More so every day!

Nevertheless, he suddenly became engulfed in one of those discourses deliberately founded upon abstruse themes for the purpose of boring her or interesting her intellectually, either being an antidote for love. But she was not bored, though it could not interest her in any way. While he talked, she did not take her eyes off him, but meanwhile, she continued to think of whatever came into her mind. When he least expected it, she interrupted him with:

"You know, that doe you gave me? She wasn't very good. She's going to have fawns."

Santos made some answer and went on eating in silence; but, suddenly, he burst out laughing. She could not find any explanation for his hilarity, and gazed at him in surprise. Finally she caught the meaning and her cheeks reddened, while she hurriedly sought something to make him think of another subject; but the only thing that came to her lips was laughter, and there was no way in which Santos could succeed in putting another face on the matter, for the minute he commenced to say anything, she burst out laughing again, and he ended by imitating her.

But Marisela's significant laugh had been a thing as transparent as her innocent remark, as far removed from right and wrong as the doe's misconduct. She was naturalness itself, without either good or evil, but the man of the city could not so accept her.

There were, on one hand, the reflections which anyone else, gifted with a moderately good judgment, would have made: Marisela, offspring of an illegitimate union and possibly inheritor of the regrettable qualities of both father and mother, could not be the woman in whom a judicious man would centre his love—and on the other hand, the inevitable reflections of a Santos Luzardo. Simple as nature herself, but at times disquieting too, like all monstrosities of nature, Marisela seemed to have the springs of tenderness sealed up in her heart.

Happy, gay, and expansive as she was, he had never seen a gesture of filial love in her relations with her father. She usually showed herself indifferent to his sufferings, or at most, when she came near Lorenzo, she made some playful remark in baby talk, but without any real tenderness showing through the words.

"This girl has no heart," Santos often said to himself. "She may not have the bitter cruelty of her mother, but she has the playful cruelty of a cub, and from one to the other, with a little intervention of circumstance, there's only a step. Perhaps it's lack of proper education, something that only a woman can give her."

But he was obliged to confess to himself that these pessimistic reflections displeased him. He found them too severe, too savage, and somewhat cruel to himself. It was a grateful change for him, disregarding reason, to give the poet in his heart a chance and repeat the metaphor of the miser's gold.

XII

SONG AND STORY

BUT with all this, the imaginary solutions had done nothing but make the problem more complicated, and life in his house had become unbearable for Santos.

Fortunately, there was still much to be done outside of it. Herding finished, the branding began. The clamour of the *desmontrencaje,* that is, the separation of cows and yearlings in two adjacent corrals, commenced at daybreak. The cows mooed, the calves gave pitiful cries, as though they foresaw the torture prepared for them. Pajarote's iron was already red-hot; he announced it with a line from a ballad and the peons began to hobble the animals. They threw them to earth, notched their ears with the mark of the ranch, and stood on the calves' heads to keep them still while Pajarote applied the hot iron to their flanks, dedicating to each a stanza in accordance with their colour and markings — reminding them of their particular pastures, the division of the herd to which they belonged, the round-up they came in;

the history of each beast, as well-known to the Plainsman as his own.

With each application of the brand he made a mark with the point of his knife on the piece of leather where the reckoning was kept, for everything in Altamira was still done as it had been in the days of Don Evaristo.

Reflecting upon this, Luzardo said to himself that it was high time to put into practice his projects for reforming the Plain, to play his rôle of civilizer.

When the branding, occupying several days in succession, was over, Antonio said to him, showing him the brander's tally:

"The business has turned out better than we hoped. Three thousand yearlings and over six hundred unmarked strays. Now we can get to work on the dairies."

This required scarcely more than erecting a certain number of posts beside Bramador Creek, covering them with a thatch of straw from the savannahs, making, out of a steer's hide, the vessel used to churn the milk, and, out of woven palm leaves, the presses for moulding the cheese; then they strengthened the palisades of some abandoned corrals, placed a number of domesticated cows in the enclosure with some wild ones captured in the rodeo at Mato Oscura, and turned everything over to the care of old Remigio, a Guarican dairyman who had arrived to look for work in company with his grandson, Jesusito.

When Santos saw how rudimentary was the undertaking in the "house on stilts" isolated in the open prairie, in the same place where the very same sort of building, dedicated to the same use, had existed twenty-odd years before, and when he realized that everything in the dairy was going to be done with the ancient routine of a primitive industry, he was ashamed of himself. Was this, then, the way Altamira was going to be converted into a "modern establishment"—his own words when he decided to devote himself to the management of the ranch—"equipped with all the improvements of the cattle industry in civilized countries"?

"This is the way dairies are managed here," replied Antonio. "With the things the Plain itself furnishes—posts of *caramacate* or *macanilla* wood, palm leaves, and steer's hide."

"And the routine of centuries," added Santos. "It's a miracle that herding has lasted, because that was an innovation, introduced by the Spanish settlers. It's a hard thing to say, but the Plainsmen have done nothing to improve the industry. Their ideal is to change everything that comes into their hands into money, put it in a pitcher, and bury it. That's what my forefathers did, and that's what I'll do too, because this land is a grindstone that dulls the edge of the hardest-tempered will. It's the same with this business of the dairy; we'll begin just where we were twenty years ago. And in the meantime, the breed is degenerating from lack of crossing, and the plagues that kill a tenth of the herds. They still pretend to cure worms with prayers, and since there are magicians in plenty and even the intelligent people end up by believing in them, no remedy is found."

"That must be just as you say, Doctor," Antonio answered. "But now that you mention crossing, try crossbreeding the herds (and I've heard that that's necessary, ever since I was a little fellow). In the end the revolutionists will eat them. Leave it a pure domestic breed, Doctor, because the minute the meat gets a little better, there'll be more revolutions, and other things that aren't war, but look a good deal like it—the authorities, for instance, that want everything for themselves."

"Those are all fallacies," Santos replied. "Rationalizations of the laziness of the Indian that we all have in our blood. These are all just the reasons why the Plain must be civilized, and why we've got to get rid of quackery and the caciques and put an end to crossing our arms in the face of nature and man."

"There'll be time for everything," said Antonio. "The dairy, just as it is, will give results. We'll get enough out of it if we only tame the herd. The whole thing is to break in the cattle quick."

The Guarican Remigio was a man of long experience in managing this sort of establishment, but to break in for dairying a herd as wild as that at Altamira was an arduous task.

"Maravilla. Maravilla. Maravilla. Punto Negro. Punto

Negro. Punto Negro," he would say all day long, stroking the wild cows tied to the posts, without ceasing to call them by their newly-found names, so that they might get used to hearing them.

And every time he or Jesusito passed any one of them, in the corrals or in the pasture, they would call its name.

"Botón de Oro. Botón de Oro. Botón de Oro."

Soon some of the cows began to know their names. It showed in the gentleness of their gaze when he called; but the greater part of the flock showed nothing but pure wildness in their bloodshot eyes.

And while the civilizing of the herd's barbarity was going on in the dairy, the lassos never ceased to whirl among the strays. The clumps of wild mint shook under the trampling of the herds surprised by the attack of the cowboys, but sometimes the beasts would become angry and turn upon the horses, and then, despite the skill of the horsemen, many horses would be killed in the encounter, or fall stunned by the pain of a fearful thrust from a steer. Many of the bulls, too, died of sheer apoplectic rage at finding themselves mastered by men, or succumbed to the misery of castration, rushing into the thickets to await death by hunger and thirst, and giving muffled roars as they thought of their lost rulership of the wild herd, and of the free, savage life of their mates in the inaccessible clumps of mint.

Santos shared the danger of these attacks with his men, and his intense emotion made him once more forgetful of his projects. The Plain was good thus, rude and wild. It was barbarism, but since the life of one man was not sufficient to put an end to it, why should he waste his in struggling against the past? After all, he said to himself, barbarism has its enchantment, is something beautiful and worth the trouble of living, in its fullness and intolerance of all limitation.

María Nieves was doing a giant's work at his task of leading the herd across the fords of the wide streams where death lay in hiding; exposing himself to the deadly teeth of the alligators, with nothing but a goad in his hand and a song on his lips.

The corrals at Algarrobo Pass were full. A part of the herd was to be taken over the Arauca, and the horsemen were already in place along the barriers to defend them against the assault of the trampling cattle. María Nieves was now in readiness to lead them across to the other side, to guide them swimming. He was the best "waterman" in the Apure country and was never so happy as when he was in the stream up to his neck, with the scarcely visible horns of the flocks behind him as he guided them across the ford and on, far over there on the other bank, for the river was wide.

Already in the water, riding his horse bareback, he carried on a shouted conversation with the canoers who paddled by the side of the herd to keep it from scattering downstream. The shouting of the peons driving the cattle could be heard in the corrals. Now the steers were coming down the barrier, with the troop of greenhorns behind them. María Nieves burst into song and jumped into the water, for his horse would just serve him as a buoy to be held with his left hand while he swung the right, grasping the goad to defend himself from the alligators. Then the trained leaders flung themselves in and commenced to swim, with their horns and noses barely above water.

"Hold on! Hold on!" the cowboys shouted. The horses shoved and the steers tumbled into the river; they roared in fright, and some tried to turn around, while others were borne away by the current, but the men on the bank and the boatmen in the canoes in mid-stream held them back and forced them into line. A tangle of horns indicated the oblique path of the ford, with María Nieves' head in the lead, next to that of his horse. His song could be heard from the middle of the wide river, in whose muddy waters were lurking the treacherous alligator, the electric eel, the ray, and voracious schools of caribs, with the vultures hovering overhead.

At last the herd reached the opposite bank, hundreds of meters away. One by one the steers were dragging themselves out of the water, giving piteous cries. They stood dejectedly on the bank, huddled together, while the guide went back into the river to fetch another lot.

The corrals at the Pass had been emptied, and on the other side of the Arauca, on a dismal, dry bank, under a sky the colour of slate, rose the mournful wailing of hundreds of jostling cattle—to be taken to Caracas, across leagues and leagues of flooded savannah, step by step, to the tune of the drivers' songs.

> Come, come, my little bulls
> Follow in your leader's tracks,
> Count your steps to where the butcher's
> Waiting for you with the axe.

As many more had been sent in a different direction towards the Cordilleras, as if it were the heyday of the old Luzardos, when Altamira was the richest ranch in the Arauca basin.

This was the beautiful and vigorous life of the wide streams and vast savannahs, where man always goes singing in the face of danger; the Epic itself, the Plain under its most imposing aspect: the winter demanding the last bit of patience and daring, the floods making the risks a hundredfold greater, and making the immensity of the desert all the more apparent from the stretches of high land above the sea of water; but also accenting the immensity of man's stature and the powers in attendance upon him, when, unable to hope for anything from anyone, he resolves to confront what may come.

It rained, and rained, and rained. For days nothing else happened. The cattlemen who had been outside their houses had returned to them, for the creeks and streams would overflow into the prairie and there would soon be no negotiable path. Nor any need to travel one. It was time for "quid, cup, and hammock," and beneath his palm thatch with these three things, the Plainsman is happy, while out of doors the clouds are falling in an endless pouring rain.

The return of the wild herons began with the first days of rain. They appeared in the south — whence they migrate in the winter, though no one knows where they go — and the numberless flocks were still arriving. Wearied by their long flight, they rested, swaying on the flexible branches of the forest trees, or, being thirsty, flew to the rim of the marsh, so that the woods and waters were covered with white. They seemed to recognize each other, and to exchange impressions of their journey; herons of one flock greeted those of another returned from some distant land, stretched out their necks, flapped their wings, gave their shrill cries, and then stood still looking at each other, their agate eyes round and immovable. At times there would be a scuffle for a branch of the roosting-tree, or the remains of a nest built the year before.

The wild ducks, the scarlet flamingos, the blue herons, the *cotuas,* the *gavanes* and the wild blue chickens, none of whom had migrated, flew up to greet the travellers, in other numberless flocks coming from the four corners of the sky. The cranes had also returned, and were telling of their voyage.

The marsh was full to overflowing, for the winter had set in with a will. One day the black snout of a crocodile rose to the surface, and soon there would be alligators too, for the creeks were rapidly filling and they could travel all over the prairie. The alligators came from far away, many of them from the Orinoco; but they tell nothing of their journeys, for they pass the entire day sleeping or pretending to be asleep. And it was a good thing they were silent, for they could have related nothing but crimes.

The moulting commenced. The home of the herons was a snowy forest. In the trees, in the nests built in them, and around the pools, was the whiteness of thousands and thousands of the herons; while on every side, in the branches, in the shoals floating over the muddy water of the swamp, lay the white frost of feathers shed during the night.

At dawn the collecting began. The pickers start out in canoes, but end up by jumping into the water; up to their waists in it, they defy death in a dozen hidden forms, shouting and singing, for the Plainsman never works in silence. If he does not yell, he sings.

Rain, rain, rain! The creeks had overflowed and the pools were full. The human beings began to fall ill, stricken by malaria, shivering with cold, their teeth chattering. They became pale, and then green, and crosses began to spring up in the Altamira cemetery, which was no more than a small rectangular plot with a barb wire fence in the middle of the prairie, for the Plainsman, even after death, is content if he may lie in the midst of his plains.

But the rivers commenced to go down at last, and the ponds on the river banks to dry up; the alligators began to abandon the creeks, some for the Arauca, some for the Orinoco, from wherever they had come, to gorge themselves on the Altamira cattle. The fever was dying out, and the guitars and rattles, the ballads and stories could be heard once more; the wild, merry soul of the Plainsman singing his loves and his work and his trickery.

"Where does the Plainsman get the strength, when he's so anaemic?" asked Santos. "He stands a whole day's hard work on horseback, riding after cattle, or in water up to his waist. And his bright spirits, so that he can show a good face in bad times?"

"I'll explain that, Doctor," said Antonio Sandoval, "from the moral of the story I'm going to tell you. An old fellow from the Cunaviche came here one day, looking for work. He offered himself as a specialist in roping strays, no less, and he came badly mounted. I tell you the old plug could hardly stand, with the best will in the world, and the harness was rubbish. I looked him over and said: 'All right friend, I can offer you a horse, one of those bronchos running wild over the prairie. Set your eye on the one you like best and train him for the saddle, but you'll have to worry about the rest yourself.' 'I've got everything,' says the man, putting his hand on his rubbish. 'The stirrup buckle is missing, and the saddle bag's lost, and they swiped my saddle-bow. I don't know what happened to the cinch, but I've got the sweat blanket.'" Antonio concluded, sententiously: "That's how the man answered me, and who do you suppose he was — Pajarote. All he had left whole was the sweat-cloth, and he said he had everything. So fit the story to the case. That's the will to go to work. That's where the Plainsman's strength comes from."

And so it seemed to Luzardo. There was the lowly, brutish tobacco-planter on the little strip of land he planted; and the light-hearted, swaggering herdsmen in the midst of the wide prairie, sharing the morsel of meat and bit of yucca their frugality demanded, treating themselves only with a cup of coffee and a quid of tobacco, resigned to the hammock and poncho as long as their horses were fine and their harness handsome, plucking the banjo, strumming the guitar, singing at the top of their lungs at night when the rude toil of starting and pursuing the herd was over, and dancing the *joropo* wildly until dawn in houses where there were girls whose attractions deserved the spicy quatrain:

In the tale of a bull, it's the curve of the horn,
In the tale of a horse, it's the speed,
But in telling of girls who are pretty,
It's the *girth* and the *croupe* that you need.

Luzardo saw that the Plainsman was indomitable and yet worsted in the contest with life, lazy yet indefatigable; impulsive yet calculating in strife, undisciplined yet loyally obedient to his superiors. With his friends he was suspicious and self-denying, with women, voluptuous and harsh, with himself, both sensual and sober; and in his conversations, both malicious and ingenuous, incredulous and superstitious — in every case merry, yet melancholy, a realist and yet imaginative; humble afoot, proud on horseback — all these at once, without any clash, like the virtues and faults in a newborn soul.

Something of this shines through the ballads in which the singer of the Plain combines the boastful jollity of the Andalusian, the smiling fatalism of the negro, the stubborn melancholy of the Indian — all the peculiar features of the souls that have gone to make his. And what was not clear to Luzardo, or what he had forgotten, he learned from the tales he heard his peons tell while he was sharing with them their hard work and boisterous leisure.

So, from these things, and because his faculties were open to the vigour, beauty, and pain of the prairieland, he was invaded by the desire to love it as it was, barbarous but lovely, and to surrender to the Plain, let himself be moulded by it, abandoning his constant vigilance to adopt the simple rude life of the savannahs.

Certain it is that not a single colt is broken nor a bull lassoed and thrown with impunity; whoever has seen it through belongs from then on to the Plain. Yet, in Santos's case, the Plain had done no more than recover him. Antonio Sandoval had said it: A Plainsman will be a Plainsman for five generations. But there was something else too, something not included in his reflections, but in his soul, nevertheless, changing the feelings of this civilized man, overcoming all obstacles: there was Marisela, who seemed the spirit of the Plain, of its ingenuous, restless soul, wild as the *paraguatán* flower that perfumes the thicket and sweetens the honey of the wild bees.

XIII

THE EVIL-EYE AND HER SHADOW

TOWARDS nightfall, as she was going to the kitchen to prepare supper for Santos, who was already entering, Marisela heard what Eufrasia, the Indian woman, was saying to Casilda.

"Why should Juan Primito insist on finding out exactly how tall the *señor* is? Who could it interest, unless it's Doña Barbara. Everybody says she's in love with the master."

"And you believe there's something in it, sister?" Casilda inquired.

"I should say I do believe it. Don't you think I've seen proof of it? The woman that ties a man's length around her waist can do what she likes with him. That Indian, Justina, tied Dominguito's length around her waist, and made a fool of him; Dominguito who came from Chicuacal. She measured him with a piece of cord, and tied it to her girdle. And that was the end of Dominguito!"

"Woman!" exclaimed Casilda, "and if you believe that, why didn't you tell the Doctor not to let Juan Primito measure him?"

"I did think of it, but since the Doctor won't believe in these things and was so much amused over the booby's antics, I didn't dare say anything. My idea was to take the string away from Juan Primito, but he threw dust in my eyes, as they say, and when I went to look for him, I couldn't even see the dust. He must be way off now, although that was just a little while ago. When he gets going, nobody can follow him."

This was the most ordinary and primitive practice of witchcraft conceivable, but Marisela felt herself grow tense when she heard about it. In spite of the persistent pains Santos had taken to combat her belief in these frauds, and although she herself declared that she didn't give any credit to them, superstition was deeply seated in her soul. Besides, the words of the kitchen maids, which she had heard with bated breath and with her heart ready to leap out of her breast, had changed into certainty the horrible suspicions that had often crossed her mind: Her mother was in love with the man *she* loved.

She choked back the exclamation of horror that was about to escape her, clapping a trembling hand to her mouth, and forgot her purpose in coming to the kitchen. She crossed the patio towards the house, turned, retraced her steps, and went back again, as though the horrible ideas in her head, rejected by her conscience, were changing themselves into involuntary movements.

At that moment she saw Pajarote coming. She went out to meet him, and asked:

" Haven't you seen Juan Primito on your way in? "

" I passed him on the other side of the cork-trees. He must be near El Miedo now, because he was going like the devil with a soul in his bag."

She thought a moment, and then said:

" I've got to ride right now to El Miedo. Will you go with me? "

" And the Doctor? " Pajarote objected. " Isn't he here? "

" Yes. He's in the house. But he mustn't know about it. I'm going in secret. Saddle Catira for me, without letting anybody know about it."

" But, Marisela, my child — " Pajarote demurred.

" No. That's no use, Pajarote. Don't lose your time trying to make me give up the idea. I've got to go to El Miedo right now. If you're afraid — "

" Don't say any more. Wait for me behind the banana tree; there no one will see you going."

Pajarote decided that something very important was in the wind, and because of this and because Marisela had said, " If you're afraid," he made up his mind to go with her without any more question. No one had yet been born who could say: " Pajarote doesn't dare to do this."

Hidden by the banana tree, they rode away from the house unperceived, as night was coming on. The desire to avoid seeing her mother face to face made Marisela ask:

"Do you think, if we hurry, we might catch up with Juan Primito before he gets there?"

"We won't catch up with him even if we ruin the horses," answered Pajarote. "With the start he has, and the length of his stride, if he isn't there yet he's pretty near to it."

As a matter of fact, Juan Primito was at that moment arriving at El Miedo. He found Doña Barbara at the table, alone, for it had been some days since Balbino Paiba had allowed himself to be seen there, fearing, as he did, that his presence would provoke the rupture that was imminent.

"Here's what you sent me for," said Juan, taking the roll of string from his pocket and putting it on the table. "It's not a hair's breadth long or short." And he told her how he had contrived to take Luzardo's measurement.

"Good," said Doña Barbara. "You may go. Get anything you want from the commissary."

She remained seated in thoughtful contemplation of that bit of greasy cord which held something of Luzardo and was to bring him to her arms, according to one of her most deeply-rooted convictions. Desire had changed into passion, and since the longed-for man who was to give himself up to her "with eager steps" was not directing them towards her, the grim determination to secure possession of him through sorcery had risen from the turbid depths of her superstitious, witchcraft-ridden soul.

In the meantime, Marisela had neared the house. At last breaking the silence of the journey, she said to Pajarote:

"I've got to talk to — my mother. I'll go into the house alone. You wait out here, a little distance away, so that if I find myself in trouble, you'll hear me call you."

They stopped behind a group of protecting trees. Marisela dismounted and went resolutely forward, along the fence of the sheepfold. For an instant, her determination weakened as she entered the gallery of the house she was visiting for the first time. Her heart seemed to be paralysed, and her knees trembled. She was on the point of giving the cry agreed upon with Pajarote; but she was already on the threshold of the room, a combined living and dining-room.

Doña Barbara had just risen from the table and gone into the next room when Marisela put her head in the door. She took one step, another, and then another, silently, looking behind her. The beating of her heart made the blood pound in her temples, but she was no longer afraid.

In the little room she used for her magic, before the shelf full of holy pictures and rude amulets on which a lamp, just lighted, was burning, Doña Barbara stood gazing at the cord while she mumbled the incantation:

"With two I gaze upon thee, with three I bind thee: With The Father, Son, and Holy Ghost. Man! I shall see thee before me, more humble than Christ before Pilate." And untying the roll of cord, she prepared to wind the string around her waist, when it was suddenly snatched out of her hands. She turned swiftly and stood there, petrified with surprise.

It was the first time mother and daughter had met face to face since Lorenzo Barquero had been obliged to leave the house. Doña Barbara well knew that Marisela had become quite another person since she had been living at Altamira; but her surprise at the girl's unexpected appearance united with the effect produced on her by her daughter's beauty, and she was for a moment unable to fling herself upon Marisela. She was about to do it, as soon as the moment of disconcerting surprise had passed, when Marisela swung around to prevent her, seizing the cord, exclaiming:

"Witch!"

The conflict in Doña Barbara's heart, when she heard from her own daughter the insulting epithet no one had ever dared pronounce in her presence, was like the collision of two masses hurtling together and falling shattered in ruins. The consciousness of wickedness and ardent desire, what she was and what she wanted to be, so that Luzardo would love her, crashed, in a formless confusion of primitive emotion. Marisela, meanwhile, had darted to the shelf and had swept to the floor, with a single movement of her arm, all the horrible confusion of holy pictures, Indian fetiches and amulets resting on it, the taper burning before the image and the chimney of the little lamp. She was shrieking,

"Witch! Witch!"

Doña Barbara, infuriated, seized the girl and tried to take the cord away from her. Marisela resisted, struggling in the grasp of the powerful, man-like hands that were tearing her blouse, baring her virginal breast, as they fought; when suddenly a vigorous, calm voice ordered:

"Let her go!"

It was Santos Luzardo who had just appeared on the threshold.

Doña Barbara obeyed, and tried, with a superhuman effort at dissimulation, to transform her sinister expression into one of affability. But instead of a smile, there appeared on her face a hideous, forlorn grimace at the failure of her attempt.

So profound was her spiritual upheaval that she could not even converse with the "Partner" that night.

She had picked up from the floor and put back into place on the shelf the holy pictures, clumsy fetiches, and amulets, flung down by the sweep of Marisela's arm. The votive taper was once more burning, but with a continual crackling caused by the mixture of oil and water seeping up through the wick and with a flickering flame, although not the slightest breath of air moved in the tightly closed chamber. Several times had she formulated the words at which the familiar demon had always shown such obedience, but he did not come quickly, for, as in the wick of the votive lamp, there were irreconcilables mingled in the thought summoning him.

"Be calm!" she admonished herself mentally. "Be calm!" And immediately she had the impression of hearing a phrase she herself had not succeeded in pronouncing:

"Everything returns whence it came."

These were the words she had thought of saying to quiet her agitation; but the "Partner" had wrested them from her lips and spoken them with that intonation, at once strange and familiar, of her own voice changed into an echo.

Doña Barbara raised her eyes and saw that the black silhouette of the "Partner," flung on the wall by the fluttering light of the votive lamp, was now in the place formerly occupied by her shadow. As was usual, she could not distinguish his face, but she *felt* it contracted in that hideous and forlorn grimace of a frustrated attempt to smile.

Convinced that she had heard the words proceeding from that phantasm, she again formulated, now as a question, the phrase which, tranquillizing when she had thought of it, had become cabalistic when pronounced by the apparition.

"Everything returns whence it came?"

Then should she renounce the feelings she had acquired at Mata Oscura, unnatural feelings which would never be really hers? and should she, instead of trying to conquer Santos Luzardo only by means of the rightful arts of a woman in love, take possession of his will, as she had done with Lorenzo Barquero's, or overcome him by armed force, as she had overcome all the men who had dared to oppose her designs?

But, she asked herself, were those longings for a new life that had come into her heart, with the same overpowering vehemence as her perverse instincts when they were loosed in her — were they really unnatural desires? Was not her real self, with all the force of its nature, concealed in that wish to bury forever the forbidding Amazon of the bloody hands, the *witch,* as Marisela had just called her? The answers rose from the two parts of her divided spirit, from what she was, and what she wanted to be, perhaps would have been if the Toad's dagger had not cut Hasdrubal off from life; from the darkness where arose the living spectre of a man degraded by her arts, and where another lay on his face in a pit with a dagger buried in his back — dark night without a star; and from that other mist receiving the fitful radiance of the light of pure love which had burned for a fleeting moment in her youth.

"Does the moccasin return to his pool, or the river to its source?

"The steer goes back to the fold and the wanderer back to the cross roads where he lost his way.

"Was I lost at Mata Oscura that day? or years ago in the arms of the tonka traders?"

And she could not tell when she asked and the shadow of the "Partner" replied, for she herself did not know where she had lost her way. She searched for it, and though she never ceased to search, never found it. She wanted to hear what the "Partner" counselled, but no sooner did he begin than she had the answer formulated, and the two phrases overlapped and became confused, and both seemed to her ears like the speech of another person, although she heard them as her own — as though her thoughts were flung by the ebb and flow of a furious sea from her to the phantasm and from the phantasm to her.

This was unusual conduct for the familiar spirit, whose counsel and warnings had always been clear and distinct, like ideas springing from a mind with no immediate communication with her own, words pronounced by another and heard by her, thoughts which had never entered her mind; while now she felt that everything he said was already within her, possessing the warmth and intimacy of her spirit, in spite of which they were incomprehensible, as though losing whatever they held of her.

"Be calm!" she admonished herself. "We can't communicate this way."

She hid her burning forehead in her icy hands, and remained a long time, silent and without thought.

The flame of the lamp crackled more sharply — it was about to expire — and these words came to Doña Barbara in her hallucination:

"If you want him to come to you, give up your plans."

She raised her eyes again to the shadow which had at last told her something she had not already thought; but the lamp had gone out, and all around her was shadow.

PART III

I

THE TERROR OF THE SAVANNAHS

MELQUÍADES could be kept at work for a year without pay, so long as the work consisted in harming someone; but he soon tired of any other activity, no matter how well rewarded. The most innocent of the occupations he was destined for by Doña Barbara was horse-hunting at night.

This meant surprising the studs asleep on the prairie, and pursuing them all night — and sometimes for several days and nights — in such a way as to make them run into a concealed corral ambushed in the thickets. Because he was known to be a *brujo,* or sorcerer, and because of the fact that it was he who introduced into the region this simplification of the task of catching wild horses, the hunting at night was called *brujeando,* and he was called *el brujeador,* the wizard.

Another advantage of this night work was that it was easy, in this manner, to lead the studs out of neighbouring ranch lands without any risk of discovery. The Altamira studs had enjoyed a respite from the persecutions of the Wizard ever since the arrival of Luzardo, on account of the truce Doña Barbara considered convenient to her plans of seduction, and now Melquíades, in view of the length of this peace, which was causing him to grow rusty, was thinking of leaving El Miedo, when Balbino brought him the order to renew his activities.

"The *señora* asked me to tell you to get ready to go to work tonight, and that you'll find a good stud in Rincón Hondo."

"And has she come from there?" asked Melquíades, who never received orders from Balbino with good grace.

"No. But you know that she doesn't have to see things with her eyes to know where they are."

Balbino himself had seen the stud referred to a short time before, but he gave the other explanation because this was the usual proceeding of Doña Barbara's overseers to prevent the servants' belief in her powers as a witch from languishing for a single moment. Melquíades did not deny that the *señora* was skilled in some of the things she was given credit for, but from that to the point where Balbino treated him as though he were Juan Primito was a long way. Nor did he need to believe in those powers to serve her loyally, for he had the soul of a real henchman, in whom two qualities, apparently irreconcilable, must be joined: absolute unscrupulousness and unflinching loyalty. Thus he served Doña Barbara not only in hunting horses by night, an office anyone else could have taken from him, but in more serious affairs; and in thus serving her, he was not, properly speaking, moved by the thought of money, for to be a henchman is not a trade; it is a natural function.

Balbino Paiba, on the other hand, could be everything but what Melquíades was, for he thought of nothing but his own profit and was treacherous by nature. He belonged to another class of men, for whom Melquíades felt the most profound contempt.

"Very well. If it's the *señora's* orders, we'll get ready to work tonight. And since it's a good ways from here to Rincón Rondo, it's best to saddle up at once."

When he started off, Balbino stopped him and said:

"Melquíades, see if you can put a few bronchos in the La Matica corral for me. It's to make Señor Luzardo angry. But don't say anything to the *señora*. I want to give her a surprise."

The La Matica corral was the place where Balbino kept the steers and horses he stole from Doña Barbara. Since these thefts were the acts of overseers, those at El Miedo spoke of them as "overseeing."

Balbino had never before dared to make such a proposition to Melquíades, and the latter answered:

"You must be making a mistake, Don Balbino. I never have liked *overseeing*."

And he rode off over the prairie at a moderate trot, the accustomed gait of his horse, used to having on his back a man who never changed his plans or hurried for anything. Balbino growled something inaudible to the peons who had witnessed the little scene and who had exchanged malicious glances.

In Rincón Hondo, that is, Deep Corners, a depression of the prairie, the Wizard found the stud mentioned by the overseer. It was a large one, and the horses were sleeping on the ground, trusting the keen ears of the leader.

The stallion gave a shrill neigh upon becoming aware of the proximity of a man, and the mares and colts got swiftly to their feet. Melquíades frightened them from a direction which would make them take flight towards El Miedo.

Excited by the dazzling brilliance with which the moon of the plains troubles the senses, awakened and pursued by the silent horseman whose shadowy persistence filled them with terror, the horses galloped off over the prairie, while Melquíades, with his mantle thrown over him to protect him from the dampness, followed them at the quiet trot of his mount, certain that they would stop further on, thinking themselves delivered from persecution.

They did as he had expected. At first, when he gave them enough time, he found them lying down again. But at each encounter the terror of the stud increased, and soon they no longer dared to lie down, but merely stopped. The mares and colts, in an immovable group with the leader at their head, and with upraised heads and ears thrown back, all looked at that shadow which was slowly, silently approaching, black and immense in silhouette against the brightness of the sky. This lasted all night.

Day was beginning to break when Melquíades succeeded in driving the stud towards a corner of the prairie at whose end, hidden between the edges of the thickets at the gap, which looked like the end of a narrow passage, was the enclosure of the false corral. So that the animals would run into the entrance without fearing the trap, he stampeded them in, rushing after them and shouting.

The stud had already followed the leader into the enclosure, but, noticing a part of the palisade poorly concealed in the thicket, the stallion stopped suddenly, and giving a short neigh, which the stud understood, bolted back to the open prairie. But the Wizard was already upon them and was able to prevent their flight. Only the leader and two fillies succeeded in escaping. Melquíades swung the gate to and went away so that the frightened, imprisoned horses might quiet down. As he was going, he saw the leader at the extreme other end of the corner of the savannah, head erect, looking defiantly at him. It was Black Mane.

"What a beautiful animal!" Melquíades exclaimed, stopping to look at the stallion. "And a good leader.

This is the biggest stud I've ever brought from over there. Perhaps I can catch him by tempting him with his own mares, because he might want to come and look for them."

But Black Mane had stopped only to engrave on his memory the image of the man on horseback, and after regarding him for a while, this living bundle of nerves under a shiny coat, shaking with rage, his eyes bloodshot, his jaws open, whirled around and went away with the fillies accompanying him.

"He'll come back," Melquíades said to himself. "But let somebody else come from over there to watch him. I've done what I was supposed to, and it's my turn to sleep now."

The corral was within the boundary of El Miedo and not far distant from the ranch-houses. When Melquíades reached them, he met Balbino, who was waiting for him to make him forget the imprudent proposition of the previous night before he could bear the tale to Doña Barbara. He received Melquíades with unusual friendliness.

But Melquíades, dry as ever, had only a few words for him.

"Send some peons to throw a lasso over the leader; he managed to get away, and he seems to want to come and visit his mares. It's worth the trouble of trying to get a rope even on him, because he's a fine horse and the *señora* will like him for her saddle."

But Balbino, without even knowing the animal, had immediately decided that he would like him for his own, and set off at once for the corral to lasso him.

Black Mane, however, had already found a way to make reprisals. After he had gone a little way, he spied a stud as large as the one he had lost, cropping grass and frolicking in the soft morning light. He ran up, announcing to the leader, with his tremulous neigh, that he had come to conquer. The leader, a dappled grey, hastily gathered his mares and colts, scattered about the pasture, and placing himself at their head, waited for the attack.

Black Mane charged impetuously. He had the advantage of height, and of fury doubled by his anger at the spoliation he had just suffered. The horses pawed each other, raising a cloud of dust, and their neighing vibrated over the prairie; the hammer-strokes of the grey's vicious snaps rang out in the air. Black Mane's teeth had caught hold of the flesh on his neck, and now came a second attack at the neck, and a third, without giving him time to recover himself. The grey's legs were beginning to weaken from so much stamping, and the other was finally biting him wherever he wanted to. Black Mane finally shook him, furiously. The grey at last succeeded in getting loose and fled. Black Mane pursued him for some distance, and then returned to the stud, which had witnessed the struggle without moving from its place. He urged them on, running around them and showing his teeth, and thus drove them on to the place where he had left his fillies; then, with these incorporated in the new stud, he set off in the direction of his old haunts in the Altamira pastures.

The grey followed at a distance for a while, but finally stopped short in the middle of the prairie, standing there until he saw the dust of his lost followers disappear on the horizon.

Some nights later, in his task of stealing the Altamira studs, the Wizard pursued one that gave him plenty to do, for the leader drove for the open prairie, avoiding the thickets, going at a steady gallop. Besides, there was a thick mist making it impossible to see more than a short distance. When the day came on, the stud was back in the same place where Melquíades had raised it, and he saw that the leader was Black Mane, who had already cheated him. This was the first time a horse had fooled the Wizard, and as this seemed to him like an evil omen, he went to tell Doña Barbara about it.

She placed the same interpretation upon it. "Things return whence they came—" the "Partner" had said. Nevertheless, she replied angrily:

"You too, Melquíades? The stud turned you around without your noticing it?—It's known that there's a man at Altamira who isn't afraid of the terror of the savannahs."

The confusion of emotions reigning in her spirit

showed through these words. Melquíades listened impassively, and then replied:

"When you want to prove to yourself that Melquíades Gamarra is not afraid of any man, you only have to tell him: Bring him to me, alive or dead."

And he turned his back and left the room.

Doña Barbara remained wrapped in thought, as though she were trying to make room for a new purpose in the whirl of her emotions.

II

THE WHIRLWINDS

IT ISN'T the play of the winds over the sand, but the evil tornados which sweep away one's hopes.

Marisela was no longer the capricious, merry soul of the house. She returned crestfallen from El Miedo that night, and it was useless for Santos, after he had reproved her, to attempt to comfort her.

"Well. The scolding is over. Raise up that head. Cheer up. The only thing you've done that's really bad was giving credit to such commonplace and grotesque superstitions. No harm could happen to me on account of that piece of string you have there. Otherwise, you've been noble and brave and I have to be grateful to you. If that's the way you defend the measurement of my height, I wonder how you would defend my life if you saw it in danger!"

But she remained crestfallen and silent, because she had had an experience at El Miedo which had banished the enchantment her life was founded upon. For in the innocence of her untutored state and in the bewilderment of a new way of life and a love, which her unnamed passion might very well be, since it rested on a point of equilibrium between reality and dream, she had never stopped to think what it meant to be daughter of The Evil Eye. If she had to refer to her mother — and she very rarely did — Marisela called her simply " she " or " her," and these words awoke no feeling of love, nor hate, nor shame in her heart. It was when she had asked Pajarote to go with her that she had called her " mother " for the first time, and she had been obliged to make an effort to bring the sound from her lips, unused as it was and void of all feeling, as though lacking in any meaning.

On the other hand, it had now acquired a hideous significance, and it kept coming to her lips every moment, accompanied by an instinctive gesture of repugnance. It was her spirit, uncontaminated, yet not any longer in the state of nature which knows neither good nor evil, which rejected violently all that was monstrous in being the daughter of the Circe who, to crown all, was enamoured of the very man she loved.

Little by little, by virtue of being ever present in her young, untainted mind, the hateful idea began to cover itself over with feelings of pity. Wasn't she too a victim of her mother? But, at all events, the enchantment had vanished, the point of equilibrium no longer existed. There was no dream now, there was only cruel and implacable reality.

Meanwhile Santos had been going around deep in thought, and when he came to the end of his reflections one day, he said to her:

"We've got to have a serious talk, Marisela."

She thought he was going to tell her what she had once longed to hear, and hastened to interrupt him:

"What a coincidence. I had to talk with you, too. I am very grateful to you for all you've done for us; but now Papa wants to go back to the palm grove . . . and I want you to let me go with him."

Santos looked at her for a long time, without a word. Then he replied, smiling:

"And if I don't let you go?"

"I'll go anyway." And she burst out crying.

Santos understood, and took her hands in his:

"Come here. Let's talk frankly. What's the matter with you?"

"It's that . . . I'm the daughter of The Evil Eye!"

The protest, a just one, seemed to him devoid of any natural feeling; it roused the same displeasure in Santos as the absence of tenderness he felt in Marisela had caused him, and, involuntarily, he let go of her hands. She rushed off to her room and locked herself in, and it was useless for him to call through that door to conclude the interrupted conversation, or to try to recommence it later, for she did not come out of her prison as long as he was in the house.

Even if he loved her, there was nothing Santos could

say to her that would compensate for the destiny which had begotten her in the accursed womb of that woman.

And in the meantime, outside, too, the whirlwinds were bearing away other hopes.

The dairy was rapidly being established. The herd still had to be driven to the corrals, but every day more cattle came in, the cows were already answering to their names, and fear no longer dried the milk in their udders. The milking began with the first cockcrow. Jesusito, shivering with the cold, would take his place at the gate of the yearlings' corral, while the milkers entered the cows' enclosure, pail and stick in hand. Someone sang—

Light of the morning
Lend me your ray,
To light my lover
Upon his way.

The calf-tender called, his child's voice ringing out in the sweet air:

"Claridad! Claridad! Claridad!"

The cow he had called mooed, and the calf hurried to her as he heard the maternal summons, putting his head through the bars of the gate; the tender swung it open to allow him to pass, and the little animal lowered his head, plunging his muzzle greedily against the full udder. The milker, stroking the cow, kept saying to her: "Come on, Claridad, come on," and when the udder swelled up — the calf's legs tangled up in those of his mother, while she licked him caressingly — the milking began and soon filled the pails.

Then there would be another song:

Who drinks water from a gourd
Or takes a wife in a foreign land
Can't tell how the water's poured
Or if the girl's the proper brand.

Again the boy called: "Azucena!" and another cow came up to be milked.

As the air of the chill morning, bearing the odour of cow dung and the snatches of song of the milkers, began to stir in the broad silence of the prairies, and the day commenced to brighten, diverse sounds and perfumes filled it: the fragrance of the mint thickets, sweetened by the dew, the scent of flowering *paraguatáns,* the sharp cry of the crane in the woods beside the creeks, the distant clarion call of a cock, the silver song of the troopial and the lark.

At evening the flocks returned to the corrals, accompaned by the songs of the herdsmen, as the sunlight began to stretch out over the plains in long slanting bars. The cows' udders would be full, and there would be soft, hungry little jaws waiting at the gate of the corral where the calves were gathered. Remigio looked at the cows and estimated the production of cheese; Jesusito, sitting on the gatepost, gazed dreamily over the prairie and listened to the songs, to their lingering cadence, the music of broad, lonely lands.

But one day Remigio came to the ranch-house, looking very gloomy, and sat down without saying a word.

"What brings you here, old man?" Santos asked him, and the dairy-man responded, slowly and gravely:

"I've come to tell you that last night a tiger killed my grandson. The milkers had gone away to a dance and we were alone in the dairy, Jesusito and I. When I woke up hearing the boy's scream, the tiger had already broken his neck with a blow of his paw. I was able to get my lance in him, and they were both dead in the morning, Jesusito and the tiger. So I've come to tell you that I haven't anybody to work for any more."

"Close up the dairy, Remigio. There's no one here who can take charge of it. Let the herd stay wild."

The gathering of the heron feathers had been finished, and Antonio told him the result.

"Fifty pounds. Now you'll be able to have that fence. With the price feathers are bringing today, more than twenty thousand pesos will come in. If you haven't made any other arrangement, I'll send Carmelito with them. He can buy the barbed wire we need for the fence, at San Fernando. I've already got the amount figured. In the meantime we can begin to set up the posts the fire burned down. That is, if you're still thinking of that."

Here were the ideas of the civilizer germinating in the mind of the man of routine. With Antonio Sandoval convinced of the necessity of the fence, a long start had been made, and Santos returned to his ambitious projects, postponed by the demands of daily toil.

Two days later a pair of horsemen came into view.

"Those aren't people from around here," Pajarote observed.

"Who can they be?" Venancio asked.

"We'll find out when they come up, because they're heading in this direction," Antonio concluded.

The strangers came up. One of them was leading a horse by the bridle.

"That's Carmelito's horse," the Altamira peons said, while Santos hurried out to the gallery.

"Are you Dr. Luzardo?" one of the newcomers inquired. "We've come on an errand for General Pernalete, Chief Magistrate of the District, to bring you bad news. Over there by the El Totumo ranch a man was found dead in a thicket of chaparral, and it seems that he was from here. He couldn't be identified, because the body was already decayed, and half eaten by the buzzards, but this horse we're leading was found later on the prairie, and your brand is on him. The General ordered us to bring him to you and give you the news."

"They've murdered Carmelito!" exclaimed Antonio, torn between rage and grief.

"His brother was with him. Where is he? And what

happened to the heron plumes they were carrying?" Pajarote demanded.

The messengers looked at each other.

"Over there it isn't known that the dead man had anybody with him or that they were carrying anything that might be stolen. They think that he had an attack of sickness in the middle of the prairie, but if you say that there was valuable property we'll tell the General. He'll have to make an investigation."

"Hasn't it been made yet?" Luzardo asked.

"As I told you, they think over there — "

"Yes. Don't go on. They always think everything over there that will help the crime to go unpunished," said Santos. "But not this time."

And the next day, he set off for the head village of the district. It was high time to begin the struggle for justice in the vast stronghold of violence.

As soon as Marisela knew that Santos had gone she decided to carry out her plan of leaving his house, where it was no longer possible for her to stay, and to return to the hut in the La Chusmita palm grove and the life she had formerly lived there, the only one she was fit for, according to the maxim which was never absent from her lips: "Better broken than mended."

Lorenzo Barquero accepted the proposition with feverish alacrity. It was time to put an end to the falsehood of his moral regeneration. His life was irremediably ruined. There in the hut in the palm grove he would be able once more to give himself up to drunkenness, there was the bog that would some day swallow him up. "Yes, we'll go tomorrow," he said, and the next day, taking advantage of the absence of Antonio, who would not have allowed them to get away, father and daughter rode off to the palm grove of La Chusmita.

They made the journey in silence, Lorenzo lurching as his horse strode along, Marisela gloomy; and only when they had arrived at the edge of the grove did she turn her head, and seeing that the Altamira houses were no longer within view, she murmured:

"I'll pretend that it has been a dream."

When she reached the hut whose squalor was now repugnant to the taste and habits she had acquired in Luzardo's home, while her father went off to stare at the quagmire as he had used to do between his drunken fits, she unsaddled the horses which were to remain there until someone came from Altamira to fetch them. She was about to tie her mare up when, remembering how Carmelito had compared his task of breaking the filly with Santos's undertaking to rid her of her boorishness, it occurred to her that Catira ought likewise to return to her former condition. She took off the mare's bridle, caressed her mournfully, and said to her: "This is all over, Catira. You go back to your pasture and I go back to my woods," and having frightened the mare away, she sat down on the curb of the well and gave free rein to her tears.

Catira trotted a short distance, trying her freedom with prudent short spurts, for she was not yet very certain of having recovered it. She rolled over in the sand, shook it from her white coat with a quiver of pleasure, neighed, and ran on a little farther, to stop and stand with her neck arched, her ears together, and her head turned towards Marisela, until she finally convinced herself that she was really free. Then, taking leave of her mistress with another neigh, she sped away and was soon lost to sight in the wide prairie.

"Good," Marisela said to herself. "Now to gather kindling as I used to." She thought of a proverb: "Don't sing songs to the one who was born to be miserable."

But if Catira was able to return to the free life of the wandering stud, Marisela could not so easily return to her old condition. The necessities of the moment and the preoccupations of the future had complicated her life. The former were so many and so imperious that upon finding herself face to face with them, she was frightened at what she had done in returning to the palm grove. It was not only kindling she had to have, it was the skill to make a fire with it and to find the things to be cooked on the fire when meal time approached, and all the other things that were lacking in the dwelling, if such a name could be given to the miserable hovel. With her mind preoccupied by the obsession her despair had nourished — to abandon Luzardo's house — she had not foreseen that mealtimes would come around in the palm grove and that there would be nothing to eat, and bedtime, with no place to sleep; for now the mat could no longer serve her for a bed, nor was it for that matter even a mat, it was now so dilapidated.

As for Lorenzo, he had lived so long outside of reality that it was impossible for him to foresee the need of these indispensables. For the rest, as long as he did not lack brandy, and Señor Danger was there to supply that, he could do without the other things.

Certainly, as before, the *chigas* and *quereveres* in the thicket would furnish flour for their rude bread and yuccas and bananas might still be found if she hunted around in the copses. But now her palate rejected such coarse food and she was no longer that creature, as wild as a tapir, who did not fear the task of securing it in the lonely wood and was willing to plunge into its recesses, crunching the underbrush beneath her broad bare feet, or who climbed up the trees and disputed with the monkeys for her wild food. She did not lack the will to do it, but she had learned at Altamira to make better use of that will. It could no longer be a case of climbing trees like a monkey to appease her hunger, it would have to be a matter of securing a certain and permanent means of subsistence. For her imagination had begun to function, and because of that uncertainty for the future, it made the privations of the moment more painful. Considering all this, it was necessary for her to give thought to a source of provision, and her first idea was this:

"Papa, have I got the right to demand that my mother look out for me? While she's burying kettlefuls of gold pieces, here we are with nothing to eat."

Lorenzo made an effort to gather his thoughts.

"Rights? None. Because you don't appear as her daughter in the Civil Register. She didn't want to be mentioned and I presented you—"

She did not let him finish. "Do you mean to say that I haven't even the right to prove that I'm the daughter of The Evil Eye?"

Her father looked fixedly at her for a few moments and then mumbled:

"Not even the right. . . ."

The words, a simple mechanical repetition of those she had used, had not the faintest suggestion of a feeling of responsibility, and when he had delivered them, Lorenzo left the hut, going in the direction of Señor Danger's house. Repenting of the cruelty of that accusing question, Marisela stood there murmuring:

"Poor Papa," while he went his way with an uncertain step and his arms hanging limp beside his body. But when she realized that he was going to the American's house, she ran after him to stop him, and said:

"No, Papa, don't go to that man's house. I beg you

not to go. Is it liquor you're going to ask him for? Wait here, I'll go get it for you at Altamira. I'll be back soon."

But while she was saddling the horse Lorenzo had ridden, he went off to satisfy the imperious necessity for alcohol, forgetting that nothing remained to him to pay Señor Danger for the drink he was going to ask for except his daughter.

Indeed the whirlwinds had swept every hope away.

III

ÑO PERNALETE

MUJIQUITA had his motives, if not reasons, for wanting to conceal himself under the shop counter when he saw Santos Luzardo coming. First of all, his friendly interference in Santos's case against Doña Barbara had resulted in Ño Pernalete's withdrawal of the Secretaryship of the Civil Magistrature. Secondly, he could not be unaware of what his former fellow student was coming for, and he saw in danger the pittance Ño Pernalete had restored to him after much begging on his part and his wife's, and many promises that he would not again involve himself in quixotisms.

But Santos did not give him time to hide himself, and Mujiquita was obliged to pretend that he was glad to see him.

"Well, you're a good sight for sore eyes! You sell yourself dear, old boy. What can I do for you?"

"If I haven't been misinformed, you already know. I've been told that you're Judge of the District."

"Yes, old fellow," said Mujiquita after a pause. "I

know very well what you've got on hand. The death of the peon, isn't that it?"

"Of the peons," Luzardo corrected him. "Because two were assassinated."

"Assassinated? You don't tell me, Santos! Look here, come over to the courthouse and tell me how it happened."

"Why should I have to tell you?"

"No. Excuse me. So you can give me a little light on the matter. So you can tell me what I'm to do."

"But, Mujiquita, you still don't know after all this time?"

"But, old boy," Mujiquita protested, and his expression as he replied furnished the superfluous words with overwhelming eloquence:

"Don't you know where we are?"

They went over to the courthouse. Mujiquita, with a shove, opened the warped door, and the two entered a straw-ceilinged, whitewashed room containing a desk, a cabinet, three chairs, and a setting hen in the corner. In offering Santos a seat, Mujiquita filled the room with dust as he shook the thick deposit off the chair. It was easy to see that no one made a habit of coming to that place of justice.

Santos sat down, worn out more by his despair, by the impression the village, the courthouse, and the judge produced on him, than by actual fatigue. Nevertheless, he pulled himself together, and, trying to enlist as much sympathy as possible from Mujiquita, he explained that Carmelito had been accompanied by his brother Rafaelito, and informed him of the amount of heron plumes they were carrying to San Fernando.

Mujiquita scratched his head, and then, taking his hat and making for the door, he said:

"Wait here a moment for me. Let me go tell the General this. He must be at the Magistracy. I won't keep you very long."

"But what's the Civil Magistrate got to do with this matter?" Santos objected. "Haven't the required number of days passed for the case to go to the proper judge?"

"*Caramba,* old fellow," Mujiquita exclaimed, "look here—the General isn't a bad sort, but between you and me, he likes to lead the band in everything around here. In civil matters as well as criminal, nothing is done here unless he directs it. It's got into the General's head that the man died of an attack, as he says—that is, of heart failure. And apropos of that, because anything can happen, you didn't notice if the peon was a cardiac sufferer?"

"Cardiac, the devil!" Santos exclaimed, jumping to his feet. "The one who is going to have heart failure pretty soon, if you haven't it already, is *you.*"

Mujiquita smiled.

"Don't get excited, old boy. Put yourself in my place,

and in the General's, because you've got to take everything into account in this life. Some days ago a circular came from the President of the State to the Civil Magistrates under his jurisdiction, giving them a little soft-soaping about several crimes committed in the unpopulated districts without anybody's being able to catch the culprits, and exhorting them to better fulfilment of their duties. The General answered that it had nothing to do with him, because in the district under his authority no criminality existed. I wrote out the statement for him, and he was so pleased with it that he had it printed on separate sheets, which you must have seen around here. As you must realize, in the case of your peon, or peons, I should say, I haven't been slow in assuming that it was a murder. But at this time, just after the statement has come out, it's impolitic to say that there's a case of crime and—"

"And since you're here to please Ño Pernalete and not to administer justice—" Santos added.

Mujiquita shrugged his shoulders. "I'm here to get the rest of their daily bread for my children, because I don't get it all from the shop," he said, and going out, he added: "Wait for me a minute. Everything isn't lost yet. Let me try my hand."

He returned unceremoniously a few moments later.

"What did I tell you? I know my stuff. The General is not pleased at your coming to me instead of going to him. So I advise you to go over there and put yourself under his wing. That's the way to get things done with him."

Before Luzardo could protest against this advice, the Civil Magistrate entered.

As Mujiquita had said, he had not been pleased at Santos' going to the judge instead of coming to him; and, as an additional aggravation, submitting information which would invalidate his convenient assumption of natural death. These were things he could not tolerate in anyone conceiving authority otherwise than the barbarian understood it, and he could much less tolerate them from one who had already dared to invoke the majesty of the law against his misdeeds.

He entered the courthouse with his hat on and both hands occupied, the left with his pipe, which had gone out, and the right holding a box of matches. Besides this, he carried under his left arm the leather-sheathed sword, which he lugged everywhere with him without rhyme or reason.

Not deigning to greet Luzardo, he went up to the table, laid his machete on it, and said, while he was striking the match and holding it to his pipe:

"I've already told you, Mujiquita, that I don't like my affairs meddled with. I'm working on this case the *señor* has on hand, and I know what my duty is."

"Allow me to point out to you that this matter is within the jurisdiction of the judicial authorities," said Santos, doing the exact opposite to what Mujiquita had counselled, since to tell Ño Pernalete that anything was not within his jurisdiction was equivalent to making an open declaration of war on him.

"However, Santos," the Judge intervened, almost stammering, "you know that—"

But Ño Pernalete needed no help.

"Yes. I've heard something like that around here," he replied ironically between puffs of his pipe. "But what I've always noticed is that where a judge and a lawyer get together, if they're left alone, what was clear becomes muddy, and what was going to last a day is not finished in a year. Therefore, whenever a suit, as you call it—I call 'em shakedowns—whenever a suit comes around here, I go outside to find out who's right, and then I come here and say to the *señor:* 'Dr. Mójica, So-and-So is right. Pass sentence in his favour immediately.'"

Concluding this explanation, he laid the full weight of his sceptre-machete on the Judge's desk, from which he had previously removed it for use in pointing the details of the scene he was describing.

Santos, momentarily losing his self-control, replied:

"Although I haven't come here to bring suit, but to ask for justice, I'd like to know what you call it when you handle it in such a manner."

"I call it dotting my e's," replied Ño Pernalete, who was a jocose fellow at heart. "You don't know that story? I'm going to tell it to you, because it's right to the point. He was one of those men they call ignorant, but he was very far from being a fool. He didn't know his spelling very well, and he didn't say "get" but "git" and not "endeavour" but "indeavour," and when his secretary—because the man was a magistrate and had a secretary—when his secretary would write one of those words for him with an 'e,' which didn't sound to him like a word beginning with 'e' but with 'i,' he'd say to him: 'Good, but dot those e's for me.'"

While Mujiquita was laughing at the General's sally, Santos replied:

"If that's the *spelling* you use around here, I've lost my time coming to ask for justice."

Ño Pernalete found it expedient to strengthen his position.

"Justice will be done," he said in a tone with no small hint of threat in it.

A despot by nature, but crafty too, if Ño Pernalete did not tolerate refutation of his opinions or criticism of his procedure, it was also certain that if he found contrary opinions convincing he would immediately adopt them when there seemed to be any advantage in so doing, but always leaving it to be understood that they had already occurred to him, and presenting them as his own. In the case in question, and because of the President's circular, his own interest counselled him to drop for the time the assumption of natural death he had caused to prevail and to say, but in the same tone of insolence:

"It wasn't necessary for you to come from so far away to let us know that the man was accompanied. That's the clue we're following."

But Santos, understanding that now he was going to intrench himself behind the assumption that Rafael was Carmelito's murderer, replied quickly:

"Carmelito's companion was his brother, and I had the utmost confidence in both. I don't hesitate to affirm that Rafael was murdered too."

"You saying it is one thing and it's being true is another," Ño Pernalete retorted, feeling himself trapped by a new blunder, and after telling the mournful looking Judge: "Dr. Mójica, you know better than to stir up the wasps' nest," he went out of the courthouse, leaving behind him a silence of indignation on Luzardo's part, and fear on Mójica's—but such an utter silence as made audible the faint pecks with which the chickens being hatched by the brooding hen in the corner began to break their shells to bring themselves out into the enjoyment of this delightful world.

Mujiquita, after the precaution of a glance into the street to ascertain if Ño Pernalete had really gone, said:

"You say the peons were carrying fifty pounds of feathers? Something like twenty-thousand pesos' worth, right? But that's not lost, Santos. Whoever has those feathers in his possession will try to get rid of them easily for whatever he can get, and the business will be discovered that way."

Santos, however, was attending to his own thoughts and he expressed them thus as he rose to go:

"If my mother, instead of taking me away to Caracas, had left me here to learn the kind of spelling Ño Pernalete tells about, I would not today be Doctor, but Colonel Santos Luzardo, at least, the equal of that savage, and he wouldn't have dared to speak to me as insolently as he did."

"I'll tell you, old fellow," Mujiquita said insinuatingly, "the General's not so—" But he did not venture to go on, such was the look Luzardo gave him, and concluded: "All right. We'll go and take a little drink, if you'll come."

This invitation at such a moment displayed an utter cynicism, and Santos, after looking him over from head to foot, said:

"Of course it's true that there wouldn't be Ño Pernaletes if there weren't—" He was going to say "Mujiquitas" but he realized that this poor fellow was likewise a victim of the ogress Barbarism, and with his anger changed into pity, he replied to the innocent invitation:

"No, Mujiquita. I'm not going to begin drinking brandy yet."

His former fellow-student stood looking at him with

the same air of incomprehension he had shown when Santos had tried to explain the lessons on Roman Law, and then, with an uncertain smile, said:

"Ah, Santos Luzardo! You haven't changed. I'm so anxious to have a long talk with you. To bring back those times, old fellow. You're not going yet, I suppose? No, old fellow. Don't start out now. Put it off until tomorrow. Rest a while now and then go over to the inn. I can't go with you because I've got to attend to an important affair."

And when Luzardo crossed the street at the corner, Mujiquita closed the courtroom and went over to the Civil Magistrate's office to find what was Ño Pernalete's attitude concerning him. He found the Magistrate alone and considerably agitated, walking up and down from one end of the room to the other and soliloquizing:

"I didn't like that Doctor fellow a bit from the first time I laid eyes on him. These shysters! I'd keep them all in jail if I had my way about it."

"Mujiquita," he said, as the latter appeared. "Bring me here the summary of that—stew about the death at El Totumo."

Mujiquita went out and returned with the brief. Ño Pernalete was still walking up and down.

"Read me that so I can see how it stands. Skip the preliminaries to where it tells how the body was found."

Mujiquita read: "'The body presented symptoms of advanced decay.'"

"'Symptoms?'" interrupted Ño Pernalete. "It was rotted away to dirt. You're always putting your poetry into everything to tangle it up more. Well. Go on reading."

"'Neither wounds nor contusions could be noted.'"

"Didn't I tell you?" Ño Pernalete took off and replaced his hat, and walked up and down more rapidly, snorting. "'Couldn't be noted?' And what were you there for then, if you couldn't note what there was? How's this about it 'couldn't be'?"

"General," Mujiquita murmured. "Remember that you told me—"

But the Magistrate did not allow him to finish.

"Don't come to me with 'you told me.' What need have I got to tell you what you ought to do in fulfilling your duty? That's what I pay you your salary for. Or do you want me to go and do the work that belongs to you as Judge? so that Doctor fellow can come afterwards to tell me about 'jurisdiction.' Didn't you read the statement I sent a while ago to the President? The rules of my conduct as a public official were clearly expressed in that report, because when I write I don't bother with all that nonsense of fine words, but I say things clearly. And now after receiving that paper of mine, the President's going to find out that we wanted to bury the El Totumo corpse without finding out definitely if the man died because he died, or whether someone killed him. Let's see! Show me that summary."

He jerked it out of Mujiquita's hands and began reading, accompanying this labour of the eyes with swallowing movements. Mujiquita, who had gathered from the foregoing that Ño Pernalete was "putting a bridge" under himself, summoned energy to say:

"Please notice, General, that it doesn't say that it was a natural death."

But in the matter of abandoning an opinion he had sustained, Ño Pernalete was like one of those horses which after throwing the rider, kick him while he is lying on the ground. He turned on Mujiquita.

"Do you say so? Perhaps you can be sure that the man wasn't murdered? A judge of court proceedings doesn't have to mix himself up in these details; he's only obliged to put in the brief what he saw with his own eyes. Maybe you're ready to give an opinion about the cause of the death?"

"Absolutely not, General."

"Well, then, what are you excited about? If you did your part well, you can rest easy about it. I've already told your friend the Doctor to rest easy because justice would be done. You go to him, you must know where he's put up, and tell him this, as if in your own words:

That justice will be done, because I'm taking charge of the matter. Then, he'll go home quietly and won't try our patience any longer."

"If you like, General, I can also ask him who are the persons he suspects—" Mujiquita suggested.

"No, sir! Do what I tell you, and nothing else."

"On my own account, I meant."

"How long are you going to keep on being a fool, Mujiquita? Hasn't it occurred to you that if we start to fooling around, we're going to find Doña Barbara's hands in the thing?"

"I meant on account of that business of the President's circular," Mujiquita mumbled.

"What did I tell you? They're going to bury you in a white coffin, Mujiquita, you're so innocent. Don't you know that circulars don't touch El Miedo because the President is a friend of Doña Barbara's? He owes her favours that can't be forgotten, saving one of his boys from death with some sort of herbs that she knows, and other things too that weren't exactly medicines. Go do what I tell you. Go give your friend a bone, so he'll go home satisfied to his house, while we look over the cards here."

Mujiquita left the office, convinced that he was going to be buried young for all the shots he had taken at the General for God and the Devil.

"Poor Santos Luzardo! He won't see a single real, it seems to me, out of those twenty thousand pesos he was going to get for his feathers. And here I've got to tell him to go home with his mind at rest."

But when he arrived at the inn, Santos's foot was already in the stirrup.

"In such a hurry, old fellow? Put off the ride until tomorrow. I've got a lot to tell you."

"Tell me when we see each other again," replied Santos, already mounted. "That will be when I can come with a machete in my hand and put it on your desk and tell you: 'Dr. Mójica, So-and-So is right. Pass sentence in his favour immediately.'"

As though he were hearing such a thing for the first time in his life, Mujiquita inquired:

"What do you mean by that, Santos?"

"That I'm being driven to violence, and I'm accepting the direction. See you later, Mujiquita. Maybe we'll meet again soon."

And he rode off, raising a cloud of dust under his horse's hoofs.

IV

THE CROSS ROADS

ONE of the messengers who had brought Santos Luzardo the news of the event at El Totumo had received the following secret instructions from Ño Pernalete:

"On your way, go over to the El Miedo ranch-house under some pretext or other, and tell Doña Barbara the story in the course of the conversation, as if it were your own idea. It's good that she should know it, too. But only tell *her, sabe?*"

The first thing that occurred to Doña Barbara when she received the news was to rejoice at the harm Santos Luzardo had suffered from the affair. Some hours later, news was brought to her that Marisela had returned with her father to the hut in the palm grove, and when she received that information, the "Partner's" cabalistic utterance rushed into her mind, but with a hopeful interpretation: Marisela, the rival who was taking Santos Luzardo's love away from her, returning to the hut in the palm grove, meant *the things which were to return whence they came.* She saw in this an indication that her lucky star was still in the ascendant, and said to herself:

"God had to keep on helping me."

She was already prepared to map out a plan adequate to the new circumstances when Balbino Paiba came up to her and asked:

"Have you heard the news?"

Quick as a flash the inspiration to interrupt him leapt into her brain:

"That Carmelito Lopez was murdered in the chaparral thicket at El Totumo."

Balbino looked surprised, and then immediately exclaimed in a flattering tone:

"*Caramba!* There's no chance of selling you fresh news. How did you know it?"

"It was reported to me last night," she answered, leaving him to understand by this impersonal use and a mysterious tone, that it was the "Partner" who had told her.

"But you were misinformed," Balbino replied, after a short pause. "Because, as it seems, Carmelito was not assassinated, but died a natural death."

"And isn't a stab in the back or a shot from behind something a natural death for a Christian in a place like the El Totumo thicket?"

Balbino was so disconcerted at hearing these words, accompanied by a mocking smile, that he committed the blunder of saying:

"There's no question about it. You're helped by things more powerful than men."

Doña Barbara's frown at this allusion to her powers as a witch was brusque and menacing, but Balbino had begun and had to finish.

"Dr. Luzardo proposes to do away with smuggling cattle from the open prairie, and Carmelito dies in the chaparral at El Totumo, while the wind carries away the feathers that were going to bring in the money he needed to fence Altamira."

"That's so," she replied, resuming her mocking attitude. "There's always a lot of wind blowing in those El Totumo savannahs."

"And since feathers are very light—" Paiba added in the same sarcastic tone.

"So it seems," she concluded. She looked steadily at him for a while, smiling, and then burst into a laugh. Balbino allowed himself to be betrayed by his characteristic involuntary gesture, and as this seemed to make Doña Barbara want to laugh all the harder, he ended by losing his poise and asked:

"What are you laughing at?"

"At the sly fellow you are. You came to tell me about that business in the chaparral thicket, which you must have known was no news to me, but you take good care not to mention your own villainy. . . . Why don't you tell me what you've done during these days you've spent without showing your face here?"

Balbino was frightened and showed it.

"I have also been told that you're having a little fling with one of the girls at Paso Real. I know that you've been there dancing and joining one night to another in a single spree. Why don't you tell me about that, instead of giving me news that doesn't interest me?"

Balbino's soul returned to his body, but when he recovered his serenity he merely became more stupid than usual, and thought that what really interested his paramour were his nights at Paso Real.

"That's just slander invented by my enemies. By Melquíades, certainly, because I've already noticed that he goes around watching every step I take. I *was* two days at a *joropo* at Paso Real, but I didn't give the party and it's not true that I'm making love to any girl there. The real truth is that since nobody has been able to come near you these last days without getting his head bitten off, the best thing I could do was not to show myself in your house."

He stopped a moment to judge the effect upon her of the freedom of speech he had ventured, a thing she was accustomed to tolerate only when he was making love to her, and as he did not see any manifestation of her displeasure, he became even bolder.

"So much so, that I was actually thinking of going away from here altogether, because the rôle you've made me play since Dr. Luzardo arrived hasn't been a very fine one."

Doña Barbara, with her usual impenetrability regarding her motives, assumed the attitude of a jealous woman in love, and replied:

" Mere excuses. You know very well what I propose to do with Santos Luzardo. But you and that girl at Paso Real are making a mistake if you think you're going to make a fool of me. I've already sent word to her that if she keeps on coquetting with you I'm going to teach her a lesson."

" I assure you that it's just slander," Balbino protested.

" Slander or anything else, I've already told you what I had to tell you, that nobody can make a fool of me. So don't get any idea of going to Paso Real again," and she turned her back on him, saying to herself: " This fellow will never see the trap he's going to fall into."

Balbino actually was entertaining these reflections:

" I managed things very well. I killed two birds with one stone. The *joropo* at Paso Real gave me a good excuse for going to El Totumo without raising any suspicions, and brought this woman back to pasture by making her jealous. Now I'm going to be cock-of-the-walk at El Miedo, but if she tries her tricks, I'm going to try mine too. I managed things very well. There's not so much as a trace of Rafaelito left, because what the alligator didn't like was nice for the caribs at Chenchenal, and now he's the one who will be blamed for the death of his brother and the theft of the feathers. And meanwhile, they're buried safe there and I can wait for time to pass before I start selling them; and meanwhile, here, the El Miedo business is coming along."

At the same moment, Doña Barbara was saying to herself:

"God had to help me! I'd no more than begun to ask myself: Who could have been the murderer? than in comes this vagabond to tell me the tale, with guilt for the crime written all over his face. I'll lead him on until I find out where he's got the feathers hidden, and the minute I have sufficient proof in my hands I'll tie him up like a mummy and turn him over to Dr. Luzardo to do what he likes with him."

She was ready for everything—to give up her plans and change her life, for no momentary caprice was moving her now, but a passion, vehement as hers always were and as December loves always are; but it was not all thirst for love, but a desire for rebirth too, a curiosity to see what another kind of life would be like, the urge of a strong nature to realize latent and delayed possibilities.

"I'll be another woman," she told herself again and again. "I'm tired of myself and I want to be different and know another kind of life. I feel young still and I can begin again."

She was in this state of mind when, two days later, on her way home at sunset, she spied Santos Luzardo returning from the village.

" Wait for me here," she said to Balbino Paiba, in whose company she now managed to be constantly, and crossing a glade which separated her from Luzardo's path, came up in front of him. She greeted him with a faint nod, without any smile, and inquired:

" Is it true that two of your peons who were carrying a load of feathers to San Fernando were assassinated? "

Santos, with a contemptuous glance, replied:

" Absolutely true, and your question is very pointed."

But she had not waited for the end of his sentence to ask another question.

" And what have you done about it? "

Looking her straight in the eyes, and clipping off his words, he answered:

" I've wasted my time thinking that justice could be obtained, but you may rest easy as far as legal ways are concerned."

" I? " exclaimed Doña Barbara, reddening suddenly, as though she had been struck in the face. " Do you mean that you — "

" I mean that we are taking another road," he replied, and spurring his horse, he continued his journey, leaving her there in the middle of the prairie.

V

MAN'S HOUR

SOME moments later, Santos Luzardo burst into the Macanillal house, revolver in hand.

The house was in the same place where Doña Barbara had ordered it placed, but not where it should have been, in strict justice, for the decision of the judge in establishing that boundary had been arbitrary. The two surviving Mondragons of the dangerous trio of brothers were stretched out in their hammocks having a peaceful talk when Santos, without giving them time to arm, ordered them to surrender. They exchanged understanding glances and the one called The Tiger said, with treacherous meekness:

"All right, Dr. Luzardo. We surrender. What shall we do now?"

"Set fire to the house," he said, and throwing a box of matches at their feet, "Let's go!"

The order was imperious, and it did not escape the minds of the Mondragons that the one giving it was a Luzardo, descendant of men who had never taken a weapon in hand to make threats which would not be carried out.

"*Caramba,* Doctor!" exclaimed The Lion. "This house isn't ours, and if we set fire to it, Doña Barbara will make us pay damages."

"That's my business," Santos replied. "Go ahead and don't give me any back talk."

Meanwhile, The Tiger had succeeded in slipping over towards the corner where there was a rifle, and was leaning over to seize it when a well-aimed shot from Luzardo, striking him in the thigh, laid him on the floor, cursing. His brother, with an enraged leap, tried to fling himself on Luzardo, but the revolver held against his chest in the right hand whose efficiency they had already sampled stopped him, and, turning livid with rage, he said to his brother:

"We'll get our chance to pay this back, brother. Get up off the floor and help me set fire to the house. Every man has his hour and Dr. Luzardo is enjoying his. Our turn will come later. Take half of these matches and let's do what we're told, you on that side and I on this. It serves us right for letting ourselves be caught off guard."

When the thatch roof was lighted, the prairie wind whipped it into a raging blaze. The house, which was nothing but four posts and a roof, was destroyed in a few moments.

"Good," said The Lion. "The house is burning up, as you wanted it to. Now, what's next?"

"Take your brother up on your back now and go along in front of me. I'll tell you the rest when we get to Altamira."

The Mondragons looked at each other again, and as it did not seem to either one that the other was disposed to risk his life in a rash effort at resistance, especially as Luzardo had the advantage of being armed and mounted and had an air of desperate resolution, the wounded man said:

"You don't need to carry me, brother. I'll walk, and that will bleed the wound on the way."

The sons of the Barinas plains, where they had committed crimes left unpunished through their flight to the Arauca and the protection Doña Barbara had extended to them, were now going to expiate those misdeeds, for Santos proposed to turn them over to the authorities, and he told them so when they reached Altamira.

"You know what you're doing," replied The Lion. "I've already said you're having your hour." And as Santos, without paying any attention to the insolence of his words, ordered Antonio to attend to the wound, he answered:

"Don't trouble yourself, Doctor. The blood I've lost was only the bit too much I had. Now I'm down to weight."

Pajarote intervened:

"Well, it will be all the easier to drive him." And he turned to Luzardo, giving bluster for bluster: "Give me this little job, Doctor. Two bits of rope to tie 'em back to back, that's all I need. I'll supply the rest. And so much the worse for him if the man is as light as he says, let's see if he takes a notion to run. I suppose you're going to send a letter with them, and if that's so, go write it now, because I'm soon going to be driving them on. It's best not to let them wait until morning, though I don't think the others will dare come tonight for these two. And it wouldn't be bad if they did. If I could split myself in two, one half would go ahead with these beauties and the other half would stay here to wait for the ones at El Miedo to come for them. But you don't need me here, because you've shown well enough that one *Altamireño* is enough and to spare for driving two of these fellows from El Miedo. They'll all sing the same tune over there from now on."

Santos had been in the house for some time and had not yet noticed that Marisela and her father were not there.

"They went away when you left for the village," Antonio explained. "It was Marisela's idea and I wasted my time going to get her. She wouldn't come for any reason."

" It's the best thing that could have happened to her," said Santos. " We're on a different road now."

He immediately gave orders to proceed, next day, with the erection of the palisade at the Gap, which Señor Danger was putting off in accordance with the trick Ño Pernalete had recommended.

" In spite of that document he showed you? " Antonio inquired.

" In spite of everything and in the face of everything against it. Fight fire with fire. That's the law of this country."

Antonio became thoughtful again.

" I have nothing to say, Doctor. You know that I'm following the same road with you." But he said to himself, as he went out: " I don't like to see Santos like this. I hope it's only thunder showers."

That night, while the dogs scampered around the table, a woman reeking of kitchen grease was the one who served Luzardo's dinner. He tried only a few mouthfuls of Casilda's wretched messes, and then, as he could not stay in that house where, in the dismal light of the lamp, things which had formerly shone with cleanliness already had a thick coating of dust and were covered with flies, he went out into the gallery.

The prairie slumbered in the darkness of the cloudy night. There was neither guitar, nor song, nor story to be heard. The peons were thinking in silence of their taciturn companion who had been murdered in the chaparral thicket at El Totumo — the " sealed-up " man upon whom they could nevertheless always count, for he never left anybody in a scrape, although he had to risk his life; the good fellow who had been obliged to take justice into his own hands, and who was not getting it even after his death.

They thought too of the master, despoiled of the money he was going to use for the work he had founded so many hopes upon, and who had come back changed into another, into a bitter, gloomy man.

Far away could be heard the shrill cry of the bitterns marking the late hour, and Venancio broke the silence:

" Pajarote and María Nieves must be pretty far away with their men."

Another, referring to the violent deeds into which the master had thrown himself, said:

" That's the way things have got to be done in this country, because the remedy has got to be like the disease. In the Plain, a man ought to be able to do whatever any man can do. I hope the Doctor will leave off once and for all thinking about fences and what they do in other tame countries, and do what everybody has always done around here: smuggle off all the unmarked cattle that put their feet on his land, from newborn calves up."

" And go into other people's land," added a third, " and drive whatever he comes across with hoofs over to here. That's what they're doing on his land, and fair exchange is no robbery."

"Well, I don't see it the way you fellows do," said Antonio Sandoval. "I'm for what the Doctor has shown me is right. Fences all around and everybody taking care of his own cattle on his own land."

When he heard these words, Santos experienced the same impression as when he had seen the melancholy gleam of the lamp on the furniture Marisela had abandoned. That conviction of Antonio's was the work of a man who no longer existed, who had come from the city cherishing projects for civilizing the land, respecting legal procedure although the law upheld the acts by which Doña Barbara went on taking his cattle away from him; a man who was an enemy to reprisals, the suggestion of which his watchful conscience rejected. He had a horror of the spiritual catastrophe to which they might lead him by setting at liberty the man of impulse breathing within him, and this although he was in danger of making himself a victim of the violence reigning over the country.

The man listening now to the conversation of his peons thought and felt like the one who had just said: a man ought to be able to do what any other man can do. And he had proved that he knew how to do it; the house at Macanillal no longer existed, and the Mondragons had gone to render account of their crimes before the law, both of these the work of his armed hand. It would be Señor Danger's turn next day. Since it was man's hour and not that of principle, and the desert placed no limits on individual action, or violent and arbitrary deeds—the man, then, would assert himself. A blow here, a blow there, one right after the other; an affirmation of force, at every opportunity presenting itself to him, and the great stronghold would be his for the future work of civilization. It was the beginning of righteous lordship of the Arauca—man's hour well employed.

VI

THE INEFFABLE DISCOVERY

SANTOS had been three days absent from the ranch, and during all that time Marisela had nursed the secret hope of seeing him come to get her as soon as he returned to Altamira and did not find her there. Stubbornly clinging to the bitter despair which had driven her to return to the hut in the palm grove, she did not like to admit to herself that she was sheltering such a hope, but nevertheless, she did not accept her new situation as final. She attended only to the necessities of the moment, as though she were there merely in passing, and spent the rest of the day seated on the curb of the well or wandering about the grove, constantly looking in the direction of Altamira.

At times her mood of black melancholy would vanish and she would burst into a laugh as she thought of Santos's annoyance when he found her no longer in his house, and thought that she had merely indulged a childish spite to pay him back for the harsh scolding he had given her as a reward for trying to protect him from the evil spells of her mother; but when she arrived at this point in her soliloquy, the hateful memory of that scene once more depressed and embittered her.

Finally she learned that Santos had returned. Two days went by, and the little gleam of hope in her breast went out for ever.

"I knew very well that he wouldn't come to get me," she said to herself, "or bother himself any more with me. Now it's really true that it was nothing but a dream."

On the other hand, Señor Danger was there every other moment. He was less audacious than formerly, for he was restrained by her dignity and seriousness in his presence, and no longer dared to put his hands on her, but each time he circled closer and closer around the prey that had returned within reach of his claws. He was greedier now, and the insolent attitude of a purchaser who has already paid alternated with his usual good humour.

At moments, despair induced Marisela to be content with the thought that it would be her destiny to fall sooner or later into the arms of this man, but the repugnant prospect would immediately lead her to seek swift and certain ways to remedy the situation.

One day she spied Juan Primito, who prowled around without daring to approach the hut, fearing that she had not forgiven him for his part in the business of measuring Luzardo's height. She called him to her and sent him on an errand.

"Tell—her. You know who I'm referring to, the *señora,* as you call her. Tell her that I've sent you to say that we're back in the palm grove, but that I want to go away from here altogether. Tell her to send me money, but not just a few cents, because I'm not asking for alms, but enough money to go to San Fernando with Papa. What are you going to say? . . . Repeat what I've told you. . . . Good. Say it just like that, and don't ever dream of coming back here if you don't."

Juan Primito went off repeating the message so that he might not forget a single one of "little Marisela's" words, and delivered it, exactly as he had received it, to Doña Barbara, whose first impulse was to reply with utter silence or with some sort of outrageous answer. But upon second thought, she realized that it was convenient for her to have Marisela go away to San Fernando, and taking a fistful of coins from her cabinet, money she had just received from a sale of steers, she gave them to Juan Primito.

"Take these. Carry them to her. Say that there are three hundred pesos here. Tell her to go away from here with her father and to do every possible thing to keep me from ever hearing of her again."

Juan Primito nearly choked to death with the breathlessness of his return and his joy at the success of his mission. He took out the handkerchief in which he had wrapped the money.

"Feel it, Marisela, my child. That's *gold!* The *señora* sends you three hundred pesos. Count them to see if they're all there."

"Put them on the table," Marisela told him, for she felt humiliated at having been obliged to take this means of escaping Señor Danger and at the necessity for accepting the charitable provisions Antonio was continually sending her from Altamira.

"Is it the handkerchief that disgusts you, Marisela, my child? Wait, I'll give them to you all clean," said Juan Primito, going to wash the coins with water from the cistern.

"No matter how much you wash them, it will always disgust me to touch them. Leave them there. It's not the handkerchief that I mind."

"Don't you be a little fool now, Marisela, girl," replied the simpleton. "Gold is gold and no matter where it comes from it's always bright. It's three hundred pesos! You could buy a business with these coppers. There's a shop for sale at Bramador Pass, on the other side of the river. If you want me to, I'll go right over there and ask how much they'll sell it for. It's a good business. Everybody over there stops at that shop and at least you'll get a living out of it. If you buy it I'll go there to be your clerk, and you won't have to pay me anything. Let me go and ask."

"No. No. Let me think about it first, and now you go away. I'm not in any humour to talk with you today. Take one of the coins for yourself and leave the others there on the table."

"*I* take one of those pieces of money for myself? What an idea, Marisela, child! *Ave Maria Purísima!* Let me think a little better of myself! Ah, I'd forgotten that the *señora* told me to tell you . . . Nothing. Nothing. Do what I tell you: buy the shop on the other side of the river and go away from here right away."

Juan Primito went off, the money remained where he had put it, and Marisela sat thinking of what he had suggested.

"Shopkeeper! But what more can I hope for? Shopkeeper! . . . Finally I'll marry or go to live with a peon, and Dr. Santos Luzardo will come there some day and ask for — no, not brandy, because he doesn't drink, but for something or other, and I'll sell it to him and he won't even notice that it was Marisela, the same Marisela, who waited on him."

Some hours later Danger appeared. He joked a bit about the coins still on the table, and when he was about to go, took out of his pocket a paper on which something was written and presented it to Don Lorenzo, saying to him:

"Sign here, old boy. This is the contract we were talking about yesterday."

Lorenzo raised his head with great effort and looked

fixedly at him out of the depths of his drunkenness, without understanding what he had said; but the foreigner put the pen between his fingers, and holding his shaking hand, compelled him to put his signature at the bottom of the page.

"All right!" the latter exclaimed, putting the pen in his breast pocket, and reading the paper aloud: "I hereby declare that I have sold my daughter Marisela to Señor Guillermo Danger for five bottles of whisky."

This was one of the brutal jests he was accustomed to make, but Marisela took it seriously and tried to tear the paper away from him, while Don Lorenzo sank back into his lethargy, with an uncomprehending smile, and a trickle of saliva running out of his mouth. Don Guillermo let her take it, and burst out laughing as Marisela ripped it to shreds, but his laugh only heightened her indignation.

"Get out of here, you insolent pig!" she screamed, her eyes flaming and her face crimson, and as Don Guillermo, standing with his legs wide apart and his hands on his hips continued his booming guffaws, she flung herself on him to shove him out of the house. But her strength was insufficient to move such a mass solidly planted on the floor, and this roused her fury to an even greater pitch and made her more beautiful than ever. She showered a rain of blows on Don Guillermo's deep chest without interrupting his roars of laughter or changing his position in the slightest, and as she succeeded only in hurting her fists against his powerful ribs, to the point of bringing tears to her eyes, she seized the fountain-pen from his breast pocket to plunge it into his throat. He grasped her arms and held her immovable; then, still laughing, he lifted her up and, turning on his feet, made her describe dizzy circles in the air. When he set her back on the floor, stupid with dizziness, she burst into tears; he stood in front of her, his arms akimbo, but no longer laughing. He was breathing heavily and looked at her with eyes inflamed with desire.

While this had been going on, Lorenzo, awakened by the screams of his daughter and Danger's laughter, had with great effort sat up in the hammock; and succeeding in getting hold of a machete blade stuck in the wattled wall of the hut he flung himself upon Danger, with the look of a man in delirium. But Marisela cried out in horror, and Danger turned swiftly, and with a blow made the drunken man lose his balance and crash to the floor with a shriek of pain and impotent rage. Danger took out his pipe, lit it quietly, and said between puffs, turning his back to Marisela:

"Just a joke of mine, Marisela. Señor Danger doesn't like to take things by force, but you know very well that he wants you for himself." And as he was going out, he added: "And don't you ever pick up a machete for Señor Danger, Don Lorenzo, because then there'd be an end to whisky and brandy and everything."

When the American had gone, Lorenzo got up from the floor, swaying on his feet, went to the corner where Marisela sat sobbing, and taking her by the arm, said in a dull, painful voice:

"Let's go away, daughter. Let's get away from here."

For a moment Marisela thought that he was speaking of going back to Altamira, and she allowed herself to be raised from the floor and went out, wiping her eyes; but Don Lorenzo continued:

"There . . . there's the quicksand where everything ends. Let's go there and put an end to this miserable life . . ."

Marisela tried to smile through her tears.

"No, Papa. Be quiet. It was just the *señor's* joke. Didn't you hear him say that? Be calm. Go back to sleep. It was just play. But promise me that you won't drink any more, and that you won't go to ask that man for liquor again."

"No, I won't go again, but I'm going to kill him. . . . It wasn't a joke. . . . It wasn't a joke . . . we'll see. . . . Give me . . . Give me that bottle!"

"No. You've already promised me that you wouldn't drink any more. Go to sleep. . . . It was just a joke."

She sat on the floor near him, passing her hand over his clammy, sticky forehead and softly smoothing his hair, rocking his hammock, until she saw that he had fallen into a deep sleep. Then she wiped off the foamy spittle that was running out of his mouth, kissed his forehead, and felt, as she did so, that a new change had come over her soul. She was no longer the careless, pleasure-seeking girl who had been able to live at Altamira with a laugh and a song on her lips at every moment, indifferent to that spectacle of repugnant and heart-breaking physical and moral misery, entirely distant from the torments of that spirit, because before her own a bright world was opening, full of lovely images, dazzling in its splendour. Santos had shown her that world, which was really her heart with its illusions, and he alone occupied it. He had wiped the dirt from her face with his own hands, had revealed with his words the beauty she had never imagined; he had ended her awkwardness and ignorance with his lessons, and had led her to acquire good manners and finer tastes; but there had remained at the end of this shining grotto that was her heart a little corner hidden in darkness: the spring of tenderness, and that had been left in the darkness, because only sorrow could reveal it to her.

Now it had come to her, and a new Marisela sprang up, dazzled by this self-discovery, with a light of goodness on her face and the softness of tender affection in the hands that had for the first time caressed her father's troubled brow, with genuine filial love.

Don Lorenzo had long sunk with all his misery in the peaceful sleep his daughter's caresses had brought him, and she was continuing to stroke his head with her hand while her distraught eyes were fixed on the coins gleaming on the corner of the table where Juan Primito had placed them, when Antonio Sandoval appeared on the threshold.

Marisela put her forefinger to her lips, jealous of her father's peaceful sleep, and then rose from her place on the floor and went outside to greet him where the conversation would not disturb Lorenzo. Her expression and the quietness of her movements betrayed the deep spiritual change she had undergone in a certain gravity which struck the attention of Antonio.

"What's the matter today, Marisela? There's something odd in the way you look."

"If you only knew, Antonio, how different I feel, too."

"I hope you haven't caught fever from the bog."

"No. Something else. But the bog there has it too. . . . Peace. . . . A delightful restfulness. . . . I feel peaceful all over, the way the pool there must feel when it reflects the palms and the clouds and sky and the herons on the edge."

"Marisela, child," said Antonio, more surprised than ever, "let me tell you how I feel. I've never heard you express yourself like that. And I'm glad to find you in such a mood, because I'll feel more free to tell you what brings me to your house today. You're missed at Altamira, Señorita Marisela. The Doctor has started out on a road that's not the right one for him and won't take him to a good end. Before, you know, he was known as a man who respected other people's rights, even if they were badly secured, and wanted everything to be done legally. And now, on the contrary, there's no arbitrary act that he don't want to do. That's got me worried, because blood is a serious thing when it begins to tell, and I'd be very sorry to see him end up like all the other Luzardos. I don't say that he oughtn't to make people respect his rights, but there's no need of trampling over everything, either. Everything in this world has its too much and too little, and the Doctor has gone out for too much now. This affair with Don Guillermo, true as it is that Don Guillermo is a bad number, was pretty ugly. I wouldn't say it to anybody else but you, but that's the truth. For him to order the putting up of the palisade, although Corozalito don't belong to him any more, was bad enough; but saying to him, 'Do you want me to shoot it out with you?'—that wasn't made for the mouth of a Santos Luzardo. I won't say anything about the bad results it may have, because these foreigners always have something behind them that the native hasn't; but it's what words such as that mean when a man like the Doctor says them. Don't you think the way I do? And now, there's this new thing he's just started, starting rodeos in Doña Barbara's lands without complying with the law and asking her permission. It was his own cattle that he took out, but the natural thing for him to do was to ask as everybody is supposed to do when he goes to collect his herd from somebody else's land. It's not that I'm going to pull him up, because I've already told him: Wherever you go, you can count on my following you. It's just that every tree bears its own fruit, and it's not natural for Santos Luzardo to proceed as Doña Barbara would."

"And do you think that if I'd been there, this would not have happened, Antonio?" Marisela asked him.

"Now look, Marisela, child," Antonio replied. "A man may not be educated, but he may not lack enough sharpness to catch on to certain things. Putting aside what there may be between you and him, and it's not my business to find out whether it exists or not, what I can tell you is that . . . How shall I say it? Well, I'll say it in my own way. For the Doctor, you're like the song for the herd, making the best of things, because if the herd don't hear singing, it wants to stampede every minute. *Sabe?*"

"Yes, I understand," Marisela answered, blushing with pleasure at Antonio's comparison.

"Very well, then. I'll finish where I began. You're missed at Altamira."

Marisela thought a moment, and then said:

"I'm very sorry, Antonio, but for the present, I can't come back to Altamira. Papa wouldn't agree to return, and besides, I've got another duty to perform. I want to take him with me to San Fernando, to see if the doctors there can give him some remedy that will cure him of his drinking and give him his health again, because he's very, very weak."

"I don't see why one prevents the other," Antonio observed.

"Yes, it does. Papa doesn't want to go back to Altamira and I don't want to cross him. Besides, the test was made at Altamira and you see yourself that it didn't work out. Look at the condition he's in. Perhaps I'm missed there, as you say, but there's more need of me here."

"That's true. Your father, first of all. But, what means will you have for going to San Fernando and taking him to see the doctors? Do you want me to speak to the Doctor about it?"

"No. Don't say anything to him about it. I have enough money. I asked it of the person who had a right to give it to me."

"Well," said Antonio, rising, "Santos will be without his song, but you're right. Your father before everything. I hope you'll find remedies for Don Lorenzo. But to make that trip you need horses and someone to go with you. If you don't want me to speak about this to the Doctor, I can send you a peon on my own account, in secret, and two good horses for you and your old father. Although it would be better to take him in a boat, because it don't seem to me that Don Lorenzo is in any condition to stand such a long trip."

"That's true. He's very much run down."

"Then let me manage that for you. Between today and tomorrow a boat from up the Arauca ought to pass here.

I think it's going back empty, and you can go to San Fernando in it."

Antonio took his departure. Marisela went back into the house, stood a moment by the hammock where Don Lorenzo was sleeping, and gazed with loving eyes at the sunken features she had never before contemplated as she did now. Then she took from the table the gold coins that would make it possible for her to carry out her plan, and felt no repugnance whatever at taking them in her hands. Juan Primito had not managed to wash them, but purifying waters from the newly found springs of tenderness had touched her mother's money.

VII

INSCRUTABLE DESIGNS

THE slanting rays of the sun gilded with their tawny gold the trunks of the trees in the patio, the posts of the corrals and those of the cabins under the violet shadow of the dark roofs, and when the brilliant disk had hidden itself on the horizon there remained above the huge wheel growing dimmer and dimmer to the prairie, long clouds like bars of molten metal, round, massy clouds of warm colours, and the firm black silhouette of a lone distant palm against the splendour of the west.

Altamira lay in that direction and Doña Barbara's gaze was turned towards it, losing itself in the distance.

Three days had passed since the news of the destruction of the house at Macanillal and the abduction of the Mondragons had reached El Miedo, the brothers were already in the keeping of the authorities to whom Luzardo had sent them, and the latter had twice entered the territory of El Miedo with his peons to hold a rodeo without complying with the required request for permission. Doña Barbara's peons were still awaiting her orders to begin reprisals.

Seeing that she was making no move to give them, Balbino Paiba finally decided to ask her to, in his capacity of overseer, and went over to the palisade where she stood absorbed in silent contemplation of the landscape. But before broaching the question, he consumed considerable time with pretexts for conversation. She responded only in monosyllables, and the pauses of the dialogue became longer and longer.

At the time, a herd was coming towards the corrals. The song of the herdsmen could be heard floating over the silent open land. The first of the beasts approached. The leader, a light brown bull, came to a sudden stop before the fig tree planted before the door of the sheepfold and bellowed significantly. He had smelled the blood of a steer slaughtered there that morning. The herd commenced to mill around and take fright, while the leader went in circles around the tree, pawing the earth, sniffing it, assuring himself of the horrible thing that had happened in that place, and when no doubts remained to him, he bellowed again, but in anger this time, and the herd rushed away to the open plain.

"Who's idea was it to take the sheepfold gate for slaughtering a steer?" roared Balbino, flaunting his position as overseer, while the herdsmen gave free rein to their horses and sped away to head off the scattering cattle. They managed at last to subdue the beasts and drove them again to the corral situated a little beyond the fig tree. The herd, though shut in, continued to bellow mournfully, and Doña Barbara said suddenly:

"Even the cattle are horrified by the blood of their fellows."

Balbino looked at her out of the corner of his eye, with a gesture of surprise, and asked himself:

"And does she say that?"

Several minutes passed.

"Hm! There's no spying into this woman's mind," Balbino reflected. "You can discover what even a horse is thinking, beast that he is, just by looking to see which of his ears he lays down, but with this woman, you're always dancing on a tightrope." And he quitted her.

But not only Balbino Paiba, who was quite stupid; Doña Barbara herself could not have told what her own plans were.

Once more, her deeds had come before her, obstructing the road she was determined to follow. Santos Luzardo's haughty words were still ringing in her ears — the words he had used to fling his suspicion in her face, at the very time when she was going to tell him that she thought she had discovered the criminal and was going to turn him over, personally, as soon as she had gained possession of the *corpus delicti*. It was an unjust and slanderous suspicion; but yet, justice itself was lurking in the depths of it, for was it only in El Totumo that the thickets kept secrets of murderous ambuscades? and if it had been Balbino Paiba who had done the deed there for his own sake, had not Melquíades, in other places, discharged mortal shots, planned by her, at unwary travellers? And was not Balbino Paiba, too, the instrument of her deeds? Wasn't he, indeed, her own deed, shutting her off from a better road?

Stinging rage lashed her heart, during those three days — against the paramour whose crime Santos Luzardo attributed to her, against the sinister assassin who kept the secrets of those he had committed, against the very victims of her greed and cruelty who had crossed her path, making it necessary for her to put them out of the way, and against all those who, as though she had not had enough of crime, now came to her to suggest reprisals: Balbino, Melquíades, every one of her peons, her gang of thugs, accomplices, and tools, whose looks, fixed on her, were asking every minute:

"What are you waiting for to order us to kill Dr. Luzardo? Aren't we here for that? Haven't you agreed to give us blood to spill?"

Juan Primito started off for Altamira with this message for Luzardo:

"Tonight, when the moon rises, a person who has something to tell you concerning the crime at El Totumo will be waiting for you in Rincón Hondo. If you aren't afraid, come there alone to hear what that person will tell you."

Juan Primito went, and returned with Luzardo's response.

"Tell her all right. I'll be there alone."

That was in the morning. A little later she had called Melquíades.

"Do you remember what you said to me a few days ago?" she inquired.

"I still remember it, *señora.*"

"Very well. Tonight, when the moon rises, Dr. Luzardo will be in Rincón Hondo."

"And I'll bring him here to you, alive or dead."

Night was coming on. Soon her sinister henchman would be setting out, but still Doña Barbara had not succeeded in discovering what plans she was following with that ambuscade, nor with what emotions she was waiting for the appearance of the moon on the horizon.

Until that time, she had always been the sphinx of the savannahs for others. Now she was that for herself, too; her own designs had become impenetrable to her.

VIII

RED GLORY

IT did not fail to occur to Santos Luzardo that only a mind in a bad state of confusion could have brought forth the idea of inviting him, in such an absurd fashion, to fall into a trap; but he too gave indications of having lost his reason, in deciding to make use of the occasion to demonstrate to Doña Barbara that she would gain nothing by trying to intimidate him, since if he could not recover his trampled rights before the authorities who were subordinated to the violators, he would in future be able to defend them with the wild law of the savage — armed force. And with this rash determination he went forth alone on the evening of that day, riding in the direction of Rincón Hondo, and planning to arrive there before the hour set, to mock the treacherous attempt made under cover of the night.

But when he came within sight of the place, he saw a horseman at the edge of the woods bordering the lonely corner of the prairie, and he said to himself:

"She's always ahead of me."

Then he discovered that the horseman was Pajarote.

"What are you doing here?" Luzardo demanded authoritatively, as he joined the man.

"I'll tell you, Doctor," the peon answered. "This morning, when Juan Primito came up to you to give you his message, I suspected that it couldn't be anything good and went after him, letting him get out of your sight first, and then I caught up with him. I put my gun against his ribs, only to scare him because I know that he's ready to cash in when he sees a revolver, and forced him to tell me the message she had given him for you. I found out from him that you had promised to come, and I was tempted to say to you: Don't do it, Doctor. But I saw determination all over you, and I said to myself: The only thing is to get there first and face the music with him."

"You've done wrong to meddle with my affairs," Santos answered, drily.

"I don't say anything to the contrary, but I'm not sorry either. Because if you've got more than enough nerve, I think you haven't got enough suspicion. Do you know if it's one man that's coming to talk with you?"

"I don't care if there are several. Go back home."

"Look, Doctor," Pajarote replied, scratching his head. "A peon is a peon, and it's up to him to obey when his master gives orders, but let me remind you that a Plainsman is a peon only when he's working. Here, at this time and place, we haven't got a man and a peon, but one man, that's you, and another man who wants to show him that he's ready to give his life for him, and for that reason didn't look for companions to come and face the music with you. I'm that man, and I don't expect to move from here."

Moved by this rude demonstration of loyalty, Santos said to himself that he wasn't sure that armed force was the only law of the Plain, and he accepted Pajarote's company, shaking his hand in silence.

"And you can make use of this as experience, Doctor," Pajarote concluded. "A Plainsman can go alone when he's told: Come with a companion, but never the opposite. And spurs ready. I've looked all through these woods. They haven't come yet, but they won't delay much longer. They ought to arrive in the direction we're looking. We'll lie in ambush behind this bit of marsh, and when they heave in sight, as soon as they come out here we'll go after them, but knocking down and gelding, because the man that shoots first shoots twice."

They concealed themselves in the spot chosen by Pajarote and remained there a long time watching the clearing between the thickets where those coming from El Miedo would appear. The men were silent beneath the excited, wailing little monkeys, trooping in bands to their sleeping places. The night closed in, and the moon had begun to shine above the edge of the savannah when the silhouette of the Wizard arose against the light.

"He is alone, after all, and I have someone with me," Luzardo muttered with a gesture of annoyance. Pajarote, to relieve him of his scruples, replied:

"Remember what I just told you, Doctor — spurs ready, always. That man is alone, if his partners aren't ambushed around here, but that's the Wizard, and they never send him to *talk* with anybody. And if he does come alone, that's the worst of all, because he never goes accompanied when he's sent to execute certain orders. Let him feel confident and come out into the open so we can go after him. Although I'm going to tell you to leave him to me. I'll undress that *Terror* all by myself, with all the reputation he's got, because better men than him have left their shirts in my hands."

"No," Luzardo protested. "The man has come for me, and it's I alone that he should meet. You stay here."

He rode swiftly out of the clump into the open prairie.

The Wizard advanced at his usual steady pace, but stopped suddenly. Luzardo did the same, and they remained so for a brief period, looking at each other from a distance, until, as the man seemed disinclined to come nearer, Luzardo put the spurs to his horse and negotiated the space between them. As he came quite close to the Wizard, he heard him say:

"Then I've been sent here so you and your men can

shoot me like a dog? If that's the case, come out of there immediately."

Santos understood that Pajarote had come behind him, in spite of the fact that he had been told to remain in hiding, and he was about to turn his head to tell him to go back when he saw the gleam of the revolver the Wizard was taking out of the poncho thrown across the pommel of his saddle. With a swift movement, he drew his own. The shots rang out simultaneously, Melquíades tumbled over the neck of his horse, and the animal, taking fright, threw him off on the ground, where he lay inert, face downward in the grass.

The stunning realization came to Luzardo like the stroke of a club: He had killed a man!

Pajarote joined him, and after looking for a moment at the body lying there on the ground, he murmured:

"Well, Doctor, what'll we do with this corpse?"

The words, although he heard them clearly, required a long time to reach the depths where Luzardo's consciousness had fled, and Pajarote answered his own question.

"We'll sling him across his horse, and I'll tie it to mine, and when we come close to the houses at El Miedo I'll let him loose, shy him off that way, and yell: 'Here's something from Rincón Hondo!'"

Coming out of his stupor, Luzardo dismounted.

"Bring that thug's horse here. I'm the one who's going to take his corpse to the person who sent him for me."

Pajarote looked at him from head to foot. The intonation with which the words had been pronounced made Luzardo's voice sound strange, as strange as the grimly fierce expression on his face, which did not seem like his own.

" Do what I tell you. Bring the horse here."

Pajarote obeyed, but when Luzardo leaned over to lift up the body, he interfered.

" No, Doctor. That's not your job. Take him to Doña Barbara, if you want to make her such a present, but the one that's going to put this dead man on the horse is Pajarote. Hold the beast while I throw him over."

When this had been done, and the Wizard's horse had been tied to Luzardo's, Pajarote, availing himself of his knowledge of the region, so that his master might not refuse to let him go along, proposed:

" There ought to be a cattle track leading straight to the El Miedo houses. Let's go along it."

Santos agreed to let the man accompany him, but when they came in sight of Doña Barbara's house, he said:

" Wait for me here."

At last, and against his will, that presentiment of a sudden return to lawlessness, the torment of his youth, had begun to be realized. All the efforts he had made to free himself from the menace he saw hanging over his life, to repress the impulse of his blood towards the violence of the Luzardos, who had all been men-at-arms with no other law than armed force; and all the efforts he had made, on the other hand, to acquire the viewpoint of a civilized man in whom instinct was subordinate to the discipline of principle, all the bitter obstinate struggle of the best years of his life — all vanished now, overthrown by the rash display of courage which had impelled him to go to the snare laid for him at Rincón Hondo.

He felt not only the natural scruples of a man who has been obliged to kill in self-defence, the horror of the brutal situation which had made it imperative for him to perform an act repugnant to the principles most deeply rooted in his spirit, but horror at the eternal loss of these principles, at having undergone an irredeemable experience, at belonging, actually belonging for life to the tragic group of men under the cloud of crime. The first, the act itself, although it had been in his power to avoid it, had its extenuating features. It had been an act of legitimate self-defence, since Melquíades had been the first to draw. But the second, which was not an act of will nor of overwhelming impulse, but resulted from a conspiracy of circumstances possible only in the breast of barbarism on which the Plain was flung: entrance in the fateful circle of men who had been compelled to execute justice with armed force — this, certainly, could have neither remedy nor extenuation. His name would swoop over the Arauca surrounded by the red halo the death of Doña Barbara's dread henchman gave to it, and from that moment on his whole life would be jeopardized by that glory, for barbarism never releases the man who tries to master it by adapting its own procedure. It is inexorable. Once a man has armed himself with it, he must accept everything from its hands.

But, when he had resolved to devote himself to the ranch, renouncing his dreams of a civilized life—had he not then proposed to become the ruler of the Plain so that he might repress the savage lordship of the caciques, and was it not with the red glory of bloody deeds that he had to struggle with them, to stamp them out? Had he not said that he accepted the path along which he was being stampeded into violence? It was too late to go back.

He rode on alone with the grim burden he was leading. Alone, and a changed man.

IX

AMUSEMENT FOR SEÑOR DANGER

SEÑOR DANGER was ready to retire when his dogs barked and he heard the hoofbeats of a horse.

"Who can be coming here at this hour?" he asked himself, going to the door and looking out.

The moon was rising, but over the savannahs of The Lick a dense darkness hung beneath a cloudy sky in the suffocating air.

"Oh! Don Balbino!" Danger exclaimed finally as he recognized his untimely visitor. "What brings you here at such an hour?"

"Just to see you, Don Guillermo. As I was passing by, I said to myself: I'll go over there to say how do you do to Don Guillermo, because I haven't seen him since he came back from San Fernando."

Danger was not likely to believe in the sincerity of any demonstrations of friendship from Balbino Paiba, nor did he value them very highly; for, apart from certain collusions, Balbino was merely one of those he called friends of his whisky, and he received him sarcastically.

" Oh! *Caramba!* What an honour to have you come to see me when I was going to bed! Many thanks, Don Balbino. That deserves a little swig. Come in and sit down while I pour it out. There's no more danger of the jaguar, because it died, poor thing! "

" Really? What a shame! " exclaimed Balbino, sitting down. " A pretty animal, that cub, and you were very fond of him. You must miss him badly."

" Oh, you can imagine. Every night, before I went to bed, I used to play around with him a long while," replied Señor Danger, while he was pouring two glasses of whisky from the recently uncorked bottle on his desk.

They emptied the glasses. Balbino wiped his moustache and said:

" Thank you, Don Guillermo. May it give you health. . . . And what have you been doing? You stayed a long while in San Fernando this time. To forget the jaguar? They were already saying around here that you'd gone back to your country. But I said: Not if I know Don Guillermo he won't go away from here. He's more of a native than we are and he'd miss the uproar, the *guachafita*."

" That's it, Don Balbino. That's the pleasant thing about this country. I always quote that general of yours, I forget his name: The one who said: ' If the disorder ends, I'm going,' " and he laughed from ear to ear of his red face.

"Didn't I say so? You're more of a native than *guasacaca.*"

"The *guasacaca* is very nice too. Everything beginning with *gua* is nice. . . . *Guachafita, guasacaca* sauce, pretty *guaricha.* . . . *Guá,* Señor Danger! Let's have a shot, as my friends always say when they're with me."

"Ah, Señor Danger. I wish all the foreigners that come here were like you," said Balbino flatteringly, laying his ground.

"And you, how are things with you, Don Balbino? How's business going?" Danger inquired, taking out his pipe and giving it a preliminary puff or two. "Is Doña Barbara still the same handsome girl? That doesn't begin with *guá,* but it's nice, eh, Don Balbino? You rascal, you!"

They laughed together like any two rascals applauding their knavery, and Balbino broached his subject, after the preliminary characteristic stroking of his moustache.

"Business hasn't been altogether very bad this year. But you know, Don Guillermo, a poor man is a poor man, and he's never without need of money."

"Oh, don't begin crying about that, Don Balbino. You've got money buried safe. Lots of money."

Balbino made an involuntary movement and hastened to reply:

"If that was only so! I make a living, that's all. There's no way of saving money with the kind of twopenny business I'm able to do. That's all right for Barbara and you, because you've got land and take out plenty of cattle. I've hardly been able to get hold of some forty strays this year. And now that we're speaking of it, buy them from me, Don Guillermo. I need a bit of cash and I'll let you have them cheap."

"Are the brands well burned off?"

Burning off the original brand of cattle to sell them as his own was one of Balbino Paiba's accomplishments, and although he did not mind having it mentioned between friends, Danger's question did not strike him pleasantly at this time.

"They're entirely mine, hair and hide," he said haughtily.

"That's another story," replied Señor Danger. "Because if they were Luzardo cattle, I wouldn't mix myself up in the business whether the brand could be seen or not."

"All this caution, Don Guillermo?" Balbino asked in reply. "You've always bought Luzardo cattle that were smuggled without making a fuss about it. Has this Altamira dude hobbled you too?"

"I don't need to tell you if he's hobbled me, as you say," retorted Danger. "I've merely said that I won't buy Altamira cattle, or horses, or feathers. That's all I have to say."

"I'm not offering you feathers," Balbino hastened to remark.

The other man was about to answer, when something happened which attracted his attention: the dogs lying on the gallery in front of the room where the interview was being held, leapt up and ran off, without growling or snapping, as though they were going out to meet someone they knew well.

Balbino did not notice this, as he was sitting with his back to the door, and Danger, to ascertain what it was, said:

"Another shot, friend Paiba?" and taking the glasses they had drunk from, under pretext of going to throw out the rest of the liquor they contained, he went out to the gallery and explored the night with a rapid glance, by which he discovered Juan Primito, poorly concealed behind a tree and surrounded by the dogs, his friends, as were all those in the houses in the locality. The explanation came swiftly: "This fellow's been sent to spy on Don Balbino," followed by a perverse inspiration: "We'll make this vagabond talk"; and without revealing anything, he went back into the room, filled the glasses, emptied his, sat facing Balbino, and remained a while in silence, puffing repeatedly at his pipe. Then he said, recommencing the interrupted conversation:

"I mentioned feathers because you sold me some last year. You remember?"

"Yes. But, unfortunately, I wasn't able to buy any this year. Just as I told you, forty steers is my whole capital."

" And you'd be right if you said ' fortunately ' because after that business at El Totumo and until they find out exactly what it was that went on there, it's dangerous to offer plumes for sale. Isn't that so, Don Balbino? "

" *Is* it dangerous? "

Danger sat back easily in his chair, stretched out his legs, and said, without taking the pipe out of his mouth, as though it were a sudden thought:

" Now that the conversation's turned on it, Don Balbino, haven't you ever been through the chaparral thicket at El Totumo? "

Plucking up heart, Balbino replied in the tone one uses for things of no importance:

" Through the chaparral? well, not exactly. I've been close to it, when I've had to go to San Fernando."

" Strange," said Señor Danger, scratching his head.

" Why do you think it's strange? " Balbino demanded, fixing a penetrating look upon him. But this was the answer he received:

" Well, I have been through there. Just now, when I was coming back from San Fernando, the day after the authorities had been there. I hunted through the whole thicket, and convinced myself, once more, that the judges in this country have their eyes for ornament, as one of my friends at San Fernando says."

While he was saying this, leaning back, with his head on the high head-rest of the extension chair, apparently looking at the smoke from his pipe, but without losing sight of Balbino's face, he opened a desk drawer and took out something his interlocutor could not see, because he had it hidden in his huge fist.

Balbino lost all notion of time, and it seemed to him that he had taken long to reply, when, on the contrary, he answered the very instant Danger had finished speaking.

"What was it you saw that the authorities didn't see?"

"I saw—" But he interrupted himself immediately, to look at the object he had taken out of the desk, with the air of one who suddenly finds in his hand something he did not believe he had. "Isn't this yours, Don Balbino? I think this little *chimó* box is yours." And he displayed one of those little boxes cut out of black wood, in which those accustomed to use *chimó* carry the vile stuff.

Balbino involuntarily tapped his pockets to see if he had the box, without remembering that he had lost it some time before.

"Yes," Señor Danger continued, after observing the monogram on the cover of the device. "This is yours, Don Balbino."

Losing control of himself, Balbino sprang to his feet, with his right hand on his revolver; but Danger replied, jokingly:

"Oh! There's no need of that, Don Balbino. Take your box. I hadn't any idea of keeping it."

With a visible effort to calm himself, Balbino demanded:

" What does all this mean, Señor Danger? "

" It's very clear, man! That you forgot and left this box, and that I found it and said to myself: ' This is Don Balbino's, he'll come here to look for it. I'll keep it for him.' But I see quite well that you've imagined something else. No, Don Balbino, don't worry. It wasn't in the chaparral thicket at El Totumo that I found this box, nor at the foot of the *paraguatán* at La Matica, either."

He referred, in speaking of the latter spot, to the place where Balbino had buried the feathers.

" I managed things very well," the latter had said to himself. " I didn't leave a trace of myself in the chaparral and as for the feathers, no magician that ever lived could find out where I've got them hidden! "

But here it was, although he didn't believe that he had carried the box with him to the chaparral, he couldn't say for certain if it was there that he had lost it; and for the rest, the allusion to the *paraguatán* tree at La Matica left no room for doubt — Danger was in on the secret of the crime and knew where he had hidden the feathers.

" Curse it! " he thought. " Who told me to come and ask this man to buy my cattle? Greediness, that always lets the cat out of the bag! "

For Balbino, upon leaving Doña Barbara a short while earlier, after he had heard her remark that " Even the cattle are horrified at the blood of their fellows," had decided to flee from the ranch with his booty and go to the Colombian frontier; and he had only been waiting for the favouring darkness to go to La Matica and dig up the plumes. But as he also had a certain number of steers in that place, the fruit of cold-blooded thefts of his paramour's property, greed told him to offer them to the foreigner.

Understanding that, now that it was discovered, the best thing was to come out bare-faced with the matter, he inquired:

"Tell me something, Don Guillermo, what did you mean by what you said about the *paraguatán* at La Matica?"

"Oh. Very simple. An accident, purely an accident. That night I was hunting a tiger they told me was hanging around there, and I saw you burying a box at the foot of the *paraguatán* I don't know what's in the box."

"Yes, you do know, Don Guillermo. Never mind those pretenses with me," replied Balbino, decidedly. "At this time and place, and with the kind of man I'm talking to, let's call a spade a spade. I haven't come to offer you cattle, but heron feathers. Fifty pounds complete and first class. Make me a reasonable offer and they're yours. They won't be the first stolen plumes you've bought."

But Danger burst into a loud laugh.

"You're making a mistake, Don Balbino," he said.

" I've only wanted to amuse myself a while with you. This *chimó* box, you left it here, on my desk, some time ago. I haven't been in the chaparral thicket at El Totumo. It was all a joke of mine, except that about the *paraguatán* at La Matica, eh? "

Purple with rage, Balbino replied:

" Do you mean that you've picked me out to take the place of your jaguar cub? Don't you know that that sort of playing is very dangerous? "

But at that moment the dogs growled, and the blood of bad temper drained out of Balbino's face. He looked out of the door, trying to pierce the obscurity, and although he saw nothing, he said:

" Someone who was listening to what we said has just gone away."

Señor Danger laughed again.

" Don't you see, Don Balbino," he concluded, " how bad it is to show fright these days? The most dangerous thing there is nowadays is to offer heron feathers for sale. Mr. Danger won't talk, not because he's afraid of your threats, but because he doesn't care a rap for what happened in the chaparral at El Totumo. And now. . . ." And clicking his teeth, he showed Don Balbino the door.

Balbino desired nothing more; but he did not leave without giving a furious look around him, accompanied by the indispensable stroking of his moustache, and once outside, he leaped upon his horse and took the road towards La Matica, saying to himself:

"Now there's no time to lose! I'll get to digging up my feathers right away, and then, the bird's as good as flown. Travelling by night and hiding in the thickets in the daytime, I'll be over the Colombian border before they get on my tracks."

Meanwhile Danger, alone in his house, was saying to himself between guffaws:

"Juan Primito must be at El Miedo already with the tale of what he's heard. Now Doña Barbara will want Balbino to divide the feathers with her. Poor old Balbino!"

After this heathful exercise of his good humour, he slept deeply and quietly, as he had been accustomed to do when the jaguar was alive, after their frolic on the mat.

X

WITHDRAWAL

IT WAS some time since she had heard, in the profound silence of the night, the reports of the shots at Rincón Hondo; and yet Doña Barbara, torn by her anxiety to know what had happened there and missing the extraordinary intuition of distant events attributed to her, was still walking up and down the gallery, from one end to the other, extremely agitated, and trying to pierce the darkness of the prairie at every moment, when Juan Primito arrived out of breath from the haste with which he had brought his news.

"The feathers are buried at La Matica at the foot of the *paraguatán*."

He went on immediately to explain how he had found this out, but he had hardly commenced when Doña Barbara, who had been paying little enough attention as it was, hastily left the gallery and went out. At the same time the dogs ran out too, barking at the horseman they met leading a horse tied to his own.

"Melquíades?" she inquired.

"It's not Melquíades," Luzardo replied, and pulling his horse up, he commenced to untie the bridle of the other, with the same grim calm the Wizard would have displayed had the situation been reversed.

Barbara joined him, and after taking a rapid survey of the assassin's body, as of a thing of no importance, she fixed her gaze upon the man, who was attentive only to the task his hands were busied with. That gaze at once expressed astonishment and admiration. This new and unexpected visage of the man she desired overthrew and mingled all there was in her of love and longing for righteousness in a single monstrous emotion.

"I knew you'd bring him," she murmured.

Santos turned his head sharply. The complicated plan of this Amazon had just become clear to him: she had wanted to rid herself of the assassin who was the accomplice of her crimes, and had sent the man to Rincón Hondo so that he, Luzardo, might kill him. She had converted him, then, into her tool, and now had the boldness to let him understand it. Morally, he actually belonged to the troop of cut-throats of the woman cacique of the Arauca.

The momentary impulse to rush upon her, driving his horse over her so that he might overthrow her and trample her on the ground, seized him; but immediately the savagery boiling in his breast underwent a brusque abatement, and tossing the bridle of the Wizard's horse at her feet, he gave rein to his and rode off buried in gloom, going over and over the reflection which had just occurred to him: The affair at Rincón Hondo had not given him the red glory of the rulers by blood and fire, but the dismal reputation of the assassin, the executor of that infamous woman's designs.

The Wizard's horse with his grim burden lying across the saddle stood a long time quiet, with his head turned towards Doña Barbara, as though awaiting her decision. The dogs, too, after they had sniffed at the feet and hanging hands of the corpse, stood quiet, in an expectant group, their gaze fixed on the face of their owner. But as the latter remained absorbed, looking in the direction of the disappearance of Luzardo's shadowy form into the night, the horse decided to walk over to the harness cabin, step by step, as though to avoid feeling the tragic weight he bore, and the dogs trotted after him, growling.

Doña Barbara remained immobile, but that look of astonishment and admiration had entirely disappeared from her face, and her frowning forehead now indicated the gloom of troubled thought. Once more it appeared as though her instinct had guided her aright, since despite the absurd fashion in which the Rincón Hondo plan had been formed, it had turned out in the manner most convenient for her schemes. Not because that solution was in reality the one she had sought, for in this, as in nearly all her plans, there had been nothing but a simple impulsive provocation, a hit-or-miss blow with any possible result, to put an end to a complicated situation. But, as always happened to her, she deceived herself, in the face of the chance outcome, telling herself that it was this she had foreseen, this she had sought.

She had been in part the prey of contradictory feelings with regard to Luzardo: passionate love and a desire for vengeance; and in part torn by furious despair at the fatal way in which former deeds rose before her wherever she might be, blocking her path; and she had planned the snare for him at Rincón Hondo to facilitate the workings of chance. The death of Luzardo, or the death of the Wizard—either was a solution on which her fate depended.

It was certain that she now had Luzardo's fate in her hands, for accusing him of killing Melquíades and setting in play a little of her influence over judges and other authorities of the country would be enough to ruin him and send him to jail. But this would have been a definite renunciation of the good, a return to her deeds of old, from whose fatal influence she wanted to free herself.

She had already begun to renounce them. The Mondragons had been left to their fate, Melquíades was lying across that horse. . . .

The excitement of the peons interrupted her reflections. One of the cowboys was coming from among the cabins to tell her the news. As she turned around she saw Juan Primito, who had watched the entire scene from the gallery, stiff with horror and crossing himself, and with a sudden inspiration she said to him:

"You haven't seen anything, *sabe?* Get away from here this instant, and look out if you get the idea of telling what you've seen."

The simple fellow vanished in the darkness of the prairie with his long strides, and Doña Barbara, as though she knew nothing of what had happened, and with the habitual impassive expression she used so well to hide her thoughts, listened to what the cowboy told her and then turned her steps towards the cabin.

Awakened by the shouts of the peon who had seen the arrival of the horse with the dead Wizard on his back, the other cowboys, the kitchen maids, and the children of one and the other, formed a circle around the horse, making comments and bursting into exclamations, but when Doña Barbara joined them they became silent and stood looking anxiously at her, hanging on the slightest movement of her enigmatic face.

She went up to the corpse and after having noticed that it bore a wound in the left breast, out of which was running a trickle of sticky black blood, she said:

"Take him down and put him on the ground to see if he has any other wounds."

This was done, but while one of the peons was examining the body, she appeared to be attentive to the thoughts which clouded her face, rather than to what he was doing.

"Only the wound in the left side," the peon finally said, getting up. "A noble wound, too. It must have killed him — like that."

"The one who fired the shot had a good eye," another observed, "but anyone can see that he wasn't face to face with him. Certainly they were shooting at him from behind some tree or other."

"Or it was someone at his side," replied Doña Barbara, turning to look at the peon who had made the remark.

"That could be, too," murmured the cowboy, accepting the interpretation from one who did not have to see things to know how they had happened.

Doña Barbara again fixed her gaze on the corpse, on whose bloodless face were mingled the pallid moonlight and the livid gleam of a candle held by the trembling hands of one of the women. Meanwhile, the silent circle of watchers awaited the outcome of her reflections. Suddenly she lifted her eyes and looked around her, as though she were seeking someone.

"Where is Balbino?"

Although all knew that Balbino was not there among them, every eye sought him in the group with a simultaneous involuntary movement, and then, with unanimous suspicion, aroused in their hostile minds by that artful question, they exchanged glances which plainly asked:

"Could it have been Balbino?"

"It is!" Doña Barbara said to herself, as she saw that

her words had produced the desired effect; and then, with the dreamy intonation, with which she assisted her reputation as a witch, she turned to two of her peons, either one of whom she might very well have chosen as Melquíades Gamarra's successor.

" At La Matica, at the foot of the *paraguatán,* the heron plumes belonging to Dr. Luzardo are buried. Balbino must be there, unearthing them. Go there, quickly. Take two Winchesters and . . . bring me the feathers. Do you understand? " She turned immediately to the others. " Take up the body. Take it to his house and lay it out there."

She went off to her house, leaving the peons with a rich field for comment during the gathering for the Melquíades death-watch.

" And let me tell you that if it was Balbino, there must have been some pretty thick trees for him to hide behind, because man to man, the dead man had it all over him."

" We'll see now if he can get the ones that are going after him from behind trees."

For a long while, expectation kept them silent, harkening to distant sounds. Finally, they heard shots from the direction of La Matica.

" The *Guinchestes* have begun firing," said one.

" There's a revolver answering," added a second. " Wouldn't it be a good thing for us to go over there to help the boys? "

Several were ready to depart for La Matica, when Doña Barbara appeared and said to them:

"It's not necessary. Balbino's already done for."

The cowboys looked in each others' faces again, with the superstitious uneasiness the "second sight" of the dreaded woman inspired in them, and when she had re-entered her house, one of them ventured an explanation:

"Didn't you notice that the revolver was the first to stop firing? The last shots came from the *Guinchestes.*"

But who could get it out of the heads of the servants of the witch of the Arauca that she had "seen" what was going on at La Matica?

XI

LIGHT IN THE CAVE

IT WAS already midnight, and they had ridden in silence for over an hour, when Pajarote remarked, as they came in sight of the palm grove of La Chusmita:

"Light at this hour in Don Lorenzo's house? Something must be happening there."

Santos, who had come from El Miedo cast down and insensible to anything around him, raised his head, as though he were just coming out of a dream. Three days had passed since that other night when Antonio Sandoval told him that Marisela had gone away to the hut in the palm grove, and not for a single instant had his mind, confused by the plans of violence which had recently reached a crisis in the depression now making him silent and gloomy, harboured any idea of the privations and dangers to which the girl might be exposed; and yet, she had beyond question been the overmastering occupation of his thoughts for several months.

He realized that he had done wrong in abandoning her to her fate, and finding relief from his torments in once more giving place in his heart to generous feelings, he turned towards the grove. A few moments later he stopped on the threshold of the hut before the sorrowful picture lighted by the dying light of a candle: huddled in his hammock in a shapeless heap lay Lorenzo Barquero with the seal of death on his features, and near him Marisela, seated on the floor, was stroking his forehead, her beautiful eyes fixed on his face.

Thus caressing him, she had helped him to die easily, with the tender support of love, although it was some time since his forehead had ceased to feel the soft touch of her hand.

More than the sadness of the scene — the dramatic life whose light had gone out, the poverty, the troubled, weeping face of the girl — what touched Luzardo's heart was the tenderness he saw, the caressing hand, the loving look of the eyes filled with tears, the tenderness he had thought Marisela incapable of feeling.

"Papa's dead!" she exclaimed, with a heart-rending accent, as she saw Santos, and covering her face with her hands she threw herself face downward on the floor.

After making sure that Lorenzo was really dead, Santos lifted Marisela up onto a chair, but she flung herself upon his breast, moaning and crying. They were silent for a long time, and then Marisela, with the loquacity of sorrow, began to explain.

"I meant to take him tomorrow to San Fernando to see the doctors. I thought they could cure him and I wanted to take him with me. I told Antonio, who was here this afternoon, and he offered to arrange for a boat which was coming from up the river. Antonio had just left and I had come in to have a look at Papa before I made his supper, because this morning he was very weak and I was afraid to leave him alone for very long, and suddenly he made an effort to sit up in the hammock, and looked at me with his eyes wide open, and shouted: 'The quagmire! It's swallowing me! . . . Hold me up, don't let me sink!' It was a frightful cry, and I seem to be hearing it still. Then he fell back again in the hammock and began to die, and kept saying every minute: 'I'm sinking! I'm sinking! I'm sinking!' And he caught hold of my hand, in a terrible agony."

"That was his idea," Pajarote observed. "That the bog would swallow him up."

Santos remained silent, reproaching himself for his unjustifiable abandonment of Lorenzo and Marisela; she went on excitedly:

"I meant to take him to San Fernando tomorrow. Antonio had offered to secure a place for us in a boat going there. . . ."

But Santos interrupted her, holding her against him as a father might have done.

"That's enough," he said. "Don't talk any more."

"But I've suffered all this night from not being able to talk. Helpless and alone all night watching him sink and sink and sink. Because it was just as if he was really sinking in the quagmire. My God! What an awful thing death is! And I, helpless and alone, helping him to die easily. And now, helpless and alone for life! What can I do now, my God!"

"We're going back to Altamira now and then we'll see what we'll do. You haven't been left as unprotected as you think. Pajarote, go get enough men and a horse saddled for Marisela. And you go to bed for a while to rest and try to sleep."

But Marisela did not wish to move away from her father, and went to sit down on the stool where Lorenzo had been seated the afternoon of Santos' first visit, leaving the latter the chair he had then occupied. And thus, separated by the hammock in which the dead man was lying, they sat a long time without a word.

Outside, the moonlight beamed upon the silent palm grove extending around the little house, immobile in the stillness of the night, reflected, a little distance away, in the quiet water of the quagmire. The peace brooding over the moonlit scene was clear and deep; but the hearts within were troubled and felt it crushing and forbidding.

Marisela sobbed from time to time, and Santos was thoughtful, frowning and gloomy; he repeated to himself the words Lorenzo had spoken that afternoon when he had visited the La Barquereña house for the first time: "You too, Santos Luzardo! You've heard the call too?"

Lorenzo had already succumbed, a victim of the ogress, which was not so much Doña Barbara as the implacable land, the wild land, with its brutalizing isolation, the quagmire where the pride of the Barqueros had wallowed; and now he too had begun to sink in that other quagmire, that of barbarism which never releases those who throw themselves into it. He too was now a victim of the ogress. Lorenzo had ended his subjugation; *he* was just beginning.

"Santos Luzardo, look at me! This land never relents!"

He looked at the sunken face, covered with the clayey patina of death, replacing, in his imagination, his own features for those of Lorenzo and saying to himself:

"Soon I shall begin to pass my days in drunkenness to forget, and soon I shall be like this, with hideous death drawn on my face, the death of a man's spectre, the death of a living corpse."

And having taken Lorenzo's place in this way, he was surprised that Marisela spoke to him as to a living being.

"They tell me you've been very strange these days, doing things that you weren't meant to do. . . ."

"They haven't told you anything yet. I killed a man tonight."

"You? . . . No! It can't be."

"What's odd about it? All the Luzardos have been murderers."

"It isn't possible," Marisela replied. "Tell me about it. Tell me."

When he had told her about the evil event, as he saw

it in his excited imagination — as it had happened, but badly interpreted in his confused mental state, she repeated:

"Don't you see that it wasn't possible? If the thing happened as you tell it, it was Pajarote who killed the Wizard. Didn't you say that he was on your right, face to face with you, and that the wound was in the left breast? Then no one but Pajarote could have shot him on that side."

The presence of the scene before his imagination for hours, and persistent reflection over all its details had not sufficed to make Santos take account of what Marisela had inferred in an instant; and he sat and looked at her with the hopeful bewilderment of a man lost in the depths of a dark cave who sees the salvation of a light coming towards him.

It was the light he himself had set burning in Marisela's spirit, the clarity of intuition in the intelligence he had brightened, the spark of goodness directing her judgment to carry comforting words to his troubled soul. It was his work, his real accomplishment, for his was not to crush out evil with blood and fire, but to discover, here and there, the hidden springs of goodness in his people and in his land. It was his work, unfinished, and abandoned in a discouraged moment, which was returning good for good, restoring his self-esteem — not because the material fact that it had been Pajarote's bullet and not his own which had killed the Wizard altered the situation, so that his spirit had reacted against the confusion violence had done to it; but because coming from Marisela, the comforting persuasion of those words had sprung from her confidence in him, and that confidence was part of him, the best part, sown in another heart.

He accepted the gift of peace, and gave in exchange a word of love. And that night light came down into the depths of the cave for Marisela, too.

XII

DOTTING THE E'S

THEY were cutting lassos in the clearing between the cabins, late in the afternoon, when Pajarote, after gazing out over the prairie, said:

"I don't know how it is that there can be Christians that like to live in the hills or in towns with walled houses. The Plain is God's country for the children of the devil."

The others suspended the work of the knives with which they were cutting the raw, stinking leather used for strips and looked questioningly at the cowboy whose ideas were always so amusing.

"But it's perfectly clear," he continued, "clear as a pool in the sand. In the Plain, you can look far away and know what's coming before it arrives, while in hilly country you're always caught between the turns of a road like a bull's horns, and as for walled houses, a Christian is like a blind man who asks who it is after he butts into him."

With a unanimous suspicion, all directed their gaze

towards the prairie and descried a horseman coming towards the houses.

The Altamira peons, knowing of the affair at Rincón Hondo, had been expecting every moment to see appearing on the horizon the posse coming to arrest Luzardo, and though it was not likely that one single man would be coming for that purpose, it was inevitable that the advent of a stranger should make them uneasy.

Pajarote, on the other hand, gave every sign of a total lack of interest, taking up his work again and laughing to himself at the effort it was costing the others to make out who was the approaching rider. From the moment the horseman had appeared on the horizon, Pajarote had been observing him, from time to time, without the others having noticed it, and getting ready to run and hide in the thickest part of the woods as soon as he should find that it was anyone suspicious. But his eyes, accustomed to the long distances of the plains, had already recognized the stranger as a friend, a cowboy from one of the ranches of the upper Arauca, who had stopped there some days before on his way to the head village of the district.

" That's little Encarnación," the others said finally.

" It's about time you found that out," said Pajarote, in his usual shouting tone. " You fellows are fine watchmen. And my partner María Nieves can put a field glass to his eye."

" *Saint Fear* works miracles," replied María Nieves.

"Even the blind see when they owe money and are waiting for somebody to come and collect it."

"Laugh that one off, bowlegs. Look how the fair-haired boy has pulled your leg," said Venancio, urging him to make a retort, as he usually did to amuse himself with the jibes with which the two always tormented each other. But Pajarote did not need to be goaded.

"Nobody doubts that *Saint Fear* works miracles, but anybody can see how cock-eyed this cowpuncher is. At least nothing ever happened to me like what happened to a friend of mine, a blond herd-leader. And just to show you, he was caught as blind as an armadillo one night after he'd lighted a cigar. And not for lack of *Saint Fear,* either, because he was close enough, according to what the man himself told me, but because he just didn't have the savvy Pajarote's got. Now, when *he* is out at night and has to have a cigar, he only keeps one eye open, so that when he's blinded by the light he can go on without falling all over himself, by using the eye he had shut."

"Giddap, María! Just see how that ape is throwing the dirt on you," Venancio again intervened, alluding to Pajarote's way of going ahead, when he was riding in the summertime, so that he might be at the head of the cavalcade and thus free from the clouds of dust raised by the other men's horses. On the other hand, in the winter he always managed to be the last, so that, when they had to cross a swollen creek, the ones in the lead would have to do all the work of finding the fords; and this was what María Nieves referred to when he replied:

"Now he's riding behind, waiting for somebody else to find the way."

But María Nieves's retort had also a meaning which only Pajarote was able to see. From the latter's description of the Rincón Hondo affair, María had deduced that it had not been Luzardo's bullet which had killed the Wizard, and that if Pajarote did not claim the glory for reasons of the rough etiquette of barbarism, since this was a deed many envied and he did not want to take the credit away from the Doctor, he was also willing to give it up because when it came time to answer to the law, Luzardo would find it easier to escape unpunished.

Both men were accustomed to abuse each other without mercy; but Pajarote had not expected that María Nieves would come at him with that, and was plainly disconcerted; this making the onlookers exclaim:

"The nigger's on his back now! Tie him up, Whitey! you've got him."

But María Nieves, realizing that the joke had gone too far, answered:

"My pard knows that he and I never rub it in."

Pajarote smiled. In the others' eyes María Nieves had worsted him, but between the two of them, his friend knew that he had "plugged" the Terror of the Savannahs, and although he was the best of the men there, admired him and envied him.

A few moments later Encarnación arrived in the clearing. Pajarote and María Nieves went out to meet him, and the latter inquired:

"What brings you here, friend?"

"Wanting to sleep under a roof, if you'll let me, and a message I was given to bring to the Doctor. A letter from the judge."

"*Ah, caramba!*" exclaimed Pajarote. "Since when have you had to ask permission in this house to swing your hammock wherever you like? Get down and settle yourself where you like best, and give me that letter you've got for the Doctor."

With the missive in his hand, he went in to Luzardo.

"Look how things have turned out, Doctor," he said. "This is for you, from the judge."

The letter was from Mujiquita and told of some unusual occurrences.

"Doña Barbara came here yesterday with the fifty pounds of heron plumes which were stolen from you at El Totumo and made the following deposition: That having been led to suspect that the author of the crime was a certain Balbino Paiba, whom you discharged from the position of overseer at Altamira upon your arrival there, she gave orders to several of her peons to watch him; and that two of them, obeying her said orders, followed him to the place known as La Matica and there surprised him *in flagrante delicto* unearthing a box which proved to contain the plumes in question; that they ordered him to surrender, and as he drew on them, shot at him and killed him, immediately after which she took horse for here, with the *corpus delicti* and with the purpose of informing the authorities of what had happened, as well as of the death of Melquíades Gamarra, alias The Wizard, assassinated, by the aforementioned Paiba, shortly before the event at La Matica, and because of the vigilance above described."

Mujiquita concluded by informing him that Doña Barbara, wishing to attend to the entire matter herself, had set out for San Fernando to deliver the plumes to the broker to whom Carmelito had been going, and by congratulating him on the settlement of the affair, in such a ticklish state a few days before. The postscript was in Ño Pernalete's handwriting:

"Didn't I tell you, Dr. Luzardo? The e's are all dotted now. Your feathers are in good hands, in those of a friend of yours, who will bring you the money for them. This is what you should have done at the beginning. Your Friend, PERNALETE."

The perusal of this letter left Santos sunk in perplexity. The heron feathers recovered, Balbino the cause of Melquíades' death, and all this done by Doña Barbara!

"Now you see, Doctor, that you didn't have to get your brains in such a fever!" Pajarote exclaimed. "Now that everything's arranged, I can tell you that it was my bullet that killed the Wizard, because, as you must remember, you shot from the lasso side and I from the stirrup side, and that was the side he had the wound on. In the left breast. You remember? Well then, it was I that put an end to the bugbear; but now the judge says it was Balbino, and Balbino it will be."

"But this is not right, Pajarote," Luzardo protested. "Our right to defend ourselves was legitimate, since Melquíades was the first to draw, and either of us, since you've acknowledged it, could rest with a good conscience. But now this injustice to Balbino removes the right for that easy mind, if we don't immediately go before the judge to depose the truth of the affair, and put the dots over the i's and not over the e's, as they are in this letter."

"Listen, Doctor," Pajarote replied, after a dubious pause, "if you go and confess the truth after what they've said there, Ño Pernalete will be sore, and he's capable of having you sentenced to keep you from being so innocent next time. And last of all, all this that has happened and seems so ugly to you wasn't done by Doña Barbara, nor by the judge, nor by the Civil Magistrate, but by God Himself, and He knows what He's doing. Consider this, Doctor: We shoot the Wizard, you or me" —at this moment it did not seem convenient to insist that it had been himself—"because, who can tell if the dead man turned his head, or not, just when we shot at him? But he was well plugged, anyway, and the one to get the blame for his death is Balbino, and nobody knows how many he ought to get the blame for. God has His own way of arranging His affairs, and He's a demon when it comes to punishment."

In spite of the gravity of the matter, Santos could not help smiling. Pajarote's God, like Ño Pernalete's friend, had no scruples about dotting e's.

XIII

DAUGHTER OF THE RIVERS

IT HAD been some time since Doña Barbara had visited San Fernando.

As always, as soon as the news of her arrival went around, the lawyers busied themselves, glimpsing one of those long and troublesome suits the famous monopolizer of the Arauca was accustomed to bring against her neighbours, and in which, if the rogues got their share—since, to retain other peoples' lands, she had to disburse in exchange her precious gold pieces into the hands of the judges and counsel for the defence or into the pockets of political higher-ups who had lent their influence—the honourable members of the profession likewise gained much from research and the exercise of subtleties necessary for defending the clear and evident rights of the victims against the sophistries and knavery of the subsidized authorities. But this time the pettifoggers were disappointed. Doña Barbara had not come to open quarrels, but, on the contrary, to carry out an unheard-of plan for making reparation.

However, it was not only among the men of law that excitement was stirred up. The eternal commentaries began to simmer the instant it became known that she was in the town, and the thousands of tales of her amours and crimes began to be told once more. Most of them were pure inventions of popular fancy, in whose exaggerated versions the Amazon acquired the character of a heroine, dreaded, yet at the same time fascinating, as though the ferocity under which she was represented displayed a close devotion on the part of her countrymen rather than hate or repugnance. Inhabitant of a distant region lost in the depths of the lonely fastnesses and allowing herself to be seen only from time to time and only for evil purposes, it was almost as a legendary figure that she excited the city's imagination.

Given this sympathetic attitude, the news that she had come to turn over, personally, the goods stolen from her enemy by her lover, and the report that she intended to restore to Luzardo the lands seized from Altamira, it was inevitable that she should arouse the town. As the inhabitants were people of impressionable temperament and susceptible to hints of the extraordinary, like the imaginative people of the Plain, they immediately began to soften the truculent anecdotes which painted her as a sinister and hateful being. And as each invented whatever he took a notion to make up, but always in opposition to the former versions, new accounts of episodes in Doña Barbara's life began to circulate, nearly all of them edifying. Nothing else was spoken of during the entire afternoon, the women gossiping in the houses, and the men around the tables of the cafés; and that night the street where her hotel stood was full of strollers.

It was a hotel with a gallery on the street, situated in front of one of the plazas. Doña Barbara was sitting in a rocking-chair, in the fresh breeze blowing from the river a hundred meters or so distant, alone, her head resting against the back of the chair, in a languid attitude and with an expression of utter indifference to everything around her.

But around her was the city's curiosity. The men of the town had stopped on the sidewalk in front to look at her, and the mute, ecstatic group was already a large one. Under the balconies of the hotel and by the neighbouring shops which stretched down to the bank of the Apure, little knots of young ladies and matrons passed every moment, having come out of their houses for the sole purpose of seeing her. The girls, when their modest eyes rested upon her, blushed, stricken with fear that the men nearby might surprise them in the act of gratifying their malicious curiosity. The older women examined her at their leisure and exchanged impressions between malevolent smiles.

She wore a white waist adorned with lace, which left exposed her finely formed arms and shoulders, and as they had never seen her so feminine in appearance, even the most irreconcilable conceded:

"She's still attractive in her way," while one heard, on the other hand:

"She's marvellous! What eyes she has!"

And if someone commented:

"They say she's head over heels in love with Doctor Luzardo," the bitterness of disillusioned honesty was not lacking when another added:

"And she'll marry him. Those women succeed with everything they start out to do, because men are all fools."

At last they became tired of admiring and murmuring, and the street gradually became empty. The moon shone faintly on the tops of the trees in the plaza, freshened by a recent shower, and was reflected in the pools which had formed in the streets. At intervals the breath of a breeze swayed the limbs of the trees and cooled the air. The passersby had gone home, and the neighbours enjoying the fresh air, obstructing the sidewalks, in rockers and folding chairs, began to exchange farewells with the other groups:

"Until tomorrow, then. To bed, the day's over."

And in the silence settling over the city, this languid invocation to sleep had all the quiet gravity of the drama of forlorn towns, where the act of going to bed is a solemn event, at the end of an idle day, one less day for hope, although the people always murmur:

"Tomorrow is another day."

So thought Doña Barbara. She had abandoned the

deeds which had blocked her path, and now she saw the road cleared. She dreamed, like a young girl in her first love, toying with the illusion of having been reborn to a new and different life, forgetful of the past, as though that had disappeared with the sinister servant whose hands were dyed in blood, and with her gross lover. What would be her feelings towards tomorrow's events? She prepared for them as for some marvellous spectacle; the spectacle of herself in a way of life different from that she had hitherto traversed, of her heart open to unknown emotions, and this pause was like a light in the darkness of her soul which was beginning to reveal itself, and where calm images were passing, wandering shadows of the broken love of the girl who had glimpsed, through her first lover's words, a world of emotions apart from those which ruled the savage river pirates with whom she lived.

But now, in the midst of her fantasies, an idea crept furtively in; an impression, perhaps of some word unconsciously heard; it was like a small foreign particle in the cogs of the machine which suddenly upsets its operation and brings it to a stop. Whence came this sudden bitterness to make her frown involuntarily, this well-known taste of forgotten rancour? Why did the sudden memory of a bewildered bird falling as the fires were all at once extinguished, come to assault her? Her heart, dazzled by the light of her illusions, had suddenly become blind to the flight of her dreams.

Was it not enough, then, to have abandoned her plans?

In the people grouped on the sidewalk in front of her, she felt the ingenuous admiration and malicious curiosity of the city which wanted to make her remember the past she had determined to forget. It seemed to her that the words: To be loved by a man like Santos Luzardo it is necessary to have no past, had been whispered in her ear.

And hers came into her mind, as always, from its starting point: She dreamed that she was on a pirogue which plied through the great waters of the rubber forests. . . .

She left the gallery of the hotel and went slowly along the rows of shops which led to the shore of the Apure. An obscure necessity carried her towards the river scene; the daughter of the rivers was commencing to feel again its mysterious attraction.

A cloudy sky filtered the moonlight, leaving it without a gleam on the façades of the houses by the river, on the roofs of thatch covering the huts farther away, on the woods upon the river banks, over the still surface of the turbid Apure, whose waters, at their lowest level during the drought, left wide sandy beaches exposed to view. On the beach of the right bank, a launch and a rowboat stranded since the last period of high water, lay at the foot of the levee. Along the shore, moored to poles stuck in the mud, were the rafts for crossing, built over canoes, a few black pirogues, laden with wood and plantains, and an empty river-scow, recently painted white, on whose cabin a boy lay asleep on his back.

The men who had been seated under the trees beside the river, in front of the cafés, drinking and talking, had long gone to their homes, and the waiters were gathering the chairs and closing the doors, shutting off the reflections of the lamps in the water.

Doña Barbara commenced strolling slowly up and down the deserted street.

On the raft, the pirogue boatmen were talking with the men from the scow, and their words were slow like the current of the river running over the level stretches of its bed, like the progress of the dreamy night of mists—like the footsteps of Doña Barbara, a wandering silent shadow on the bank.

There was the side of the gorge, still and dark in the serene night; the river, flowing down from the far-away mountains, gliding silently past; the cry of an approaching gull flying over the sleeping water, and the conversation of the boatmen, tales of the terrible things that had happened on the streams which go through the Plain. These were what Doña Barbara saw when she came, slowly, walking in the faint bluish shadow of the trees. And she found these same things when she returned; the side of the gorge, the silent night, the river gliding noiselessly down to another far away stream. She heard the cry of the sleepless bird, now lost to sight, and the drowsy talk of the boatmen — things that bring solemn thoughts, the things that have happened in the wild lands beside the wide, mysterious waters. . . .

But for Doña Barbara the city sleeping on the right bank of the stream had ceased to exist. She was attentive only to what had suddenly taken possession of her soul: the fascination of the river scene, the instant attraction of the mysterious rivers where her story had begun. . . . The yellow Orinoco, the red Atabapo, the black Guainóa! . . .

It was close to midnight. Roosters were crowing, the dogs of the town were barking. Then silence fell again, and the flight of owls could be heard. No one was talking any longer on the raft. But the river had begun to whisper to the black pirogues.

Doña Barbara stopped and listened:

All things return whence they came.

XIV

THE GLEAM OF A STAR

THE decline had already begun. The indomitable woman who had stopped at nothing now found herself in the presence of something against which she could not struggle. The plan for the meeting at Rincón Hondo had been the sweep of a claw in the dark, and the impulse which had led her to make the Wizard's death fall on the dead Balbino was the starting point of definite surrender.

She saw the downfall of the hopes she had placed in the abandonment of her plans, and the fatalism of the Indian in her blood made her look now, in spite of herself, towards the path of renunciation. The images of the past, of her rude childhood on the wide rivers of the wilderness, were veiled forms of her new idea — were retreat.

Nevertheless, overcoming her momentary depression of spirit, she resolved to undertake the return to her ranch, with the letter in which the broker to whom she had delivered the feathers in Luzardo's name informed the latter that he had received them and listed them at the current price, a higher one than they would have brought when Carmelito set out with them. She had also a deed drawn up by her lawyer providing for the sale of the Altamira lands she had snatched from him in unjust legal judgments. In these papers were placed her last hopes, though they were hopes without definite form, for she no longer aspired to that love which had led her to do so much. From moment to moment, when she had been beside the river, Santos's image had become confused with that other indistinct image of Hasdrubal, and now one seemed as far away as the other, a shadow receding farther and farther, and vanishing in the wavering light of an unreal world.

But she wished to carry out what she had planned. She needed to, and the need was overwhelming, for an unrealized plan at this time would have been the finishing blow to her already uncertain reason for existing.

The drought had begun to hold sway. It was now the time for driving to the water holes the cattle who had never known them, or had forgotten them in the agony of thirst. The rutted beds of creeks long dried up ran here and there through the brownish weeds, and between the whitening crusts of the cracks the putrid marshes were like pestilent ulcers which had scarified without healing. In some there still remained a little oozy, warm water, in which were putrefying steers, who, maddened by thirst, had leapt into the deepest part of the holes and there, gorged, swollen with overmuch drinking, had been trapped and had died. Great bands of buzzards, eager for the carrion, wheeled above the pools. Death is a pendulum swinging over the Plain, from flood to drought and from drought to flood.

The parched chaparral crackled, the prairie glowed with heat within the circle of mirages which gave the illusion of blue lakes, waters which drive to desperation the thirsty who go towards them, remaining always at the same distance away on the round horizon. Doña Barbara was riding by forced marches towards the mirage of impossible love.

When she reached the ranch, despite the fatigue of her journey and the fact that night was near, she stopped only for the time necessary to replace her worn horse, change her clothing, and to make herself neat for the interview with Luzardo, which her impatience would not allow her to postpone until the following day. She saw that the cabins were deserted, the kitchen closed, and the corrals empty. There was only Juan Primito there.

"What's happened here?" she asked him. "What's become of the people?"

"They all sneaked away," replied the simple fellow, not daring to approach her in his fear of the fit of rage his words might produce. "They said they didn't want to work for you any longer, because you're not the same as before, and that you were going to turn them in bound hand and foot one of these days."

The woman's angry gaze flashed, and Juan Primito hastened to give his other news:

"Do you know that Don Lorenzo's dead?"

"It was time. He lasted a long time. And the girl? Where is she?"

"Little Marisela? At Altamira again. The Doctor took her with him to his house, and from what I've heard tell he's going to marry her right away."

Suddenly the woman of overwhelming impulses reappeared completely in Doña Barbara, and without a word, and with a suddenness charged with sinister intent, she remounted her horse and rode off towards Altamira.

Juan Primito stood there crossing himself, and then, seized by his mania, rushed off to seek the pans where he was accustomed to put the drinks for his birds.

Meanwhile, borne along at a gallop, with which the winded horse, with the last ounce of his flagging strength, responded to the bloody application of the spurs, the furious Doña Barbara raved aloud to herself:

"Does this mean that I've lost my time giving up all my plans? Well then, I'll take them up again, to the grave! But we'll see who triumphs. Nobody has been born yet who can snatch what I've said was my own away from me! I'll die before I'll be beaten!"

In this condition, she reached the Altamira ranch-house. Under cover of the dark night, she approached the house and saw, through the door opening on the gallery in the rear, Luzardo, seated at the table with Marisela. They had finished dinner. He was speaking and she was listening to him, gazing at him in delight, her elbows on the table and her cheeks in her hands.

Doña Barbara rode up within revolver range and pulled up her horse. Slowly, and with a murderous pleasure, she took the weapon out of the saddle holster and pointed it at the breast of the girl, white in the lamplight.

The gleam of the sight, in the treacherous darkness, was like the light of a star, helping the grim eye to find Marisela's heart. But, as if that tiny beam held all the weight of the star from which it was reflected, the revolver descended without a shot, and slowly returned to its place in the holster. With her eye squinting along the sight levelled at the heart of her daughter, Doña Barbara had suddenly seen herself, bathed in the glow of a fire burning on a deserted beach in the wilds, listening, as Marisela was listening, to Hasdrubal's words, and the bitter memory wiped out her fury.

She remained a long time gazing at her happy daughter, and the longing for a new life which had so long tormented her took the form of a maternal sentiment, unknown to her heart.

"He is yours. May he make you happy."

Hasdrubal's love, the pure shadow wandering through her darkened soul, had at last come to rest in a noble emotion.

XV

MANY HORIZONS, MANY PATHS

THAT night the lamp was not lighted in the room where the interviews with the " Partner " were held, but when Doña Barbara came out to the patio, Juan Primito and the two peons who had accompanied her on the trip to San Fernando — the ones who had killed Balbino, the only ones still faithful — did not recognize her. She had grown old in a single night, her face was sunken from the effects of insomnia, but she nevertheless displayed, graven on her features and unmistakable in her gaze, the tragic calm of a supreme resolve.

" Here is what I owe you," she said to the two men, who hung on her words, putting some coins in their hands. " Anything extra is for the time you may not have work. There is nothing more to do here. You may go away. You, Juan Primito, take this letter to Dr. Luzardo. And don't come back here. Stay there if they'll let you."

Hours later, Señor Danger saw her pass, at the lower end of the Salt Lick. He saluted her at a distance, but obtained no response. She rode along absorbed, her gaze fixed ahead, at a steady slow trot, the loose reins in her hands resting on her thighs.

Dry lands, broken by ravines, and riven with cracks. Thin cattle, with weary gaze, were here and there licking, with an obsessed desperation, the slopes and bare spots of the forlorn spot. Whitening on the ground were the bones of those who had already succumbed, victims of the salty land that had drawn and held them until they had died of hunger, forgetful of food, and great bands of buzzards soared above the stinking carrion. Doña Barbara stopped to contemplate the persistent aberration of the cattle, and with her own thoughts materialized into sensation, she felt in the ill-tasting dryness of her tongue burning with fever and thirst the bitterness and sharpness of the earth the obstinate animal tongues were licking. So had she felt in her terrible longing to taste the sweetness of the love that was consuming her. Then, with an effort to free herself from the fascination that thirst and the spectacle before her had for her spirit, she spurred her horse forward.

Something unusual was happening in the quagmire, where ordinarily a deathly stillness reigned. Numerous flocks of ducks, *cotuas,* herons, and other waterfowl of various colours flew around the pool in panicky circles, giving cries of fear. Every moment, those able to fly higher disappeared over the palms, the others descended to the edge of the grim pool, and the silence, reasserting itself, gave the impression of an anguished pause; but immediately, some would again take wing and others would reappear to wheel once more around the centre of their terror.

Despite the profound absorption in which she was plunged, Doña Barbara quickly drew up her horse. A young steer was struggling, with frightened cries, at the edge of the bog, clasped around the throat by a huge water snake whose head was scarcely above the level of the swamp. His trembling legs rigid, hoofs buried in the soft earth on the margin, his neck stiffened with his desperate effort, his eyes staring with terror, the captive beast was consuming his strength in the struggle against the formidable contraction of the serpent's coils, and was bathed in a mortal sweat.

" He'll never escape," murmured Doña Barbara. " The quagmire is eating today."

Finally the boa constrictor began to stretch himself out, drawing his powerful body out of the water, and the steer began to pull away, struggling to free his throat; but then the snake began again to contract his coils, slowly, and the victim, already tired out, gave up and allowed himself to be drawn in. He commenced to sink down in the bog, with horrible cries, and disappeared under the foul water, which closed over him with a sound like the smacking of hungry lips.

The terrified birds flew around and shrieked without

ceasing. Doña Barbara remained impassive. Finally they flew away, silence recovered its reign, and the troubled quagmire regained its habitual tragic calm. Scarcely more than a faint ripple marred its surface, and in the spot where the green scum around the shoals had been broken by the steer's hoofs, little globules of marsh gas rose to the top. One large bubble remained on the surface in a yellowish bulb, like an eye jaundiced with rage. And that angry eye seemed to stare at the fascinated woman. . . .

Word flew from mouth to mouth: The cacica of the Arauca had disappeared.

It was supposed that she had thrown herself into the quagmire, because she had been seen going in that direction with the shadow of a tragic resolve on her face; but people also spoke of a boat descending the Arauca, on which someone or other thought he had seen a woman. What was certain was that she had vanished, leaving her last will in a letter for Dr. Luzardo, which said:

"I have no other heir but my daughter Marisela, and I hereby recognize her as such before God and men. Take charge of arranging all the details of the legacy for her."

But as it was well known that she had a great deal of money buried, and the letter made no mention of that; and since, besides, signs of digging up had been found in the earthen floor of the conjuring-room, the assumption of suicide was replaced by that of mere disappearance, and there was much talk about the boat. It had gone by night, and indeed, several people had heard it pass on its way down the Arauca. . . .

The barb-wire purchased with the proceeds of the heron plumes arrived, and the work commenced. The posts were already set up, the lines of wire were reeling off the rolls, and in the land of uncounted paths, the wire fence began to trace a single straight way towards the future.

Señor Danger, when he saw that his salt licks were going to be closed up and that other people's cattle would not longer be able to come to lick the salty bitterness of his gullies and fall under his lasso, shrugged his shoulders and said to himself:

"Your time is over, Mr. Danger."

He took his rifle, slung it across his back, mounted his horse, and on his way past them, shouted to the peons working on the fence:

"Don't waste all that wire, fencing the licks. Tell Dr. Luzardo that Señor Danger is going away too."

The time required by law for Marisela to wait before taking possession of the legacy left by her mother, of whom no news had ever come, passed; the name of El Miedo disappeared from the Arauca, and all the lands once more became known as Altamira.